TO BE A FOOL

A GHOST'S MEMOIR

BOOK 2

THE FOOL

TO BE A FOOL

A GHOST'S MEMOIR

BOOK 2

ROBERT J. MCCARTER

Little Hummingbird Publishing
Flagstaff, AZ

To Be a Fool
A Ghost's Memoir, Book 2

Version 1.1, October, 2016
Version 1.0, October 2013

ISBN: 978-0-9642096-7-1

Find out more about this book at: www.ShuffledOff.com
Visit Robert's website at: www.RobertJMcCarter.com
Visit Steve Staal's website at: www.sswebworks.com

Published by:
Little Hummingbird Publishing
P.O. Box 23518
Flagstaff, AZ 86002
www.LittleHummingbird.com

Little Hummingbird Publishing is a division of Arapas, Inc. Find more about Arapas at: www.Arapas.com.

*This one's for Jake, Matt, Lew, Herb, and Konrad.
And Wayne, of course, always for Wayne.*

"The fool doth think he is wise,
but the wise man knows himself to be a fool."
As You Like It: Act V, Scene I, by William Shakespeare

Editor's Note

We have arranged this book in a slightly different order than the SECI transmissions came into our facility to aid in its comprehension. Besides that, along with some grammatical cleanup and some changes in names to protect identities, these are the words JJ Lynch wrote.

References to JJ's previous memoir are available in *Shuffled Off: A Ghost's Memoir, Book 1*. Viki Dobos's story is told in *Drawing the Dead*.

Tamara Watson and Jin Shi
Tucson, Arizona
July 2013

Prologue

NATE LUCA PACED AS JIN SHI AND TAMARA WATSON SET up the video gear. He was nervous. As a friend, Nate knew that at times you signed yourself up for some hard duty. As a best friend, even more so. And even though Nate's best friend, JJ Lynch, was dead, was a ghost, Nate was still obliged to him. Obliged to do what was right, to do what he needed to do.

He paused, rubbing his sweating palms on his jeans and tucking his white T-shirt in again for the fourth time. "Is there a problem?" he asked.

Jin mumbled something that Nate couldn't hear, and Tamara stepped away and walked over to Nate. "It's just not turning on. The battery is fine, but it won't come on." Nate studied her expression as she spoke. It lacked any trace of surprise.

Nate looked around the mostly empty building that housed Afterlife Communications. It had tall ceilings and a concrete floor. The kind of place you might find used as an auto shop or a small printer. In one corner sat the SECI chamber, the device JJ had used to communicate with them and to write his memoir. Next to it were the skeletons of two more SECI chambers in the process of being built. SECI: The Search for Extra-Corporeal Intelligence. It is a project that Tamara and Jin had started at the University of Arizona (UA) and now were taking private. The three SECI chambers and the adjoining offices were the start of Afterlife Communications, Inc.

"Do you think it's a ghost?" Nate asked, a shiver going down his spine. He knew enough to justify his concern.

Tamara shrugged and smiled, as if having a ghost interfere with her electronics was the most normal thing in the world. "Could be. Just be patient, Nate, we'll get it going. We've got another camera we can dig out if this one doesn't respond soon."

"It's just—" Nate began.

"I know, Nate, I know," she said, her hand lightly touching his muscular arm. "It's a hell of thing to have to tell him."

Nate nodded, "Rhiannon... I just can't believe it. She's so young. I'm afraid of how he'll react. He'll probably lose it." Nate paused as he stared at the SECI chamber. "Do you think he'll be back? Do you think he'll get the message in time?"

Tamara ran her hands through her shoulder-length black hair, pulling it back into a ponytail. "I hope so. We've got the 2.0 SECI chamber up and running for him. I hope he finds it and uses it. And if he does, this video will be in the chamber with instructions for him on how to trigger it and he'll hear what you need to tell him."

Nate nodded again, retucking his shirt in for the fifth time. It fit tightly across his broad chest. "Thanks for letting me do the greeting."

"Of course, Nate. You have some important news, it's only right. Do you remember what to say?"

Nate pulled the piece of paper out of his back pocket, his eyes scanning the notes. "Yeah, I've got it. I'll tell him this stuff first, before—"

"Got it!" Jin shouted from behind the camera. "Let's do this before it decides to turn itself off again."

Part 1

Jesus and Javier

"Sweet are the uses of adversity,
Which, like the toad, ugly and venomous,
Wears yet a precious jewel in his head."
As You Like It: Act II, Scene I, by William Shakespeare

THE FOOL

Video Transcript #1
Nate Luca speaking to JJ Lynch
Recorded on 2011/10/16 2:13 p.m.
Playback triggered on 2012/01/11 9:15 p.m.

HEY, BRO, WELCOME BACK. JIN AND TAMARA ARE LETTING me do this introduction for you. They first asked me to write it, but you know me. Unlike you, I couldn't write my way out of a paper bag—it would take me days to write this down. And it would be even harder to tell you...

But, I'm getting ahead of myself. I'm here to introduce you to SECI 2.0 and to give you some news.

Since your book, *Shuffled Off,* came out SECI has taken off. There are lots of ghosts trying their hand at the SECI Chamber and a few are even able to use it. They are getting transmissions in all the time. Tamara got worried that with the traffic in the chamber now you would have trouble getting through if you wanted to. And everyone wants to hear from you again.

So we were having dinner one night and Tam and Jin were talking about making another chamber for you and hiding it so the other ghosts couldn't find it. They were talking about a few improvements, and I suggested they make you a real keyboard. Like when you made that little light and hovered it over the keys to my laptop, back when you first started to communicate with me. I thought it would be easier than making all those crazy symbols you had to make for the original SECI chamber.

Well, they liked the idea, and here we are. SECI 2.0. It's just like a big keyboard and any unusual electromagnetic radiation in the rectangle of the key will register the corresponding letter. It should be a lot easier on you and a lot quicker.

So, that's the intro, and now I have some news for you.

I won't lie to you. It's been tough. I've been in counseling since... since... God, JJ, that night. I don't really even know how to talk about it. I was crazy with grief and then you showed up and started to communicate with me. Well, I was off my nut thinking that I wanted to be a ghost too. That druggy tried to steal the tow truck and what did I do? I tried to get him to shoot me. And he would have killed me, but you tapped into the electricity of the Prius and moved his hand just enough so he didn't shoot me in the head. He died from electrocution, you nearly destroyed your ghostly form, and I nearly died from the gunshot wound to my chest.

It's been over a year and I still have nightmares about that night. About what I almost did and what you did do to save me. I...

I miss you, man. I miss you bad. I mean, it is comforting knowing you are out there, but I miss sitting and talking with you. Working on cars. Having a beer or two. Hanging out.

But, you know, things are getting better. Slowly, but surely, they are getting better.

Your mother, Ma, is doing good. Not "good" in the sense of skipping around and singing, but good in the sense of having buried both her husband and her son and getting her feet under her. She's got a part-time job and does some volunteer work. I'd tell you more, but I know she would rather do it herself. Once we know you're back, Tam and Jin will get her in here to record a video for you.

Speaking of volunteering. I am on the board of the "JJ Lynch Foundation." Anna-Beth and William—well, mostly Anna-Beth—have started a foundation in your name. Who would have thought this would come out of them being in the car that killed you.

They've collected a lot of money, and we are going to help "at-risk" teens with vocational education. Sounds fancy, but basically we are going to teach troubled kids to fix cars. Get them dirty, give them something to do.

This is all Anna-Beth, bro. What she went through with you, what happened with you and her... Well, it changed her in a big way. She's... She's...

God I wish you were here. I wish we could talk about shit like this. I am doing my best to implement the patented "JJ Lynch's slowly grow on them" method, but there are some subtleties I am not sure of. I enjoy spending time with her and I am doing my best to be her friend and let things go from there. But...

William is still in the picture, but I don't think for much longer. Maybe they'll break up, and I'll be there like you were for Rhiannon...

Shit, JJ, this is so damn hard. Tam isn't letting me do this so I can babble on about Ma and me, about the little pieces of our lives. She is letting me do this because I have something important to say. Something I would love not to have to tell you.

It's Rhiannon, bro, she's real sick. I... You...

Ah, hell. This sucks. She's got a tumor in her brain. It's got some damn fancy name that I can't remember, but it's killing her, bro. It's killing her.

They discovered it about eight months ago. She had surgery and chemo and it looked pretty good, but it's back now, and they're saying they can't operate. They're gonna do radiation, but reading between the lines, it's not hopeful. This thing is a killer, almost no one survives it for very long.

I'm so sorry to be the bearer of these bad tidings. I can just imagine how you are feeling. But listen to me, I know it hurts but you've got to take care of yourself. Don't go all JJ-apeshit on me. Don't go doing crazy things.

Look, the reason I am telling you this is... Well, because I know you would want to know. But, also, so maybe you can be there if she does... you know... die. You can be there to help her along if she's earth-bound like you. If she's a ghost.

I can't imagine you wouldn't want to be there. So, in case you haven't mastered traveling, that "popping" thing you talked about in your book, Jin is going to put some maps on the end of this. She's still in Texas, and the maps will show you how to get to her.

I am going to keep tabs on things and go out there at some point before...

Take care of yourself, bro, and keep your head on.

I sure hope you come back. I hope you get this message in time. I hope you're OK.

Transmission #1
Received 2012/01/11 21:42:03

THIS IS JOSEPH JEFFERY LYNCH. I DON'T KNOW WHAT TO say. I have so much to say. So much has happened, but I just saw the video of Nate talking about Rhiannon.

The world doesn't ever stop, does it? Not for a damn minute. Not for anything, and certainly not when you need it the most.

Tam, I've got your fiancé John here. I found him, I... well, it's why I came back. He's the reason you started the SECI project, the reason I can write my stories, but... It's a long story and I'd love to tell it to you... I'd love to...

Listen, I have to go. I can't stay here banging on your ghost keyboard when Rhiannon might be dying or be...

Now if that isn't something, here I am a ghost and I don't want to say the word 'dead.' Unbelievable.

OK, this is hitting me now. I'm a mess but I don't want to leave you hanging too badly, Tam, so here's a message from John.

"Honey, I'm OK. I am so very, very sorry for what happened and how it happened. That you saw me die that way, that I left so many things unsaid. JJ will come back with me later and we'll tell you the whole story. For now just know that I love you and I'm OK."

I'm starting to lose it here. I'm going to get John back to the graveyard and go find Rhiannon. Alive or dead, I'm going to find her. I'll be back as soon as I can.

Transmission #2
Received 2012/01/30 01:12:42

I'M BACK AND I HAVE A STORY TO TELL, BUT BEFORE I start I need to get something off my chest. Something that I must say and I hope that you will indulge me.

Life is grief.

Think about it, it is. Not in a "hide my head in the sand and be depressed for the rest of my existence" way. No, not like that. But like gravity. As in the natural order of things, as in, just the way it is and there is nothing you can do about it.

Like gravity, you can fight it, you can expend tremendous energy and counteract its forces briefly, but no matter how hard you try it's not going to go away, it's not going to change, and there is not a damn thing you can do about it.

Grief is a natural reaction to change. Things change and we grieve. That crappy old dorm room you left for your first professional job. You think you're done, you're glad to be out, but you sometimes miss it. You miss the simplicity of life in college that the dorm room represented. You miss the goofy stoner who lived across the hall from you and told the worst jokes. You miss the boneheads pulling the fire alarm in the middle of the night because you had some of the best conversations of your life while half-awake in the quad under the moonlight.

You grieve the end of that life even as you are excited about the beginning of a new one. Change results in grief. There is no getting out of it—just like gravity.

And in life there is no getting out of change, no matter how hard you try. And believe me, I was the expert at resisting change, floating along in my life like a rudderless ship just hoping nothing bad happened. Doesn't matter, change comes. Change came to me when my dad died, change came when Rhiannon, the love of my life, kicked me out, and change certainly came when a car full of drunk coeds slammed into me, killing me instantly.

Life = Change. Change = Grief. Life = Grief.

You can pretend otherwise, but you know what that is gonna cause you? More grief.

I apologize if this kind of rambling isn't what you were looking for. I really do. I know you want to hear cool stories about ghostly powers, graveyards, and grand adventures. And those are coming, and I fully understand if you need to skip ahead a few pages. But indulge me. I feel the need to set the stage like the narrator does at the beginning of Romeo and Juliet. I am your humble thespian laying out the view of the landscape we are about to cover.

So before we get to the grand adventure and breathless realizations, I need to step onto my soapbox for a moment. What? You think that bit I just said was me on my soapbox. Nope, but here it is.

It's hard when someone you care for dies. So hard. It is

a broad spectrum of reactions that goes from an emotional hiccup, to the shape of your life never being the same again.

If it's a big change, grief is required. One way or another, whether healthy or not, you will grieve. No choice. It's like gravity, remember?

So here comes the soapbox part. When it comes to grief, you, the living, have it easy.

I don't care if it was your firstborn child, a career, a cherished dream, or your partner of fifty years. You have it easy.

Now wait, before you throw the book across the room, let me explain. It's not that grieving the death of your child or your lifelong partner is easy. It is anything but. It is just not nearly as hard as dying.

Here's the thing. In most cases you lose one thing at a time. Your life may be changed, your world may be rocked, but it's usually one thing at a time. Not always, and I am not speaking in absolutes here, I am just pointing out that the scale goes higher, much higher, than what the living regularly experience.

When someone dies they aren't giving up one person, they are giving up *every* person. When someone dies they aren't giving up a job or hobby or dream, but *every* job and *every* hobby and *every* dream. When someone dies they aren't losing one thing, they are losing *every*-thing.

Sure, plenty of souls move directly on and don't end up as an earth-bound spirit, or a ghost, like me, but the ones that do end up as ghosts are on that far end of the spectrum of grief. Is it any wonder that so many of us end up as slack-jawed apparitions stuck in our own personal hell? We call that place the "bardo" around the graveyard.

Think about it. Did you like to read? Well, you can't turn pages anymore, making reading quite difficult. Were you a writer? Well, except for the SECI project that is enabling me to type this manuscript, you are out of luck. Did you garden, play sports, love to go shopping? Nope, can't do that here. Did you love facebook or twitter, or fooling around at your computer? That's gone too. Did you value the kindness and support of friends, having long conversations with them over food and drinks, roughhousing with your kids? Gone, gone, gone.

Look, I am in no way trying to minimize the grief you have been through. I had some whoppers in my day when I was still corporeal. I am just trying to give you a sense of scale, of perspective.

And one other thing. Someday a friend of yours or a family member is going to have a slow death. That person is going to have some time to think about all this, to get their affairs in order, and to say their good-byes (or not). And that friend or family member will be going through a lot—really as much as you can go through.

And you will be going through your own experiences around their upcoming transition. You will be having a difficult time, you will be seeing ahead to a life that is barely recognizable. You, in a word, will be grieving.

When this happens—and if you are lucky enough to stay in a body long enough, it *will* happen—remember how much more that dying person is giving up. While you are about to give them up, they are about to give up *everything*.

One moment they will be alive, and the next moment they will be dead and gone. And when that happens your life will be changed, but their life, as we commonly define it, will be over.

So if they grow withdrawn and distant, and you need to be close; if they need to talk, and you need to be quiet;

if they want to pretend it's not happening, and you don't; if they need to share feelings, and you need to bottle it all in—go with it. If whatever they do gets in the way of your grieving, do one thing for me. Get Over It. I am not saying to not have your process, to not grieve, to not try to get your needs met. I am saying put the dying person first. What the dying says goes. End of story. Period.

Yes, your world is about to change, maybe beyond recognition. But their world, it's about to end.

It's not like when you left college and started work, or when you had your first child, or when your kids left the house for good. Sure, your world changes in a huge way, but many things stay the same. Like your family and friends, your history and abilities, your hopes and dreams. It's not like that when you die. Everything changes, even down to the laws that govern the world you are living in.

It's a lot. That's all I'm saying. It's a hell of a lot.

Transmission #3
Received 2012/01/30 03:11:16

OK, NOW THAT I'VE GOT THAT OFF MY CHEST, I GUESS I should back up, back way up.

My name is Joseph Jeffery Lynch, but everyone calls me JJ. I died on August 22, 2010, when a car full of drunk coeds plowed into me, pinning me to the jungle gym at a Mickey D's.

I found myself a ghost and went through a lot coming to accept that and dealing with the life that I had left behind and my loved ones. I've already written about all of that so I won't go into it now.

I'm back because... well... I'm back because so much has happened, and the last time I did this it really helped me to get my head screwed back on.

To belabor the metaphor, my head is anything but screwed on right now. I am a huge mess. I have promised to tell the story of John for Tamara, so I was going to come here and do just that and nothing else. Let John talk, say what he needs to say, and just type it out.

But Banquo wouldn't hear of it. Banquo is... well, I guess

you would call him my mentor. He is the one that has been showing me and my best dead friend Jesus the ropes.

Jesus's name is pronounced "Hey-Zues," not "Gee-Zus," as he is often fond of saying when he explains the pronunciation, "I don't want be confused with the big fellow."

You see, ghosts like me can move on. Moving "on" is a euphemism around here for, well, moving on to the next level. And just like the living talking about dying, there isn't too much of a consensus about what that "moving on" is, just that it's the next step. Those who die at peace move on right away and don't end up like us ghosts. But moving on, answering the Call, is generally accepted to be a good thing, the next step. But I am not ready to answer the Call, I don't want to move on, I don't want to leave this world yet. And while I am here, I want to do something worth doing.

So I asked Banquo to be my mentor, to train me, to take me on as his apprentice. If I'm here, if I'm a ghost, I want to do things that matter. But, you see, I'm still kind of a mess from what I've just been through. Me being here and writing this is my way of processing it all, of getting over it, of grieving. And Banquo won't teach me until I'm done.

Banquo used to be a professor of English Literature, and he has structured lessons he teaches to the newly dead, like me. His lessons are: 1) Cutting the Cord; 2) Appearance Matters; 3) Awareness, Awareness, Awareness; 4) Traveling; and 5) This is Not the End.

I am badly stuck on Lesson #4 and am eager to figure that one out. It is really a pain to have to fly everywhere and not be able to "pop" from place to place like most everyone else.

So, I'm going to be here day in and day out until I tell

my story, until I can get some perspective, until I can move past it.

To be honest, I don't know if what I am doing is a good idea. I mean, it's good for me, but I worry about what it means for the world, for those that believe, for those that come to know there is an afterlife. It's heady stuff, and frankly more philosophical than I am suited for, but the question rumbles around my mind. What happens when people "know" there is an afterlife and just don't "believe" it? There is a huge difference between believing and knowing, and I am not so big a fool that I don't know that such a transition could get messy.

So here I am and there is so much to tell. As I flew over I thought about how to tell the story and make it understandable. I really want to leap ahead and talk about Rhiannon, but honestly I think that it is too fresh and that I will lose my way if I try to do that. So, I am going to start right where the last story ended. I'll take you through the whole thing and hopefully it will all make sense.

Transmission #4
Received 2012/01/31 01:16:13

In late December 2010, I signed off and finished writing my... my... Well, I guess there is nothing to call it but a "memoir." It feels funny, you know? I never thought my life interesting enough to tell the story of, but things have gotten decidedly interesting since I "shuffled off this mortal coil."

As I flew away from the SECI chamber, having completed my memoir, I felt this sense of peace. I felt satisfied. I felt happy, really happy. What I had done seemed impossible. I had gotten over much of what had haunted me in my meat life and was feeling ready to start my ghost life.

It was a beautiful moment, it really was. It ended, of course, but that feeling of peace and balance and belonging did stick around for a while. For that I am grateful.

When I got to the graveyard, the Midnight Circle—the nightly gathering of the ghosts—was just breaking up. They had performed Romeo and Juliet, and I was sorry I missed it. It was one of Shakespeare's plays in the rotation that I hadn't seen yet.

Jim the cowboy, one of the longest dead, played Romeo. Jane, his constant companion who ran a speakeasy in the twenties, played Juliet. Those two are constantly together and clearly in the throes of the sloppiest kind of love. I'm sure they played the parts brilliantly, but if truth be told it just would have made me maudlin to watch a love story, even a tragic one.

Banquo with his English Literature background leads the Midnight Circle. He plays the narrator, teaches everyone their lines, and sometimes plays a part or two himself.

"So?" Jesus asked when I got back. He had a big smile below his black mustache and his brown eyes sparkled. In answer, I just nodded and smiled. "Way to go man, way to go."

"Yup, I finished it," I said. "I'm ready to move on... Umm, but not, you know, to move 'on,' just to do something different."

"We should celebrate, my friend. Something like this is cause for celebration."

"What?" I asked. "How should we celebrate?"

Jesus shrugged, "Anything you always wanted to do? Anywhere you always wanted to go?"

The memory of the time Nate and I hiked down the Grand Canyon flashed through my mind. We weren't exactly city boys, but we weren't the outdoorsy type either. We were blue collar through and through, and didn't have the funds or the time to buy fancy gear and go walking around outside.

But we did it anyway. We had heard how amazing it was so we got reservations at Phantom Ranch down at the bottom of the Grand Canyon, put on our best shoes—just your regular, average, tennis shoes—got some cheap backpacks and filled them with water and snacks and went.

Hiking the Canyon is unforgettable. When you are at the top of the Grand Canyon looking in, it is breathtaking, stunning, but when you are walking down all those layers, it is... Well, it is breathtaking and stunning, but it is a different experience. A richer experience and a much longer and much more nuanced experience.

"Have you ever seen the Grand Canyon?" I asked Jesus.

"No, only pictures."

"Well, it's time to do something about that. Let's tell Banquo to come find us when he's ready to go."

It was an indulgence, what we did, a celebration. We were celebrating not just the finishing of my memoir, but our successful deaths. Or maybe a better way to put it was our successful transition to the afterlife.

Well, that's the way it seemed at the time. From where I am now, I can see that we were both a bit naïve. We still had Jesus's killer to find and many more challenges ahead. But that naïveté was actually good—it afforded us some well-earned R&R.

WE FLEW UP SEVERAL HUNDRED FEET INTO THE CLEAR night sky and headed north-northwest. The Grand Canyon is a big target; we figured we could hit it without having to follow a road, even at night.

From Tucson to the Grand Canyon, as a ghost flies, is about 250 miles. We put on a good pace and got there just before dawn.

Have you ever seen the Grand Canyon? Have you flown over it in utter silence while the sun rose? Have you done aerial swoops down the narrow side canyons? Have you stood on the top of one of the huge rock formations in the middle of the canyon just as the sun kissed the top of it?

No? You haven't done all that? Well I can tell you that sometimes it is good to be a ghost. Better than good, beyond good.

As the sun slowly rose in the sky, Jesus and I ended up settling on the top of a formation called Vishnu Temple. It's one of the taller pieces that jut out of the canyon. It has a rounded look with a pointed top that looks somewhat like a temple.

The Grand Canyon experience is usually a pretty humbling one. It's so vast, so big, so old, that it applies this scale to your life that makes you feel small. Not in a bad way, just a level of perspective of how the normal day to day things just aren't that big of a deal in the vast sweep of time. And I felt that, but I felt something else. The Grand Canyon was no longer difficult to access or explore. It was right there, and I could easily see any part of it I wanted. I could fly over the river, I could sit on every peak and temple, I could explore every side canyon.

So I felt the vast sweep of time, but I felt a subtle empowerment that came along with it. It was a glorious feeling. I think Jesus was feeling it too, but we didn't really talk much. We sat there on top of Vishnu Temple and soaked in the sun and the stone, the blue sky, and the red rocks.

It was one of those moments you live for, one of those moments that anchor you when your life (or death) moves into more troubling territory.

Banquo's Rules of the Dead #1: *Enjoy the good times when they come, they often don't last long.*

Banquo doesn't literally have rules, not like that. He lectures endlessly, but doesn't come up with anything punchy or concise, unless, of course, he is quoting Shakespeare. But, I have been distilling his lessons into rules that make it easier for me to understand them. Being grateful for what you've got is the first one.

A "POP" JOLTED US OUT OF OUR REVERIE ATOP VISHNU Temple. I looked around and saw Banquo standing right behind us.

"Well gentlemen, it's..." he began, his words stolen by the beauty that surrounded us.

The rock we were atop was like a little island in the sea of geological beauty that is the Grand Canyon. With the sun high in the sky the colors were not as spectacular, but it still took the breath away.

"This is nice," he said when he found his voice again.

"Amen to that," Jesus added.

The three of us sat there in silence for some minutes. It felt like the silence that fills those big Catholic churches with the huge vaulted ceilings in the middle of the day—a deep and pervasive silence, punctuated by the soft hiss of the breeze and the reverberating caws of the ravens.

Jesus said it all. Amen.

After a few more minutes, Jesus called us to action. "Shall we?" he asked. After nods from Banquo and myself, he continued, "Banquo, can you pop us back to the graveyard? Our initial destination is in Tucson, and we can fly from there."

And just like that our little celebration ended. The time had come to get down to the serous business of finding Jesus's killer.

Transmission #5
Received 2012/01/31 02:23:56

THE HOTEL—OR DO YOU CALL IT A MOTEL, I NEVER CAN remember what the difference is—stood before us, a two-story L with peeling blue paint and a tired, desperate look. It sat a bit off of I-19 in the southern part of Tucson west of the airport. There were a few cars parked in front of some of the rooms, but not many.

Jesus led us to the second floor, room 202, and stopped in front of the door. He looked anxious, his ghostly form going a bit wispy as he hesitated.

"Where are we?" I asked.

"This is where I died," Jesus said flatly, but his even tone could not hide his fear. I could relate. I hadn't visited the site of my death since... well, since I died. Both Jesus and I experienced a violent death and the place of its occurrence has some weight to it.

"Why are we here?" Banquo asked.

"I..." Jesus began, his form continuing to degrade. If he degraded too much further he was in danger of going bardo.

Perhaps I should explain. There are a lot of ghosts that

are lost. They look like the classic wispy, diffusely formed ghost. You know, the ones that are gape-jawed and moan and wail. They are clearly not having fun. These ghosts are in the bardo, the bardo being their own private hell. Their forms may be here, but their minds are trapped in a world controlled by their fears and regrets.

Bardo is a concept that comes from Buddhism. I really don't know much about it, but I've been there a few times, and believe me, it makes the regular pain and suffering of life look like a day at the park.

So, Banquo and I were watching Jesus closely. We wanted to prevent his descent into the bardo, because getting someone out of the bardo can be very difficult.

"Jesus," Banquo said. "Get it together. Look at me. Why are we here?"

"I..." Jesus began and then looked at Banquo, his form coming into focus and getting more solid.

"That's more like it," Banquo said.

"I want to show you guys where *it* happened. I have a solid lead, but this seems like the place to start."

Banquo nodded and continued to stare at Jesus. It's the kind of stare he gives that I don't like being the target of. He was doing that looking at/looking into thing to determine if Jesus was ready for this. "Normally," he began, "I would recommend against this," he finally said. "You are still pretty young as a ghost. But, I think you can handle it."

Jesus nodded and walked through the door, as did Banquo and I.

The room wasn't much: a bed, a small table and chair, and a grim bathroom. The shag carpet was a multicolored brown that was several decades out of vogue and the TV looked nearly as old.

Jesus walked—actually he wasn't walking very well, he mostly floated. You see, us ghosts have no mass. Walking as a ghost is something like making a puppet look like it's walking. We do it consciously, with effort and practice.

It's part of Banquo's Lesson #2: Appearance Matters. Looking and acting as much as possible like we did when we were living keeps us in balance and out of the bardo. Jesus and I had, for the most part, mastered Lesson #2, and his "floating" was another sign that he was flirting with bardo-land.

He walked/floated across the room near the bathroom door and looked at the carpet. Following his gaze down, I could see a darker area on the carpet. They hadn't gotten all his blood out.

"Talk to us, Jesus," I said. "Walk us through this."

Jesus was the first ghost I had met at the morgue. His advice to "keep walking, keep talking" kept me out of the bardo for that first day of my death. I was just trying to return the favor.

"Right," he said, as he started to slowly walk back and forth. "The bounty on this guy was a good one. He was wanted for the murder of a teenage girl. The girl's family had some money so they put a sizable price on his head..." he trailed off, his pacing stalled as he stared at the carpet.

I looked to Banquo, I wanted to know if it was time to get him out of here. He gave me a small nod and said to Jesus, "What is his name?"

"Javier. Javier Medina." Jesus resumed his pacing. "The murder happened in Mexico City, where I lived. He was the family's gardener. Her parents were out of town with only the housekeeper to watch out for her. He... It was ugly, let's just say that, and when I found out about the bounty I started looking for him.

"He had jumped bail and I caught his trail heading north. I spent months tracking him all the way to the border. He had hired some Coyotes to get him across, so I did the same. I picked the trail back up in Nogales, on the Arizona side, and caught him just outside of Tucson." Jesus was gaining momentum now, his walking speeding up, as was his story.

"Being here illegally," he continued "I couldn't just take him to the police. My plan was to get some sleep, take him back to Nogales and hand him over to the authorities at the border.

"I picked this place to stay because they took cash, they didn't even mind the pesos, and didn't ask questions. Javier asked to use the bathroom, so I uncuffed his legs, but kept his hands cuffed, and let him go in. I kept the door cracked and stood outside. Everything seemed OK, but he was taking an awful long time washing his hands. I opened the door to say something and that is when he stabbed me in the eye with an ice pick." Jesus trailed off, his hand coming up to his left eye.

You might be wondering what all of this has to do with catching Jesus's killer. Well, if you remember all that I went through coming to terms with my death, Jesus was now doing the same. We weren't here to just help him catch Javier, we were here to help him come to terms with the fact that he died and how he died. Think about it. It's kind of a big deal.

Transmission #6
Received 2012/01/31 03:45:21

His story over, Jesus's head fell as he stared at the large ovoid stain on the carpet. His form went wispy and his eyes grew wide. I looked at Banquo, I could tell he was about to say something, but I shook my head. I stepped forward and said, "Man, you are a bleeder."

"Huh?" Jesus said.

"I mean, look at the size of this stain. Who knew someone could bleed that much out of his eye." Jesus looked away from the stain and at me, a look of confusion on his face. "What are you? Some kind of hemophiliac? Some prissy little girl that bleeds a quart at the slightest prick?"

"Hey!" he shouted, a trace of red flicking along the edges of his form. He was getting angry at me. "He stabbed me in the eye, JJ! This wasn't 'the slightest prick.'"

I shook my head, "I don't know, Jesus. So he took your eye out and that was it? You just laid there bleeding like some spoiled little baby. You didn't get up and fight? I don't know..."

"What?" Jesus shouted. "What is wrong with you? Ice

pick to the eye, into the brain, that was it. I was out of my body and stood here, right here, and watched the blood pour out of my eye, the handle of the pick sticking out... I... I..." The red flickering went away, and his form became even more diffuse. He was right on the edge of going bardo. I could feel Banquo's presence behind me but was grateful I couldn't see him. I had no idea what he thought of the tactic I was taking with Jesus.

"Prissy little girl, bleeds just like a pig," I chanted in a singsong tone.

The red flicker came back, his gaze returning to me, "You know, I am getting real tired of this, JJ."

"Prissy little girl, bleeds just like a pig."

"Have you no respect for the dead?" Jesus asked as he crossed himself and looked back at the stained carpet.

"Really?" I asked as I laughed at him. "I am dead too, you know. That little rule doesn't apply. The living should have respect for the dead. But the dead? Nope, not needed, you prissy little girl. You poor excuse for a bounty hunter. You border-hopping wetback illegal alien. You church-loving fool."

Yes, I was insulting him intentionally. When Jesus and I were first in the morgue with only a couple of bardo-brained ghosts for company, we spent quite some time trading insults to keep us from going bardo.

"Well at least I didn't die on the grease-stained floor of America's blight on the world, fast food restaurants," Jesus said, his attention fully on me.

"Yeah? Well at least where I come from we have grease-stained floors and don't all live in huts with dirt floors." I backed up slowly, and Jesus kept pace.

"At least those dirt floors gave me some perspective, and

I'm not some privileged red-necked American sucking up more than I deserve."

I was slowly backing up as I continued to taunt him. "At least I'm not enslaved to a church that is stuck in a world that passed it by a thousand years ago."

"And at least I'm not some heathen that believes in nothing but my own self-satisfaction and can't see beyond my own problems to the problems of his so-called friends and loved ones!" Jesus yelled.

That one hurt, but I knew the reason for this and I kept focused on that. I was getting close to the door and kept moving. "OK, boy-o, the gloves are off. I may be a self-centered heathen, but at least I don't support a religion that doesn't believe in contraception when the world is bursting at the seams with mouths to feed."

"And I'm not supporting a country that shoves its ideals down the throats of the whole world, by gunpoint if needed."

We were outside of the room, the sun bright above us. Jesus's form was looking better, the red had gotten brighter. Out of the corner of my eye, I could see red flickering along the edges of my own form. At that point, though, I didn't care. This was a fight, and I never back down from a fight. Never. It didn't matter that I started it, that I had a good reason for starting it, and that that reason was now past. The fight was all that mattered.

I opened my mouth to continue when Banquo intervened. "Now boys," he said, sounding like my mother. "I think that is quite enough."

"At least my—" I began.

"Enough!" Banquo shouted, surprising us both. The red flicking on Jesus's form died out and his form firmed back up. Banquo didn't raise his voice often, so when he did, it was effective. "You are both to be commended. Jesus, well done on facing the most difficult of circumstances and staying conscious. JJ, your methodology in helping Jesus was unusual, but innovative and effective."

I nodded my head, coming back to my senses, and pulled my form together—it had gone somewhat diffuse.

"Thanks, JJ," Jesus said.

"Any time," I answered.

"OK," Banquo began, "what is next, Jesus?"

Jesus turned and looked at the door of the room we had just exited. I could tell by the look on his face, a combination of dread and curiosity, that part of him wanted to go back in. I suspect it's kind of like that feeling when you stand at the edge of a precipice. Fear of falling, but this odd impulse to jump anyway.

"Umm..." Jesus began as he fought that feeling. "Yeah, just over here." Banquo and I followed him as he slowly led us away with a few looks over his shoulder.

The Fool

Transmission #7
Received 2012/01/31 05:01:02

JESUS LED US TO WHAT LOOKED LIKE A STUDIO APARTMENT right behind the motel's office. When they built places like this, probably forty years ago, they had built them with housing for the managers.

Two ratty recliners dominated the room, with two ratty people sitting in them watching TV. They had a glazed look in their eyes as they watched and discussed one of those trashy shows they put on in the middle of the day. The kind where people air their dirty laundry out publicly. It might have been Springer, or Maury Povich, or one of those guys. I couldn't tell—they're all the same to me.

"This is Ann and Frank Maston," Jesus began. "They run this place. When JJ was writing, this is where I started. I, fortunately, didn't go into the room where it happened, but started here.

"Normally I would have asked around, but in my current state that is not possible. I spent a week with this lovely couple, waiting for them to talk about what happened."

I looked at the couple that Jesus called "lovely." I wasn't

sure, because of his flat delivery, but I thought it might be sarcasm. Ann was rail-thin and twitchy, Frank was doughy and slouched in his recliner. I kept an eye on them as Jesus continued—they would occasionally make nasty comments about the poor family on the show, or snip at each other. "Lovely" indeed.

"And they did, finally," Jesus continued. "Javier robbed them after he murdered me, and they saw him running north as they were calling the police."

We left the Mastons and moved north ourselves. We went through an industrial area and eventually came to an old, run-down neighborhood. Jesus narrated how he had spent days lurking in this neighborhood waiting for someone to talk about Javier.

The neighborhood is a tough one, filled with old houses built with cement blocks in various states of disrepair. They were the type of houses built back in the seventies, uninspired rectangles with a garage on one end and small yard in the back.

Don't get me wrong, it's the kind of neighborhood I feel at home in. The kind where some neighbors you want to know and share a beer with on the weekends, and other neighbors you don't want to have anything to do with, and yet others you'll have to call the cops on when the fighting gets too loud.

It wasn't a pretty neighborhood, with the reality of everyone's humanity hidden behind fresh paint and rows of identical houses. Nope, the evidence of it was right out in the open for everyone to see.

Some houses had perfect, manicured yards, and others had bare dirt left over from grass that had died in years past.

Some windows were barred, some broken, some boarded up, and others just fine.

It was the kind of neighborhood where you had to keep your head on and your eyes open.

Jesus eventually brought us to a grim little house. It had once been a cheery yellow with a bright green lawn, but now the paint was peeling and the grass was brown.

"This is Mick's house. He's... well, he's... Let me just show you."

Jesus led us around the back of the house to what I thought was a bedroom. "Mick is—" Jesus began again.

"Why are you taking us around this way?" I asked.

"Mick is a bit of a hoarder. I don't really like going through it. This is the quickest way to him." With that, Jesus carefully positioned himself to the left of the cardboarded window and walked through the wall. Banquo looked at me and I shrugged my shoulders and followed.

I guess I should talk a bit about walking through walls. It's fun, yes, but it can also be disconcerting. A ghost can see, but doesn't have eyes. No, that's not some sort of Zen saying like "what is the sound of one hand clapping?" it's just the way it is. We have a visual sense, without eyes. Our forms have the appearance of eyes, but they aren't "real" eyes with retina and optic nerves. When I close my "eyelids" on my "eyes" I can still see. The presentation of eyes is just a nicety. But, even without eyes, in most cases our perception of vision is directional. You move your ghost-eyes and you see something different. As a side note, it doesn't have to be that way, and I have experienced it differently, but that is a serious, and dangerous, violation of Banquo's rule #2: Appearance Matters.

So, back to walking through walls. When your form is

completely immersed in darkness, when there is no light, then you don't see anything. Makes sense, right? Even though ghost-vision is much more sensitive than human-vision—we can see just fine at night with only a few stars—we are still limited by the need for light.

So, it's not some cool special effect where you see every layer of the wall, the brick, the wiring, the insulation, the sheetrock, etcetera. It's just that you can see, then you can't, then you can.

And the trouble is when you can't see you have no point of reference, no sense of movement. It can cause problems. Imagine if you "popped" deep into the earth, how would you ever get out? How would you know which way is up?

When I "walked" through the wall at Mick's house I became disconcerted because it seemed to be taking way too long. But, I stuck to my training and just kept my momentum steady. It took a few seconds and then I was out in a dimly lit room. On one end was a narrow pathway that wound through piles of... Well, it's hard to describe. The room was filled with junk: newspapers, boxes, stuffed trash bags, old furniture, fast food wrappers. This stuff was stacked everywhere with a small pathway out of the room.

On one wall of the room was a desk with a police scanner, CB radio, phone, and an old-fashioned reel-to-reel tape recorder. A large corkboard hung behind the desk covered in papers and maps with colored pushpins stuck into the maps.

Set up next to the desk was a recliner with a body in it. At first I thought the person was asleep until I noticed the silver cord snaking from the belly of the body to the figure standing and studying the maps.

The three of us stood there taking in the scene. I was

stunned by the sight of it, Banquo was wide eyed, and Jesus looked puzzled.

The ghost turned, his body wispy and indistinct, his eyes wide. "Who are you? Get out of my house!" He surged forward, but only got a couple feet until he got to the limit of his silver cord and was snapped back to his body in the recliner. "What the?" he said. "I'm calling the cops." He reached down and tried to pick up the phone, but his poorly formed limb just went through the cordless phone that was sitting there.

"Sorry, man," Jesus said holding up his hands. "Wrong house." He then walked through the stacks of junk until we were out of sight and flew straight up to the roof. Banquo and I followed.

I was left wondering what the hell had happened and how this ghost factored in to finding Javier.

Transmission #8
Received 2012/02/01 02:12:23

A BIG YELLOW SUN HUNG ABOVE US IN THE MIDDLE OF THE grubby Tucson sky. Things were quiet, the day-oriented people were out working, and the night-oriented people were sleeping.

"He was alive last time I was here, just a few days ago," Jesus said.

"Why are we here?" Banquo asked.

"The police scanner," Jesus said, pointing down. "He's obsessed with the police scanner, and neighborhood watch, and the most mundane crimes in this area. I spent about a week with him listening for signs of Javier. If he's still in the area he's going to be getting into trouble."

Banquo nodded and was silent for a time, his eyes going back and forth from Jesus to me. After a time he sighed and began lecturing, "Lesson #3, Awareness, Awareness, Awareness." It always bothered me when he said it that way, like he was repeating himself. As if saying "awareness" three times is much more effective than saying it once.

"You have both done well with the first two lessons,"

Banquo continued. "You both cut the cord, and you do a pretty good job at 'Appearance Matters'. It's time to move on to the most important lesson. In many ways the only lesson."

I looked at Jesus, he was nodding his head and looked excited. And really, I was too, because you never knew when Banquo was going to bestow you with a lesson, but the timing seemed odd. Banquo had started to open his mouth to speak again when I interrupted. "Excuse me, Banquo," I began. "Umm... we are kind of in the middle of something here. You know, tracking down Jesus's killer. Is this... I mean, I'm sure it is, but is this..." I trailed off. It sounded more lame coming out of my mouth than it did in my head.

"Yes, JJ, it is relevant and important. Actually I hadn't planned on getting into this for a while, but it appears to be time." Banquo in his suit and tie sat down on the peak of the black shingled roof. Jesus and I followed his example and sat below him. I'm not sure we all did this intentionally, but it certainly communicated the order of things.

"Awareness, Awareness, Awareness is a three-fold teaching, that is why 'Awareness' is repeated three times." I groaned. It's eerie sometimes how he seems to be able to read my mind, to answer the questions I haven't dared to ask. "The three aspects of Awareness you must master are: Awareness of Self; Awareness of Others; and Awareness of All.

"In reality everything I have taught you thus far falls under Awareness of Self. Cutting the cord and keeping your form sharp and clear are Awareness of Self. And I am sure you've sometimes wondered why I am so strict about this." He pointedly looked at me. "And the answer is simple. If you are not very aware of yourself—and we use our ghostly form as a focal point for this—you can't move on into the other levels of Awareness."

I nodded, it made sense.

"So, on to Awareness of Others. What did you notice about Mick down there?"

"He doesn't know he's dead," I said. Obvious, yes, but important.

Banquo nodded.

"He didn't know we were dead," Jesus said. Less obvious, more important.

"Good," Banquo said, his gaze turning to me.

I thought back. New vapory ghost, police scanner, hoarder, maps of the area with push pins. I licked my lips and hesitated before saying, "If we could get him to cooperate, he would be even more useful to us as a ghost than when he was alive."

Banquo smiled, "OK, why?"

"We can talk to him," I answered, "ask him questions."

"But he is scared of us," Banquo said, "he doesn't want to talk to us."

I nodded, going silent. It was true, he could be a good resource, but I didn't know how to get him to cooperate.

"If only we could dress up like police," Jesus said.

Banquo was silent and stared at him.

"We can? We can dress up as police?" Jesus asked, but Banquo didn't answer.

"Of course we can," I said. "We can just change our forms to look like police uniforms."

"Of course!" Jesus said.

"If it's that easy, JJ," Banquo said, "show us."

That brought me up short. As ghosts our forms are very malleable, but hard to keep sharp and clear and consistent.

The "clothing" Jesus and I wore were chosen to be simple to maintain, and we had been using them for long enough that it had become easy. Jesus was dressed in jeans with a white T-shirt and cowboy boots. I was in jeans, a long sleeve black T-shirt, and brown hiking shoes without the laces. I would occasionally add a blue jacket if I wanted a challenge.

All that ran through my mind, but Banquo had challenged me, I had to try. I stood up and focused on my pants, changing the blue jeans into blue dress pants. That took a few minutes, but worked. I then focused on the brown hiking shoes, turning them into black dress shoes. That worked too. Onto the shirt, a navy blue dress shirt with buttons, shirt pocket, and cuffs. This was giving me a bit more trouble, but I was slowly getting there. I looked up at Banquo and saw him shaking his head.

"Shoes and pants," he said. I looked down and my shoes and pants had reverted to normal.

I let my shirt go back to normal and sat back down ready to listen.

Banquo nodded and smiled and began lecturing to us again on form, this time under the heading of "Awareness of Self," instead of "Appearance Matters." He must have spoken for several hours, because the sun was going down when he finished. I won't make an attempt to transcribe the lesson here, it wouldn't really do any good—it was meant for Jesus and I and wouldn't translate well. A few things did become clear. Looking different and holding it takes practice, of course. The best trick he gave us was to focus on the "feel" of what we want our appearance to be, which gives us one thing to focus on instead of a thousand little details. Because of Mick's level of confusion, he thought that while our police disguise would not have to be perfect, we would have to act the part.

With Banquo's help we spent the rest of the night on the roof learning how to look and act like Tucson police officers.

Transmission #9
Received 2012/02/02 01:48:28

When the sun came up, Jesus was "dressed" in a short-sleeved white shirt with yellow patches on the shoulders, blue dress pants, black shoes, and one of those blue policeman's hats.

I was "dressed" in blue shorts, a white long-sleeved polo shirt with the yellow patches, and a bike helmet. It was a compromise for me. I just couldn't get the policeman's hat to work with its odd shape, small bill, and yellow piping. So, I decided to be one of these newfangled policemen on a bike. And keeping this form wasn't easy, my legs were bare, and that took some doing. I had to eventually give up on the leg hair and make like I was one of these crazy bikers who shaved their legs. The hair was just too hard to deal with. Unlike the hair on my head, which is short, and more of a "mass" of hair, I just couldn't manage thousands of individual hairs.

Banquo looked us over slowly nodding his head. I was afraid he was going to tell us it wasn't good enough. And if truth be told, it really didn't seem to be good enough to me. The yellow policeman's patches on our shoulders were indistinct, like they might be in a dream. They were the right shape, you could tell there were symbols and writing on them, but you just couldn't quite make them out. We also had batman-type—well, in this case policeman-type—black leather utility belts. It wasn't bad, but it wasn't up to Banquo's usual standards.

"I think that'll do," he finally said. "Remember, focus on being a policeman and don't get caught up in the little details too much. Those will be good enough if your head is in the right space."

Jesus smiled at me, he was clearly having fun. And from his perspective I could see why. A dead Mexican bounty hunter in the country illegally impersonating a Tucson police officer. Fun.

I was having fun too. You know me, I like a challenge, and this was definitely a challenge, and it had opened up Banquo enough to start teaching us again.

Our lesson-related mission was clear. Awareness of Self: I am a Tucson police officer. Awareness of Others: Pay strict attention to Mick and what he is emoting.

"I'll meet you guys back up here when you are done," Banquo said, and with a "pop" he was gone.

"Shall we?" I asked.

"Let's do this, Officer Lynch," Jesus said with a grin.

We flew down to the front door and walked through. The sea of junk was disconcerting. I had known, of course, that there were people like this, I had just never come up against it before. There was junk everywhere. And I would love to give you a better description than "junk," but really there is no better description. Empty boxes, trash, broken furniture, unopened mail, boxes stuffed to bursting, newspapers and magazines, and on and on. Junk.

"Mr. Mercer," Jesus said loudly. It didn't take long to find out his last name, there was a huge pile of unopened mail just inside the door. "Mr. Mercer, Tucson PD, we've been canvassing the neighborhood and have some questions for you."

"Umm..." said the ghost, a few rooms away. "Yes, yes, I'm here. I'm back here."

"Mr. Mercer," I said loudly, "may we have permission to enter the premises? We are searching for a criminal and have heard that you are the person to talk to about criminal activity in the area." I hoped I sounded like a policeman.

"Why, yes. Yes, of course. Yes, you may come in. I am back in the office."

Jesus in the lead, we slowly wound our way through the mountains of junk back to the room where we had first met Mick Mercer. I took a proverbial deep breath before entering, and said to myself, "I am a policeman."

Mick was there just as we had left him. His body was slumped in the office chair while his wispy, ghostly form hovered near it. I was glad to be a ghost, right then. I was pretty sure his body was getting rank by now, and I was grateful not to be able to smell it.

Yeah, ghosts can't smell. I didn't realize it at first, but over time it dawned on me. I think it has something to do with the biochemical nature of the olfactory sense. Light is an electromagnetic phenomenon, and sound is a vibratory phenomenon, but smell requires a biochemical reaction. And not having a biological body, that just isn't possible.

When we entered the room, the recently deceased Mick stood there wide-eyed and nervous, hovering over the stinking, rotting piece of meat that used to be him. "Mr. Mercer," Jesus began, "I am Officer Dominga, this is Officer Lynch."

Mick nodded his head, but didn't comment, his eyes darting from Jesus to me and back again. I focused on our Awareness lessons, trying to be sensitive to what he was feeling.

He was scared, that was easy to spot, but I got the feeling that he was worried we were there for him. Not a big leap, I know—most folks have that reaction to the police—but it was an unusual level of sensitivity for me. The Awareness thing seemed to be working.

"Mr. Mercer," I said, letting my voice become deep and soothing. "We've been canvassing the neighborhood talking to everyone. There was a dangerous criminal that we think came through a few weeks ago, and we were wondering if you noticed anything."

"Criminal?" he said. "Yes, yes, crime happens around here all the time." He turned to the map on the wall and pointed at the push pins. "Red is for a domestic disturbance, way, way too many of those. Yellow is for a robbery. Black is for a homicide—haven't had one for a while, that's a good thing. Crime yes, yes, I know about the crime around here, yes I do."

It was clear that this was the right tact for Mick. He was obsessed with this and it was the information we wanted.

"That's a fine police scanner," Jesus said. "Do you listen to it often?"

"Oh, yes, yes, I do. I listen to it all day, some of the night. Except when I sleep." His face went a bit vacant and his form further wisped out as he continued, "Except lately I don't need to sleep, or eat, or... I... I... Well, I just stay in my room and listen to the scanner."

He was starting to lose it. I pulled a pad of paper and a pencil out of my pocket and flipped through it. "Good thing we found you, Mr. Mercer. Listen, we are looking for a dangerous man by the name of Javier Medina. He's about five foot ten, 250 pounds, dark hair and skin, a native of Mexico. Have you heard reports of someone like that?" I stood there with my pen poised above the pad.

"Umm... umm... well, let me think." His wisp of a hand came up to his head in what was probably an attempt to scratch it as he turned to his map. "I think yes... maybe, maybe."

"This is important, sir," Jesus said. "We really could use your help."

"Yes, of course, of course. Anything for Tucson's finest." He turned back to his map and studied it, mumbling for some minutes. "Aha!" he said finally. "I remember now. It was a mugging about three weeks ago." His hand, which actually had come into focus, was pointing at a yellow push pin on the big map of Tucson.

"May we approach and get a closer look?" Jesus asked.

"Of course, of course. Umm... Well, you see, I called in about this. I called in, I am surprised you don't have the report." He was looking at us closely, too closely.

"It's a big department, sir," I began. "Can I be honest with you, Mr. Mercer?"

The ghost nodded, his eyes wide.

"This is a bit... a bit personal for us. You see, Mr. Medina assaulted officer Dominga here. We asked our lieutenant to put us on the case, but he refused. This is... well, I hope you can help us out, Mr. Mercer."

"Oh, sorry, so sorry." He looked at Jesus and added, "He didn't hurt you too bad, did he?"

"No sir, I'm still standing," Jesus said with a wry grin. "Now, if you could help us I would really appreciate it."

Mick nodded enthusiastically and began to give us an in-depth report on that incident and crimes in the area. It went on for over an hour, and the experience of it was something like walking through his house. He didn't give us a little information, he gave us an avalanche of information, with constant tangents about every little thing. But, in the end, Jesus gave me a sharp nod and I knew he had gotten what he needed.

"Mr. Mercer," I said, "I am going to put you in for a citizen's commendation. You have been most helpful."

"Me? Really? Well I... I just... you know, I just care about this community."

"And it's people like you that make our job easier," Jesus said.

It took us five more minutes to say good-bye to Mick. I don't think he wanted us to go, poor guy was lonely. We finally got out of there and flew up to the roof. It was time to really start looking for Jesus's killer.

Transmission #10
Received 2012/02/02 02:56:39

WE WERE EXCITED BY OUR LITTLE VICTORY WITH MICK. We felt, and acted, kinda like a couple of kids that had gotten away with something. You know, stayed up late, went to that R-rated movie when we were ten, cut class in high school.

And, I think, for some of us ghosts there is a reverting to a younger age. The ghost life is so very different. We don't have to work all day so we can keep a roof over our heads and feed our family. We need neither roof nor food. So, we are left with lots of extra time and, depending on the ghost's personality of course, we play. We play a lot.

"That was amazing, man!" Jesus said when we got to Mick's roof. "Where... How did you do that pencil and paper thing?"

"Oh that," I said with a feigned nonchalance, like a boy showing off the frog he had just caught, "I was focused on being a policeman. They always have a little pad of paper and pen, at least on TV, so I didn't really think about it. I just focused on being the policeman and pulled it out of my pocket." As I described it, I did it again. And sure enough I had a little pad of paper with a little pen threaded through the top.

"Let me see what you wrote," he said.

I opened the pad and sure enough there was what looked like writing on it. But it was kind of like our badges, dream writing. It sure looked like letters, but we couldn't make them out.

Jesus brought his head close and examined it carefully as I held it out. "There's a thread here. It runs from you to the pad and the pen. This thing is part of your form."

"Just like Fredrick," I added. Fredrick is a ghost back at the graveyard. He is a former mortician who died in 1929 and wears a working pocket watch. That watch, just like this pad and pen, are part of our ghostly forms.

"Way to go, man, way to go!" Jesus said holding his hand up, which I slapped in a high five. I felt something, it wasn't the same as meat contact, more like high-fiving with a numb hand, but being a ghost, any sense of touch is a thrill. Jesus and I were good enough with our forms now so that this kind of thing didn't require a lot of effort.

I put the pad and pen back in my pocket and started to dance around Mick's rooftop. Celebrations, you've got to take them when you can get them. I started humming and before I knew it I was singing, "Spirits in the material world, spirits in the material world."

"What song is that?" Jesus asked.

"It's an old Police song. My dad would always have the radio playing in the garage."

"Police?" he asked, looking at the way were dressed. "Nice. Is the song about ghosts?" he asked.

I thought for a moment. "I don't think so, but for us, for

today, it is. I wonder..." I stopped thinking of myself as a police officer and started pretending to be a rock musician. I wanted to experiment with this "awareness" thing to see if my form would follow my imagining.

Judging from Jesus's surprised expression, something was happening. I looked down and I was back in my normal blue jeans and black T-shirt, but I was holding a guitar. It was a plastic guitar with colored buttons on the neck and a plastic bar where the strings should be. I laughed, but it made sense. My most vivid memory of being a "musician" was playing Guitar Hero.

"Now you," I said to Jesus.

He shrugged and spun around clapping his hands, when he was facing me again he was back in his normal clothes holding a tambourine. When he banged on it, it made noise. It sounded like a tambourine, but the sound was a bit diffuse, muffled.

"Wow, that is amazing," I said, there was a big grin on his face.

"Does that thing make any noise?" he asked.

Doubt leapt into my mind, but I pushed it away. It's true I had no idea how to play a real guitar, but what did that matter? We were playing, and when you played as a kid, knowing how doesn't matter at all. I focused my mind on being a musician, I started singing and working the guitar just like I did in the game.

The sound wasn't all that great, but it was a rhythmic guitar-like sound, it was enough for me.

Jesus banged on his tambourine while we made up lyrics to the tune of the Police song. We got a couple of verses going, with mostly just the chorus as we danced around the roof playing our instruments and making a huge racket.

I'm not sure how long it went on but after a while I noticed I was the only one singing, making up really bad lyrics that featured Banquo. I was about to leap into the chorus when I became fully aware of Jesus's silence.

I turned around and saw Banquo there, his arms crossed and resting on his belly.

"I... We..." I stammered.

Banquo held his finger to his lips and I was silent and became aware of someone shouting. The words were faint, but discernible, "Hey! Hey! Hello! Who's up there? I... I'm part of the neighborhood watch. I'm calling the police now!" There was pause and then, "Damn phone. What is wrong with the phone, my hand goes right through it."

Banquo's thin smile said it all. A strong reprimand, a touch of amazement, and amusement.

"Quickly and quietly, what happened down there?" he asked.

Jesus filled him in on what happened, "There is a pattern of muggings and petty theft, with a couple of eyewitness reports that are probably Javier. He seems to be limiting himself to a square mile or so. The next step is to search."

"Good," Banquo said. "You two get started, I am going to pay Mick a visit and see if I can help him move on."

"We..." I stammered again, "We were working on our Awareness. Practicing holding a view of ourselves and letting our form follow."

Banquo nodded, a frown on his face. "As you search, practice your Awareness of Others." With that he sunk into the roof.

Transmission #11
Received 2012/02/03 01:57:01

I HATED BEING CAUGHT LIKE THAT, ESPECIALLY WHEN I was having fun. Banquo is an authority, a father figure, and his disapproval is something I try to avoid just like I did with my own father. It is this tight feeling in the gut, and I hate it.

Jesus didn't seem to be bothered, so I kept it to myself. We flew up to a high altitude so we could dial in the locations that Mick had showed us on his map. We were up high enough so that we could see our entire search area and quite a bit of Tucson.

We were looking at a neighborhood bordered by I-19 on the west, train tracks on the east, the Tucson airport on the south, and Irvington road on the north.

I liked it up there, it was quiet and peaceful.

"Don't go all cloud on me, JJ," Jesus said, eyeing me.

I laughed and said, "Don't think I don't want to." He was referring to an incident above Globe, Arizona, when we were hiding from some ghost bullies. I had become as large and diffuse as a cloud, and if not for Jesus, might have stayed that way.

Jesus laughed too, but I think we both knew it wasn't a joke. It was peaceful being like that, like a cloud. I sometimes missed that feeling.

From up high we were able to clearly see the boundaries of our search area. I wasn't real familiar with this part of Tucson, so we made several trips down and back up to get the names of the four streets that were the boundaries of our search area: I-19, Valencia Road, Campbell Avenue, and Irvington Road.

"Well, this is going to take a while," I said. We were back on the ground at the corner of Irvington and Campbell. It was mostly residential, pretty dense, with parks and schools, some shopping areas and a cemetery right in the middle.

"That it is," Jesus agreed.

He seemed hesitant. "What's going on?" I asked.

"I think we need to split up."

I nodded in agreement.

"It's just that..." he began.

I studied his face, gone was the frequent smile below his big black mustache and in its place was a worried frown. "It's just that," I said, "you are afraid of what will happen if you find Javier. You don't want be alone when you face him."

Jesus nodded. I felt a bit guilty. Jesus had been witness to my many antics as I confronted my killer, tried to exact vengeance, and made a terrible mess of the whole thing. I was starting to get a glimpse of what that had been like for him as he watched me.

"Let's make a deal," I said, a plan starting to come into focus. "We'll meet at the playground of that elementary school over there every hour on the hour. We're going to be searching houses, they will have clocks, so we'll be able to keep track of time. If one of us is more than ten minutes late, the other will go looking for him."

"Sounds good," Jesus said tentatively. "And skip the stores, parks, and that cemetery."

I nodded. I really didn't want to get mixed up with another group of ghosts anyway. We needed to stay focused. "And if one of us finds him, we will go to the playground immediately. Take no action, right?"

"Right," Jesus said, a small smile returning to his lips.

"Do you want to start here?" I asked. We were at the northeast corner of our search area. "I'll start at the southwest corner."

"Right. And search each house thoroughly. Every room. Check for attics and basements. Search sheds and other buildings. Everything," he said.

I nodded and smiled, Jesus was getting back to himself.

"And we search during the day only. From what Mick said, all his activities have been occurring at night."

"OK," I agreed. "Meet you at the school playground at the top of every hour. Shall we?"

A shadow passed over Jesus's face, but he shook it off and nodded. I watched him fly to the nearest house before I took off flying to the other corner of our search area.

IT WAS STRANGE FOR ME, WATCHING JESUS GRIEVE. HE had been gracious enough to hold off this long while he helped me through my own transition. It was his turn. I was duty bound to help him, he's my best dead-friend and he needed me.

But it was a transition in our relationship. I was used to him being logical and levelheaded, while I was the one going off all half-cocked and crazy. I'm not saying Jesus was half-cocked, not at all. But he wasn't levelheaded either. His process, thankfully, was different than mine, but it was a process, and he was going through a lot.

He was going through it quieter than I did, but he was going through it. Those damn five stages of grief. Denial, Anger, Deals, Depression, and Acceptance.

I think that while I frolicked through those stages, he was in Denial. He was pushing back the grief and giving me space to go through it. Now, I would say he was brushing up against Depression. What I was worried about was Anger. I almost killed someone when my Anger came to fruition. Jesus is a quiet, gentle man, and those are the ones you have to worry about when it comes to the un-quiet, un-gentle emotions.

All these thoughts flickered through my mind as I flew to the corner of I-19 and Valencia and began my search.

The neighborhood was older so the houses had a fair amount of variation in their layout so I had to be careful I didn't miss anything.

It was a strangely voyeuristic activity. I had done a stint as a voyeur in my poltergeist/haunting stage, but this was different. What I had done previously was this gentle trickle of peering at humanity, but this was like trying to take a drink from a fire hose. Wholly overwhelming.

One saving grace was most people were at work, but a surprising number of them weren't. But even in those empty houses, I was constantly under assault by the flotsam and jetsam of a meat life.

Transmission #12
Received 2012/02/03 03:12:45

Searching those houses, I saw it all.

I saw far too many people slouching on couches, watching bad daytime TV, looking very much like the bardo-brained dead. Their faces all slack, their eyes wide and unfocused. I saw sleeping people who must work the graveyard shift, I saw people arguing over inconsequentialities, I saw mothers taking care of their children, I saw people dressing, showering, eating, making love, having bowel movements, and everything between.

It was overwhelming. From house to house to house I flew, and I began to appreciate the empty houses. I could fly through and not get distracted, having only to deal with the disorientation of all their stuff and constantly flying through walls and floors.

In some ways, the houses with people became like daytime TV for me. I found myself unable to move on when the drama presented was interesting enough.

There was this young couple, Ben and Lisa. I knew their names because they were shouting them at each other loud enough for the neighbors to hear. Ben was out of work and had been looking for close to a year. Lisa was the one keeping the household afloat, but she was pregnant and was going to have to stop working soon. The house they owned was under water and they were a few months behind on the mortgage. Lisa had come home for lunch and found Ben all slack jawed in front of the TV instead of looking for work.

They had real problems, interesting problems. I only stopped for a few minutes as they went through this mini cycle of fighting and making up, but it was fascinating.

I found some stoner college students with a basement full of hydroponic equipment and big healthy pot plants. The three of them, all male, were too busy sampling their wares to make it to class.

There was a hoarder in training, not quite up to Mick's level, who had a spare bedroom filled with unopened boxes from QVC. No one was home, he or she must have been working to pay for their little habit.

I watched a business man home for "lunch," which was nothing more than a line of cocaine.

I searched the house of some newlyweds who had called in sick so they could stay home and make love all day.

I couldn't help but watch the young mother teaching her daughter how to make cupcakes.

And on and on it went. Humanity on display a house at a time. I bet this is how some ghosts spend their days. Locked in this voyeuristic mode where they can't be what they were, so they can spend their days watching other people. Daytime TV for ghosts.

I also came across two ghosts, both in empty houses that I am pretty sure were foreclosed. The first was this bardo-brained mess wandering around one of the nicer houses in the neighborhood. I spent a few minutes trying to reach him, to no avail.

The second was a young woman in one of the simple brick houses that predominate. She was well formed, dressed in blue pants, a white blouse, and a blue jacket. She looked like a professional woman and was very out of place in the empty house.

"Hello," I said when I noticed her transparency.

She jumped back, her eyes wide as she looked at me.

"Hi, my name is JJ." I extended my hand.

"Hi," she answered quietly, backing up another step.

"Can I help you?" I asked.

She looked confused, but not bardo-ish. "Where is everyone, what happened?"

I smiled looking around, "I don't know. It looks like everyone left. I think the house has been foreclosed."

"But I live here," she said. As we talked she wandered about the house a bit, from the living room, into the kitchen, and back into the living room. When she entered the living room she would always stare at a spot on the floor.

Banquo had told me to be aware of others, and the second time she did this I asked, "Did something happen here?"

Her brow crinkled as she nodded and clutched her heart. I felt a brief, surprising spike of pain in my chest as she did this.

"I..." she began and then wandered back into the kitchen. She would go there, look around for something and then seemingly not finding it come back into the living room and stare at the spot on the floor.

I felt the spike of pain in my chest again. "Your heart?" I asked.

She nodded, her hands again coming to her chest. She was pretty, with long brown hair and blue eyes, early thirties. I wanted to get on with my search, but I felt I had to try to help her.

Banquo's Rules of the Dead #2: *If you can help, then you must try to help*. In this circumstance, the need was clear.

"Can I tell you something?" I asked.

She looked up from the spot on the floor and nodded, she seemed grateful for the distraction.

"Please don't be afraid, but I'm a ghost. I died a few months ago." I proceeded to tell her the Reader's Digest version of my death and coming to grips with it.

She listened quietly and stopped her pacing, her attention on me. After my story ended, her brow furrowed deeply for a long time and she asked, "Am I dead?"

"Yes," I said gently, "but it's not so bad. I have friends, we have fun, we help people. It's really OK, and it's not the end."

"It's not?" she asked.

"No, it's not. Can you tell me what happened?"

She looked at the floor and clutched her chest again. I felt the spike of pain as she said, "My chest it hurt, so bad, the pressure and then..." She looked back at the carpet and then walked to the kitchen. "I was in here, making dinner for my husband when I felt it. It was sharp like a knife, heavy like an elephant was sitting on my chest. I..." Her eyes started to glaze over and her form got wispy, she was in danger of going bardo.

"What happened then?" I asked putting as much punch in my voice as I could.

"Oh, I... It was Sunday, Howie was watching football. I didn't know what was happening so I came in here." She walked back to the living room and I followed. "I tried to tell him, but I couldn't talk. The pain was unbearable, I fell down on the floor and then…"

"And then you were standing here like this," I said.

"Yes. How did you know?"

"It's not uncommon, what has happened to you."

She nodded, biting on her lower lip.

"Listen, it's OK," I told her. "This is not the end. You will not be stuck here forever."

"I won't?"

I shook my head, "No you won't, I promise. Most people move on when they die. Some of us end up as ghosts for a while, but at some point we all answer the Call."

"The Call?"

I nodded and smiled. "Yes, the Call. It's like hearing the most beautiful music you've ever heard, except you are not just hearing it, you are seeing it and tasting it and smelling it. It is peace and redemption and grace. It is—" I stopped talking because I noticed two things. First, that the woman was smiling, her face went from confused and sad to happy. Second, I could almost hear the Call. As I talked and remembered it, it seemed to be coming back to me.

"I hear it," she said excitedly. "Oh my God, it is so beautiful."

"That's it, you've got it." I could sense the Call, it was wonderful and beautiful, but it wasn't quite the same. I could tell that it wasn't there for me, but I could tell that it was there.

"What do I do?" she asked.

"Just say 'yes' to it." And with a look of bliss on her face she was gone.

THE FOOL

Transmission #13
Received 2012/02/04 02:02:59

With the sun low on the horizon, Jesus and I met back at the playground of the grade school. Our hourly meetings had been brief, nothing more than a "You OK?" and back to it. Since the search was over for the day, we took some time to reflect. He was sitting on top of the monkey bars when I got there.

"Well?" I asked.

He shook his head, "No Javier... but, an interesting day."

"I'll say," I said as I flew up to him and we discussed the day.

Later, as darkness came, we scouted for a place to spend the night. You might think, you're a ghost, what does it matter? Well it does. Just like everyone, we want a place that feels private and safe to rest in.

We flew up to the flat roof of the school, but it was a dirty expanse of tar and cooling units. Not inspiring. We considered the playground, but it felt too exposed. We ended up deciding to leave the area and go for height. Downtown Tucson isn't much, as these things go, but there are a few high-rises. We ended up at the Unisource Energy Tower which was a few miles north of our search area, and settled right at the top on its blue metal roof.

So, there are two ways for a ghost to rest. The first is "fading." It is like a dreamless sleep and if you are present when it happens to one of us, we slowly fade away. The other is to... well, there is no formal word for it, but it is resting similar to how you meat folk do it on a lazy Sunday afternoon.

We find a peaceful place and relax. If you do it right, time becomes quite elastic and tends to pass very quickly. Jesus, I am sure, would call it prayer, and Banquo would call it meditation. I don't really have a word for it, maybe "zoning out" fits for me.

Jesus and I were in that state as we felt midnight approach.

OK, so another short "Ghosts 101" break. We all can feel it when it is midnight. We feel more energy, more awake for the hour before and after midnight. Most of us are active then. It's really our time.

So, shortly before midnight, there was a "pop" and Banquo was there. He looked at us both carefully before speaking, "Time for the Midnight Circle, gentlemen."

I thought he meant he was going to take us back to the graveyard for the nightly gathering of the ghosts. It was often the highlight of the day. Banquo would often lead the assembled host in performances, often Shakespeare, usually the tragedies.

I was conflicted about the prospect. While I knew I would enjoy the Midnight Circle, I wanted the three of us to stay focused on our adventure.

"I've been thinking," Banquo continued. "It is important

to have the Circle, even with just three of us." I breathed a sigh of relief. "And I know we have things to talk about, but I think the tradition is a good one and should be honored." He waved us over to the outside edge of roof. He sat on the corner, and Jesus and I sat facing him, the three of us forming a triangle, the closest to a circle three can do.

"While Shakespeare would work in a small group like this," he said, "I think we need to go back, way back, and go for something more primal, something that inspired the Bard himself."

Banquo's voice, a deep, booming baritone, seemed like it belonged on the stage. When he went into story mode it became even bigger and swept us up in whatever tale he was telling.

"Tonight I would like to start reciting to you Homer's epic poem, the Iliad."

I groaned, I didn't mean to, it just slipped out. Banquo leveled his gaze at me and asked, "Is there a problem, JJ?"

"It's just that 'poem' doesn't do much for me. Shakespeare is one thing, but epic poetry is another."

Banquo's smile was an equal mixture of amusement and indulgence. "You may not know it, JJ, but you already know the Iliad. It is a story that has never left us even though it was written in the 8th century BC. It is a tale of war, revenge, lust, betrayal, and the gods interference with mankind."

I shrugged my shoulders, I wasn't convinced.

"The siege of Troy by the Greeks, Achilles, Helen of Troy, Agamemnon, and Hector."

Recognition dawned on me, but I was still dubious.

"Tell you what, JJ. Let's try this tonight. If you're bored, we can move on to something else."

I nodded. It did no good to argue with Banquo on items like this.

Banquo took a deep breath and began.

Achilles' wrath, to Greece the direful spring

Of woes unnumber'd, heavenly goddess, sing!

That wrath which hurl'd to Pluto's gloomy reign

The souls of mighty chiefs untimely slain;

Whose limbs unburied on the naked shore,

Devouring dogs and hungry vultures tore.

Since great Achilles and Atrides strove,

Such was the sovereign doom, and such the will of Jove.

Banquo paused and looked at me. I nodded, I had to admit that it didn't sound boring. The language was strange, just like Shakespeare, but as Banquo continued to recite the "epic poem" it began to make more sense. The worst part was keeping all the names straight. Banquo would pause and explain things from time to time.

After about an hour, Banquo ended his recitation, having finished Book I. He looked at both of us and said, "So how did it go today?"

It was a difficult transition. I had been taken into the story and found the change abrupt. My mind groped for a while as the events of the day came rushing back.

"I helped a ghost move on," I began. Banquo gave me one sharp nod, so I briefly told him the tale.

"Excellent," was his reply to it. High praise.

"So what happened?" I asked. "Did I summon the Call? Was I just hearing what was already there and helping her hear it? If I really wanted to move on, could I do it that way for myself? What if—"

Banquo held up his hand cutting me off. "These are

good questions, JJ, but not what is most important about what happened."

"Huh?"

He smiled. "Awareness of All, that is what happened. That is how you helped her. You were aware of her, but it went beyond that. Well done."

My mouth moved as I tried to repeat my questions, but I was stunned to silence by the praise. For Banquo this was effusive.

Banquo laughed, the sound rumbling over the city below us. "In truth, JJ, I don't know whether you summoned it or whether it was there. It doesn't really matter. And if you are ever ready, the Call will be there."

With that he turned to Jesus, "And you?"

Jesus told Banquo about the family of ghosts he had found. "I came across this empty lot. It was strange because in a neighborhood that old you don't see empty lots. On this lot, a family—a mother and father and two kids—are going about their business like the house is there and they are alive."

Banquo's eyes narrowed; he was clearly interested. "What did you do?"

"They didn't seem to see me so I looked around the property. I found a few burnt remnants and deduced that the family had died when the house burned down. They were still going on with their lives as if it hadn't happened. I watched them for a while, they didn't seem to be distressed, but it doesn't feel right.

"As I spent time with them, the outlines of the house started to become visible." Banquo nodded encouragingly at this. "I changed my form back to a policeman and went to the door and knocked and called to them. It was weird, the door seemed more substantial than it should have."

"Did they hear you?" I asked.

"They did. The father came and opened the door—by then the house was even more visible. Not knowing what else to do, I asked them about Javier and a few other questions. They seemed OK. But it's so strange. Should we help them?"

Banquo was silent for a while, his eyes distant. "I don't know. It would be easy to make it worse, but the state they are in isn't really a good one. It's not quite the bardo, but it could easily go that way." Banquo was silent again for a time, his eyes gazing out over the city. "They are in a shared illusion we call 'maya.'"

"Do you mean Mayan?" Jesus asked. "Like my ancestors?"

He turned to Jesus. "No. The word maya, like bardo, is a Sanskrit word. It means, roughly, 'that which is not, but appears real.' Tell you what. Take me there in the morning and I'll see what I think."

Both men were quiet, lost in thought. I hated to interrupt, but Banquo was in a talkative mood and I had more questions. "Do you mind if I ask some questions about what happened earlier at Mick's?"

Banquo nodded. "Go ahead."

"What happened when you visited him?" I asked.

Banquo shook his head, looking bemused. "It was tough, but I got him to move on. He is quite the character."

"I am curious about when you saw us on the roof and we were playing the instruments." I was a bit embarrassed about the whole thing, but so intrigued by what we managed to do.

Banquo was silent and finally said, "What is your question, JJ?"

I went back over what I had just said and realized I hadn't asked a question. "How did we do that?" I asked.

"I'll let you ponder that for yourselves but will give you a few questions to get you going." He paused and looked at both of us for a moment. "How are we seeing right now? We have no eyes. How are we hearing each other? We have no ears to hear or vocal cords to speak."

I opened my mouth to say something about wanting a straight answer but closed it. After a moment I said, "We are spirits, you know. Spirits in the material world." I was still trying to explain the song, the celebration we were having. "We were dressed as police. That's a Police song."

"I know who the Police are, JJ," Banquo said, his eyes unfocused, suddenly looking like he was far, far away. "My daughter was the right age when that song came out. She had a crush on Sting."

If I had been meat I would have held my breath waiting for Banquo to continue. I could see Jesus was experiencing the same surprise and desire for more. This was the kind of thing Banquo never talked about. I wanted more, but Banquo was done talking about it.

"Well, gentlemen," he said, standing up and moving away, "get some rest, we have a lot to do tomorrow."

Everyone found their own spot on the roof, each of us resting in our own way. Jesus praying, Banquo meditating, and me doing my "zoning out" thing.

It had been a good day, a very good day, the exact kind of day I had been hoping for when this plan came together. I got to help my best dead-friend, I was able to learn and grow with relative ease, and I discovered something new about my mentor.

It was a good day, too bad things were about to change.

Transmission #14
Received 2012/02/04 03:26:22

THE NEXT MORNING BANQUO AND JESUS WENT AND HELPED the family in the lot of the burned down house. We had two more days of the same with Banquo joining us in the search when he wasn't helping ghosts move on.

In truth, after three days of this I was getting bored and overwhelmed at the same time. Bored of doing the same thing day after day, overwhelmed by the display of humanity laid before me.

It was that boredom/overwhelm that led me to changing my routine. I had just finished a section of the neighborhood and it was late in the afternoon, a few hours before our stopping time, and I had just had enough. I flew to the school playground, our rally point, and waited.

School was out on Christmas Holiday, so no one was there, which was a relief from the overwhelm but not the boredom. After a half hour sitting on the jungle gym, my restlessness led me to explore the school.

I flew down the empty halls, through the empty classrooms, through the school offices, with a few people still at work, until I came to Mrs. Turner's first grade classroom.

The room was bright with windows on one side and many crayon drawings decorating the walls. There were big letter sets, "Aa", "Bb," "Cc," on the very top of the wall. Behind the teacher's desk was a series of framed pictures.

The pictures were of Mrs. Turner and her first grade classes over the years. It started in 1979 and progressed from there. Mrs. Turner started out as a slim, young blond woman with a bright smile and transformed to an older, plumper blond woman with a bright smile. Her smile stayed the same as her face and body slowly morphed as she aged.

When I came towards the end of the display, I became aware of another ghost in the room.

At first it was just a sense that I wasn't alone. I hadn't seen anyone when I came into the classroom and I had thought it was empty. Then as I moved towards the last few pictures, I felt my form tingling along my right shoulder and arm.

I looked over and I had "bumped" into another ghost. That "tingle" was our forms overlapping. This is not something you do on purpose without permission. It would be like a meat-person touching a complete stranger.

"Excuse me," I said, looking over at the ghost.

He was a diffuse mess and gape-jawed. A bardo-brain. Well, at least this was a slight change of pace. I looked him over. He would have been tall when he was alive and handsome. He had sandy hair, brown eyes, and a crescent-shaped scar on his right cheek. As I looked at him, something tickled at the back of my brain, something felt familiar.

"So whatcha looking at?" I asked, moving a little closer so I could see the picture he was examining. It was Mrs.

Turner's 2009 class. But, being in the state he was in, he wasn't really looking at it. Maybe a small part of him was, but the larger part of him was locked in the bardo.

"The class of 2009, huh? You know somebody in this class?" It was a long shot, but you never know what's going to rouse a bardo-brain.

The sense of familiarity was starting to drive me crazy. "This classroom reminds me of my grade school," I began, just to talk. "I remember having all those letters at the top of the wall. I remember my teacher, Mrs. Walters. She was kind of tough. This was in Globe. My dad was a mechanic and my parents didn't have a lot of money so he would come pick me up after school and take me to the garage. I remember loving to ride in his '67 Mustang. He loved that Mustang."

When I said "Mustang" the ghost's eyes changed just a bit, as if I had gotten through to him.

"You like Mustangs? Great cars. My friend Nate and I used to buy old 'stangs and fix them up. Sell them to middle-aged men looking to recapture the thrill of their youth."

Part of him heard me when I talked about Mustangs. So I kept it up. I started reciting stats for different years, throwing in bits of Mustang trivia, keeping up a constant stream of words.

His face came a little more into focus, and his eyes would sometimes change just a tiny bit, but it was never much. Never enough.

After about an hour of this, it was time for me to go so I said, "Nice talking to you. See you later, John."

That "John" just slipped out. It wasn't conscious, but when I said it a memory came back to me. It was of me and Tamara having coffee when she told me of her dead fiancé

John. The one that was murdered, the one that tried to tell her something while he was dying, the one that haunted her and tried to communicate with her after he died, the one that inspired the SECI project.

"Oh my God," I said, turning around and looking at him again. "John? Are you Tamara's John?" His eyes flickered at the mention of Tamara's name.

I remember the picture of him she had on her cell phone. He had the right hair and eye color. His face was round like in the picture, and he had the exact same crescent scar on his cheek. It had to be him, it had to be.

"Shit!" I swore. "Come on, John, snap out of it. Tam has been looking for you; my God you don't know what she's gone through trying to communicate with you. Come on, John, Tam needs to hear from you."

I was a little off my nut. Tamara had moved mountains trying to communicate with him, and here he was gape-jawed and bardo-brained staring at Mrs. Turner's 2009 first grade class.

I couldn't leave him like this, I couldn't. I couldn't let Tamara wonder any longer. There was a way for him to communicate with her, Tamara had created it. If only I could snap him out of the bardo.

Transmission #15
Received 2012/02/04 04:26:31

I KIND OF FEEL BAD ABOUT DOING THIS. ABOUT COMING back and continuing my story. I tried my best on the first round to leave things tied up pretty well. I wasn't going for "happily ever after," because that would be silly, but I was hoping to leave everyone with peace and hope. Peace in knowing that I had gotten through my very difficult transition into the afterlife. Hope in the knowing there is an afterlife.

But now, here I am again and as I am writing this I am anything but peaceful. Life, as I now know it, has drug me back under and I am struggling. I am forced to return to telling my story to come to grips with it.

I think it's human to want the "happily ever after," to grasp for those moments and try to keep them. But it's like holding on to a handful of air, complete illusion. The pendulum of our lives swings back and forth, and balance comes, it does, but it is fleeting, lasting only a moment before things swing the other way.

I know this. You know this. We all know this. And yet

there is something in us that wants it all to end OK, for us to be all right. And what I have to tell you is that death is not the end, and that means that our struggle at living (whether we're "dead" or "alive") continues on beyond the shuffling off of this mortal coil.

I know, I know, this is Life 101. I get that. I also get that just because it is basic and simple doesn't mean it is easy. It's not easy at all.

For me this all comes back to Rhiannon. As I type away, I keep thinking about her.

I know we are in the middle of some crazy stuff with Jesus, but unlike the JJ I am writing about, I know what is coming. And it's about Rhiannon. I could tell you some funny stories, or some romantic stories, but you've heard those kinds of things a thousand times. What I want to tell you, and what I hope will convey something important about our relationship, is the most mundane of stories.

I was still a student but had started as a part-time janitor at UA—the University of Arizona. It was nighttime and I'm using one of these big round industrial floor scrubbers to clean one of the endless hallways in the College of Engineering. I was in the zone, bathed in the potent lemony scent of the cleaning solution. I remember the machine was called the PowerGlide. Which always amused me. Such a romantic name for such a mundane activity. I didn't mind the work, it just wasn't glamorous or anything.

Anyway, I'm working on the floor when my cell phone rings. It's Rhiannon. We had been friends for a while but had only been on a few official dates.

"Hey, beautiful," I said in greeting after I click the machine off.

"Hi, JJ. You working?"

"Oh yeah. Just cleaning the floors, doing my little part to make the world a better place. Or at least a cleaner place."

"So... Ah..." She stammered which immediately made me fear this was a "Dear JJ" kind of moment. But my insecurity was misplaced. "I'm heading out to the store and am going to pick up a lottery ticket."

I didn't say anything. I didn't understand the hesitation or why she was telling me she wants to get a lottery ticket.

"So, I thought we could pick the numbers together," she continued.

I'm sure the look on my face as I stood there with my PowerGlide was a quizzical one. Who was this girl asking me to come up with lottery numbers? "Umm... OK. You know the odds are kind of long." I've never been a lottery buyer. I don't mind it, don't get me wrong. It's a voluntary form of taxation (what with Uncle Sam keeping most of the dough), which I have no problem with. It's the odds that kept me away.

"Well, you know, someone has to get lucky," she said. I could hear the shrug in her voice. "It might as well be us."

"OK, sounds like fun," I told her and then rattled off a few numbers at random.

We chatted a little more and when the call was over I stood there in that long, quiet hallway kind of stunned. I had never had a girlfriend do something like that. And by "like that," I mean treat me as a friend in the most ordinary of ways.

What she did had nothing to do with the usual mating rituals we humans go through as we try to determine if the fit is right. You know, all the grand gestures, romantic dinners, trying to be so perfect for your potential mate. In this tiny mundane way she treated me like a real person, like a friend.

And beyond that I realized that the important moments in a relationship aren't the big romantic gestures or dramatic events that come from time to time. It's the little mundane day-to-day moments that fill up your life and make your time with that person worth living.

When I was pretty young, I became aware of this ritual my mother and father would do every night. After dinner they would go do dishes while my sister Jean and I watched TV. This wasn't something they ever asked us to do as a chore, but a little mundane thing they did together. My dad would wash—no dishwasher in our house back then—and my mom would dry and put things away. They would chat and laugh and seemed to really enjoy it. Which puzzled my ten-year-old self.

I never understood that until Rhiannon called me about the lottery ticket. It's the little mundane things that make a relationship work. And it was that lottery ticket that sunk me so much further into my love for Rhiannon.

For the first time I could imagine spending the rest of my life with someone, with Rhiannon.

Does that make sense? Her treating me like a human, like a friend, changed my understanding of what it means to be in a relationship in the most fundamental way.

That's who she is to me. The girl that changed me in the most fundamental way.

Transmission #16
Received 2012/02/05 00:58:12

I SPENT ANOTHER HALF HOUR WITH JOHN. I TRIED EVERY-thing I could to snap him out of his bardo state, but failed. I had no idea what I was doing, this wasn't something Banquo had taught us about. The only thing I knew that worked was shocking them back into this world.

I told him that Tamara was here to see him, I told him Tamara was dying and wanted to say good-bye, I told him that Mrs. Turner was here and needed to talk to him, and I told him he had won a classic '67 Mustang fastback and all he had to do was tell me he wanted it and it was his.

I went on like this until it was past time for me to meet Jesus and Banquo. I reluctantly headed out to the play-ground where they sat on the jungle gym talking.

"I found him, I found John," I said as I approached. I noticed that my form wasn't in too good of shape, a bit dif-fuse and flickering with orange along the edges, but I didn't care. "He's there, he's right there in the school."

"Who?" Banquo asked.

"John, Tamara's John. He's the reason Tam got involved in Jin's project and created the SECI chamber."

"Great, man, that's great," Jesus said with a smile. "Why didn't you bring him out to meet us?"

"He's gone, he's far gone. A bardo-brain if there ever was one. Banquo, can you help me?" The words were rushing out of me like air escaping an overfilled balloon.

Banquo paused, looking me up and down. "As I recall, this John tried communicating with Tamara after he died for a while, which stopped all the sudden. That would be—what?—two years ago? I'm sorry, JJ, but someone who's been in the bardo that long is very, very difficult to help."

"Please, just come take a look."

He nodded and then followed me back into the classroom. John was still there all vapor-like and gape-jawed, staring at the same picture.

Banquo looked him over, walking around and viewing him from all sides. He spoke to him briefly and then walked back over to Jesus and I. "He is beyond the kind of help I can give," Banquo said flatly.

"But you hardly tried anything," I said.

"That is because his condition is clear. I'm sorry, JJ, there is nothing to be done."

"Nothing? Nothing! Come on. There must be something."

Banquo was silent again, his lips a thin straight line as he stared at me. I firmed up my form, but the orange flicker along the edges remained. "There is one way," he said, "but it is difficult and dangerous to the spirit that goes to his aid."

"Tell me, I'll do it," I said without a thought.

"Why is this so important, JJ?"

Now is the point in a narrative where I should give a punchy little answer that clearly described my motives.

You know, tell a story of my past that illustrates why this is so important. It's expected in storytelling. Why else have back story besides to illuminate a character's actions? You can't have a character doing things that don't make sense, can you?

Except I'm not a character in a story. I am real, and real life is messy. It's true that even though the last few days had been exactly what I wanted, I was growing bored. It's true that I cared for Tam and would do a lot to help her. It's also true that when I was in my meat body I had the beginning of feelings for her and saw just how hard John's death was on her.

All that is true, as well as some darker things. I wouldn't have been able to put my finger on it then, but from where I am now, I think I was not enjoying my role. Don't get me wrong, I really wanted to help Jesus, but I was no longer at the center of things, and I was finding that hard.

The last part of my meat life I had been adrift, carried along by events, depressed. I had surrendered myself to that life, I had essentially given up. Dying woke me up and I had taken control of my life, I had set a course and followed it.

Since dying, I have done lots of stupid things, made lots of mistakes, but the choices have been mine. I am quite sure that part of me that had woken up didn't like being in service to someone else.

But even with all of that, it doesn't seem to be enough. A simple explanation of cause and effect just doesn't explain my desperation.

Boredom + Helping Tamara + No Longer Being the Center of Attention does not equal JJ Risking Everything to Pull John Out of the Bardo.

It doesn't seem to, but maybe it does. The human heart (even if you're a ghost) is a mysterious thing.

"I..." I stammered, trying to express what I was feeling. "I... For Tamara. I owe her, I want to help Tamara." It seemed to me that I was totally failing at Awareness of Self. I knew even then that I couldn't explain it.

"But, JJ," Banquo said slowly, "we are here helping Jesus right now."

The words fell on me like a ton of bricks. I looked at my friend and saw his jaw moving, but he didn't speak. His face showed confusion, but something deeper, fear. Jesus needed me, needed a friend to go through this with. It is not easy confronting your death, and I could not have done it without his help.

"Right. Sorry," I said. "I'm sorry, Jesus."

"OK..." he said quietly.

"I want to help you," I began and found myself having trouble continuing. "I am going to help you." I looked back to John then back to Jesus. "I am here to help you."

His face relaxed a bit but he still looked at me warily.

I turned to Banquo, "When this is over, will you tell me what I need to do? Will you help me find John if he is not here?"

Banquo looked from me to John, to Jesus, and back to me. He folded his arms and narrowed his eyes. "I will try to talk you out of it, but yes, I will tell you."

At the moment I was aware that in some ways letting this go now was out of character. That it wasn't typical of me when I was younger, and it wasn't typical of me since I've been dead. It felt like a crossroads, like a test, like maybe I was growing up.

And that may sound strange coming from someone who

was in his body for nearly thirty years, but that is what I felt. Like I had just grown up a bit. I can't confirm this, not having grown old in my body, but I suspect this feeling persists throughout life when you turn your back on who you used to be.

It felt good and it felt terrible at the same time. I hated it.

Transmission #17
Received 2012/02/05 02:04:44

THE NEXT WEEK WAS WONDERFUL AND DIFFICULT.

It was wonderful because each night Banquo, Jesus, and I would have our little Midnight Circle. Banquo continued to recite the Iliad to us, a book every night, followed by a discussion about the story, the themes, and how this work has affected so much of storytelling.

It sounds like a literary geek session, and that is exactly what it was. I am not a literary geek, but stories... I love stories and the Iliad through all its archaic language and devices is a hell of a story. Sex, lust, betrayal, fighting, courage, cowardice—you name it, it's there.

And the week was difficult. I spent my days alone going from house to house exposing myself to humanity in all its glory. It's strange, really. I mean, I identify with my own life, with my own experiences, with my own suffering. It's real, so real. What began to tweak my head was that everyone I saw, as I passed briefly through their homes and their lives, have the same sense of reality. Even those people whose lives I could absolutely not identify with.

Maybe I didn't say that very well. It's kind of an out-there concept. Let me try again. As we walk through our lives, we identify strongly with ourselves and those close to us. We have empathy for their experiences; we have feelings as a result of what we see and know about them. But that circle is not very big—the human heart doesn't seem to be able to empathize with everyone. Most people in this world are, to us, cardboard cutouts. They live, they die, and we just don't feel very much. They are not so real.

But going from house to house, breathing in humanity in all its form, function, and dysfunction, made that barrier start to break down. I started feeling bad for the hoarders and the people that couldn't get off the couch. They weren't out there "theoretically"; they weren't on some TV show or in a story of some sort. They were people, real people, with real experiences, as real as me.

And, on the flip side, I started to celebrate the good things when I saw them: a mother feeding her baby; a husband sneaking home at lunch to meet his wife for a rendezvous; a man whistling and tending his garden; a plumber greeting his clients with a smile.

And John was always in the back of my mind. He wasn't a "real" person to me, I didn't know him. But, Tamara was, and John's inability to communicate with her after he died had caused her a lot of pain, pain she had shared with me, and pain I had fully empathized with. But, I kept my promise and stayed away from Mrs. Turner's classroom, doing no more than obsessively thinking about John and about how you might rescue a bardo-brain that far gone.

So it was wonderful and it was difficult and at the end of the week Banquo found Javier.

WHEN I ARRIVED AT OUR PLAYGROUND RALLY POINT, JESUS and Banquo were already there. Jesus looked tense, scared, and his form flickered with a crimson hue.

I flew up quickly and asked, "What's going on?"

"Banquo found him," Jesus said, his mouth set in grim determination.

"Where?" I asked.

"He's in a foreclosed home, not far from here," Banquo said.

"Good," I said, although I didn't really mean it, at least not in a straightforward way. I was glad that we found him, that this endless searching was over, but I was worried about Jesus and the next phase. "What now?"

"I... We..." Jesus stammered. "Follow him, we need to keep an eye on him for a day or two. Make a plan."

"OK," I said, feeling it was anything but "OK."

"Can you guys handle this?" Banquo asked, looking first at Jesus and then at me.

He was, in his own rather pointed way, asking me if I could handle helping Jesus through this. I was, honestly, much less confident than I sounded. "Sure, Banquo. We got this."

Banquo nodded. "Good. I'll check on you in a few days." He told us where Javier was, and with a "pop" he was gone.

We sat there on the jungle gym silent for a while as darkness descended upon us. Jesus was brooding, I knew it, he knew it, but I wasn't one to jump in too quick. Besides, this called for some brooding.

"Umm..." I began after it was fully dark. "Javier is active at night, right? That's why we've been searching for him during the day, so we wouldn't miss him."

Jesus nodded.

"So, do you want to start observing him tonight? If not, no problem, we can go find a movie to watch, or something."

Jesus was silent for a few moments and then shook his head rapidly, as if trying to shake his malaise off. "No, let's go."

We found Javier just as he left the foreclosed home. He looked just like Jesus described. He wasn't tall, but he was big. He was strong, no doubt about that, but his powerful body was sheathed in a layer of fat. He had black hair, brown eyes, and a thin, straight scar on his chin. His eyes had a wild look as they darted rapidly, and he constantly rubbed the fingers of his right hand together. He walked rapidly, stopping and starting, reminding me of how a squirrel moves up and down a tree in short, fast bursts.

"You OK?" I asked Jesus, whose form was a bit diffuse with an intensely red flicker.

"Yeah, man, I'm OK."

I knew he wasn't, but I didn't think calling him out on it would be helpful. My plan was to keep him moving and to keep him talking.

Javier walked down the street, his head moving side to side, stopping every minute or so to check if he was being followed. He was, of course, but he couldn't possibly know that we were there. He would occasionally check the pistol he had shoved into the back of his jeans.

"Paranoid, isn't he?" I asked.

Jesus chuckled. "He has every right to be. But, I think there is a chemical component to this."

"Chemical?" I asked.

"Just watch."

Transmission #18
Received 2012/02/05 03:16:43

AND SO WE WATCHED. JAVIER WALKED HIS STRANGE WALK out of the neighborhood and to the south where there are some commercial properties. It wasn't a bad neighborhood, but it wasn't a good one.

He met a mousy looking man behind a gas station and there was an exchange of money for "chemicals."

"What's his poison?" I asked Jesus.

"Speed of some sort. With him it's always something speedy." I felt relieved seeing Jesus focused, more in his element. Now that we were actually doing something he seemed to be better.

After the mousy man left, Javier snorted the white powder he had bought, his head kicking back and a guttural sigh escaping his chest.

"Cocaine?" I asked.

Jesus nodded, "But not just. Knowing him, there is something else in there."

After a few minutes leaning against the dumpster, Javier straightened up and smiled. It was not a smile that warms the heart, but the kind that chills the blood.

As the night progressed, we continued to follow him. From the gas station, to dumpster diving behind a grocery store for some food, to breaking into some cars, to hanging out and drinking with what looked like some gang members in front of a Circle-K.

Towards the end of the night, Javier moved back into the residential area and went to a different house just as the sun came up.

Jesus and I spent the day on the roof of the house he was staying in. We didn't think he was going to leave while it was light, but we didn't want to take any chances.

"Why is he still in Tucson?" I asked.

Jesus shrugged. "He's wanted in Mexico, so why go back? Besides, he's burning the money he manages to come up with on drugs. He doesn't have the means to leave."

We were silent as we both thought. We had found him, now what? How do a couple of ghosts catch a meat person? "So," I finally asked, "how do we catch him?"

He sighed, "That is the question, my friend, isn't it?"

"You want the police to catch him, right?"

Jesus stared at me, giving me a look that reminded me of Banquo, all intense and searching. "Yes. What else would I want to do?"

"Well..." I wasn't nearly as levelheaded when I faced my killers, William and Anna-Beth.

"No, JJ, just the police. If the INS gets him, he'll be deported and the Mexican authorities will take care of him."

"Do you think they'll do that? Isn't he wanted for your murder?"

"I do," he said. "One illegal kills another, who's really going to care?"

That brought me up short. Jesus was murdered, surely

it was taken seriously whether he was in the country illegally or not.

"But that guy at the hotel saw it all," I said, "surely the police got a description of him."

Jesus smiled at me. It wasn't a smile that I liked to see. It was the kind of smile an older brother would give a naïve younger one when they said something stupid. "I'm sure they did, JJ. But the point is moot. Either way, we need the police, how do we do that?"

We were both silent for a long time. I guess I should have been resting, but I wasn't. I was brooding. I am not stupid enough to think I understand Jesus's life, but what he was suggesting insulted my sense of justice. If what he said was true—that his life, his death, mattered less because he was an illegal—well, then I was pissed. No two ways about it.

And I don't know about you, but for me, intense emotions require action. I can't just stay with it, I have to do something.

I opened my mouth to speak several times, but couldn't find any words to express what I was feeling. And maybe it was the whole Awareness of Others thing, but this was really getting to me. It was prejudice, pure and simple, and that was something I couldn't stand.

But the problem was I couldn't attack the prejudice, there was only one target. Javier.

I got up, still unable to speak, and sunk down into the house. I quickly searched it and found him asleep in an empty bedroom wrapped in a dirty blanket.

His face was slack, and he looked peaceful. That stopped me for a moment but not for long. I went to the nearest light switch and put my hand in. I modulated my form properly, to conduct electricity, and the light came on. I felt the electricity moving through my form, energizing me.

This was old territory. I had picked up this trick when I had haunted William and Anna-Beth and tried to exact revenge for my death. I had sworn I would never do this again, but it was the only thing I could think of.

The light didn't wake Javier up, he was really out of it, but I let the electricity flow for a while, building up in my system.

This time, I told myself, this time I will use this as a tool. I will not take it too far.

Just as I was about to pull my hand out, Jesus flew in front of me. He must have noticed I was gone and had come looking. "What are you doing, JJ?"

"Nothing much," I answered. "I'm just going to wake him up. Keep him from sleeping. Make him sloppy. That way he'll get caught."

Jesus folded his arms and said, "No."

"What?"

"No, JJ. You can't do that."

"What do you mean, 'I can't.'" I never react well to challenges.

I noticed the red flicker along the edges of my form. I was mad and anyone who could see me could tell.

I saw Jesus relax, he put his arms down and backed up a step. His eyes defocused for a moment before he said, "Your heart is the right place, JJ. I appreciate you wanting to help, but let's think this through first."

"OK," I said warily, keeping my hand in the light switch and continuing to "charge" myself.

"So, your plan is to keep him awake all day so that

when he goes out at night he'll do something stupid and get caught?"

I nodded.

"And what if that 'something stupid' is him hurting, or killing, someone else?"

"I..." I began as I withdrew my hand from the switch. The light went off. "I hadn't thought of that."

"Javier here," Jesus said, gesturing to the sleeping man, "is not the most balanced individual. Something like what you are planning could really send him over the edge. We must be careful."

I nodded, he was right. "Sorry, Jesus."

"That's OK, JJ. Come on, let's go outside and get you grounded."

The "grounding" Jesus was referring to was me literally sinking into the ground to dissipate the electricity I had built up. Having that energy running through my form can be kinda maddening if I don't do something with it.

We flew out to the front yard, and I sunk into the dirt up to my neck.

"Jesus," I began, "we should be taking your murder seriously. Illegal or no, we should be."

"Thanks, JJ, but don't feel bad. It is just the way of things."

I shook my head. "Not good enough, not for me. Each life is worth the same. The rest of it is just bullshit."

Jesus nodded, but didn't speak. He had a faraway look on his face.

"You were using that Awareness stuff on me in there, weren't you? When your eyes went unfocused, you were trying to feel what I was feeling."

He nodded and laughed. "Worked good too."

"Gold star for you today, my friend." I stayed in the ground longer than I really needed to. It felt good. I felt calm and grateful not to have gone down the poltergeist path again.

But we still had a problem. Now that we had found Javier, what were we going to do with him?

Transmission #19
Received 2012/02/06 01:15:25

Up on the roof of the house Javier was in, Jesus and I had a long discussion about being a ghost as we watched the sun set. About what Banquo had asked us when I wanted to know how we created those musical instruments.

We went rounds and rounds on it. Really, it is fascinating, this "ghost" thing. How is it that we are ghosts? That we think without a brain, see without eyes, hear without ears, and speak without lungs and vocal cords.

Banquo's Rules of the Dead #3: *There are more things in heaven and earth, Horatio, than are dreamt of in your philosophy.*

OK, so that one is Shakespeare—Hamlet for those of you that don't recognize it—and maybe I'm cheating a little bit with it, but I don't know how to put it better. Life is strange, and the afterlife even stranger.

"You know," I said after we had been at it for a while, "my memory is really good. Much better than when I was meat.

I mean, all that stuff I wrote about in the SECI chamber I did from memory. It never used to be that good."

Jesus shook his head and laughed, "Me too. And you know what? My English is much better too. I don't struggle for words like I did when I was alive."

"Really?" I asked.

"Si, señor. Really."

That surprised me, it wasn't something that I had ever thought about. Growing up in Globe I had taken Spanish in both junior high and high school. I had used it from time to time but wasn't very good at it as an adult. So, I tried speaking to Jesus in Spanish. I didn't think about it, or worry about it, I just started speaking Spanish, "Tú eres mi amigo, tú eres mi mejor amigo muerto." I told him he was my best dead friend. The words just flowed.

"Muchas gracias, y tú eres mi mejor amigo muerto," he said.

We both smiled, it was a nice moment. I am grateful for Jesus in my life (you know, I just can't resist putting in those "Jesus" lines, the name makes it so easy). And we would come back to the topic of our ghost-ness many times, but right then I had something of a brainstorm even though I had no brain (yeah, no wisecracks from the audience there).

"If you were meat, what would you do?" I asked. "What would you do about Javier, right now?"

Jesus shrugged, "That's easy. I would call the police and tell them who he was, where he was, and that he was armed and dangerous."

I nodded, thinking the idea through, letting it roll around in my head. "Well then, my best dead-friend, that is what we are going to do." He looked at me puzzled, so I continued. "You were right to pull me back from my poltergeist madness, but there are other things I learned how to do. I can get someone to make that call for us."

Jesus leveled a Banquo-like look at me and I just smiled. I wasn't going off the deep end this time. "Tell me more," he said.

"OK. I could go back to the SECI chamber, but to tell you the truth, I am not ready for that. It would be easy enough, but it's kind of public. I told them I was leaving and I just don't want to show up two weeks later. Besides, there would be a delay and Javier might have moved on."

Jesus nodded but did not comment.

"I could go talk to Nate. We have a system we worked out and that would be pretty easy too. But, that would take me too much back into my meat life. After the disaster my communications with him led us to, I don't want to risk it. I don't want to put him through anything else."

"So what, then?" Jesus asked.

"Tamara," I said, as I thought it through again.

"Tamara?"

"Yeah, Tamara. She must have read what I wrote. She'll be easy enough to communicate with and..." I trailed off, because it did get dicey.

"No, JJ. You can't tell her about finding John."

"I know, I know. I wouldn't. But, because of him, because we found him, I feel like I should check in on her."

Jesus nodded. I wasn't sure he understood the linkage I had made, I didn't think I had explained it that well. "You care for her," he said. It wasn't a question.

"I do," I admitted. "But, she doesn't run through my whole life like Nate does. She is a recent friend."

"And yet you want to do whatever this risky thing was that Banquo hinted at to get John out of bardo for her."

I nodded. "I didn't say it was simple. Look, I'll go check on her, get her attention, and get her to call the cops about Javier. That's it."

Jesus looked at me for a long, long time. I could see hints of emotions at play on his face. He wanted to say yes, he wanted to have this part of his journey over. He was also concerned about me. I don't have the best track record when it comes to making contact with the living.

"I wish Banquo was here," he said finally.

"I don't. He'd just tell me 'no' and I'd get mad and go do it anyway," I said.

"And if I tell you no?" Jesus asked.

I thought for a moment, tried to get in touch with my own feelings, tried to center myself in what I was doing here—helping my friend. "This is your show, Jesus. You're calling the shots."

He nodded and rubbed at his mustache. It was a gesture I am sure he did a lot while he was alive, and had gotten good enough with his ghostly form so that he could now do it while dead. "OK, here's the plan. You go find her, do reconnaissance and then come back here before making contact. I'll stay here and watch Javier."

I smiled. "Got it, boss." I paused and then added, "Will you be OK here alone?" It was a fair question. That was his killer in the house below, and from personal experience I knew how easy it is to go off the rails with something like that.

He nodded. "Go now, come back soon. I'll be here."

Transmission #20
Received 2012/02/06 02:58:00

I FLEW OFF AND DIDN'T LOOK BACK. I DIDN'T WANT EITHER of us to lose our nerve. I hadn't planned to start interacting with the living again and I was a bit concerned about what had happened before with William and Anna-Beth, and then with Nate.

But, there were other considerations driving me down this path. Helping Jesus, helping Tamara.

It was about 8 p.m. and there was a good chance that Tam would be home. I flew north out of the neighborhood we were in until I got past the university. I then flew right above the streets—I had only been to Tam's place a couple times and I remembered the directions, but had to do them turn by turn to get there.

She lived in some apartments off of Grant. They were pretty nice two-story adobe-style buildings with palm trees and a pool. I flew up to her door and stood there fidgeting and nervous.

The last time I had been here was for a little party she threw a few weeks before I died. We were celebrating the completion of the SECI chamber. It was a small party with Tam and Jin, of course, me, and some of the undergrads that worked in the lab with them.

The whole "extra-corporeal" part of what they were doing wasn't exactly well known. The main mission, research on electromagnetic shielding, was, and I know they had some of their sponsors by the lab and showed them the chamber. But this party had been for those in the know.

I had arrived with a bottle of wine and flowers. I remember standing at the door nervous then too. Tam and I had become friends and were starting to become close. The road we were on, at that point, was unclear, but it might have led to something more than friendship. Provided, of course, that Tamara could get over her dead fiancé, and I could get past my stalled life.

But death had come and that was the road not taken.

I took a deep breath—not really, but the ghostly equivalent of it—and walked through the door.

Things looked pretty much the same. A brown easy chair that used to be John's in the living room, a few pictures on the wall, bookshelves everywhere, and a small desk with a laptop on it.

It was a small apartment, very neat, very organized, very put together. I lingered, looking at the pictures on the wall, a 11x14 picture of Tamara and John smiling with champagne glasses in their hands. I think it was of their engagement party. I studied John, I wanted to be sure it was him that I had found. There were several other pictures of him, and I studied them until I was sure that the ghost I had found was John. There was no doubt. The handsome face, strong jaw, and crescent-shaped scar on his cheek were unmistakable.

I felt fear then. I had talked big with Banquo, that I would do anything to get him out of the bardo, that I would do that for Tamara, that I would—

My thought process was brought up short by a new picture on the wall, one that hadn't been there before. It was a picture of Tam and me in front of the nearly completed SECI chamber. She wore her white lab coat with a demure smile on her face. I was hefting the final panel above my head with a big, goofy grin on my face.

The room started to fade on me, and I could feel the bardo coming. But I wasn't a brand new ghost anymore. I had survived two trips to the bardo and come out. I knew the signs of its approach, and I knew some tricks to deal with it.

I turned from the picture and started singing at the top of my ghostly lungs. "Spirits in the material world, I'm just a messed up ghost in the material world."

I manifested my silly Guitar Hero guitar and started strumming along with my very bad singing. The goal here wasn't artistry but to keep me out of the bardo.

You see, I really do care for Tamara. Seeing that she had that picture of us on her wall sent me back into grief for my lost life and then sent me careening towards the bardo.

When I had finished my long sessions at the SECI chamber and told my story, my impulse had been to break completely from my meat life. Right then it was clear that had been the right instinct.

I WAS MAKING A HORRIBLE RACKET, THE KIND OF "WAKE the dead" racket that only the dead can pull off. So lost in my world was I that I didn't notice when Tamara came out of the bathroom. I had been so caught up in looking at pictures I hadn't gotten out of the living room to search the apartment for her.

"John?" I heard her say.

I was facing away from her and spun around when I heard her.

"John?" she repeated. She stood there soaking wet, wrapped in a towel, her shoulder-length black hair plastered against her head. She looked so vulnerable standing there clutching the towel, holding it up as she dripped on the carpet.

Fear hit me, deep and visceral, although I have no viscera to speak of. Here I was trying to contact the living and it wasn't going so good. Again.

And I guess I need to talk about Awareness some more. You see, sometimes, some people can sense ghosts, they are aware of them. When I was a brand new ghost, I went around the mortuary shouting in people's ears. None of them would "hear" me, not really, but some of them would notice something.

So, I don't think Tam "heard" my awful singing and fake-guitar playing. No, that is not what happened. But Tamara had experienced a ghost trying to contact her before and was open to it. She sensed something and after all these years she thought that something was John.

I couldn't leave Tam thinking her fiancé's ghost was back. I had to do something.

THE FOOL

Transmission #21
Received 2012/02/06 04:02:19

Back at the graveyard there is a ghost, an old one in terms of years dead, that is a gypsy. Notice that I didn't say "used to be," she is still a gypsy even though she is dead. When I was recovering from what happened with Nate and me, I would spend time with her.

Helen is a nice lady, with a cool accent, heavy makeup, flowing skirts, and a silk scarf around her head. She has a different view on the world, a view I have come to appreciate.

One day we were talking about what I had experienced post-death. I was telling her the story. She knew it, everyone in the graveyard knew it, but she was kind enough to let me tell it again.

And if you've heard my story you know that I tend to jump in feet first into anything... into everything. So, at the end of telling her the story, I said, "Only fools rush in."

"What?" Helen asked, shaking her head, "You think that is a bad thing?"

I snorted and nodded, "Yes I do."

She shook her head and looked at me like I was crazy.

At first I thought that look was about what I had done, but she made it clear that it was about my attitude on being a fool. "Do you know the Tarot?" she asked.

I shrugged. "Cards for telling the future?"

"Divination. It's not exactly telling the future, but the cards help us see where we have been and where we are going."

I nodded, unsure of what she was getting at.

"The Fool is the first card in the Tarot. It is a very important card."

"Important?" I asked.

She nodded. "Important. It is the Fool that starts us on adventures, it is the Fool that discovers new things, it is the Fool who is not burdened by the beliefs of the masses, that makes this world a better place."

"OK..." I said, not sure where the hell she was going with this.

"So it is true that Fools rush in, but this is a good thing, JJ, a *good* thing." Her gnarled hand touched me gently on my shoulder.

I slowly shook my head, I still wasn't getting it.

"Thomas Edison," she continued, "he failed how many times in inventing the lightbulb?"

"Over a thousand, I think."

"What a Fool. The Wright Brothers, what do you think people told them when they said they were going to make a flying machine?"

"Fool?" I asked tentatively.

"The Fools show us the way. The Fools embrace innocence. Being the Fool is not a bad thing."

AS IF RIGHT ON CUE, THAT NIGHT BANQUO LED SHAKE-speare's "As You Like It" for the Midnight Circle.

Now this is one of Shakespeare's comedies. And in this case I had to scratch my head a while about that. It's not really filled with laugh out loud moments, but then again, no one dies, there are women dressing as men, and a bunch of folks get married and live happily ever after. So for Shakespeare, I guess that does qualify as a comedy.

And like most of Shakespeare's works, it has quotes in it we all know. For example, "All the world's a stage." We all know that phrase, whether we attribute it to the Bard or not. It is part of a soliloquy by the depressed Jaques, that is quite poignant, that talks of life and death. I won't quote the whole thing, but let me give you a bit of it:

All the world's a stage,
And all the men and women merely players:
They have their exits and their entrances;
And one man in his time plays many parts.

Jaques goes on to list the stages of our lives and ends with:

Last scene of all,
That ends this strange eventful history,
Is second childishness and mere oblivion,
Sans teeth, sans eyes, sans taste, sans everything.

And I have to tell you, that last part got a standing ovation of hoots and hollers from us ghosts. There were shouts of "oblivion" and "sans everything." Don't get me wrong, Shakespeare was one Aware guy, he really saw life, and death, from a worthwhile perspective. But when he talks about the end and oblivion, well, we can't help but get rowdy. We are that end, we are that oblivion that Shakespeare wrote about. And while it is true we are sans teeth, eyes, taste, and everything, we aren't sans consciousness. A second childishness, now that is something I will whole-heartedly agree with.

So, in "As You Like It," there is a jester, a court fool named Touchstone. In this play he's really quite a smart guy. He seems to be there to point out the facts of life to the other characters. Anyway, he has a line in that play that has really stuck with me.

The fool doth think he is wise, but the wise man knows himself to be a fool.

It's one of those twisty self-referential things, isn't it? If I think I'm wise, then I'm a fool. If I know that I am a fool, then I am wise.

That phrase and Helen's thoughts on the Fool of the Tarot pinged around my head that evening, and have continued to.

Here is what's clear. I don't think of myself as wise. Clever sometimes, but not wise. I am often the fool, but hope I am more often the Fool of the Tarot.

Make sense? If not, maybe you need to be a bit more Fool-ish to understand it.

Transmission #22
Received 2012/02/07 00:48:51

I STOOD THERE STARING AT THE DRIPPING TAMARA FEELING like a fool. And not the capital-F "Fool" that Helen was talking about, but the regular old lowercase-f "fool."

Seriously! I had thought it would be easy to do this one little thing. That it would be simple. And, as always, I rushed in.

"John? Is that you, John?" Tamara asked, adjusting the towel tighter around her torso.

Well, having rushed in, there was nothing left to do but continue. I absorbed the guitar back into my form and modulated my hand for light. It had been a while, but I had done this so much when I communicated with Nate that it happened pretty quickly.

You see, us ghosts emanate very high frequency (off the charts, really) electromagnetic (EM) radiation. To make visible light is by no means easy, but I had figured it out. So, I lowered the vibration of my "hand" until it was a glowing ball of light about the size of walnut.

I waved it back in forth in a horizontal line. This was the

signal for "no" I had used with Nate. I had written about this, and I knew Tamara had read what I had written.

When she saw the light her mouth opened and then closed several times. She ran around the room shutting some lights off so she could see it better.

"You are not John?" she asked.

I moved the light up and down. *YES.*

"Are you JJ?"

YES!

"JJ? What are you doing here?" She paused looking at her state of dress, only a towel, and looked a bit embarrassed.

She didn't need to be, really. I had been out of my meat body long enough that flesh didn't have the same effect that it once had. Sorry to break the bad news, but no meat, no hormones, no hormones, no drooling over a wet, beautiful woman in a towel.

Don't feel bad for me. At that point I had been dead long enough for things like that to be only a ghostly memory. I understood it, but it was insubstantial.

I moved over to the laptop and bounced my light on the lid. Nate and I had done it this way.

"Oh!" she said opening the laptop and turning it on.

I made my light smaller and hovered it over one key at a time so that I could "speak" to her.

GOOD TO SEE U TAM.

Her expression was complicated. She looked both excited and ready to cry at the same time. She nodded, "Good to *see* you too, JJ."

She still looked uncomfortable in her towel so I typed, GET DRESSED. I'LL WAIT.

She nodded and scurried off. I was tempted to look

around more, to look at more photos, but stayed put. I didn't want to risk seeing something else that might unbalance me.

You see, there is a real good reason for a ghost to stay away from their former life if they can. It is a dangerous and addictive thing. You can so easily get lost in what your life once was, lost in the life your loved ones are still living. And if you are not very careful, you will end up in the bardo. Either way you are not "living" anymore. You are stuck in the past ignoring the opportunity that the afterlife brings.

Seriously, I know what I am talking about here.

Tamara came back quickly, dressed in pink socks and a fluffy blue robe. "What is it, JJ?" she asked as she sat down.

I NEED A FAVOR.

"Anything, anything at all."

I paused. I was never good with secrets and longed to tell her that I had found John. But I was not that much of a fool. I knew that at this point it wouldn't do her any good. But seeing her, years after John's death, still hoping it was him coming back to communicate with her, just hardened my resolve to help her.

So, no, I wasn't fool enough to tell her, but I was Fool enough to want to help her.

WE FOUND JESUS'S KILLER. WE NEED YOU TO CALL THE POLICE.

She nodded her head slowly. "OK. They'll probably think I'm crazy, but I will call them. What do I say?"

I spent the next few minutes giving her all the details. His name and description, the address of the house he was in, and that he was armed and dangerous.

After we were done, she asked, "Are you OK, JJ?"

YES. ARE U?

Her eyes began to tear up as her brow crinkled. "I'm so sorry what happened to you. So sorry. I... I miss you, JJ."

I paused, feeling that "sinking into the bardo" sensation again, but instead of crazed antics I just pushed it away.

MISS U 2. BUT, NOT SO BAD THIS WAY.

She nodded, her lower teeth pressing against her upper lip. "You're a good man, JJ," she said as the tears flowed freely down her cheeks. "I am glad we got to be friends."

ME TOO. THIS IS HARD 4 BOTH OF US. I SHOULD GO.

She nodded but didn't speak, rubbing her running nose on her sleeve.

THANKS FOR DOING THIS. TAKE CARE OF YOURSELF, TAM.

She nodded. "You too."

I pulled my light away from the keyboard and let it get bigger. I brought it up and pressed it against her cheek. When I removed it she had a look of surprise on her face and brought her hand up to feel the place my light had touched. The tears really started to flow down her cheeks then. She was watching closely so I went slowly first, floating towards the ceiling and then I flew fast.

Reality had that stuttering look that it has when the bardo is near. It's kind of the opposite of the Call. Instead of the most beautiful thing you can hear, see, feel, it is this creeping darkness that wants to further invade your being, that wants to take you over and snuff out your light.

As I shot up into the sky, I said no to the bardo. Actually, I shouted and screamed "No!" as I flew straight up. I shouted it over and over and over.

It wasn't just the bardo I was saying "no" to, but this pattern of mine, of keeping going back into my old life, my meat life. Back to the people and places that had meant something when I was alive.

I watched Tucson retreat below me as I screamed and felt the darkness, the bardo, retreat. Even so, it was tempting, so tempting to give in to it.

I had a realization then about the bardo. It is a horrible place, but it is also an escape. An escape from consciousness, an escape from the "real" world, an escape from confronting what is really wrong.

And that realization didn't make it any easier to say no to it, it made it harder. The darkness whispered to me of succor, of escape, of a twisted kind of peace in the midst of my horror. "At least," it whispered, "you won't have to deal with your life anymore. Come with me, and I will give you a life of such intensity you won't even remember your old life."

The bardo is a drug, an addiction, a horrible temptation.

I stopped flying and screamed, "No!" again. I looked below me at all the little lights. The houses and other buildings with their still lights and the moving lights of the cars and other vehicles. It was strange. Tucson looked like something in a movie, or a very sophisticated model. It didn't look real.

I took the ghostly equivalent of a deep breath.

Actually, not breathing is one of the hardest losses you face as a ghost. Think about it. Every moment of your meat life you are either breathing in or breathing out, or in that tiny space in between. It grounds you, it focuses you, it's this place you can always come back to. Breathe in, breathe out... it is a never ending source of calm and grounding.

Breathe in... breathe out.

Never ending, that is, until you don't have a meat-body anymore.

I looked down at my form, my ghostly chest, focusing on the "feeling" of breathing. I saw my chest rise, I felt myself fill up with something, and then my chest fell and I let go of that something that had filled me. I had known I was doing this ghostly breathing thing, but it wasn't until that moment that I became aware of it.

Ghosts talk, right? They talk without lungs or vocal cords, but they talk in the same pattern as the living. There are pauses when they inhale. Their ghostly chests rise and fall. There seems to be something that they are doing.

At that moment, floating above Tucson, I realized all of this. Ghosts have no lungs, but they look like they do when they breathe. What the hell is that?

I focused on the sensation, a mere whisper compared to meat breathing but still I felt it. The taking in of something and the expelling of something.

I had no idea what it was, but I clung to it like a drowning man, like it was a log that could keep me above water amidst the storm of my emotions.

Breathing in... something, exhaling... something.

And it was helping. Not in that deeply visceral way that focusing on your breathing can do when you are meat, but in that echoish ghostly way that many meat things are in the afterlife.

I wasn't up there long, just a few minutes, but my head was reeling from all that I had realized.

I got oriented and flew as fast as I could to Jesus.

Transmission #23
Received 2012/02/07 02:22:32

I REMEMBER FLYING AS FAST AS I COULD AND THEN I WAS there right in front of Jesus.

"Wow! Man, you just popped," he said. "How did you do that?"

"What?" I asked.

"You 'popped' in. Like Banquo does. As in Lesson #4, Traveling."

"I... What? I didn't do that. I just flew, really fast."

"No, man, you just popped."

Maybe I had popped, but it wasn't anything intentional, I had just been very, very focused on Jesus. I paused trying to remember, then I started hearing sirens and the urgency of our situation drove all of that out. "The police are on their way," I told him.

"What?" he asked, his face stern. "You were just doing reconnaissance."

"I know. I know. But she was aware of my presence." I then quickly gave him the thirty-second summary of what happened.

He nodded his head as he flew up above the house, "I was worried about that." I followed him. "The sirens might spook him, so let's keep an eye out."

I looked below and again found it comforting to see the world in miniature. We weren't that far up, but it was far enough to distance me a bit from the reality of it all. All those days we spent searching house after house, wading through the myriad expression of humanity, it really felt good to be a bit "above" that.

The police, thankfully, cut their sirens as they got close. They moved in and surrounded the place. There were six squad cars and they deployed men out back and around the sides before breaking in the front door.

We didn't go in, we stayed aloft and watched. A few minutes later they brought Javier out in handcuffs.

I looked at Jesus. He was going through something, his face made that plain. I saw traces of anger, mixed with fear and maybe confusion. His feelings were complicated, I knew he was going to need plenty of time to sort it out.

After they loaded Javier in the car, we flew down and stuck our heads in so we could hear the police officers talking.

Not that they said much. The blond-haired one was complaining about his girlfriend, and the dark-haired one was obsessed with sports.

This was just a job to them. They were transporting a prisoner. No big deal.

Javier was twitching away in the backseat, twitching worse than usual, but he didn't say a word.

We eventually pulled our heads out and rode on the roof of the police car as it wound its way through the streets of Tucson until we came to the South Tucson Police Department.

The policemen got Javier out of the car and marched him towards the front door. I followed a few feet behind. As they went through the door I stopped, realizing Jesus was not with me. I looked back, he was still sitting on the roof of the squad car.

I flew over. "¿Qué pasa?" I asked.

He smiled briefly at my use of Spanish, but the look was erased by a very blank, un-Jesus like face.

Jesus has a face that is animated and expressive. You don't really have to wonder what Jesus is feeling, it is usually written all over his face. A big frown, or a big smile. Eyes wide and alert or hooded and cautious. But not then. His face was blank and he kept looking around as if he expected something to happen. It was weird.

"So," I continued. "Are we going to follow him?"

"Follow him?" he asked, his voice dull. "Why?"

"Why? To make sure he comes to justice. To follow this thing through until it's done."

He looked at me, his eyes narrowing, but otherwise his face staying blank. "Are you prepared to spend the next year or two hanging out with Javier as he winds his way through the justice system?"

"I... well... maybe we stay with him until we find out if they are going to try him here or deport him to Mexico."

"No," Jesus said flatly, looking around again.

"No?" I asked.

"No, JJ. This is as far as I go. This is as far as I ever went. I would find them and bring them in. And then I would..." The bland mask broke as his lips pursed and his eyes seemed near to tears. "Then I would trust the system to do what needed to be done."

I looked at him the way Banquo often looks at me and the way Jesus had recently started looking at me. I gave him the "Awareness of Others" look.

Now, I didn't know if the look, that narrow-eyed, appraising look, had anything to do with it working, but it was a place to start. I wanted to know what my friend was going through.

Logically I could see why he didn't want to follow Javier's progress. It would be long and boring and extremely arduous. It also seemed to me that he might be at a loss as to what to do next, a feeling I would wholly and enthusiastically relate to. But as I looked, I felt something deeper, fear and surprise. Fear of the future, fear of the unknown, fear of grief, and surprise that something he had been expecting hadn't happened.

Jesus had done what he needed to do in this world to tie up the loose ends of his death—the ones I knew of at that time—and all that was left to do was the hard work of grieving, those glorious (that's sarcasm there, folks) five stages.

"Well," I said, "let's get the hell out of here then."

Jesus nodded, but didn't say anything. He was staring at the front door of the precinct, at the door they had taken Javier through.

"My recommendation," I began, "a movie. One with lots of senseless explosions and an even more senseless plot."

Jesus looked at me and smiled. It wasn't a real smile, just a brief note of gratitude, and it didn't stay long. "That sounds great, JJ." Except the way he said it made it seem like it sounded horrible.

We flew to a nearby theater and managed to catch the

last half of a completely senseless action movie in 2D. We picked 2D because ghosts, of course, can't put on 3D glasses. After that we went back to the graveyard and Jesus asked to be alone.

I gave him space, but not too much. I kept an eye him from afar, checking in now and then to make sure he wasn't losing it. But, honestly, I couldn't tell.

Transmission #24
Received 2012/02/07 03:57:13

WHAT DOES GRIEF LOOK LIKE? WELL, TAKE A HUNDRED people and you'll get a hundred looks to grief. Sure there are some similarities, but the actual experience of grieving something looks different on everyone.

With Jesus, he became withdrawn, very withdrawn. So withdrawn and uncommunicative that I couldn't tell which of the stages of grief he was in (Denial, Anger, Deals, Depression, or Acceptance). I didn't think it was Denial or Acceptance, but it could be Depression, but it also could be Anger. You know the quiet types, it can smolder in there a long time before it comes erupting out.

I used my "Awareness of Others" look on him so much that I expected him to snap at me, but he never did. Frankly, I didn't consider that a good sign.

We spent a week or so like this. I would go engage him several times a day, dragging him off to the movies and he would also come around for the Midnight Circle. Banquo was gone and the Circle wasn't quite the same. It was mostly the campfire/storytelling kind. Which is good and distracting, but nothing beats the tragedies and Shakespeare to soothe the soul of a ghost.

I missed the way things were that morning Jesus and I had spent in the Grand Canyon on Vishnu Temple. When we were both OK, when this afterlife was enough. Things seemed to have changed so quickly.

I even missed the endless searching of houses, looking at humanity so closely. And I really missed our little three-person Midnight Circle. I was wondering what happened in the Iliad. Epic poetry? Who cares, it's a good story, the form is not important.

So, I had a lot of time to myself (when I wasn't stalking Jesus) and my mind kept coming back to John and Tamara. It was like an itch I couldn't scratch. It just kept bothering me and bothering me.

Everything changed the day Banquo came back.

"DUDE, YOU GOTTA TALK THIS OUT," I SAID TO JESUS. We were down walking the southern part of the graveyard. I was over giving him space and was trying a more direct approach. The more I watched the more this seemed like depression to me. If I had been acting that way I would have died of depression already.

"What is there to say, JJ?" Jesus asked, his face that freaky blank mask. "Javier killed me, we brought him to justice, and I am still here. What is there to say?"

"That's not justice, Jesus. Not justice with a capital-J or a lowercase-j. That is no kind of goddamn justice." I was pushing purposefully, swearing more, trying to get some kind of reaction from him.

"What?" he asked. He actually looked confused, which I found comforting.

"OK, Javier took your life and what, two others?" Jesus nodded. "The idea of justice implies a balancing. How the hell can that ever happen? Even if you believe in capital punishment, killing him won't even the score. He killed three people, you can't atone for that with just one life. He can't make up for what he did to you. Nothing will give you your life back. Nothing will bring justice to this situation. There is no fucking justice to be had for this."

After my little speech I stood there looking at him, waiting for it. Waiting for the anger to come. But it didn't. I was angry, remembering the drunk William Author Reynolds, who ran me down, but he didn't seem to be mad about Javier.

"Nice try, JJ," Jesus said with the smallest of smiles that quickly evaporated. "I know the reality of my situation."

"Well then, get angry about it! Rage at the injustice. Goddamn it, Jesus, do something!"

"OK," Jesus said with a nod and a shrug. He walked away from me, his stiff posture making it clear that he didn't want me to follow.

I stood there fuming mad at the injustice of Jesus's death and my own. Mad at myself because I couldn't get through to him and mad at Jesus for being so damn walled off.

I looked around, looking for someplace to put my anger, something to do with it. But, there was nothing. Manicured lawns and gravestones, with a few ghosts here and there. Nothing.

I considered sinking myself into the ground, to try that "grounding" trick, but that was terrifying. There are the remnants of a lot of meat bodies down there and that is where some ghosts spend their days.

Old man Perkins is a nice enough fellow. He has a big belly and a bigger smile. I asked him once about this practice of sleeping with your bones, and he said, "The bones, your bones, the place that they rest, there is no place like it. It feels good, it feels like home."

No, not for me. I couldn't think of anything else to do, so remembering what I did when I left Tamara, I flew straight up into the air.

I watched as the graveyard receded and I could see the city that wrapped itself around our little community.

There was a funeral going on over on the west side of the graveyard. A few limos and lots of cars awkwardly parked. The casket was poised above the grave and the mourners were assembled.

I stopped going up. I was maybe a thousand feet above everything and found that it helped. The physical distance gave me some emotional distance.

I moved laterally until I was just over that casket. Even though I was quite high I could sense a lot and became fascinated with it. You know, another way to practice "Awareness, Awareness, Awareness" and to distract myself from my current problems.

First, the casket. I didn't see any cords coming out of it, so the "dearly departed" had probably moved on. I don't know why, but I found this comforting.

Second, the family. The obviously grieving widow and children, sitting in the front, wrapped in black. The other assembled friends and family huddled around them. Those shy, or less attached, standing farther back.

Of particular interest to me was a four-year-old boy on the edges tugging on the hand of his mother. He wanted to run, to play. Clearly he was too young for this death stuff to mean anything to him. Anytime was playtime, including a funeral. The mother was clearly horrified, but I rather liked the kid.

Next, the usual cast of ghosts attended the proceedings. Marilyn wandered through the middle of it looking for her cat, calling, "Motor. Here kitty. Where are you, Motor?" She had done this for my funeral and for a few others I had seen.

Fredrick was there, of course. He started this place way back when and felt responsible for everything that happened.

And there were a number of other ghosts there too. The ones that showed up for each and every funeral. I had come to think of them as death groupies. They couldn't seem to get enough of the ceremonies the living do around the recently dead. The embalming and preparation of the corpse, the calling hours, the digging of the grave, the grave-side memorial, the filling in of the grave, and then they would follow the limo back to the wake.

I just hovered there as it unfolded. While my senses were clearly better than my meat senses had been, I couldn't hear everything. But occasionally something the priest or the family said floated up.

"Alexander was a righteous man"; "Stop tugging, honey, we can't play now. Uncle Alex is..."; "Heaven has another angel today"; "So young, too young"; "Fucking cancer!" "Ashes to ashes, dust to dust."

I was thoroughly engrossed in my experience. Combining Awareness with distance. So, I was shocked when I heard a "pop" and then Banquo floated next to me.

"Hmm," he began, looking below us and then at me. "Interesting choice."

I nodded, but didn't answer. They were lowering the

casket into the ground. The act had this sense of weight, of finality, and I wanted to be "Aware" of it.

It didn't last long, but after it was over and the flower-covered casket was in the ground, the mood of the crowd began to change. They became restless, like the spell of the ceremony had been broken, and started milling about and whispering. The priest threw a handful of dirt into the open grave followed by many of the rest.

I watched closely as the widow approached. Her hand shook as she picked up the earth, but when she threw it, she threw it hard, her sobbing becoming loud enough for us to hear. Her oldest child, a boy of maybe twelve, who was carrying his sister who was about five, took control. He unceremoniously kicked some dirt into the grave, helped his sister throw a pebble in, and took his mother's hand and dragged her off.

"Almost as good as Shakespeare," Banquo said, after the mourners had thrown in the last handful of dirt and the crowd had dispersed.

"Indeed," I agreed. But I wished he hadn't said anything yet. I was lost in the meta-human experience, which is what I was coming to think of it as. Each person down there with a full life came together at this event that was changing them all. Some a little, some a lot, but this would reverberate through all their lives. I had physical distance, which helped, but I ached with their collective pain.

"So, bring me up to speed," Banquo requested.

And I did. I reluctantly pulled myself from the human tableau below and took a few minutes and filled him in on Jesus's and my activities while he was gone.

"I think he's deep in depression," I concluded.

Banquo nodded. It wasn't an "I agree with you nod," but a "maybe, let's see" nod. "Where is he?" he asked.

From this elevation the whole of the graveyard was visible. Although I didn't realize it then, I think Banquo was testing me. I think he already knew where Jesus was.

I looked around and it didn't take long to find him. He was maybe fifty yards from where I left him wandering in a slow circle. I pointed.

"I'm going to go talk to him," he said. "You stay here."

Transmission #25
Received 2012/02/07 06:01:16

I SPENT THE REST OF THE DAY AT ELEVATION OBSERVING the patterns below. The meat wagon bringing the fresh dead to the mortuary. The other funeral that happened. The families visiting the graves of the "dearly departed." The milling about of the ghosts. And, Banquo and Jesus in a multi-hour-long conversation.

In some ways it was like all that time we spent going from door to door searching for Javier. It was humanity on display, but instead of up close and personal, it was with some distance. Everything was small physically, so everything felt smaller emotionally. There was a lot to see and observe and be aware of, but it felt safer.

I watched how after the sun went down the graveyard came alive. The ghosts that rested in the ground, like Old Man Perkins, rose up once the sun had left and started their evenings.

I watched as the humans left and the ghosts took over.

I watched as the greeting committee descended upon the mortuary to check out the newly dead.

I watched the clumps of ghosts go about their ghostly socializations until around midnight, when they all gathered at the same place for the Midnight Circle.

I didn't go down for the Circle, I stayed at elevation and positioned myself directly above it.

The crowd seemed excited. Banquo was back, and I think they were hoping for something good. I know I was. I wanted to see Hamlet from above or one of the other Shakespearian tragedies. But not tonight. Banquo, with the assistance of a few of the other old-timers, did "All's Well That Ends Well."

Comedy mixed with tragedy. I had never seen it before and I did enjoy it. The play follows the lengths Helena goes through to win the love of Bertram, which involves such extremes as Helena getting pregnant by Bertram without him knowing it.

Banquo's booming voice had no trouble reaching up to my elevation as I floated there awash in Shakespeare, stewing in my own discontent while listening to the story of fictional discontent.

After it ended, the ghosts slowly started to disperse. I saw Jesus speak quietly to Banquo who pointed straight up at me.

I didn't go down. It was safer up here; besides, I wanted Jesus to come to me. I wanted to hear what he said in my territory. Odd that what I was considering "my territory" at that point was an area filled with nothing but air.

"Hey, man," he said as he flew up next to me.

"Hey, Jesus."

"I'm feeling..." Jesus began, but cut himself off with a sigh. "You know, when you were going through what you went through, I knew it was hard, but I didn't really know how hard it was."

"Thanks," I said. "And I had no idea how hard it was to watch. How powerless you must have felt when I was crazed, trying to kill people, among other ungraceful displays."

"Umm... I didn't hear the Call," he said, changing the subject.

"Oh." The statement took me aback. Had he wanted to hear the Call? Was he disappointed? Had he wanted to move on?

"I was expecting it, you know, after we took care of Javier. But, it hasn't come."

I nodded, studying him. He was disappointed and that scared me. I didn't want to lose him. "Sorry, Jesus. Maybe you have more to do."

"But that's not all," he continued. "My religion believes that we are judged immediately upon death. That didn't happen and I don't know what it means. When I first died, when I met you in the mortuary, this didn't even occur to me. We were doing everything we could to just stay out of the bardo. Now... now I can't stop thinking about it."

I blinked and studied him. He was clearly in great pain. "I'm sorry," I said. It wasn't much, but it was all I had.

Jesus nodded and we floated there in companionable silence for a while watching the ghosts move about, gather in small groups briefly, and then move apart again. I had this thought that I was a scientist looking through a microscope watching these single-cell organisms interact. It was an odd thing to think about my community, but comforting.

"It's nice up here," Jesus said.

"Yeah. I like the perspective."

"So... Ah... Listen, JJ. I've got to go."

I nodded, it made sense.

"I've got to go home," he added.

"Great. When do we leave?" I asked.

"Sorry, JJ. I've got to do this alone. You know, like with you and Nate."

I nodded again. I didn't like it, but I understood. "Where are you going?"

"Back down to Mexico City. I need to check on Sister Dominga. She's all the family I have left. She was ill when I left, and I want to see if she's OK. I owe her that."

"I'm going to worry about you," I said.

He smiled. Not a big smile, but just big enough to say he was glad that I cared. "Banquo has agreed to check in on me once or twice a week."

"Good."

We were silent again, but it was less companionable. The fact was that I was scared that he was leaving. Jesus grounded me, sometimes literally, and I was worried how I would be without him. This was feeling like it was another one of those damn growth experiences.

"When are you leaving?" I asked

"As soon as I can. I need to fade—it's been a long time since I properly rested. And as soon as I come back I am going to head south."

"OK then," I said. "Good luck, Jesus. I hope you find what you need."

"Good-bye, JJ," he said, and with that he slowly faded away.

After he left, I whispered, "I'm going to miss you, Jesus."

I stayed up there for the rest of the night, still feeling like I was a scientist observing single-cell organisms under a microscope. Things were busiest around midnight when everyone gathered, and the activity slowly faded away from there, until at sunrise there were only a few ghosts there. Marilyn was out looking for her cat, and Fredrick was heading into the mortuary to observe the day's work.

Our little three-ghost adventure was over, my future in doubt, and my mind restless and anxious. So, as the sun rose, I gave into my own fatigue and faded into sweet oblivion.

THE FOOL

Interlude

Letters from Home

Video Transcript #2
Janet Lynch (mother of the deceased) speaking to JJ Lynch
Recorded on 2012/02/22 2:01 p.m.
Playback triggered on: 2012/02/23 1:13 a.m.

JJ,

Oh, God. What am I doing? I don't think I can do this. Tamara, dear, can you please turn off the camera?

OK, I CAN DO THIS. I CAN DO THIS. JJ, I HEAR YOU ARE back, that you are writing again. I've read a little of it. It's...

I am sorry it's taken me so long to get in here and record a message to you. I think, though, you'll understand. This...

I can do this.

OK. First off, I am so sorry about Rhiannon. I am so sorry. Nate offered to take me out there to see her before..., but I just couldn't. I just couldn't. It's just too much. I... Oh...

I THINK I'VE GOT MYSELF TOGETHER NOW. AS YOU CAN

tell, this isn't easy sitting here and recording a message for my dead son, for you, JJ. This isn't easy at all.

I am sure mothers everywhere would kill for the chance to do this—communicate with their dead child—and, frankly, I would too. It's just that... It's not easy.

Nate's here helping me. He's holding up a sign right now that says "Happy Stuff." He wants me to talk about the happy stuff. The things that are going right. And, I guess, if I were you, I wouldn't want to sit there watching your old mother weep and blather. I would want to hear the positive. So here goes.

I am very proud of your sister. Jean graduated from U of A and found a job. She is moving up to Portland to work at a design firm up there. She was always the artist in the family. She is very excited, and it's really time for her to move on. She's been hanging out in Tucson since graduation doing odd jobs and some freelance web design, just to keep an eye on me.

I tell her that I have Nate here, that he'll keep an eye on me when she leaves. It's just taken a long time to convince her. I may not have birthed Nate, but he's one of mine.

So, I recently moved into my own apartment. I have to tell you, that has been strange. I lived alone in Globe after your father passed, but that was the house you and Jean were born in. Somehow this feels different.

Jean graduating has nudged me back into the world. I got a...

Wait. I think I have to back up and talk about some stuff that is maybe not so happy so you will understand.

This SECI thing that Tamara and Jin have created has made me wonder about a lot of things. It's not like they teach this ghost stuff in Sunday school.

And while some people may dismiss your writings as fiction, I know better. I was there for some of what you wrote about. Nate was there. Anna-Beth was there. We all know that it is real. That you, as a ghost, are real. That this reality, this ghost thing, is real.

And this has forced me to examine my beliefs. Now I *know*, not just *believe*, that there is an afterlife. But it raises questions. I've been going to church all my life and they don't talk about this reality, this thing that has happened to you, this bardo place, this... All of this. Why my boy is not in heaven. How he still suffers here on Earth struggling with... with all these things we struggle with.

So, JJ, I had to learn. I had to try to understand. And this is the part that Nate really wants me to tell you about. I am now a certified Hospice volunteer.

And I can tell you that this is something I never thought I would do. I never thought I would sit with people who are dying. And I have to tell you, I love it. I just love it.

A lot of times these are people that don't have any family around. My job is just to be with them. To listen to their stories, to read to them, to help them eat, or turn the channel on the television, or just sit there.

I have lost three of my hospice people now. And... and... well, JJ, it's not easy, but it seems to be helping me. It seems to be giving me some kind of purpose.

One man, his name was Larry, wanted me to tell him stories. He was a World War II vet, with nobody left alive in his family. He was at the hospice house and only had me and another volunteer to sit with him. So, I told him about you, JJ. I told him your story. I read some of your book to him. I think it helped. It eased his mind.

I know it may sound strange, but in being with the dying

I think I am becoming more comfortable with death. With this thing that is going to happen to us all.

Let me see, what else?

I have been working part-time too. I signed on with an agency and go out to do depositions. Kind of like when I was a court recorder in Globe, but a lot less work, and more variety. This is mostly corporate stuff. I'm good at it and it helps pay the bills.

I have moved... did I mention that yet? I'm still in the same apartment complex I was with Jean; I just moved into a studio apartment. Jean and I are both there, but she'll be leaving soon.

I know visiting us can be hard on you, but I want you to know where I am, just in case.

Well, I think that's about it, JJ. I... I love you, son. I know you are strong and good and will find your way.

If you can see your way to do it, I would love it if you could write me a message back.

Transmission #26
Received 2012/02/23 02:01:44
From JJ Lynch to Janet Lynch

Ma,

I am so happy to hear from you. To hear that you are helping people that are dying, that you are working again.

I wish I could explain all this to you, what it all means, why I, and so many others, are ghosts. I can only tell you that it is real and that I am OK.

Really, Ma, I'm OK.

I will admit to this journey being a difficult one, to me struggling and having a very hard time with it. That I can't deny. But I have also had some of the most amazing experiences here in the afterlife.

I have made good friends, seen amazing things, and have helped people.

Just like you are helping people die on that side, I am doing the same on this side. It is very rewarding.

And you know, I don't feel stuck in my life like I did before I died. All those years after Dad died and Rhiannon left, I was just adrift. This time, now, is harder, but I am growing, I am learning, I am...

Well, if you've read what I've written you get the picture.

I love you, Ma, with all my heart. I am so glad to hear that you are moving along with your life. I am doing my best to do the same.

I am very happy to hear about Jean. Give her my best and tell her I am proud of her too.

I love you,

JJ

Transmission #27
Received 2012/02/24 04:16:51
From JJ Lynch to Nate Luca

HEY NATE,

I didn't forget you, bro. I just have been busy typing away at this memoir. Thanks for telling me about Rhiannon—I'm glad it was you. I know it couldn't have been easy.

The Rhiannon part of the story is coming, but I thought I would take a moment and talk about your woman problem. So here goes.

Dude! Anna-Beth. Are you freaking crazy! She is so far out of your league that you would need to... need to...

Crap! I was hoping to come up with a good insult there, but I just can't find one. And besides, I was just kidding.

I have this cool idea, so before you read further, print this out and take it home.

Do it, Nate. Seriously. Don't read any further until you are home with a cold Corona in your hand.

OK. You're sitting alone with a beer in hand, so here goes.

It seriously sucks that we can't sit down over a beer and

talk about this. But, what I am going to do is write how our conversation might go, and you drink your beer and read it. Read it aloud. Maybe this will help. Maybe this will be almost like I'm there.

IT'S A QUIET NIGHT AT CASA DE LUCA. YOU'VE JUST COME off of a long shift driving the tow truck and are tired. As you head in to your little trailer, you see me driving up in my vintage '69 Mustang fastback.

Yeah, I know I never owned a '69 Mustang, but hey, I'm making this up, so it might as well be good.

You see me driving up so you head to the fridge and grab us some cold beers. We sit on your lawn chairs looking up at the stars. You are quiet, tense, your grip on the beer a bit tight, your swallows a bit longer than usual. Before I'm halfway done with mine you get up with a grumble and go grab another one.

As you sit back down, I say, "Nate, spit it out, bro. What's up?"

You sigh and scratch at your shoulder as you shrug.

"Come on. It's me. It's JJ. You can tell me anything." I'm smiling at you, but you're looking at the ground.

"It's Anna-Beth," you grumble.

"That chick from the foundation you volunteer with?" I ask.

"She's no 'chick,'" you say as your eyes meet mine. They are clearly a warning to approach this topic carefully.

"OK, not a chick," I say. "Got it. What about her?"

"I... I like her."

I almost chuckle but hold it back and turn it into an "uh huh," but judging from your glare I didn't hide the chuckle well enough. "She's intense," I say, trying to cover myself. "She's beautiful too."

"Too beautiful... for me," you say.

"Hell with that!" I say, standing up and raising my bottle. "You're Nate freaking Luca. You are the best man I know. But... ah... well, maybe not the prettiest man I know."

You take a swipe at me, but I dance back. "Shut up, JJ!"

"No, seriously, bro. You are the best man I know. Any girl would be lucky to have you. Anna-Beth would be lucky to have you."

"But she's still with that William."

"Eww," I say, making a face like I just ate worms. "Preppy-boy William may be pretty but he's got no heart, no soul. A woman like Anna-Beth, she's been through some stuff in her life, she needs depth, she needs heart. Just bide your time."

"Like you did with Rhiannon?" you ask.

"Exactly," I say smiling.

Since this is a fantasy I not only drive a '69 fastback, but Rhi and I are living happily ever after and making mad monkey love every night.

"She must know how I feel," you say. "How can she not? I show up, do this foundation stuff that is so foreign to me, just so I can be around her. Just so I can see her smile or see that look she gives me when I am not taking things serious enough and trying to make her laugh. She must see me as some dumb puppy following her around."

"Puppy?" I ask.

"Yeah, JJ. Some silly puppy."

"Dude, have you ever seen how girls act around puppies? They love them. They can't keep their hands off them. They—" I leap back as you take another swipe at me.

"Seriously, JJ," you say.

"I am being serious, Nate. Just be her friend. Be glad to be around her. That's what I did with Rhiannon. I was so happy just to be in her presence that I really didn't care if we were a couple or not. It was enough just to be with her, enough to..." I trail off, the poetic nature of my outpouring embarrassing me.

"Yeah," you say, taking a long pull of your beer as I sit down. "I do love being around her."

"So be around her and forget the rest. Be her friend. Don't put any pressure or expectations on her. Women love that."

"Yeah," you say again, a smile growing on your face.

"So, no guarantees here, bro. But at least you can spend time with her, get to know her. And she'll get to know you, know what kind of man you are."

"OK," you say, nodding.

"And if that ain't enough for her, ain't light years better than Willy-boy, then... then..."

"Then what?" you ask, your smile transforming into a frown.

"Then... then maybe she's got a nice sister or something," I say, laughing.

"JJ," you say, your deep tone a warning.

"Yeah," I continue, I can't help myself. "Maybe Anna-Beth's the ugly one. Maybe you should find out if she has a sister." I put my beer down and get up, I know what's coming.

You slowly rise, "You better stop right now," you say.

"Or maybe you should meet her mom. Yeah, maybe her mom likes younger men and is tired of her stuck-up husband and is—"

I don't get any more words out because you've got me pinned to the ground and I can hardly breathe.

"Not another word, Lynch," you whisper in my face.

I nod my head and you get off me and sit on the ground.

I slowly sit up and start laughing. I can't help it. You have always been very practical about women and seeing you all Cupid-ized is funny.

You take a deep breath and I think you are going to yell at me, but your rumbling laughter joins mine. We laugh until our stomachs hurt and then we laugh some more. We then sit there on the ground, enjoying the cool desert night and drink and talk about women until the sun comes up.

OK, BRO. THERE'S THE SCENE, THERE'S MY ADVICE. JUST be yourself and know she's lucky to have you in her life. Worst case scenario is that you make a friend, have some fun.

Anna-Beth changed a lot with what she, William, and I went through. I think she'll be ready for a real man soon. Just be there and let that be enough.

Take care, Nate.

JJ

Part 2

Bardo

"My hour is almost come,
When I to sulphurous and tormenting flames
Must render up myself."
Hamlet: Act I, Scene V, by William Shakespeare

Transmission #28
Received 2012/02/10 02:01:33

I<small>T IS PROBABLY HUMAN NATURE TO FEAR OBLIVION, LACK</small> of consciousness, an end without us. Our consciousness, our sense of self, is something we cling to with a desperation matched only by someone out on the stormy seas holding on to a scrap of wood.

Kids hate to go to sleep, afraid they might miss something, or afraid they won't wake up. Humans fight death tooth and nail just for a few more moments of consciousness, no matter how miserable those moments are. And, modern medicine being what it is, those moments are often very, very miserable.

And I used to be like that. I was one of those kids who hated to go to sleep, and I was one of those ghosts that hated to fade. But not anymore. Sometimes oblivion is just the thing.

I came to in the same place high above the graveyard. The Midnight Circle was breaking up, and Banquo stood there alone. I flew down.

"Jesus is gone," I said. I didn't phrase it as a question, but Banquo took it as one.

"Yes," Banquo said, "he left this morning."

"Will you tell me what I need to know to help John now?" I was in a mood and saw no reason to beat around the bush.

Banquo was quiet for a long time. Instead of leveling his gaze at me his eyes were unfocused, staring off into the distance. "Yes," he said.

No long speech, no trying to stop me, just "yes." "Really?" I asked.

Banquo looked at me and laughed. "Really, JJ. Let's face it. You need something to do, don't you?"

He was right. Without a task to focus on, God knows what kind of trouble I could get into despite this new level of maturity I felt coming on.

"Indeed I do," I agreed.

THE NEXT DAY WE FOUND JOHN STARING AT THE WALL, except things had changed.

On the blackboard written in big letters was "Rest In Peace Mrs. Turner" and around it were the signed names of what I assumed were her students. The handwriting looked like children did it, and there were assorted little pictures drawn too: flowers, hearts, rainbows, and the like. And towards the bottom was a shakily written "we love you."

The room was empty of students and teacher. It must have been a weekend day. When I was alive, the day of the week didn't matter all that much, and even less now that I am dead. I was just glad class wasn't going on for this.

I stared at the "Rest In Peace" for a while. At first I was offended. The only "peace" I knew was the oblivion of fading, and my post-death "life" had been anything but peaceful. And frankly, I wasn't looking for the peaceful "wings and harps" kind of afterlife. If things are peaceful for very long they become boring.

Rest in peace. Seriously? Is that the best we have to offer the dearly departed? Rest in peace. As if that absolves us all of everything. As if there being some nebulous peace ties up all the loose ends of our very chaotic lives and somehow leaves us in a "better place."

Banquo watched me as I looked at the blackboard fuming. He didn't say anything, but I am sure he had a good idea of what was going through my head.

I wasn't resting in peace, Jesus wasn't resting in peace, and Banquo wasn't resting in peace. Hell, none of us were resting, and while peace may be a part of the experience it certainly wasn't the whole experience.

I opened my mouth about to try to convey my outrage when I remembered Old Man Perkins. Spending the day with his bones, coming out at night for the party that is the Midnight Circle, spending the rest of the night hanging out with his friends. It was kind of like a retirement community for the dead. Not everyone was running around making a mess of things like me.

He was resting and he was in peace.

Maybe it wasn't such a bad wish to make. I knew I wasn't ready to "Rest In Peace," but maybe someday. Maybe Mrs. Turner was.

I sighed and got myself back to focusing on the task at hand. I was glad that Mrs. Turner, or rather her ghost, wasn't there. I felt guilty about it, because if she had been there we would have tried to help her and that would have delayed what I so wanted to do.

It seemed funny to me that after my reaction to that phrase on the blackboard, that it was better for me if it was true, if Mrs. Turner was really resting in peace.

John stood staring at the 2009 class picture, the same wispy bardoed ghost he had been the last time I saw him.

"OK," I said, diving right in, now that I was done with my mental sidetrack. "What's the big secret, how do we help him?"

Banquo gave a sharp, single nod, his posture straightening as he moved to John. "First, we try the easy stuff."

We spent the next few hours trying to snap him out of the bardo. It was what Jesus had referred to as Banquo's "scaring the shit out of them" when we first met in the morgue.

In some of its forms it was just that, doing anything to scare him. Like, telling him Tamara had just been stabbed and she wanted to talk to him before she died, or yelling and screaming at him at the top of our proverbial lungs.

But it also got more subtle than that. Like, Banquo and I having a conversation about John and his bed-wetting problem, like we were his parents. And even to the just plain bizarre. Like, speaking to him in gibberish or moving our mouths but not talking at all while wildly gesticulating at him.

We would get a small reaction from him now and again, like I got when I first found him, but not enough. Banquo let out a big sigh and walked away. We had been at it for a long time.

"So what was all that?" I asked.

"Hmmm..." he said, lost in thought.

"What was it that we were doing there? All that crazy stuff."

"Simple, JJ. We were trying to make this reality more engaging than the bardo reality his mind is locked in."

I opened my mouth to ask what the hell he was talking about, but then I thought about it for a minute. The bardo, while horrible, is nothing if not engaging. Perhaps the most engaging experience I have ever had. Even though "engaging" seems much too pedestrian a term. Maybe "can't look away horrible" better describes it, but "engaging" does the job.

I closed my mouth and nodded, it made sense. "So what's next?" I asked.

"Next we go back to the graveyard and relax. We try this again tomorrow evening." Banquo paused, I think he was waiting for my objection. But, hey, I was embracing my new and improved, slightly more mature JJ. "The next step is not an easy one. You need to be well rested," he continued as if answering the question he thought I was going to ask.

Transmission #29
Received 2012/02/10 03:48:51

THAT NIGHT I ENJOYED THE MIDNIGHT CIRCLE AND FINALLY got to see Romeo and Juliet—theatrical human tragedy is a sure winner with a pack of ghosts in a graveyard—but I was distracted. After it was over I flew back up to "elevation" and rested.

I let time slip and went back through my memories of Tamara and what I knew of John.

They were in love and engaged. John was a graduate student at UA working on some top secret project. Someone stabbed him to death in front of an ATM at night in a good Tucson neighborhood. The FBI had confiscated most of his belongings after his death. The professor John worked for had disappeared the same night he had died. He loved Mustangs. Tamara loved him.

It wasn't much. But at the time, when Tamara shared what she did about John, I knew it was a big deal and I never pressed her for more details.

The sun rose and the day blurred around me until late afternoon came and it was time to go. I brought my attention back to the present and time slipped back into its normal gear.

"I DON'T WANT YOU TO DO THIS," BANQUO BEGAN WHEN we met at the playground and moved towards Mrs. Turner's old class. "It is dangerous, very dangerous."

"Well," I said, "why don't you start by telling me what 'it' is."

Banquo stopped and sighed heavily. "There is only one way I know of to bring someone this far gone out of the bardo."

"OK," I said shrugging, "what is it?"

"You have to go in after him."

I felt dread, heavy and sharp, in my belly. "Go in after him" reverberated around my mind. Anything, I would do anything to help John, but to willingly go into the bardo...

I want to use meat metaphors here, like: I was pale as a ghost; my blood ran cold; hairs on the back of my neck stood up; and a chill ran up and down my spine. And considering that I was already a ghost and I had not blood nor hair nor spine, they seem a little disingenuous. But really, how else can I express it? I felt fear and dread and panic, and it was visceral. I felt it throughout my ghostly form. I looked and could see a flicker of the faintest chartreuse licking along the edges, and I had gone wispy.

I tightened up my form and took the equivalent of a few deep breaths.

"Tell me more," I said slowly.

"I know the procedure," he began "I know how it is done. I know what you need to accomplish, but I have never done it."

This did nothing to make me feel better. It's like the person teaching you how to drive has only ever read about it and never done it. Sounds like a recipe for disaster, right?

"How... Why..." I stammered. "If you haven't done it, how do you know about it?"

"My teacher, he goes by Monk, he told me about it."

"Monk?" I mumbled. It was another odd name, but my teacher was "Banquo" so who was I to complain. "He told you?"

Banquo nodded and swallowed hard. He looked scared, his composure, for once, not a solid wall of awesomeness. "He told me, yes. He told me when I asked him how he rescued me out of the bardo."

"You? You were in the bardo?" Shock is not sufficient to describe what I was feeling. It was like the moment when I was a teenager and realized my dad was mortal. Here I was realizing my teacher once needed rescuing.

"Yes, JJ, for a very long time I was in the bardo."

"You? Bardo? Why?" I could only speak in single word sentences.

His eyes grew sad as he slowly shook his head. "For the usual reason, JJ."

"And this Monk guy went in after you?"

Banquo nodded. "He did. And you want to know the funny part?" I nodded. "He didn't even know me. I was bardoed for over a year after my death and Monk found me and for some reason he decided that I was 'worth the trip,' as he put it."

I felt dizzy. Banquo in the bardo for a year. A ghost that casually enters the bardo when it's "worth the trip." I would have to go into the bardo, willingly, to save John. If I had had a body I would have had to sit down.

Part of me knew this was a big deal, that Banquo was sharing personal history with me, revealing weakness. It was very un-Banquo like. And suddenly Banquo's motives for teaching me and the other ghosts had a context, paying forward what his teacher gave him. But another part of me was more driven, more focused on my goal. "So where is this Monk? Do you think he will help?"

Banquo shook his head, "No, he won't help. He's about a year into a two-year silent retreat." He swiveled and pointed north. "He's up on the top of the San Francisco peaks, at the highest point in Arizona."

"Wait. Two years? Silent for two years?" Who the hell goes on a silent retreat for two years? "Is this guy, like, a real monk?"

Banquo shrugged. "He doesn't look like one, but he is a Buddhist. He's the one that came up with the term 'bardo' to describe the state of our less fortunate ghosts. Bardo is a Buddhist term as is 'maya.'"

"So let's go un-silent him," I said taking a step to the north.

"It won't work, JJ. Believe me, it won't work. He won't talk, not for any reason, not until he is ready. And if you think I am a tough teacher, you haven't seen anything."

I nodded and wandered away studying the swing set on the playground. Well, I wasn't really studying it. I was staring at it and pacing back and forth. Banquo walked to the edge of the playground and gave me space.

This was it. One of those moments that can change the course of your life. It was also a risk and a challenge and a fight. Fear gripped me, doubts assailed me, but my decision was clear. With Jesus gone and John in need of help for Tamara's sake, what was I to do? I wanted to run away, but I couldn't. Fool that I am, I walked up to Banquo and said, "OK then. Tell me how I make the trip."

Transmission #30
Received 2012/02/11 01:42:16

I'M BACK TO THINKING ABOUT MOTIVATION, WHY WE DO what we do. Like, in this case, why I was willing to descend into the bardo?

And if you are looking for clean, easy to understand motives, they are these: helping my friend Tamara; distracting myself from the fact that my anchor in this ghostly world was gone. I had come to depend on the fact that Jesus was there and, in truth, I had some grieving to do that I was in Denial about; taking on a new, and difficult challenge; having some kind of purpose and not being ready to "rest in peace" even if that purpose was fraught with peril; and utter ignorance as to the magnitude of the challenge.

And you could say all of that as the "why" and you wouldn't be wrong. But, you wouldn't be completely right either. Let me try to explain. All of those things, those motives, are stories. They are a clean word-based description around the much, much messier human reality. Yes, they convey truth, that is what stories are all about, but, no, they don't convey the *whole* truth. The lines are too neat and well defined. Reality, as opposed to story, is one messy place.

Right then and there I knew I wanted to help Tamara and that I was pathologically unable to back down from a challenge. The rest didn't register.

So, despite the difficulty, despite the personal risk, I was going to do it.

And here's the kicker. The risk was huge.

"Once you go in," Banquo told me, "you won't be able to come out on your own. You both have to wake up to the bardo at the same time, the exact same time, or you will both be locked in there."

I swallowed hard and nodded.

"And the experience John is having will change. It won't be just his bardo but a combination of yours and his. You will have to face your own worst fears as well as his."

More swallowing hard.

"And, there is nothing any of us will be able to do to help you. I don't even think Monk would find that a trip worth going on. You have to wake yourself up and wake John up and both of you have to want to leave. At the same time. That is the only way out."

Not fun. I had already decided and committed myself, and Banquo kept piling on the bad news.

I paused, letting all that he had said rattle around my brain. I was never one to back down from a fight or to not take on a bully because I might lose. In fact, a fight and a bully bigger than me just made me want to do it more.

What Banquo was telling me was having that effect while at the same time increasing my level of fear. This wasn't some junior high kid I was about to have a juvenile fist fight with. This was the bardo. This was, in many ways, myself I was about to have a fight with.

A fight with myself. There is something exciting about that, isn't there? To go fight with your own fears, to go delve into that which no one wants to look at, to face the worst this ghostly life has to offer. I wasn't a neophyte at this—I was fully informed and thought I knew just how bad the bardo could get. I smiled and slowly nodded my head while I watched Banquo frown and shake his head.

"OK, then," I said. "Consider me fully warned. How do I do this?"

FIRST, MATCHING THE QUALITY OF MY FORM TO JOHN'S. Going all wispy and diffuse, allowing my limbs to become vague shapes. Becoming transparent. And I felt a shift, I felt the bardo coming near, just by looking like a bardoed ghost.

Second, intertwining my arms with John's arms so that I could not tell where one started and the other ended. I could feel it then. Not something as definite as hearing voices or seeing images, but I could feel it on a deep level. I could feel his fear and guilt and remorse, those boat anchors of emotion that were keeping him locked in the bardo.

Third, becoming more aware of that vague feeling. Finding a piece that seems clearer and making it more real. I focused on it, made it bigger. I heard a wisp of phrase shouted by a female voice, "You did what!?" It was diffuse, a vague distant echo, but as I focused on it, tuned it in, it became louder, the emotion became clear, and I started to feel those words churn in my belly. I knew, then, that they weren't directed at me, but I felt myself starting to react to those words as if they were. "You did what!? My God, how could you? What will happen to her?"

Fourth, letting go. This was the hardest part. Not nearly as hard as getting out of the bardo, not by several orders of magnitude, but hard. Like asking someone to hit you as hard as they can in the face. It took courage and strength and a large dose of foolishness. Helen the gypsy would be proud. Right then and there I was nothing if not the Fool, completely unprepared for what was to come.

Transmission #31
Received 2012/02/11 03:10:21

A SMALL AND CRAMPED WOMAN STOOD IN A SMALL AND cramped kitchen and yelled at me. She had obviously bleached blond hair that had gone limp from not being washed. She had eyes the same brown as John's and a cigarette in her mouth.

"Jesus Christ, John," she said. "How can you do this? Sign your rights away like that. What the hell were you thinking?" The woman, John's mother, paced about the kitchen in an elaborate ritual that seemed like it was about making dinner.

I say "ritual" because it involved a lot of picking up and putting things down. Like getting frozen hamburger out of the freezer and putting it in the microwave to defrost was a holy act. First take it out and put it on the counter. Pause taking a long drag of your cigarette and shout some insults at your son. Then get a plate from the cupboard and slam the frozen meat down on it. Next lean against the counter taking another drag on the cigarette. And then decide that is one of the good plates, so take it to the sink, rinse it and put it the dishwasher. Then go back to put the meat in the microwave and realize there is no plate. Go back to the cupboard and find an appropriate plate and slam the meat down on it. Pause, leaning against the counter as if exhausted and shout some more at your son. Stub out your cigarette in the sink and go on a hunt for another one. Once found, yell at your son some more, go on a hunt for a working lighter, going through four that don't work while cursing before finding one that does. Take a drag on the cigarette and sigh as if you haven't smoked for days. Look around the kitchen trying to remember what you were doing.

And on and on it went.

As this played out I became aware that this woman, John's mom, spoke directly to me. I looked around when I first realized this and saw that John and I were... Well it's hard to explain. We were occupying the same space. We moved at the same time, we said the same things. When we spoke it was both of our voices coming out together exactly the same. At this point, John was in control of our body and our voice.

I knew I was in the bardo, I was aware of what was going on, but I was in no way in control of it.

"It's the right thing to do, Mom," we said. "I'm twenty years old. I would have to leave college. I would have to give up everything. I... I..."

"Weak. You're weak, John, just like your deadbeat father. Weak. When you have a child you take care of that child. No matter what."

We nodded. I felt John's guilt and suddenly knew what had happened. John had a brief, and wild, affair with an older woman, Alice, when he was a sophomore in college. She had red hair, wild green eyes, and bright white teeth.

She was passionate and intriguing and John's philosophy professor at UA.

"It is more complicated than that," we said.

"No, John," she said as she shoved the meat, finally sitting on its appropriate plate, into the microwave. "Some things are just black and white. This is your child. You are its father. You must take care of it."

"Alice... she... she wants it this way."

"Alice, oh yes, let's take the opinion of the woman who sleeps with her students. Let's trust her judgment. Let's do whatever she says."

"It's complicated, Mom. If this came out she would lose her job. She's a tenured professor, it's a big deal."

"Yeah?" she said, taking a long drag on her cigarette. "Well maybe she should have thought about it before she started making eyes at my boy."

I could feel us getting frustrated. Well, I could feel John getting frustrated, and it started seeping over to me. I was feeling more and more connected to his emotional process. I could also feel his youth, how everything was big and important, not that this wasn't, and how much passion he had in him. It had been a long time since I had been twenty. It was kind of heady to feel that rush, it was kind of seductive, and it was all kinds of dangerous.

"We love each other," we said. "We still do, even though it's over. Doesn't that count for something?"

Our mother went to the microwave, opening it, poking at the partially thawed meat, and closing it. She turned to us, her eyes sharp as knives and said, "Love, is it? Really, John? You love this woman, but you don't love the child that she is about to bear. How selfish is that? How immature? Didn't I raise you better than that, John? Didn't I?"

I fought to hold on to my sense of self, my sense of what was going on, but moment by moment, it became harder. As the argument escalated, as John's mother dug into us emotionally, I started to lose myself to the bardo.

"It's not that simple," we said.

"Well then, why don't you explain it me. I know I'm not smart like you, I never got to go to college, I had to work as soon as I could. But I'm not stupid, so explain it to me."

"She... she..." we stuttered. I could feel his shame welling up and his grief. It was like a rising tide spilling over onto me.

"What is it, boy? Spit it out." She was standing right in front of us, her eyes unrelenting as she looked up into ours. The microwave dinged behind her, but she ignored it.

"She wants it this way."

"What? Alice wants it this way? She wants you to sign your rights away to your child? To make it so you are legally not her father. Is that the way she wants it?" She inched closer until the smell of her cigarette breath became overwhelming. I felt another flood of emotion spill over, triggered by that smell. Years of not being good enough, years of yelling and shaming, years of questioning our value came with that scent. We felt sick to our stomachs. We wanted to run. We wanted to vomit.

"Yes, goddammit, yes! Alice wants it this way. Alice always wanted it this way."

"Say it John, say it. Say, 'Alice doesn't want me to be the father of our child.' Say it!"

"No, I won't," we said.

"SAY IT!"

"Alice doesn't... she doesn't want me to be..." we couldn't continue. We sunk to the floor, tears flowing down our cheeks. The memory flooded back. I saw Alice as John had first seen her, with glasses over her green eyes and her long red hair pulled up in the back. She had her head tilted down as she studied some papers at the podium. Class was about to begin.

I saw the shy flirtations that John initiated, talking to her whenever he could after class. Waiting until everyone had left to compliment her on her lecture.

I saw the encounter at the bar where Alice was clearly drunk and upset about something. I saw how we... how John comforted her and made sure she got home without taking advantage of her state.

I saw how she fixed him dinner as a thank you and how one thing led to another.

I saw when she told him/us that she was pregnant, that she was keeping the baby, that she wanted full legal rights to it. I felt the mixture of fear and guilty relief wash over us as a result. I tasted the greed and guilt that filled us when she offered to "compensate" us for our cooperation.

We gasped at the strength of the memories and looked up when we smelled the stench of cigarette breath again. Our mother's face was there, her eyes even sharper. "You're nothing more than a goddamn sperm donor. A prostitute. A dirty, goddamn prostitute." Her voice changed, no longer loud or high pitched but soft and low and all the more devastating for it. "I am so ashamed of you, John."

I felt the tears flow as the scene shifted. Gone was the small and cramped kitchen, it was replaced by a cramped office.

We sat in a chair across from a big desk. We were alone. We looked around at the stacks of papers and books, the diplomas on the wall, and we fixated on the baby picture on the desk. We picked it up and held it, our hands shaking, our belly tight.

"What are you doing here?" Alice asked as she opened the door. We hid the picture in our lap.

"Umm... I..." we said.

Alice went over to her desk and sat down with a sigh. "We can't keep doing this, John. We can't. You can't see her. You can't know her. And, you can't keep sneaking in here."

"Please, Alice. I made a mistake, Jill is my daughter, I shouldn't have..."

"John, you didn't make a mistake. You did the right thing. I care for you, honestly I do. But it would never work out. You have your whole life ahead of you." We bit our lip and nodded slowly as she continued, "Please stop doing this, don't make me get a restraining order. Please, John."

We looked up, but could hardly see her through our tears. We nodded and slowly got up, slipping the baby picture into our jacket as we went.

The scene shifted to a small park. We stood quietly across the street and watched Alice play with a baby. The girl had a delightful smile, it was our girl. She was so beautiful, so delicate, so awkward. We felt our hearts break and melt at the same time. We wanted so badly to touch her, to hold her, to tell her who we were.

We should have left when Alice noticed us and then was on the phone briefly. We should have left, but we didn't. A little while later the police took us away.

After that we went through counseling. It was hard and long, and seemed to last forever. It was one monumental session where we told the therapist about our mother, where we told him about never knowing our father, about Alice and how we would never get to know our daughter. On it went. On and on and on.

The Fool

Transmission #32
Received 2012/02/12 00:48:38

Even with the restraining order and the counseling, the stalking didn't stop, we couldn't stop. It was our child after all, and we had been pressured into signing our rights away. A fact our mother continued to make perfectly clear.

I continued to lose myself to the sense of "us" and "we" as I came to identify with John's life as if it were my own.

We had been in counseling for what seemed like a long time, but in this bardo reenactment there was no way to tell how long it really was. When the eternal counseling session ended it was our daughter's first birthday.

We got up that morning and looked in the mirror and grimaced. Bags under our brown eyes, sandy hair way past the need for a haircut, a week of stubble on our face. But there was nothing to be done about it because we knew it was a special day. It was her day. It was our daughter's first birthday. It was Jill's day.

It was late on a Saturday morning, and we felt the drag of too much alcohol consumed the night before. We had Fruit

Loops and orange juice for breakfast, put on a baseball cap and sunglasses, and went to go see our daughter.

We understood that we would be violating the restraining order, we knew it was stupid, but we had to do it.

The party was already started when we got there. It was held in Reid Park, a huge park in the center of the city. We saw Alice and a bunch of adults cooing over our Jill.

Her hair had grown since we had last seen her, a wispy strawberry blond, and her blue eyes were brighter than we remembered. We were being careful, we were a ways away looking through binoculars. We were sure Alice didn't know we knew about the party—we had gone through her trash a few weeks ago and found one of the invitations.

We watched as the presents were opened, as the cake was cut, as Jill smeared the white frosting on her face, and as the guests started to leave. Soon it was Alice, her brother Edgar and his family, and our little Jill.

The counseling had helped us to understand how we had gotten here, how what we were doing was wrong, but it hadn't stopped the desire.

So as we snuck closer we felt fear and guilt but couldn't stop ourselves. Edgar was loading a heavy cooler, and Alice's back was turned so we took our chance. We ran up quietly, out of eyesight of both of them, and squatted before our daughter.

"Hi, Jill. Happy birthday," we whispered to her. She was lying in her stroller.

She was so beautiful. The blue of her eyes shocked us, they spoke of an ancient wisdom. Her chubby hands reached out, her fingers reaching for ours.

We felt the tears run down our cheeks. She knew us.

She wanted us. She was the most beautiful thing we had ever seen.

"Step away, John," Alice said, her voice low. She was trying to hide her panic, but we could hear it. Why was she panicked? We were Jill's father, we would never hurt her.

We didn't move away, we leaned closer until one of those fingers touched our cheeks. Just a brush of warm flesh and a sharp little fingernail. We smelled soap and baby powder. It was the most amazing thing we had ever experienced.

"The police are coming, John. You better go now." We looked up, Alice had a phone in her hand. We didn't care. This moment, right here, was worth it.

We leaned in again as our daughter reached her fingers out, but we didn't connect. Something yanked us sharply back and pulled us up and spun us around. A meaty fist met with our face as Edgar punched us. We spun and fell, our right cheek connecting with the cement picnic table as we went down.

The last thing we saw was the face of our daughter scrunched in fear as she cried.

A MOMENT LATER WE WOKE UP IN A HOSPITAL WITH A horrible headache, bandages on our cheek, and handcuffs locking us to the bed.

The doctor said we had a mild concussion and would have a scar on our right cheek. He had the nurse give us something that made us woozy right before the big men came to take us away.

Much to our eternal shame, our mother rescued us. She arrived all blustery and loud with a man in a suit next to her. For once her anger was not directed at us. She yelled at the big men until they left the room. She yelled at everyone, the suited man waving papers at them until they let her take us back to a cramped room in her cramped home.

It was then that she started yelling at us. "Do you know what this is going to cost me? I had to hire a lawyer to keep you out of the loony bin. Jesus Christ, John. If you had just listened to me in the first place. You can't just walk away from your child and not pay the price."

And things sped up then, a blur of humiliating activity. Psych evaluations, counseling, meetings with lawyers, meetings with a judge, struggling to keep up with coursework, being forced to move back in with our mother, and our mother constantly yelling at us.

It wore me down—I began to lose what little remaining sense of self I still had.

Transmission #33
Received 2012/02/12 02:29:11

TIME LEAPT FORWARD. THIS WAS THE BARDO—I DIDN'T
get to experience the high points, the victories, only the
crushing defeats. We were past that chapter in our lives
and were now a graduate student, living on our own, and
no longer obsessed with our daughter.

We were in a lab working with equipment that John
was adept with, but I only vaguely understood. We were
happy and valued and doing something important, doing
something secret.

In the lab was a thin man with large glasses and wild
grey hair. Professor Aldridge. We liked him a lot. When no
one else believed in us, he did. He took us in and helped
us. He gave us a purpose.

Except that day he was angry at us. He was yelling and
he reminded us of our mother.

"They're coming tomorrow. Do you want us to lose our
funding? How could you be so sloppy?" he asked.

The rebuke was relatively mild, but it hurt us. He was
like a father to us, like the father we never had.

"I am sorry, Professor," we said. "I will get started on a new batch."

"We'll be at this all night," he said. There was still anger, but it made us feel warm in that "we" would be doing it together.

I DON'T WANT YOU TO GET THE WRONG IMPRESSION OF John. What I am sharing is our bardo experience, it's not his real life. It's the worst parts of his life put end to end and amplified like a bad dream. It's the nature of the experience, the worst parts are all that you get to relive. Except it's often not the way it actually happened; it is worse so that the remembered reality matches your internal emotional memory.

No one should be judged by their bardo experience. Believe me. No one.

And the experience we were having started to spin forth faster. Time was flowing rapidly because John, for a while, had gotten his life together and for the most part was happy. There was nothing to view in the bardo.

He met Tamara and they fell in love and all I got to see was their occasional fights.

He and Professor Aldridge continued to work on the top secret project which was... well, I hesitate to say too much here. The facts are clearly of a sensitive nature, and if I disclose them one of two things will happen. Tam and Jin will edit them out or there will be serious consequences to them once this memoir goes public. So, as we continue, please excuse me when I am vague about their project and expect me to fictionalize it a bit. I will, though, try to paint a picture that is, at least, intriguing.

So, as the project moved forward all the things I experienced with him were the worst difficulties, the biggest setbacks, and the paranoia. But even with that, I didn't experience much, just enough to figure out what they were up to.

As JOHN'S WORK LIFE SPUN FORTH WE WERE ALWAYS IN the lab, always at the machines, always frustrated by what was happening.

This wasn't a large crew of people—it was just Professor Aldridge and John. It was a small, risky, top secret project running on a shoestring budget and funded by the military.

John was a materials guy, like Jin. Except unlike Jin his work had nothing to do with electromagnetic shielding, but shielding of another nature. He was working on making lasers much more efficient.

And this was hard for me to follow. These people were smart, Mensa smart, and I'm... well, I'm not dumb, but I'm no genius.

So as John worked in the lab, mixing substances, pouring, baking, irradiating, and all the other processes they went through, I was pretty lost.

The first experience was that all-nighter with him and Professor Aldridge. It seemed to go on forever as they kept failing to get the mixture right. They couldn't keep the temperature steady, they couldn't control the machines well enough. It went on and on and on until it was over.

Next we were having a fight with Tamara. We were teaching an undergraduate class, and she was our student. It was the morning after the all-nighter, and we were so exhausted.

I did a double take when I first saw Tamara. We walked

in to the lecture hall and looked out at the students there, but we were only looking at one of them. Tam sat about halfway back and to the side. Her blue eyes were hard and her arms crossed.

When we saw her I felt us both react. Our reactions were different, not as closely coupled as they had been. He felt guilt, he had forgotten their date. I felt a sliver of happiness at seeing her. Her black hair was very long, and she looked younger than I remembered. Not just in years, but in terms of life. She looked innocent. She was clearly angry that John had stood her up, but it was a simple anger, uncluttered by the complexities that colored her emotions when I knew her. I felt refreshed and buoyed by it.

That all disappeared quickly when we looked at our notes to begin our lecture and found all the pages blank. The class turned into one of those nightmares of unpreparedness as we stumbled through a lecture on thermodynamics having no idea what we were really talking about.

After class ended, we found ourselves running after Tamara down a long sidewalk.

"I'm sorry, I'm sorry, I'm sorry," we said as we caught up to her.

She frowned, rolled her eyes, and kept walking.

"It was a work thing. I got stuck in the lab."

"Without a phone?" she asked.

"No," we said, looking down. "I'm sorry. It was a big deal. I screwed up and had to make it right. I got distracted."

She stopped and faced us, her eyes searching ours. "Don't take me for granted, John."

"I don't, I don't. It's just that... I made a mistake and Professor Aldridge needed me."

"Well, maybe you should date him," she said as she turned and walked away.

As we watched her I remembered John and Alice. Alice had been the teacher and John had been the student. Now that John was teaching, he was involved with his student. The age difference, in this case, was small, but the remaining "I" found it interesting.

We ran after her. She had to forgive us, we needed her to forgive us.

THE FOOL

Transmission #34
Received 2012/02/12 04:03:07

Time jerked forward again and we found ourselves walking under the midnight moon. We had just left the lab and someone was following us. Tamara was at home—our home now—and was used to our late nights.

We heard the scrape of feet on pavement. We turned but couldn't see anyone. The campus was well lit but at this hour pretty much deserted.

We put our hand in our pocket and pulled out our keys, arranging the largest key, the key to our car, so it stuck out between our fingers. We had no idea if it would help if we got into a fight, but we had a vague memory of some self-defense class we saw on YouTube.

We heard the scuff of a foot echo off the walls of the brick buildings but we never managed to spot the person. We finally made it to the parking lot and our car. We fumbled with the key, and missed the keyhole. We heard the scrape of a foot on pavement again. We didn't look around. We got the key in properly, unlocked the door, ripped it open, jumped in, and slammed down the lock.

As this sequence kept repeating itself, it got worse. We began panicking and running for the car. Sometimes we would drop our keys, sometimes we had trouble finding the keys. Each time the sequence played out the fear got worse and worse, but we never saw anyone. Just the scrape of a foot and fear in our belly. We began leaving the lab with pepper spray in hand and contemplated buying a gun. We began to regret our '75 Mustang—a new car with keyless entry would be a lot quicker to get into.

In our bardo experience, this happened hundreds of times until—

"Stay calm," the man said from the backseat after we entered the car. "I am not going to hurt you, just don't turn around and stay calm."

Our hands shook as we looked into the rearview mirror trying to get a glimpse of the person. We didn't see much, but we could tell he was middle-aged with short, dark-colored hair and bags hanging under his sad eyes.

"What do you want?" we asked, our heart beating so loudly in our chest that we doubted he could hear us.

"Just listen, kid."

We considered running but felt frozen in place. We thought about shouting for help and honking the horn, but it was the middle of the night and no one would hear.

We heard the sound of papers shuffling. The man threw some photos onto the front seat next to us and shone a dim flashlight on them. They were pictures of Professor Aldridge and showed him handing envelopes of paper to some well-dressed Asian men.

"He's selling the tech you are developing to the Chinese," the man said.

"No..." we began, picking up the pictures and looking

at them. In one Aldridge is looking over his shoulder as if he suspects someone is watching him. "No, he wouldn't do that."

"Sorry, kid, he did, and it's my job to know." He handed us a small leather wallet, in it was an FBI badge, "Special Agent Henry Franks."

"What? I... Why are you talking to me and not arresting him if this is true?"

"I know it, but I don't have enough evidence to prove it," he said.

"Prove it?" we asked.

"Yeah, kid, prove it. As in a court of law. You know, presumed innocent until proven guilty."

We felt this weight on our chest, pressing down. This wasn't Professor Aldridge, this wasn't our mentor. Our project was funded by the military; he would never give our secrets away. "I... What do you want from me?"

He nodded and we saw a crack of a smile in the rear-view mirror. "I need details, details on what he's giving the Chinese. If I know what you guys are doing, I can prove the Chinese have it and prove he gave it to them."

That didn't sound right. We opened our mouths to speak when Franks threw some more pictures onto the front seat. Our breath caught in our chest and our heart pounded. We felt a rush of energy, scary and exciting, that we hadn't felt for a long time.

The pictures were of Jill at her third birthday party. Her face had changed, it wasn't so chubby anymore, and it had elongated a bit. She had a blue dress on, and her strawberry-blond hair was pulled into a ponytail with a pink bow.

We felt dizzy and hungry and desperate as we looked

through the photos. Shots of her ripping open presents. Shots of her on a pony with Alice walking next to her holding her steady on the animal.

We blinked back tears. "What? How? Why?"

"It ain't right, kid. A man should get to see his daughter. There's two wrongs here; let's correct both of them." With that we heard him get out of the car. We stayed there for a long time looking at the pictures of Jill over and over and over again.

THREE DAYS LATER, OUR HANDS SHAKING, WE DIALED THE FBI. We wanted it to be true, we wanted him to be an FBI agent. We were desperate for him to be one. We had driven to the airport and were at one of the few remaining payphones. We wore sunglasses, a hat, and a red coat we got at Good Will, the kind of coat we would never wear, just in case they came looking for us.

When the woman's voice answered, we asked for Special Agent Henry Franks. The woman said, "Just one moment." The line clicked and rang several times, and then a voice mail greeting played. "You've reached Special Agent Henry Franks, please leave me your name, number, and reason for calling and I'll get back to you."

We slammed the receiver down, pulled our hat low, and quickly walked out of the airport. The voice was his. We felt a potent mixture of fear and excitement.

Transmission #35
Received 2012/02/13 01:34:54

"GOOD JOB, KID. GOOD JOB," FRANKS SAID FROM THE backseat after we handed him some paperwork. It wasn't much, not enough to duplicate what we were doing, but it was something. We felt guilty, but we wanted... we needed...

He threw some pictures over to us from the backseat. We looked at them eagerly, lapping them up like water in the desert. Jill on a swing. Jill holding her mother's hand. Jill crying.

"Do you think I could see her sometime?" Our voice was weak as we spoke. We hated that.

"This is a good start, kid. Get me more and I'll see what I can do."

And on it went, over and over. Secret meetings in our Mustang with Special Agent Henry Franks. We fed him bits of our research, and he gave us pictures of Jill.

Part of us knew it was wrong, that this wasn't the way it should be. "Why do we meet like this?" we asked him one night. "You're FBI, why do we have to meet like this?"

"There is someone on the inside, someone dirty," Franks

said, his voice low and conspiratorial. "We can't trust anyone else, kid. It's just you and me."

So we kept doing it for months. During that time, the rest of our life went well. Work, teaching, our relationship with Tamara. It was all good, and I knew that. I knew we were doing well, but all I got to see was the secret meetings with Franks in our Mustang. The rush at seeing and hearing Jill (he eventually provided video) seemed to keep us coming back for more. We were an addict and he was our supplier.

One day we confronted Aldridge. It was in the lab, things weren't going well, we had just burned ourselves pretty badly. As we ran cold water over our hand, we said, "Professor. I... I need to ask you something."

"Let me see that," he said, ignoring what we said. "I think we need to take you into the ER."

We nodded. It was a second degree burn and needed to be treated. "I'm afraid I did something, Professor, something wrong." The pain was tremendous, but somehow it gave us courage to do what we had tried so many times to do but couldn't.

"What?" Aldridge said, looking at our hand. "No, no, don't worry, John. These things happen."

"Not this," we said, indicating our hand. "In the bottom drawer over there." We nodded to a cabinet. Aldridge had a bad back, and we put the envelope on the bottom knowing that he wouldn't get in there unless he had a good reason.

"What?" he asked, pushing his glasses up and running his hand through his unruly grey hair.

We continued to run cold water on our hand. The pain was intense, but this had to be done. "Please, there is a manila envelope in there, pull it out."

He studied us for a moment before painfully squatting

down and opening the drawer. "At the very bottom," we said. He pulled the envelope out and brought it over to the counter next to the sink. He slowly pulled out the pictures of him with the Asian men.

"What the hell is this, John?" he asked.

"Who are those people?" we asked.

His brows furrowed as he looked from the pictures to us and back. "Potential investors. I met with them early on, before the military got involved and funded this research."

The pain in our stomach, as it clenched, briefly overwhelmed the pain in our hand. We felt dizzy and had to clutch the counter.

The Professor ran out of the lab and came back with some ice. "You're not well," he said wrapping our wounded hand with a towel and icing it down. "We're going to the ER, now."

As he drove us through the dark streets of Tucson, we told him everything. We didn't leave anything out. We cried.

We were a mess as he guided us through the doors to the ER. "I'm so sorry, Professor," we said. "I am so sorry."

"Not to worry, my boy," he said gently. "I've got a plan, but first let's get you looked at."

THE PROFESSOR'S PLAN MADE SENSE. IT SOUNDED SAFE enough, but it scared us—we had to meet with Franks twice more.

The first time we did everything the same. We did our best to act normal, but we were so scared. Franks didn't seem to notice, taking the information we gave him and giving us a few pictures of Jill.

The next time, the last time, we met with him was

different. We didn't have an envelope for him. "What's the problem?" he asked.

Our hands shook as we hit play on the recorder. It was of the last time we had met:

"I just can't believe he would be selling secrets to the Chinese," we said on the recording.

"Sorry, kid," Franks replied, "we've been over this, he did it, and he continues to do it."

"But Agent Franks, why would he do that? What is he getting out of it?"

"Money, what else..."

The playback halted as Franks ripped the recorder from my hand. "That was not smart, kid."

"Do you really work for the FBI?" we asked.

"Is this the only copy?" he asked.

We shook our head, "Lots more," we said. "So why, Franks, why?"

"Money, what else?" he said just like he had said on the recording.

"Why me?" we asked, our voice shaking.

He shrugged his shoulders. "Oh, I don't know. Some young idealist kid who signed away the rights to his own kid. You tell me?"

We felt our face flush red. "I better never see you again," we said.

"Kid, if you ever do see me again, it will be the last thing you see. And don't bother going to the cops, not unless you want to see your cute little girlfriend in a casket."

Our blood ran cold as he got out of the car and walked away. After he was out of sight, we pulled down the visor on the passenger's side and with our shaking hand checked the digital recorder. We had gotten it all.

We called Professor Aldridge and told him what had happened. We decided not to tell anyone; it seemed safer that way.

For a long time after the call we sat in our Mustang, Franks's threat echoing through our head.

Transmission #36
Received 2012/02/13 03:00:52

Tamara was mad, no, she was furious. Her blue eyes bore into us as we stood there in what was once her apartment, but was now our apartment.

We had missed dinner and hadn't called. She had tried our cell, but we had left it in the lab while we dealt with Agent Franks. She had been worried that we had been hurt.

The guilt we felt was making it hard to breathe, but we knew, we hoped, that it was over. That we could get back to a normal life.

"I'm so sorry, Tamara. I am. Really," we said.

She crossed her arms. "Sorry isn't enough anymore, John. Sometimes I don't think you are even in this relationship."

We opened our mouth to speak and closed it. We loved her, God how we loved her. Even in her anger a part of us cherished that she was even there. "I..." we stammered. We hadn't told her. We couldn't tell her about Franks or Jill. That would just complicate things. The time wasn't right. "You're right," we said. We saw Tamara relax a little at our admission. "You're right," we repeated. "I understand how you could feel that way. But I promise you I am in this relationship. I am in this more than anything I have ever been in my life."

The love we felt for her, mixed with the fear of losing her, nearly overwhelmed us.

"I don't know, John," she said, shaking her head.

"I can prove it, Tam. I can prove that I am in this relationship, that I am all in."

She crossed her arms again. "How?"

"Wait here," we said as we went into the bedroom. We opened the sock draw and looked for the grey dress socks. Our heart pounded even harder when we couldn't find it, but there it was, at the very back. It was rolled into a ball, and we unrolled it and pulled out the little velvet box inside.

We went back into the living room, fumbled with the stereo and put on our song, "Just the Two of Us." We got down on one knee, and said, "Tamara Watson, will you do me the great honor of being my wife?"

Her eyes sparkled brighter than the diamond we were giving her, and she began to cry. And this being the bardo, that quiet cry turned into a sob and that turned into a chuckle and that chuckle turned into a gale of laughter.

This wasn't right. She had cried, but then she had said yes. Why was she laughing at us?

We ran out of the apartment throwing the door open and found ourselves in downtown Tucson.

We were standing in front of an ATM and after a brief bit of confusion, we suddenly felt calm, our belly filled with good food and wine. Tamara, our fiancée, was back at the restaurant waiting for us. Franks hadn't showed up again, and we were past our obsession with Jill. Things were good.

We put our card in and punched in the PIN number and amount we wanted. We heard a rough scuff of a foot behind us. But, it had been several months since we had seen Agent Franks and our paranoia had abated so we didn't turn around.

We got our money and moved to leave when we saw the man. He was tall and skeletally thin, with a gaunt face and a Cardinal's hat pulled low. "Excuse me," we said with a small smile.

He didn't speak, but we saw the flash of metal, we felt the knife plunge into our chest, we felt the pain, deep and sharp, as we fell to the sidewalk gasping for breath.

The pain burned white hot, and we felt our warmth escaping us as we bled. For a moment the traffic cleared on Sixth Avenue, and we saw a man on the other side of the street. He was middle-aged with short dark hair and sad eyes with bags underneath. He too had a hat on and tipped it at us before turning and walking away. Agent Franks.

We thought it had ended, but it hadn't. We tried to pull out our cell phone, it was in our back pocket, but our hands weren't working right. We had to warn Professor Aldridge. Our hands stiff and awkward were still trying to find the phone when Tamara came. She screamed, "Oh my God!" as she leaned down beside us. "What!? What happened? Oh my God." She pulled out her phone and called 911. A small crowd gathered around us, gawking.

She took our head into her lap and stroked our hair. "It's OK," she said. "Just hold on, John. Just hold on. The ambulance is on its way."

We felt that burning sensation leaving as icy cold started to press around us. It was heavy and inescapable. We couldn't move our arms anymore. We worried about

Tamara, she had just bought the lovely navy blue skirt she was wearing, and now our blood was ruining it.

There was so much to say. We tried to talk, but it came out as a thin gasp. Tamara leaned close and suddenly there was just the two of us. We didn't see the crowd or hear the scream of the approaching siren anymore. It was just the two of us there. She leaned close in an intimate moment, we could smell the wine on her breath and feel the warmth of it as is caressed our cheek. There was so much to say.

"Tam, I love you, God how I love you," we said, but our voice lost its momentum and we didn't think she heard more than, "Tam, I..."

"Must tell you where the recording is," we said, but again our voice broke and it didn't sound intelligible.

"I should have told you about Jill." We tried to tell her about our daughter, but all that came out was "I should have..."

"Sorry," we said as the paramedics took us away from her. The last thing we saw before the darkness claimed us was Tamara. Tears flowed down her cheeks, and our blood stained her navy blue skirt and silk blouse as her bloody hands reached for us.

Transmission #37
Received 2012/02/14 00:59:23

THE BARDO IS UNFORGIVING, UNRELENTING, UNENDING. Seeing Tamara like that, bloody and terrified, destroyed me. Her pain ran me through and the remaining shred of "me" was gone. I was no longer experiencing the bardo as a "we," as John and I together. It was now just I. It was me.

John was still there, but I so identified with what was happening that I was completely unaware of him. *I* had just been stabbed. Tamara was *my* fiancée. Agent Franks had used *me*.

It felt like my life, it felt completely real.

And I was then a ghost watching Tamara grieve. I followed her everywhere. I watched her spend twenty-four hours in bed until her mother came to be with her. I watched the preparations for my funeral and as Tamara talked to my mother and father. I attended my funeral and wake. I watched my casket lowered into the ground.

I watched as Tamara's mother tried to get Tamara back onto her feet. Feeding her, making sure she went to her classes.

And bardo-time did me no favors. This all went moment by moment. Watching my beloved grieve was a horror to behold, most all of it bardo worthy.

And I was there when Agent Franks and some other FBI agents showed up at Tamara's door. Oh, how I wanted to hurt him, but I was nothing, just a wispy presence and could only watch as they removed all my possessions from the apartment, as they took Tamara in for long questioning about me, as she began to doubt me.

And slowly, eventually, Tamara got back on her feet, started acting more normal and bardo-time jumped forward as I tried desperately to communicate with her. She needed to know the things I had tried to tell her. She needed to know about Jill, about what Agent Franks had done. She needed to know where I had hid the recordings I had made of him.

Bardo-time finally skipped forward to when I had learned enough about being a ghost to attempt to communicate with her. Actually, it was an accident. At this point I was stuck in the apartment and couldn't leave. I learned to use my ghostly hand to turn on the TV and to change channels. I would get bored during the day and I would watch ESPN when she was gone to pass the time. I would always turn it off before she came home.

She noticed that the TV was always on ESPN when she turned it on, even though she hadn't left it that way. The fifth time it happened she looked around and said, "John?"

After that, I tried to communicate with her all the time. I would follow her around and talk to her. When she went to bed and cried at night, I tried to soothe her. I would sing to her lyrics from "Just the Two of Us," hoping that she could somehow hear me.

John had a very different style of discovering what he

could do as a ghost. While my process with my own death was decidedly logical, his was more intuitive. He didn't (I didn't, since I was him then) have a cause and effect model (i.e. ghosts emit electromagnetic (EM) radiation; if ghosts can emit that radiation in the right frequency they can make visible light), but felt his way through it. Accidents helped, but John made intuitive leaps and figured out how to do things that I didn't using my logical model.

For example, when I was alive, Tamara told me how she kept waking up at 1:16 (1/16 is John's birthday) and 3:20 (they got engaged on 3/20). Now that I was in John's bardo, I experienced the other side of it, with bardo enhancements, of course.

At night I would sit on the bed by Tamara and watch her sleep. It often took her hours to go to sleep, and she would wake up several times a night. While this was happening I would talk to her. I would tell her over and over about Agent Franks and the recordings I had hidden, about my daughter Jill, about how much I loved her.

At one point I talked to her about the stabbing. It was a big part of the story so it was natural that I told her. I looked at the clock and it was 1:16 a.m. and I said, "Well, happy birthday to me. Born on a full moon in January, murdered on a dark night in May. God it hurt, Tam, I can't even tell you how much it hurt." And I rattled on, feeling the pain again, feeling the fear and the emotion, feeling so very sorry for myself.

Tamara had been dreaming, her eyes twitching under their lids, before I started my little pity party. As I talked, the twitching got worse, so I stopped talking and the twitching relaxed. So I started talking about the night I died again, how it felt, my fear, the pain. Reliving the memory was a bit like the bardo in itself—and yes, I realize that I am in the bardo experiencing something akin to the bardo. A bardo within a bardo, very Shakespearian.

I felt horribly guilty, but the connection was obvious. I eventually felt it and spoke it intensely enough so that she opened her eyes and sat straight up. She was terrified, her eyes wide, a sheen of sweat on her face, gasping for breath. "John!" she said and then started crying. It was 1:18 a.m. It had taken me several minutes to actually wake her.

I tried to talk to her after she woke, but she couldn't hear me. She eventually went back to sleep and when 3:17 rolled around I tried again. This time I was able to wake her right at 3:20 a.m.

And this went on and on, night after night. I tried everything I could think of to wake her, to reach her, but only the horror of my death would do it. Only reliving my pain and fear would reach her in her sleep state.

And as bad as I felt about it, I kept it up. I was desperate to reach her. Each time I did it, I would see her fear and swear I wouldn't do it again, but the next time 1:16 or 3:20 approached I just couldn't help myself. It was the only way I seemed to be able to reach her, so I did it. Eventually Tamara started to notice.

At first the bardo was gentle with this, probably because it was horrifying enough in its own right. But eventually the experience began to get worse, enhanced by the bardo. Tamara would wake up, rip off the covers, and there would be a knife in her chest just where I was stabbed. She would grasp at it, pulling, desperate to remove it, but she couldn't. It just made it worse. She would scream in agony for what seemed like hours.

Or she would wake up, look right at me, and say

something like, "I'm so glad you're gone, John." And then she would lie back down and fall into a peaceful sleep.

As bardo-time progressed through the worst of John's (my) haunting of Tamara, I eventually was able to leave the apartment, but I had to stay with Tamara. I would ride with her in the car and sing "Just the Two of Us" to her. This being the bardo, those outings, that were actually joyous when they really happened, started that way, but didn't stay that way. They started out normal and nice, like a horror movie, but just like a horror movie, ended in something terrible. Like Agent Franks flagging us down and stabbing Tamara in the chest, like seeing her all grey faced in a casket, like the horrible car accidents that we kept having.

But that peaceful beginning was always there. And one day as I was singing "Just the Two of Us" to her I had this flash of intuition and using my ghostly finger turned on the radio and the lyrics that I had been singing were playing.

I was as shocked as Tamara when it happened. I had no context for understanding it, but it's clear to me now that this falls under Banquo's "Awareness of All" lesson. Somehow John had stumbled into it.

We did it many times, and that part of the bardo experience gave us joy until the horrible horror movie aspect of it took over and felt all that much worse for having felt the brief joy.

This went on until the day I left Tamara.

THE FOOL

Transmission #38
Received 2012/02/14 02:34:12

I DIDN'T MEAN TO LEAVE TAMARA, I DIDN'T WANT TO, BUT one day I saw Jill.

She was older, a lot of time had passed since I had seen her with my own eyes, and some time since I had seen Frank's pictures of her. She was six and dressed in pink shorts, a white shirt with a big flower on the front, and had a small Hello Kitty backpack on. She stood by the road holding her mother's hand, waiting for traffic to stop so she could cross the street.

Suddenly I was there with Jill and Alice. I was just feet away from my daughter, but she had no idea I was there.

I cursed being a ghost, I so wanted to smell her, but I couldn't. I wanted to smell that fresh, soapy, girly smell. But I could see her and hear her and my heart soared.

"I'm scared, Mommy. What if they don't like me?" she said, her voice tiny and high.

"It's OK, honey. It's OK. You're going to be fine," Alice said.

"But what if I need you?" she asked as she grasped her mother's hand tightly.

"You'll see me after school. Mrs. Turner will take good care of you. You remember her? We met her last week." Jill nodded. "She is very, very nice. She will take good care of you."

When the light changed I followed as they crossed the street and went into the school and Alice left her daughter at Mrs. Turner's class.

Mrs. Turner was plump with grey hair and bright blue eyes. She greeted each student, Jill included, warmly. I stayed there basking in the warm glow of being near my daughter, but it didn't last long, maybe an hour.

Each moment of joy I experienced highlighted the six years that I had missed. Pounded home what I had given up and what I had lost. Eventually my joy turned to shame and guilt. Eventually the classroom faded and my mother was yelling at me about signing my rights away to Jill. Eventually I sunk into the bardo.

Yes, I know, this was the bardo already, but like a dream within a dream I sunk deeper into the bardo.

Back to the small and cramped kitchen, back to my mother yelling at me, back to experiencing the whole thing over again. Except now I had no distance, it was no longer "us" but "me." This was my life, my bardo, my eternal shame.

Transmission #39
Received 2012/02/14 04:03:12

JOHN AND I WERE TWO LOST SOULS EXPERIENCING THE bardo as one. And that experience eventually began to change. Slowly my presence started to have its effect on the experience.

It was small things at first. Like as I sat on that floor of that small and cramped kitchen, the person yelling at me, asking me if I was a prostitute, was *my* mother, Ma. Her plump form replacing the thin form of John's mother, although, she had an uncharacteristic cigarette hanging from her mouth.

Or when I proposed to Tamara, I would look up from the ring to her and it would be Rhiannon. Petite Rhiannon with her hair up in a ponytail and her fingernails painted purple.

The first time it happened, it woke me up a tiny bit. Enough to know something wasn't right. I think it woke up John some too, and for a moment it was "us" again instead of "I." We shook our head and blinked, but when we looked again it was Tamara, and we fell back asleep, the "we" going back to "I."

At Jill's first birthday party, after Alice's brother, Edgar, punched me, I got up and punched him back. It is not what John would have done, but it is what I would have done. For that brief moment I was aware of being JJ as Edgar and I traded punches.

But things would always get back on track. In the middle of the fight I was suddenly in the hospital handcuffed to the bed, woozy from the drugs they had given me.

Or sometimes Professor Aldridge would look like Banquo. Aldridge's thinness and wild grey hair replaced by Banquo's hefty belly and short-haired baldness.

Clearly this is because Banquo was my mentor, just as Professor Aldridge was John's. But, when Banquo leveled his gaze at me and said, "I expect better of you," it woke me up, all the way up.

Suddenly I remembered that I was JJ, not John, that this was his bardo experience, not mine, and that I had come in to wake him up.

But how? How could I possibly wake him up?

"Banquo?" I said, "Banquo, help me." For once it was me talking, not John and not we, but me.

The neat hair on Banquo's head started to grow rapidly as the fat melted from his belly. Seconds later Banquo was gone and Professor Aldridge was there. "John? Are you OK? What are you talking about?"

And as soon as Banquo was gone, I was gone again too.

But my presence continued to make a difference. Sometimes Rhiannon held me as I lie dying on the sidewalk with a knife in me.

Sometimes after being stabbed I found myself a ghost looking at my body pinned to the kiddie's jungle gym at Mickey D's with Anna-Beth and William stumbling out of the car. While it was my death, it was colored by John's. When this happened, Agent Franks would be there examining the body with an eerie calmness while he ate a burger.

And as we experienced these events over and over and over, they began to mix up even more. Sometimes things would happen that had never happened to either of us.

I found myself sitting down to dinner in Globe with my mother and father. This was years earlier when I was in college. It was a big moment for my family, but not one I was witness to. I had been in Tucson at the time.

My parents were talking, my father discussing some garage business with Ma as I sat at the table with them. I spoke, but they didn't seem to hear me. My father was irritated, and he kept rubbing his left arm near the shoulder.

"What is it, honey?" Ma asked.

"Nothing, dear, nothing," he said, dismissing her even as he rubbed it again. "Probably just strained it a bit at the garage."

A cold sweat covered my body as I realized what was happening, what day this was.

"I talked to Rhiannon this evening," Ma said with a smile on her face.

"Oh?" Dad said, taking a bite of his pork chop.

"I love that girl, she is so good for JJ."

"So what are they up to?" Dad asked.

Ma shrugged, "Not much. They're getting back into the rhythm of school, last semester, you know." Dad nodded and rubbed his arm again, this time his face forming a grimace of pain. Ma didn't notice. "Rhiannon is applying to medical school. You know, I worry a bit about JJ. If he's not careful she's going to leave him behind, he doesn't seem to—"

My father surged up, his hand going to his chest as the chair he had been sitting in clattered behind him. The look on his face was equal parts pain and terror as he fell to the floor, his mouth moving but no words forming, only guttural grunts coming out.

Ma rushed to his side, "George, what is it? What's happening?"

I tried to get up, to go to his side, but I couldn't move. I tried to speak, but no sound came out of my mouth. I sat there helpless as I watched my mother, tears flowing now, rush to the phone and call 911. "My husband, he... I think he had a heart attack. Please... please hurry." She went back to him. He was still now, his eyes slowly blinking as tears ran down his cheeks.

Ma was crying. "Please, George, please don't leave me. Please!"

This was my nightmare, not John's, and it woke him up. I was gone, totally lost, but I felt a presence that I didn't understand. It scared me. "What is this, where am I?" The words came out of my mouth, but they weren't mine. "Who are these people?" It just confused me more as John struggled to grasp where he was as I watched my father die on the kitchen floor.

But, ultimately it wasn't enough. Soon we were back to haunting Tamara, and we were both lost to the bardo again.

Transmission #40
Received 2012/02/15 01:44:25

I COULD GO ON DESCRIBING THE BARDO, OUTLINING THE ways in which John's and my fears and pasts further intersected and collided as we struggled and suffered, but I think you get the idea.

It was horrendous. It was terrible. It seemed to last forever.

But, it didn't. Eventually a miracle happened. I can't say that it was some mighty feat on my part—beyond the knuckle-headed stubbornness that had me enter John's bardo in the first place—it was totally luck.

As our two psyches mixed, sometimes I would be awake and sometimes John would be. The trend, as bardo-time passed, was things getting stranger and stranger. Eventually something happened that was so bizarre we both woke up at the same time.

A few blocks east of the university is a nice little Italian restaurant. It was a favorite of John and Tamara's and also a place Rhiannon and I had been to a few times. They have this wonderful fettuccine Alfredo. It is a great date place with red brick walls, dim lighting, and candles burning on the tables.

One time, when John and Tamara were there, Alice came in. This was before Agent Franks entered the picture and a period of time when John was at peace with his life. He almost choked on his pasta when he saw her and what proceeded was a brief and awkward conversation between Alice and John while Tamara and Alice's date watched.

"Who was she?" Tamara asked after Alice left.

"Oh, no one," John said, his cheeks flushed red. "No one."

Tamara laughed, sharp and high. "If she's no one, then I'm... I'm no one too." She laughed again, but naturally this time, as if embarrassed she couldn't come up with a decent metaphor.

"We dated, briefly when I was an undergrad," John said. "It was a huge mistake."

Tamara's eyebrows raised and she didn't comment further, but as the night wore on John would catch her staring at Alice.

So that is what really happened to John and Tamara. In the bardo it played out differently.

"Hello, JJ," Rhiannon said as she walked up to my table. On her arm was a tall kind-looking man she introduced as Thomas.

I choked and coughed, but it didn't make sense. Something was wrong.

"Umm... hello, Rhiannon," we said when I recovered. The "I" that had been in the bardo for so long snapped back into a "we." Rhiannon was the wrong person to be here, it wasn't right and this caused John to start to wake up.

"How have you been?" she asked as she bit her thumbnail. Thomas, standing behind her, stared at the floor.

"Well... you know," we said. "Busy with school, doing some work for a professor."

"How's Ma?" she asked. Ma? How's Ma? Ma is my mother, not John's. My vision rippled as I began to wake up just a little bit. This wasn't right, which was beginning to mean that this wasn't real.

"Who's Ma?" John asked. At this point we were one body, but two voices.

Rhiannon opened her mouth and furrowed her brows. "What's wrong with you, JJ?" she asked.

"JJ? Who's JJ?" John said using "my" mouth.

"OK, then," she said, crossing her arms. "If you didn't want to talk you could have just said so." She turned to walk away.

"Wait, Rhi!" I said as I stood up. "Wait. I've missed you, God how I have missed you. It's just that..." I shook my head trying to clear it. "Something is wrong here."

"You've missed her?" Tamara said. She was standing now glaring at us. "Who the hell is she, John?"

"She's..." John stuttered, now in control of our voice. "She's... I don't know who she is." He turned to Rhiannon. "Who are you?"

I couldn't believe the strange words coming out of my mouth. I got control back and said, "I didn't say that, I didn't mean that. Please, Rhiannon, I love you, can't we just talk?"

"You love her?" Tamara asked, her arms folded across her chest, voice strident. "You *love* her?"

"No... No, of course not, Tam. I don't know who she is," John said.

"Seriously, JJ," Rhiannon said. "What is going on with you?"

This battle between John and I continued, each confused by the other, each trying to placate one of the women, each being thwarted by the other when we spoke with our body.

Eventually we stood alone in the restaurant, both women had stormed out, and everyone still there stared at us.

It was horrible, yes, this was the bardo after all, but it was also funny. I laughed until tears were running down our cheeks. And then, still in the bardo, John and I proceeded to have a conversation.

"What's so funny?" he asked.

"What's not funny about that?" I answered.

The stares intensified because John and I had one body and it looked like we were talking to ourselves.

"Well, I don't know if Tamara will ever forgive me for that," John said.

"And you think Rhiannon will forgive me?"

"Who is she?" John asked.

"The love of my life," I said. "The one that got away."

"But I'm with Tamara."

My own memories of Tamara came rushing back and the stories she had told me of John. I woke up fully and knew where I was and what I was doing.

"John, listen to me," I said ignoring everything but what I was saying. "My name is JJ, and I am here to help you."

"Oh Christ," John said, "I think I've finally lost it."

"I'm here because of Tamara, John. She wants to talk to you."

"Oh, I doubt it," he said. "She must think I'm crazy."

"I can help you, John, I can help you tell Tamara about

Jill, about what happened with Agent Franks, about what happened after you died."

"I died..." I could feel him remembering. "I'm dead?"

"John, listen to me. I am a ghost, my name is JJ Lynch. I'm a friend of Tamara's. She's still alive and I can help you communicate with her."

"I'm dead?" he asked again. I could feel him fading, going back to sleep. I thought furiously, I needed to find a way to wake him up further. The restaurant was starting to fade.

Shit. I needed to do something and fast.

This was the bardo, and for once, I was awake, really awake. I knew John's fears, they wouldn't take me by surprise any more. Maybe I could influence the experience.

We were back in the small and cramped kitchen with John's mother yelling at us.

"Jesus Christ, John," she said, a cigarette dangling from her mouth. "How can you do this? Sign your rights away like that. What the hell were you thinking?"

"Shut up, Mom," I said, taking control over our voice. "Just shut the hell up."

She backed up several steps, her hand shaking as it went to her cigarette. "Johnny," she said, "don't talk to your mom like that."

"Then stop yelling at me. Stop treating me like a child. I made a decision and it was my decision to make, it was the best decision I could make. I'm not ready to be a father." I could feel John trying to speak, but I didn't let him. This may be his bardo, but I was fully awake and maybe by changing the experience I could wake him all the way up.

"But that little girl..." she continued as she fumbled for another cigarette.

"Is better off without me. Look, Mom, I know you are

disappointed. You think I am just like my father giving her up like this. But you know what? I am not my father, and Alice is not you. She will do a fine job raising her child. She wanted a baby, not me. This is for the best."

The scene shifted and we were in Alice's office at the university. "What are you doing here?" Alice asked as she opened the door. "We can't keep doing this, John. We can't. You can't see her. You can't know her. And, you can't keep sneaking in here."

"You're right," I said. "You are absolutely right."

Her eyes widened and her hand went to her mouth. I could hear that John wanted to plead with her, but I didn't let him speak. I was awake, I knew what was happening, I could stay in control. "What do you want, John?" she asked.

"I want to say good-bye. I want to say good luck. And I want to tell you that I think you are a wonderful mother."

Alice stood there, her mouth open and her eyes wide.

"And I am glad something good came of our time together." I went and kissed her on the cheek and walked out the office door and walked into—

Nothing.

We were in a grey space with diffuse light coming from everywhere.

"What the hell is going on?" John asked. We were still of one body and in the greyness we talked.

"This is not real, John."

"I... This..."

"We can keep doing this," I said gently. "We can keep going through this, but I won't be along for the ride anymore. I will not let this be a horror to you anymore."

"What? What is going on?"

"You're dead, John, and so am I. This place is in your mind. You are reliving the worst parts of your life."

"This is not real?"

"No, it's not. We can leave this place. We can communicate with Tamara. She wants to hear from you, John. You have no idea what she has gone through to hear from you."

"Tamara..."

"Yes, Tamara. She needs to hear from you. She needs closure. I can help you."

"Who... who are you?" he asked.

"My name is JJ Lynch."

"Why? Why are you doing this?"

I laughed then. I couldn't help it. I didn't have a particularly good explanation. I didn't understand it well enough myself to explain it.

And the laughter was contagious. I soon felt John laughing. I don't think he knew why he was laughing but was happy to let out some of the pent up angst that had been fueling his bardo trip.

We laughed hard and long until we were standing in what used to be Mrs. Turner's first grade classroom.

Transmission #41
Received 2012/02/15 03:23:10

FREE OF THE BARDO AT LAST, JOHN AND I STOOD THERE staring at each other and blinking. Not that the blinking did us any good, it was just a carryover from our meat bodies.

We were like a couple of inmates just released from solitary confinement and seeing the first sunshine we had seen in years. It was shocking.

I looked around at the classroom, and things had changed. Gone was the "Rest In Peace" message on the blackboard and in its place were signs of the holiday season. A small tree sat on the teacher's desk and "Happy Holidays" was written on the blackboard. They must be on their Christmas break.

That thought sunk into my belly and started to stomp around with its cleated shoes. Christmas. It had been late January when I entered the bardo and now it was the holidays. How long had I been in there? Eleven months at the very least.

I looked at John. We stood in the exact same position

when this started, in front of Mrs. Turner's 2009 first grade class's picture. A picture that I now know had Jill in it.

I slowly separated my arms from him and brought my form into focus.

"Hi, John," I said doing my best to smile. "I'm JJ. Welcome back to the world."

He looked around, his eyes taking in the changes, many changes from when he had entered the bardo back in 2009. The pained look on his face made me worry he was about to fall back into the bardo.

"John, come with me." I began to walk towards the outer wall of the building, but he didn't move. I walked back over. "Tamara. I have a way to talk to Tamara."

His brown eyes snapped into focus, and he studied me. I must admit that his stare made me uncomfortable. John knew many of my darker moments just as I knew many of his. Our time in the bardo was extremely intimate.

"You love her, don't you?" he asked.

"What?"

"Tamara. You love her. Why else would you…" his voice trailed off, his eyes defocussing again.

"Come rescue you?" I offered in conclusion.

He nodded in answer.

"Look, we have to get out of here. It's important. Just come with me and I'll answer any questions you have."

Yes, I was putting off answering that particular question, but it was important to get him out of there. Having been so long in the bardo there, it would be easy to slip back in. I could feel it too, kind of like the way alcohol used to call to me. I knew it was bad, but I wanted it anyway.

He nodded, the barest of nods, and followed me out to the playground.

I wasn't sure what to do with him. He needed help, lots of help, except I didn't feel qualified to deliver that help. I wasn't a psychologist. I wasn't prepared to help him through the grieving he needed to do, to help him acclimate to life as a ghost, to help him accept the Call when it came.

Banquo's Rules of the Dead #4: *You must finish what you have started.*

I wanted to run away, leave him there. I had paid a much higher price than I thought I would—fool that I was—when I started. But I knew Banquo would tell me to stick with it so I looked him over. He was still a wispy mess, and his eyes told me he was in danger of going bardo.

"OK," I began, taking a tone I had heard many times in Banquo's voice. It was his "teaching" tone. "There are some basic lessons to being a ghost. Lesson 1: Cutting the Cord—you've already taken care of that. Lesson 2: Appearance Matters. Lesson 3: Awareness, Awareness, Awareness. Lesson 4: Traveling. And, Lesson 5: This is Not the End."

John looked confused, but he was listening. I walked backwards as I talked, walking him around and around the playground. It was important to keep him moving.

"Today's lesson," I continued, "will be on Appearance Matters." I looked his form over and shook my head. "The way you appear, your ghostly form, is the key to your well-being."

"The key?" John asked. I breathed a sigh of relief, he was talking and not about what we had just been through.

"Yes, the key," I said, making my voice as deep and authoritative as I could. "When you are a wispy mess like that, you are just asking for the bardo, that place we just got out of. Your form, your ghostly body, should look as close to your meat body as possible. It should be crisp, well formed, and as solid as possible."

"But why?" he asked. "I don't have a body, what does it matter what I look like?"

I rolled my eyes. "Oh my God, you don't know a damn thing, do you? OK, here it is: staying grounded without a body is hard. What do you think all that dense meat did for us? We don't have the meat, but we do have our ghost forms. We must maintain them."

He still looked puzzled. "I don't understand."

"Well, you know what? You don't have to understand right now. You just have to clean up that form." I couldn't stand the confusion on his face, so I tried to explain it again. "Look, John. I know this is a lot. But let me ask a question. When you were alive did you walk around in dirty clothes? In ripped clothing? Did you avoid bathing for months at a time?"

"No, of course not."

"Why not?" I asked.

"That would be just gross. I wouldn't feel human if I didn't bathe, didn't have clean clothes."

"Exactly," I said. "That is precisely what you are doing right now. You are unbathed in dirty, ragged clothing. How can you feel like yourself when you look like that?"

Revelation dawned on his face, and I walked him through cleaning up his form. First we got him looking like a person and then we added clothing. It was a struggle for him, and if he tried too hard his form would reset to the bardo-like wispy mess. I guess because he had been that way for a long time, it was harder for him to hold his form.

What we settled on was John in a long white lab coat. His face and hands were properly formed if rather transparent, but his feet didn't exist. It wasn't where he needed to be, but it was a good start and not so far away from his bardo norm that he couldn't hold it.

Hours had passed, and I could feel midnight approaching. I longed to be back in the graveyard, but given how much it had taken to get John out of the bardo, I wasn't going to let him fall right back in.

"How do you feel?" I asked.

He nodded slowly and smiled. "I understand now. I feel more like myself."

"Good work, John. I know this is hard."

"So, can you answer my question now?" he asked.

"About Tamara?"

He nodded.

"Tam's my friend, John. You want to know if I loved her? Well, yes, I loved her as a friend." John frowned and narrowed his eyes. He wasn't buying it. We had been too long in each other's heads for me to get away with a half-truth. "But, was I 'in love' with her?" I shook my head. "I think if I had lived long enough, I would have been. Infatuation? Yes. In love? No."

John slowly nodded and grew silent.

"That's your only question?" I asked. I couldn't believe it. Me, I always had a ton of questions for Banquo.

"You said there is a way for me to talk to her," he said.

"Yes, there is."

"When can we do that? I need to tell her..." he trailed off. I already knew everything he wanted to tell her. I had lived it with him over and over again.

"Soon, John. We need to get you used to being a ghost for a bit first. But, soon."

And I hoped it would be soon. I needed to get back to the graveyard.

Transmission #42
Received 2012/02/16 00:58:31

HERE'S WHAT JJ LYNCH IS LIKE AS A TEACHER: PATIENT, articulate, attentive, and somewhat mysterious. Only giving the student just enough information and letting them make the crucial leaps themselves.

In other words, he's a lot like Banquo.

Suddenly I had a better understanding and empathy for my own teacher. Suddenly I understood a lot of the reasons why Banquo acted the way he did. Suddenly it was clear just how hard it is to be a teacher. Suddenly I felt the burden of that responsibility.

It was really, really annoying.

This wasn't what I had intended. While John figured out, in his intuitive way, how to do a lot of things when he was haunting Tamara, he really didn't have the basics of Appearance Matters down at all.

And he had just come out of a several-year stint in the bardo. I couldn't just leave him to his own devices, he would end up right back there.

So there I was, day after day, in the playground of the

school teaching John about form and telling him about some of the other crucial things: fading, popping, Midnight Circle, the Call, and the bardo.

I was itching to go back to the graveyard. I so wanted to see Jesus and hoped after all these months he was back. I really missed Banquo and would have killed for one of his stern, teacherly looks. I longed for the comfort of the Midnight Circle. And, I was getting desperate to fade.

But I stuck with it. John needed me, and in my best estimation, he wasn't ready for a graveyard full of ghosts yet.

Early on, I tried to take him out of the playground, away from the school. But, that didn't go well, I almost lost him to the bardo. So there we stayed. When the kids came back from their holiday, we just moved up a hundred feet and avoided the chaos when they were in the playground.

After a week of this I felt a bit strung out, and John's form was finally decent with hands and feet and real clothing. He was too transparent still, but he had a form and was starting to learn how to walk and not just float.

It was just after midnight, and we were moving into rest mode. "It's time," I said.

"Time?" he asked.

"Time for you to meet some other ghosts."

"I..." he began.

I smiled and nodded slowly. "It'll be OK, John. This is the next step we need to take." I didn't specifically mention Tamara. She was a bit of a wildcard. Sometimes it would motivate him and sometimes it would send him careening towards the bardo. "At first light we'll make our way over." I turned and walked away, ending the discussion.

He didn't follow me and I was glad. These kinds of moments were hard for me. First, it's not really in my nature to be like that, to draw sharp lines. Actually, I had never really been in the role of a teacher like this. And John's knowledge of me made it that much more complicated. He knew about my weakness and fears—he had experienced them with me in our shared bardo. He knew me for the imperfect person that I was in a very real way.

As I rested, letting time slip past, I realized, deep in my gut, just how hard what Banquo does is. I resolved to be a better student if he chose to teach me again.

JOHN AND I FLEW SLOWLY OVER TUCSON. THE WINTER sun rising, its yellow light bathing the waking city below us. He was just learning to fly, so we had to go slow, but I liked it. I also took us up about a thousand feet. The city looked so much simpler, so much safer from that height. I also did this as a precaution so we wouldn't run into anything that could trigger him or distract me.

"You're ready," I said as the graveyard came into sight.

"I am?" he asked, his voice that of a child's.

"Yes, John. You are. Community is important, even when you're a ghost. Especially when you're a ghost."

He nodded but I could see the doubt in his downcast eyes and his wispy form.

"Get dressed," I said. He looked at himself and firmed up his form pretty quickly. I suppressed a smile; he was starting to get it. "Feel better now?"

He nodded.

I positioned us directly over where the Midnight Circle occurs but didn't make a move to go down.

"What are we waiting for?" John asked.

I shrugged. Not to be mysterious—well, OK to be a bit

mysterious. I stayed there because it seemed liked I needed to stay there. I don't know if this was my own fear, some kind of "awareness," or just a lame dramatic flourish, but I felt strongly it wasn't time to go down yet.

The graveyard was quiet. I saw Marilyn looking for Motor and a few other ghosts heading towards their plots so they could "rest with their bones." But other than that there wasn't anything going on. So we waited.

The sun rose and the employees arrived at the mortuary but still we stayed there.

The hours melted away and I didn't budge.

When the sun was directly overhead, John made a move to go down.

"Don't," I said.

"Why?" he asked.

I paused, putting myself in his position. I would want a full and logical explanation, not just a vaguely expressed feeling. "Just don't," I said, despite my empathy for him.

He sighed and came back up to where I was. I could hear the exasperation and knew exactly how he felt. But it wasn't time to take him down and I knew it.

I did my best to let my Awareness expand, to let it tell me why I was keeping us up there, to give me a reason not to go down, to help me not feel silly about my behavior. But, just like I didn't give John a reason, this feeling, this Awareness, did not give me one either. So, noon melted into afternoon and afternoon melted into evening.

The sun went down and the ghosts came out.

They started rising from the ground and coming out of the crypts. Some of them "popped" in and others came walking or floating from areas we couldn't see.

John gasped.

"Greeting committee," I said by way of explanation.

"Huh?" he mumbled.

"Watch."

We watched as a good number of them descended on the mortuary.

"What... what are they doing?" he asked.

"Greeting committee," I said again. "They are checking out the newly dead." I laughed, and added, "They scared the hell out of me the first time I saw them."

I looked at John; he was blinking, his form rapidly devolving into the wispy blob he was when I found him.

"You might want to put on your Sunday best," I said nodding towards him. "At some point we are going to be noticed."

It didn't take long. It was Fredrick, of course, that noticed us first. He came out of the mortuary and looked around, his eyes finding us. He flew quickly up.

"JJ! My God, JJ. Back from the bardo after lo these many months, and you've brought your prize. You must be John. I am Fredrick, this is my place."

"Hi," John replied.

"Good to see you, Fredrick," I said with a stupid grin on my face. "I can't tell you how good it is to see you."

Fredrick nodded. "Decided to ease him in, I see," he said, referring to our elevation. "Good choice. I tell you what. You two stay right here, and I'll send one or two up at a time to say hello."

As Fredrick moved to return to the ground, I was dying to talk to him, to get some news of Jesus or Banquo. I wanted to know how my meat family and my ghost family were doing. But I stayed put. This wasn't about me. This was about John.

Transmission #43
Received 2012/02/16 02:22:31

FREDRICK WAS GOOD TO HIS WORD. FOR THE NEXT FEW hours, a sizable portion of the un-corded, un-bardoed ghost population of the graveyard flew up to greet John. And then ensued the standard ritual between ghosts in which they get to know each other. "So, how did you die?"

I had been through this with all of them but not in such a concentrated burst. It was kind of illuminating. A lot of the deaths were violent, sudden, or messy in some way: "Car wreck;" "Goddamn cigarettes;" "Shot;" "Sky diving accident;" "Drowned... in my Jacuzzi;" "Gunfight;" "Valley fever;" and lots of varieties of cancer.

There were two ghosts that stood out because of their deaths and their interactions with John. The first was a bespectacled man who appeared to be in his early sixties. I loved that he had glasses, or at least the rims of glasses, as part of his form. Glass is not an effect we can pull off—convincing glass has to interact with light, magnifying it and refracting it. Ghosts can't do that, so while he had the frames, there was no glass in them.

"My name is Anton, Anton Weis, you must be John," he said, speaking quickly, his words running together. "Welcome to our humble little community. I think you'll like it here. It's a great bunch of spooks, just stay away from the crypts. I used to be an engineer. Taught at the university a few decades back. What did you do, John?"

"Umm... I..." John stammered, his mind catching up with Anton's words. Well, I guessed his mind was catching up. I know my mind was. "Don't you want to know how I died?" John asked.

"Why?" Anton began. "Waste of time. Everyone knows how you died. You were stabbed to death. A thing like that travels through our community like wildfire. Everyone's just being polite by asking you. Our community of ghosts is kind of like a throwback. All verbal communication, no written word. So we know how to gossip around here. We are damn professionals at it. So, of course I know how you died."

Fredrick smiled as he watched the interaction. It was the same reaction that Anton usually got. You had to work pretty hard to keep up with him.

John didn't speak and Anton leapt into the void. "Want to know how I died?" he asked. He waited maybe half a second before answering. "I killed myself, that's what I did. I was losing my mind, yes sir, losing my mind—dementia, you know—and what is a life without a mind? So I took pills, the perfect dose, went peacefully asleep and—boom!—woke with my mind back and no body. Not a bad trade, not a bad trade at all. Not that I am advocating suicide. Most of the poor bastards that do that end up long-term in the bardo. But not me, no sir. So what did you do when you were alive, John?"

"Umm... I was a graduate student, doing some research into lasers."

"Lasers! Lasers, don't you mean 'light amplification by stimulated emissions of radiation'? Just kidding, of course you know what a laser is. We've got to talk, yes we do, we've got to talk. I worked with Peter Smith on the Imager for Mars Pathfinder back in the nineties. Lasers, my good fellow, lasers. I think we will—"

I am sure the conversation would have continued, but Fredrick guided him away.

"I think he liked you," I said.

John smiled and nodded. "He reminds me of Professor Aldridge."

"Really?" I asked. "I don't remember him talking that fast."

John blinked and stared at me for a moment. I was coming to realize that references to our shared bardo experience were more than a bit awkward. "No, not the speech pattern," he said, "but the passion."

Later, towards the end of the "meet and greet," came old man Cooper. Everyone called him Coop. He was short with fluffy grey hair, sharp hazel eyes, old man pants pulled up too high, a deeply wrinkled face with skin the texture of an orange, and fluffy slippers. Of all of us here, he had lived the longest in his meat body and was accorded an elder's respect. Which, in some ways, was odd. Jim, who had been dead about two hundred years, was the oldest soul here, but he died young so did not get that kind of respect.

"What am I doing up here?" Coop said, looking around. "Why the hell are we in the air? Nothing natural about that."

"This is John," Fredrick said. "He's the newest addition to our family. JJ rescued him out of the bardo."

Coop's hazel eyes turned to mine, and I felt exposed under the old man's gaze. I had met Coop, of course, but we hadn't interacted much.

He grunted, a kind of "oh really?" grunt, frowned and turned his gaze to John.

"Very happy to meet you, Mr. Cooper," John said. "How did you die?"

"What?" Coop said, leaning close and holding his hand to his ear. Yeah, how can a ghost be hard of hearing? Seems odd to me too, but we bring plenty from our meat life here.

"How did you die?" John asked, his voice louder this time.

"Oh... that. Old age, what's it look like?" His head swiveled around looking just like someone having a senior moment and forgetting where he was.

"Don't you want to know how *he* died?" Fredrick asked. It was only polite.

"Eh? You want to know how he died?" Coop said. "Well that's as obvious as that big nose on your face, Fredrick. He was stabbed, right here." And then his bony finger pointed to the exact spot where John had been stabbed.

While John had told everyone that he had been stabbed to death, he hadn't given any specifics. The shock on John's face was evident, as I am sure it was on mine.

"Get that damn watch out, Fredrick. I think it may be QVC time."

After Fredrick and Coop left, John turned to me. "QVC?"

I shrugged. "Yeah, there is someplace near here where some meat folks watch QVC every night. A group of ghosts go over and watch it with them. Coop loves QVC."

"And how did he know?" John asked, pointing at his chest.

And in truth, I didn't know exactly how he knew, but I was beginning to understand. "That falls under Lesson 3: Awareness, Awareness, Awareness."

John just shook his head and prepared to meet the next ghost.

AFTER WE RAN OUT OF GHOSTS FOR JOHN TO MEET, THE two of us lingered up there for a few more minutes. John's demeanor had changed. He was smiling, shaking his head, and looking excited, even a bit joyful. "Wow," he said summing it up.

I laughed. "They're a good bunch. This is a good place, John."

He nodded. "I see that. Thank you for doing it this way."

"You're welcome." I saw Fredrick waving at us and pointing at something, so I slowly flew down with John following.

"I found it!" Fredrick said triumphantly.

He pointed at a small granite stone in the ground. It said, "John Evan Fisher. Beloved Son and Fiancé. 1/16/1979 - 6/13/2009."

"You see, John, you do belong here," Fredrick said. "You are one of us. I thought I recognized your face from when they brought your body in."

This is the kind of thing that sends you bardo, so I watched him carefully. He seemed fine. He kneeled and looked at his gravestone closely, his ghostly hand tracing the letters.

He stood up and said, "Thank you, Fredrick. Thank you for finding this. And thank you for orchestrating such a wonderful greeting. I do feel like I belong here."

I looked at Fredrick, he was blinking back ghostly tears.

I saw his impeccable form go just a touch less transparent so it was nearly solid looking as he straightened up. He pulled his pocket watch out of the breast pocket of his period three-piece suit and said, "Right... Yes... Well... Well you are most welcome. It's almost time for Midnight Circle. I should be going." With that he turned and walked quickly away.

"Did I say something?" John asked, a confused look on his face.

"I'll say," I said.

"What? What did I say?"

"The exact right thing, John. You said the exact right thing. Fredrick does a lot around here, he feels protective of this place, but he often doesn't get the thanks he deserves. Well done."

I was starting to relax about John, he had handled himself well. But I was still worried about Jesus and wondering what was next for me.

Transmission #44
Received 2012/02/17 02:15:45

I TOOK JOHN TO HIS FIRST MIDNIGHT CIRCLE. BANQUO wasn't there to lead a play, so various ghosts got up and told stories of their meat life. Kind of like what happens around a campfire. While it was good to see everyone and to hear them tell stories of their lives, it wasn't the same.

I longed for the tragedies of Shakespeare, they have grown to be such a comfort to me.

I longed to see Jesus, to just sit and talk, or to just sit. I wanted to know how he was doing, how his quest to resolve his death and his past was going. I worried about his desire to answer the Call. I just didn't know if my afterlife could work without him.

I longed for Banquo's appraising look and difficult lessons. I missed him all the more for being in a mentor role with John and understanding Banquo all the better.

"How are you doing?" I asked John after it was over and the assembled host of ghosts slowly dispersed.

"Good. I'm... I'm... tired? I feel tired, but it's different."

I nodded and looked at him, his form becoming more

transparent. "It's just time to fade, go with it. You need the rest; you'll feel much better when you get back." And before I finished talking he was gone.

I seriously needed to fade myself, but I couldn't yet. I found Fredrick, he was just finishing up a conversation with Marilyn, who had Motor in hand and was happy as could be.

"Do you have a minute?" I asked when he was alone.

"Of course, JJ," Fredrick said.

"Do you have any news on Jesus or Banquo?"

Fredrick nodded and smiled gently. "Jesus is still in Mexico. The nun that helped when he was young, Sister Dominga, died and Jesus has been dealing with the aftermath of that. Banquo... well you know, he's off doing his Banquo thing. He'll be back around soon."

I nodded and walked the graveyard for a bit avoiding the other spirits. I didn't want to be alone, but since I couldn't be with Jesus or Banquo, and John didn't need me, alone was the best alternative I had.

I thought of flying off to check on my family, but that, as my experiences with the living keep teaching me, can get complicated real fast.

As dawn came, I gave into fatigue and let myself fade into the arms of my friend, oblivion.

GHOSTS CAN MANIFEST IN ALL SHAPES AND SIZES. WHICH is to say the path I have chosen (not sure "chosen" feels like the right word here) is not the only path.

Take, for example, Emily. She died when she was four years old, and her ghostly form looks like she is still four years old even though she has been dead for nearly eighty years.

Talking to Emily can be an odd experience. I find myself constantly confronting the disparity between her appearance and her experience. And to complicate it, Emily sometimes acts like a wild four-year-old and at other times acts like a wise old woman.

"Do you know what your problem is, JJ?" she asked me not long after John and I had returned to the graveyard. She spoke with a trace of a lisp, her words slightly mangled, causing you to listen carefully to her.

"No, Emily, what is it?" I asked. I was reacting as if she was four, as if her telling me something like that would be cute. I squatted down so I could be at her level.

"You don't think in the right amount," she said, her eyes sparking mischievously.

"Huh?"

"You know. You either don't think enough and jump right into the biggest messes—Mr. Bardo Adventurer—or you think way too much and become a brooding dark cloud over our lovely graveyard, being all serious about what you have been through and what you are experiencing." She ended with her fists balled and on her little hips.

That's Emily, she lures you in with cute, and then—boom—gets all grown up and serious on you. "I.. well... you know..." I stammered.

"I think that's enough, Emily," Walter said. Walter is another interesting ghost. He used to be a dentist, but was murdered and had become this accidental ghost detective trying to track down his killer. He died while I was in the bardo, so I hadn't gotten to know him well. For some reason Emily had attached herself to him; they were almost constantly together.

"It's true," Emily said looking up at Walter with a sheepish grin.

"Yes it is," Walter said with a smile, "but it is rude."

"I've been dead for eighty years," she growled, sounding like a feisty old woman, "I don't have time to beat around the bush anymore." She turned to me and said, "And neither do you." With that she stuck her tongue out at me, going all four-year-old, and stalked away.

I stood up and shook my head.

"She means well," Walter said. He has a kind face with short curly black hair and brown eyes. His ghostly form is a long beige trench coat, and he kind of looks the part of the detective.

"And she's right," I said with a sigh.

We stood there in silence, watching the ghosts gather for the Midnight Circle.

I saw an odd-looking ghost and asked Walter, "Who is that?"

He chuckled and nodded his head. "He's new. He goes by Blinky."

My jaw opened as I watched him float around the gravestones. He looked like a cartoon version of a ghost. Huge blue eyes, a red form that looked kind of like the classic "holes cut in a sheet" ghost. "No..." I began.

"Yes," Walter said, his chuckle deepening into a laugh.

"Seriously? He's being the ghost Blinky from Pac-Man?" I couldn't believe it. It flew in the face of Appearance Matters, but at the same time it was brilliantly done.

"Seriously," Walter echoed. "If you want to make his day, make yourself look like Pac-Man and let him chase you around the graveyard."

I stood there watching Blinky float through the gathering

crowd until the Midnight Circle started. At that point his form morphed into something more normal. He looked like a middle-aged geek with a big belly and a long grey ponytail.

I could go on, but you get the picture. This ghost life can take many forms. Things are a lot more pliable here, and it is harder to judge things by their appearances (and really rather better not to in the first place).

I WATCHED OUT FOR JOHN FOR THE NEXT FEW DAYS AS he acclimated to the graveyard. He spent a lot of time with Anton—he seemed to enjoy the man's breathless monologues and even managed to say things that Anton would listen to very carefully. It was scientist stuff, way over my head.

Old Man Perkins talked to him about "resting with your bones," and he started doing that during the day.

He made friends with Jim and Jane and spent time with a lot of other ghosts.

He was fitting in shockingly well. After five days of this, I decided it was time for us to find the SECI chamber so he could get his message through to Tamara. He was with Anton, having one of their science-geek blab-o-thons when I heard a "pop" right next to me. It was Banquo.

"Banquo!" I said. "I am so glad to see you." He gave me that thin-lipped appraising look, but I didn't care.

He nodded, looking around, his gaze lingering on John. "He's fitting right in, I see," he said.

I nodded. I wanted to jump right in and ask about Jesus, but that wasn't the way it worked with Banquo. "Yeah, he's doing great. I think it's time to take him to the SECI chamber so he can say what he needs to say to Tamara."

He looked back to me and then to John and nodded. It wasn't much, but it was clearly him agreeing with me. It felt good.

"Jesus sends his best," he said.

"How is he? Does he know I'm out of the bardo?"

He nodded. "I was here when you were faded and heard. I was just visiting Jesus and told him. He sends his regards."

"Does he... should I go..." I stammered.

"It hasn't been easy for him but he's getting through it. He doesn't want you to come," Banquo said.

I nodded. I was disappointed, and I'm sure it showed.

"It looks like you've got your hands full, anyway," Banquo said, nodding towards John.

Banquo spent the next few hours with me as I told him about my time in the bardo with John and what it was like mentoring him. After it was over, he smiled, a broad un-Banquo-like smile and said, "I'm proud of you, JJ. Amazing, truly amazing."

I stood there, my mouth open like some fool. I wasn't expecting such a direct and unambiguous compliment. I, of course, wanted his approval, but the reality of it was like spending your life looking for Bigfoot and finally finding him. It left me speechless.

He laughed, the sound of it rumbling out of his big belly. "And with that, ladies and gentlemen, my job here is done." He bowed with a flourish of his hand and with a "pop" he was gone.

Transmission #45
Received 2012/02/17 04:20:35

JOHN AND I FLEW SLOWLY OVER TO THE UNIVERSITY OF Arizona. We took our time because John was still learning to fly and besides, I figured he could use the time to get his head together. I knew he was eager to see the SECI chamber, to send a message to Tamara, but he was nervous too. Understandable, he had left a lot unsaid.

When we got there my heart dropped. The lab, the lab where I used to clean up, the lab where Tamara and Jin worked, the lab where I helped them build the SECI chamber and typed my memoir, was empty.

The SECI chamber was gone. The computers were gone. The file cabinets and the papers were gone. Everything. Gone.

"Shit!" I said. I didn't mean too. It wasn't exactly proper etiquette around my student. But sometimes there is nothing that can say what needs to be said but the proper curse.

"Is this the wrong lab?" John asked.

I looked around and doubted myself for a moment. "No. I worked here, I spent a lot of time here. This is the place."

I searched for something familiar. On the wall I spotted one of the posters Jin had put up. A *Ghostbusters* movie poster. It looked a little more ragged than I remembered and one of the corners had come loose and was curled up. "There, that poster. Jin put that up. This is the right place."

I worried about showing my emotions to John. Banquo was always so cool, and here I was about to lose it in front of my student. How the hell does Banquo keep calm all the time?

I paced around the room trying to think, but my mind was mush. Jin and Tam were gone. The SECI chamber was gone. How the hell was I going to get John's message to Tamara?

I knew that I could take him to her house and use the "typing on the laptop" trick, but I feared it would be too much for John, that it would send him back into the bardo. I discarded that idea and continued to pace.

I felt John's stare as I traveled about the room, and it made me wish Jesus was with us. It made me wonder what Jesus would do.

I stopped and laughed. It was a bit manic, this laughter, but at least it was laughter.

"What?" John asked.

"My friend, Jesus, I told you about him. He was a bounty hunter when he was alive. He would know what to do in this situation." John nodded and I continued. "His name is pronounced Hey-Zeus, but in my mind I heard the more traditional pronunciation: What would Gee-Zus do?" I started laughing again.

John just stared at me.

"What would *Jesus* do? Don't you get it? Christians love

to ask that question. It's on bumper stickers. What would Jesus do?"

John just slowly shook his head. Clearly my Hey-Zues/ Gee-Zus humor didn't work for him. "So?" he finally asked. "What would Jesus do?" He went back to the Hey-Zues pronunciation.

"Well... He would go over every inch of this place, every scrap of paper and look for clues. If he found a clue he would follow it. If he didn't he would search every building in the whole damn city looking for what he wanted." I didn't tell him that Jesus would go to Tamara's place and follow her.

"OK, then," John said as he started to look around the room.

Still chuckling, I joined him and resolved to find out what made the guy laugh. You gotta laugh, you just gotta laugh.

We spent hours at it. There wasn't much left, but we read every word of every scrap of paper in the room. There was nothing that made sense. Scraps of old magazines and newspapers, invoices, receipts, and other assorted garbage.

After we finished, I stood in the middle of the room shaking my head. I just didn't believe they would have left without giving me a way to find them. It just didn't make sense.

The curled up edge of the *Ghostbusters* poster caught my eye. I thought I saw some writing on it. The poster was up high enough that someone standing on the floor would have a hard time reading it. I flew up and looked closely. It said, "JJ, we've moved," followed by an address.

THE SUN HAD GONE DOWN WHEN WE GOT THERE. THE building was one of those metal structures you find in an industrial park, with high ceilings and a big door you can roll up and move large items through. There were multiple occupants, but as we flew past the doors, one of the company names stood out. "Afterlife Communications, Inc."

"Well, this must be it," I said. "They must have gone private with the technology."

We flew through the door into a hallway that had a few offices on either side. I kept moving, Tamara might be in one of those, and I didn't want John to see her. The door at the end of the hallway led to a high-ceilinged, cement-floored warehouse-type area.

My jaw dropped when we entered. I saw three SECI chambers sitting there, I also saw ghosts, a lot of them. They seemed to be in a rough line that spiraled out from the SECI chambers. There must have been forty or fifty ghosts.

"What the..." I said. Next to me John was silent.

It all seemed quite orderly with groups of ghosts chatting with each other. Off, away from the line, there were a few bardo-brains floating around. I walked over to the closest portion of the line to a well-formed ghost who was looking at us.

"Excuse me," I said. "I need to get in there."

He smiled. "Tell me about it," he said with a thick Brooklyn accent. "I've been here for two weeks. I figure I got at least a week to go."

"Three weeks to get in?" I said, dumbfounded.

"Depends, you know," he said with a grin. "Some don't have much to say. Some can't do it for long before fading out. Some get the swing of it and can be in there for a long time."

"But, I'm..." I began.

"Sorry," the ghost interrupted. "Forgot my manners. My name is Jack, Jack Ramsey. I died of cancer."

"Oh, yeah," I said. "I am JJ, JJ Lynch and I died when a car rammed me into the kiddie gym at Mickey D's. This is—" I was about to introduce John when Jack's eyes went wide. The ghosts around us whispered to the ghosts around them, and the noise spread throughout the warehouse.

"Seriously?" Jack asked. "You're JJ? You're not just saying that to move up the line, are you?"

"What? No. Of course not."

He looked at me closely, his eyes squinting. "Yeah, you look like him."

"I... I... What?" I asked.

"You look like JJ Lynch. The book, I read the book that you wrote in that thing." He pointed at one of the SECI chambers. "Came looking for it as soon as I died." He stopped and spoke loudly, his head swiveling around. "Hey everyone. This here is JJ Lynch. *The* JJ Lynch."

A murmur swept through the warehouse, and then the murmur became a babbling of ghostly voices. I could hear snippets of what those close to me were saying: "Goddamn, JJ Lynch in the flesh"; "Did you really kill that dude at Picacho"; "I've heard this thing is hard to use, can you give me some tips"; "Are you as crazy as that book made you out to be?"

I was overwhelmed and felt fear creeping into my belly. I wanted to fly straight up and distance myself from all this. It was too much. These people knew about me. They knew *all* about me. Sure, I understood when I was doing all that writing in the SECI chamber that Tam and Jin might publish it. But, I had not factored in the reality of ghosts I didn't know, knowing all about me. It was completely unnerving.

"Look," I said to Jack. "I just need a little time in the chamber. An hour tops."

Jack's smile disappeared from his face. The ghosts around him whispered to the ghosts near them, and a wave of whispers spread throughout the warehouse until it was stone silent.

I flew up a few feet so everyone could see me. "Look, I don't need much time, but I... we have an important message to get out."

The assembled ghosts just stared at me, many of them shaking their heads. I flew back down to the floor.

"Look," Jack began, "I feel for you, I really do. We all have important messages to get out. Me, I left things a mess. There was too much I didn't tell my wife. She's got to know this stuff or dealing with my death is going to be horrible for her. She'll lose the house if I don't get in there soon."

I nodded my head. John's message was important, but I couldn't say that it was urgent. My time spent going house to house searching for Jesus's killer had changed me. I knew everyone here had a story; that everyone here was doing something that was important to them.

"I'm sorry, JJ," Jack said. "There is only one way this works. You'll have to wait in line with everyone else."

I nodded, mumbled a thanks, and walked away. John followed, he was asking me questions, but I didn't really hear him. We walked out the way we had come in and then slowly flew back to the graveyard.

"What are we going to do?" John asked when we got back.

"I don't know," I told him with a smile. "Let's enjoy the Midnight Circle, then we both should fade. After we've rested, we'll talk again."

I hated lying to him, but I had to.

Transmission #46
Received 2012/02/18 02:21:54

I SNUCK AWAY BEFORE THE MIDNIGHT CIRCLE EVEN started. The whole situation with the SECI machines being overrun with ghosts bothered the hell out of me. I had to go back to the SECI chambers without John.

On one hand, I was frustrated. I couldn't do what I wanted to do. On the other hand, it made me uneasy. What will it mean if hundreds of ghosts started communicating in a believable way with the living? I've read enough science fiction to imagine that it won't be all rainbows and smiley faces.

I flew back fast, much faster than John could fly. I didn't have a clear idea of what I wanted to do, I just knew I wasn't done with the place.

As was becoming a habit, I was flying high when I spotted the Afterlife Communications building, and on the white roof I saw two rough, black letters: "JJ."

I don't know whether to chalk this up to Awareness or dumb luck, but it sure surprised me. I flew down and found the letters were made out of black rocks arranged on the white roof. They were about six feet high. Tam and Jin must have put them there. They had put that note on the poster in the lab, and they had done this too.

I noticed a piece of laminated paper weighed down by rocks in the middle of the "JJ." It read:

JJ, We hope you are well and find this note. We have created a new SECI chamber just for you, but because of the popularity of these we need to make this a bit of a scavenger hunt so only you can find the new chamber.

We all are looking forward to hearing from you.

Here is the clue to where you will find your next set of instructions: Go where one mustang sleeps and one waits, where the bear sleeps in his cave.

Love,

Tam and Jin

I felt my belly tighten with excitement. Something to do, something focused, something challenging, something different. The clue was an easy one, and I shot up into the air until I was about a thousand feet up, until things looked comfortingly small below me, and headed west.

I FOLLOWED I-10 WEST OUT OF TUCSON TOWARD PICACHO Peak. I veered off the highway until I sighted the little single-wide trailer and the two cars, one tarped, in front of the shed. Nate's place.

He was the bear the clue referred to, and the two cars were the mustangs. One was for parts (sleeps) and one was the last car Nate and I worked on together (waits).

Relief washed over me when I saw that the big red tow truck was not there. Nate was gone, and I wouldn't even be tempted to communicate with him.

I spotted another laminated piece of paper weighted down with rocks on the roof of the trailer. I flew over and read it:

Location #3: Was one then two, then one again. It was a cradle and a grave, but now all that you cared for is gone from there.

I groaned after I read it. Someone was having fun with the clues, too much fun. My guess is that it was Jin.

But I understood. I had revealed so much about my past that they couldn't just tell me where to go. I am sure other ghosts found the first clue and this one too.

I thought about it. One then two then one. Cradle and grave. It didn't take long, it wasn't that hard of a clue. I flew up and to the east, cutting across some open land until I hit state route 77. I headed towards Globe, Arizona.

I CAME IN AT ELEVATION AGAIN AND STOPPED JUST ABOVE my childhood home. It was originally built as a single family home, but at some point it was turned into a duplex. When my parents bought it they turned it back into a single family home (one, then two, then one again). It was also the place I was born (cradle) and the place my father died (grave).

I stayed at elevation as the sun rose and did my best to expand my sense of Awareness. I didn't want to run into the ghostly bullies Jesus and I had met when we had been there before. I also waited for the light, because ghosts tended to be less active during the day.

I didn't see any ghosts, so I flew down quickly, got the clue off of the roof of the house and flew right back up to elevation.

At this point I am going to fast forward to the end of

this scavenger hunt. While I was having a good time with it, I realize the details are probably boring. But I loved it. I got to interact both with people I loved and with my past at the same time.

But, my real reason for skipping forward is that the SECI chamber I am now using will get overrun with ghosts if I reveal all the clues.

So all you soon-to-be ghosts, this SECI chamber is mine. Hands off. If I find you here you will have to deal with me. I will defend my territory, and those of you who have read my other memoir know I am pretty good in a fight.

When I found the new SECI chamber I felt both excited and sad. Excited to reach the end of the quest. Sad that the quest, and the focus it afforded me, was over.

I entered the building and stared at the SECI chamber, a sense of dread tunneling into my psyche. Finding it was a victory, but something told me using it was not going to be simple.

Awareness? Maybe. Fatigue? Undoubtedly, it had taken me several days to follow all the clues.

With a sigh, I flew straight up until things became small and safe and I faded. I knew I would need to be rested for what was to come.

Transmission #47
Received 2012/02/18 04:36:11

JOHN AND I STOOD THERE STARING AT THE NEW SECI chamber. It was larger than the old one, but still recognizable. The panels that made up the walls were the same—they were roughly square about two feet on a side, made of grey metal.

The chamber dominated the otherwise empty small room. The electronics that monitor it must be located somewhere else.

And no, I'm not going to tell you about the building it's in. I'll tell you again, this SECI chamber is mine, don't come looking for it after you die.

"Are you ready?" I asked John.

"I think so," he said, nodding his head a bit too fast. I could tell he was nervous and scared. Hell, so was I. I was beginning to approach any encounter with the living, with my past, with great trepidation.

"So, those panels shield EM radiation. It's going to feel a little funny walking through it."

He nodded, "OK."

Inside I stopped and stared for a minute. Instead of the panels with the complicated symbols to make for each letter was a large keyboard inscribed on the back wall with a flat screen panel above it. Each key was about two inches on a side. They weren't actual keys, but little black pieces of glass embedded into the wall with a white letter on them.

On the other side of the chamber was a smaller flat panel display, and below it another one of the "keys," this one with a triangle pointing to the right, like "play" on a DVD player, and a note taped to the wall.

Welcome JJ,

This is SECI 2.0. It's just for you. We redesigned it to make it easier for you to communicate. We also want to be able to communicate back to you, so we will be placing videos here that you can watch.

This first one is from Nate. It will orient you more on SECI 2.0 and catch you up on some things.

You trigger it by lowering your frequency a bit and passing your form (a finger should do it) through the black glass.

We look forward to hearing from you.

Tam and Jin.

I stood there blinking, and then I read the message again. I was touched. I mean, how could I not be? My friends, these people I loved, had gone through a lot just so I could type more messages to them. I was moved, not just because of the money it took to build this thing but because of the time and effort they put into creating it and the clues that led me there.

I must have been standing there for a while because John asked, "Are you going to play it?"

I nodded, but didn't make a move. I was touched, yes, but afraid too. The thought of watching Nate talking to me was terrifying. I had made such a mess of our communication after I died, I didn't think I was ready to see him, to have even a one-way conversation with him.

But, there was nothing to do about it. I modulated my right index finger, like I used to do for the first SECI chamber, and passed my finger through the glass of the play key.

The video came to life and there was Nate. He looked the same, his kind face, his big chest stuffed into a white T-shirt. He looked good, but he looked nervous.

"Hey, bro," he began on the screen, "welcome back. Jin and Tamara are letting me do this introduction for you. They first asked me to write it, but you know me. Unlike you, I couldn't write my way out of a paper bag, it would take me days to write this down. And it would be even harder to tell you…"

Why was Nate giving me the orientation? What was it that was going to be hard to tell me? The unease that I had been feeling multiplied and I wanted to run away, but I didn't, I watched.

I loved hearing about Ma and Anna-Beth and Nate. It was wonderful, but I knew something bad was coming. Nate had essentially said it and his pinched face told the story.

When the news came, that Rhiannon had a brain tumor, that she was very ill, that she was dying, I…

This is going to be hard to explain so please bear with me. As I have documented, I had been going through this "growth" phase. I helped Jesus find his killer and bring him to justice (such as it is). I helped John get out of the bardo and was showing him the ropes. I was learning to be a teacher, learning to be aware of others and how they are feeling. I was growing, maturing, I really was.

But, when I heard about Rhiannon, all that went out

the door. I snapped back to the JJ I used to be—passionate and impulsive—and wanted to leave that very second. I wanted to leave John where he stood and fly as fast as I could to Texas.

I felt fear and anger course through me. I saw red flickering on the edge of my form. I was desperate to "do" something and not just stand there.

The video ended and John said, "I'm so sorry."

I looked at him, and he looked scared. He had seen my transformation, he might not know exactly what it was about, but he must have known I was going through something.

I nodded, modulated my finger and played the video again. It didn't have any other controls, and I needed to see the directions to Rhiannon's again.

It felt like torture waiting for the end. As much as I loved Nate and loved seeing him, all I wanted were the damn directions so I could be sure I had them and I could leave.

When the video stopped I looked again at John. On his face I saw fear, but mostly I saw compassion. His mouth moved. I am sure he was searching for words to say, but none came out.

And, in truth, John could relate to what I was going through in a way that few could. We had spent all that time in bardo together, and my feelings and passion for Rhiannon had been made entirely clear.

"Look—" I began.

"No, it's OK," he said. "She's the one that got away. You have to go to her. I understand. My message can wait."

That disarmed me. The red flicking along my form didn't go away, but it subsided some. I took a deep breath and sighed. "Thank you, John. I am really sorry."

"I understand. It's been a long time now. I am sure Tamara isn't even expecting a message anymore."

When he mentioned Tamara, visions of our shared bardo experience came back. How at times Rhiannon and Tamara filled the same role, the role of lover and mate. I felt torn, obliged to help Tamara and desperate to see Rhiannon.

I marched over to the keyboard on the wall, modulated my index fingers and started typing. "This is Joseph Jeffery Lynch. I don't know what to say. I have so much to say. So much has happened, but I just saw the video of Nate talking about Rhiannon."

I typed furiously, the letters appearing on the flat screen above the keyboard. In the back of my mind I really appreciate the changes they had made for me, making it easier to type. But I stayed focused, letting John get a short message to Tamara. Not the message he needed to send her, but enough.

"Thank you," I said as we flew out the ceiling and headed back towards the graveyard. "Thank you for understanding."

He smiled, it was a shy, gentle, John-like smile, "How could I not understand?" he asked.

When we got to the graveyard, I found Fredrick and gave him the scoop. He said he would tell Banquo what was going on and would keep an eye on John.

With that done, I didn't say a word. I flew up, straight up, until the graveyard was small and tiny like a toy. I paused for a moment, even though I could feel this irresistible force pulling me east.

I took some deep ghostly breaths. After having spent nearly twelve months in the bardo, I wasn't able to fool myself into thinking I knew what the future was going to bring. I had to be honest with myself, I didn't even know if

I would make it back to the graveyard. With Rhiannon dead or dying, everything changed for me. Everything.

I hoped I was in time, that I would get there before she died. And then—

And then I had no idea what to hope for. That she died well? Whatever the hell that was. That she moved on right away? And then I wouldn't get to talk to her again. That she stayed as a ghost? And then had to deal with all the shit that I had been dealing with since dying.

When I thought of her being a ghost, something stirred in my chest. I'm a ghost, and if Rhiannon was a ghost too, we could be together, we could—

I brutally shoved the thought down and thought of Rhiannon until she was all that I could see. Her petite body, her purple nail polish, her brown hair perpetually in a ponytail, the shape of her red lips, the feel of her hand in mine, the way her smile made me feel, the way her laughter made me happy to be alive, the smell of the lavender oil she used to wear as perfume, the way she would tease me about Nate and call it a bro-mance, the way her body used to feel against mine. And then—

And then I was no longer floating above the graveyard, I was in a small room in Texas.

She was there, Rhiannon, but it wasn't the woman I remembered. Her fingernails were painted purple, but almost everything else was different. Gone was her long brown hair, and in its stead was a purple bandanna wrapped around her head. Her face wasn't thin anymore but puffy, and there was no life in her body.

Well, not "no life," but not much life. It was clear she was alive, but she wasn't "alive." Her eyes were closed and her body was covered up to her neck with a sheet.

The room was cheery enough in appearance with flowers and pictures of her family, but it was heavy. Heavy with grief, heavy with fear, heavy with the knowledge of impending death.

"Oh, Rhi," I said. "God, I am so sorry."

Interlude

Tamara and John

Transmission #48
Received 2012/01/29 16:15:31
From John Fisher to Tamara Watson.
Transcribed by JJ Lynch.

OK TAMARA, IT HAS BEEN A LONG TIME COMING, BUT I am finally back and have John here and I am going to type his message to you.

MY DEAR SWEET TAMARA,

I have had a lot of time to think about what to say while JJ was gone dealing with Rhiannon. I have written this little letter to you a thousand times in my mind, but here we are, and I have no idea what to say.

JJ is being kind enough to transcribe my words, to encourage me to do this, but...

But it's hard. How can it not be?

This moment, right here, I am getting the chance to do something unprecedented. To reach beyond the boundary of life and death and to say what I need to say. But there is so much to say. So much.

First, I love you with all my heart. I know I wasn't perfect, nor was our love. I loved you to the best of my ability, and I still love you. So there is that. I don't want you to ever doubt that.

Second, I am sorry. There is much I kept from you and for that I am sorry. Some of it I had to keep from you, some of it I was too ashamed to share.

JJ tells me that he will be documenting our time together in the bardo, including what happened with Professor Aldridge and Agent Franks. So, I will let that stand. Suffice it to say that at first I couldn't tell you, and then when things went sideways, I feared for your well-being and chose not to tell you.

But what I really need to tell you, what I tried so hard to tell you when I was dying, and when I was a ghost, is that I have a daughter. Her name is Jill, Jill Moore. She has strawberry blond hair and beautiful blue eyes. She is...

I can't tell you the whole story, I don't have the courage, but JJ will tell what he saw of it, and that will fill in the blanks for you.

This daughter of mine is the big secret. It wasn't the FBI, or top secret project, it was this thing, this shame of mine. That I fathered a child and gave her up.

Can you see why I might not want to share that with you? That I was afraid you might not see me as a fit father for our own children if you knew. That you might not marry me, that you might not love me.

Can you understand, Tamara?

And I regret this. I regret holding back anything from you. I don't know how you would have reacted to knowing about little Jill, and I don't know if I would have lost you over this. But I do wish I had told you. I do wish I had had the courage to tell you.

As I lay there on the cool sidewalk, my blood flowing out of me, as you held me and cried, as we waited for the ambulance to come, I focused on two things. You and Jill.

I was afraid I was dying, and afraid of losing you and regretting that I had, long ago, lost Jill.

Being dead has afforded me some perspective. Predictable, yes, but important nonetheless. There is nothing more important in this life, or this afterlife, than love. Nothing.

Even though I never got to know my daughter, I loved her. Even though I am dead, I still love you.

Don't worry, I am not haunting you, and I am not going to. The danger in that is very clear to me. Nor am I going to haunt Jill or her mother Alice.

Actually, I don't know what I am going to do. I am staying, for now, in the graveyard with JJ, Banquo, and the gang. I am giving myself time to heal. But what is next? I have no idea.

I do have a favor to ask of you, and it's a big favor. I don't ask it lightly, and I don't expect you to do this. I hope you can, but if you don't I won't think any less of you.

Can you check on Jill for me from time to time?

I... I don't even know what I expect you can do, but I want some part of me to be there for her, and you, Tamara Watson, are the biggest part of me that I have left.

It's crazy, right? Alice may not let you, she may not understand. But can you at least try? Can you tell Alice how sorry I am for how badly I acted? Can you let my little girl know that someone out there in this big world loves her?

You know, I am trying to let go of all these regrets. How if I had handled things differently I might still be alive, I might have had a relationship with my daughter, with you.

These are heavy things, and try as I might, I have not been able to let them go.

And I know what I have asked of you is not fair, and you are well within your rights to say no. But I don't know what else to do. I need something still—it's why I am still here, still a ghost. If you can't help, don't worry about it, I will find a way.

I love you so much, Tamara. I miss you desperately. But, I hope you have moved on with your life, you must. You must find love, you must cherish it, and you must nurture it. You are an amazing woman, and you deserve to have an amazing man in your life. You deserve love that you can touch.

I hope you are well. JJ will add contact information for Alice and Jill that I trust will be edited out if this is to be published.

All my love, John

Video Transcript #3
Tamara Watson speaking to John Fisher
Recorded on 2012/01/31/10:16 a.m.
Playback triggered on: 2012/02/01 1:31 a.m.

MY DEAREST JOHN,

Thank you for finding your way back to this world and writing your letter to me.

I... Oh, excuse me, I promised myself I wouldn't cry. You... We... Oh hell, John, this is hard, so hard.

I thought that if we could just talk, if we had the chance to say good-bye, if I just knew what you wanted to say to me when you were dying that this would all be OK.

But it's not.

It's been nearly three years since you died. I did so much for so long trying to communicate with you, but the timing... God, the timing, John. I just can't believe that now you are here, now you are ready to communicate.

After I created the SECI project, after JJ wrote his memoir, I finally felt something release. I finally was able to let you go, to move beyond the grief that had so plagued me.

Jin and I are out of the university now. We have formed

a company and are taking the SECI technology and using it. It's an odd start-up, just imagine what our presentations to investors look like, but we are making progress. I have found work that I value and love doing.

And I met someone, John, I finally met someone. Six months ago I met a man. He's... we...

Oh hell, and now here you are. Don't get me wrong. I am so glad you are all right, that you are communicating. It's just that I finally moved on with my life and... and now I am remembering and feeling and grieving you again.

Look, that's all I can say right now. I am thinking about what you have asked for concerning your daughter. I...

Damn it, if I keep recording this, I'm just going to keep crying. Let me get my act together, and I will communicate again.

Video Transcript #4
Tamara Watson speaking to John Fisher
Recorded on 2012/02/19 7:12 a.m.
Playback triggered on: 2012/02/21 2:12 a.m.

JOHN,

I'm sorry. I know it's been a few weeks. I was reading what JJ wrote about his time in the bardo with you and I had to wait until the entire story unfolded. Then I needed a few days.

After you died I was angry at you for a long, long time. After the FBI came and took most of your possessions away, after I stopped being afraid and paranoid, I became angry. Angry that you had withheld things from me. Angry at what the FBI said you did. Angry that I had trusted you.

Having read what JJ and you wrote, you might think that I would understand and feel fine about it. But I don't. I am even more angry. Actually, I am furious. Five stages of grief, you know.

And I'm scared now, too. Actually terrified. I now know who killed you. I have found where you hid the recordings, and I have no idea what to do. This could have been so much simpler if...

I keep wondering why you didn't trust me. Why you didn't tell me about Jill and Alice. Why you didn't come to me when Agent Franks started extorting your work from you. Why?

I, at first, fell into depression, thinking it was all about me. But—you know what?—it wasn't. So maybe we didn't share everything, maybe I'm not the most open person in the world. But, Jesus Christ, John, you kept a lot from me. Too much. Way too much.

I'm sorry, this is probably not what you want to hear, not what you need. But it is what I need to say. I don't know any more if I really knew you, knew us. I thought I did, but with all of this...

We all have secrets, dark little places we keep to ourselves. But what you kept from me, John, was too much.

I'll have more to say, but not right now. This is enough for now.

Take care of yourself, John.

Transmission #49
Received 2012/02/21 05:42:21
From John Fisher to Tamara Watson.
Transcribed by JJ Lynch.

TAMARA,

I feel like an idiot. I didn't realize what kind of danger knowing the story of my death might put you in. I am sorry for that as well as many other things.

I talked with Banquo and JJ, and they think you should get Nate involved in this situation. Don't try to deal with this alone, like I did. Get help. Nate knows some people on the Tucson PD.

I know you, and I know you won't be able to let this be. But, don't feel like you need to do something about Franks for me. I'm dead, nothing is going to change that. But you, you have so much to lose here. Please be careful.

John

Video Transcript #5
Tamara Watson speaking to John Fisher
Recorded on 2012/02/27 9:10 a.m.
Playback triggered on: 2012/02/28 1:44 a.m.

WELL, JOHN, IT'S OVER. NATE HELPED, GOT HIS POLICE friends involved, and they have arrested Agent Franks. I can't tell you how relieved I am. I could hardly sleep knowing he was out there, knowing he knew where I lived. Knowing what he did to you.

What happened to Professor Aldridge is still a mystery. He disappeared the night you died, and no one knows what happened to him. If I find out anything new about him, I will let you know.

I hope this helps. I hope this gives you some peace, knowing that justice will be served.

That said, I am still so angry with you. Going through this thing with Franks has just made it worse. Why didn't you trust me, John? Why?

Transmission #50
Received 2012/02/28 04:16:38
From John Fisher to Tamara Watson.
Transcribed by JJ Lynch.

I AM RELIEVED BEYOND WORDS TO HEAR THAT FRANKS IS behind bars. Not for myself, but for you. It means everything to me to know that you are safe.

I still wonder about Professor Aldridge and hope that he is OK. Maybe after I learn more about this ghost stuff I will go look for him. I, at least, owe him that.

Beyond that, I don't know what else to say. I am sorry, I truly am. I wish I could have lived my life differently, made different choices. But you know what? I didn't.

I will not wallow in regret, I will not. I am doing my best to grieve my life, to learn from my mistakes, to move on. But if what you want from me is... Actually, I'm sorry. I don't know what you want from me. I am sorry this isn't what you wanted, and I am not who you thought I was.

I'm human. I made some huge mistakes. That doesn't negate the love we shared.

And honestly, Tam, that is what I have left. I loved you

and I know you loved me. That is all I have left. In the end, that is all any of us have left.

Be well, Tamara. I am here if you want to discuss this more.

Video Transcript #6
Tamara Watson speaking to John Fisher
Recorded on 2012/03/02 3:23 p.m.
Playback triggered on: 2012/03/03 2:58 a.m.

JOHN,

I met Jill the other day. I am sure as you watch this video you are quite surprised given my last message.

I was angry and feeling betrayed. I still feel that, but it has died down some. You are right about what is important here. It is that we loved each other. And truthfully, John, I will always love you. Your intelligence, your graceful hands, how you always made me laugh... often when you were not trying. We did love, you and I, we did. And that is what is important.

The rest of this will eventually fall away. I know that. I deal with the dead talking to the living all the time. Please don't be too hard on yourself. I am grateful that we had a chance to love.

So back to Jill. She is nine now, and is a bit of a princess, favoring frilly dresses and glitzy barrettes in her long hair.

But, let me tell the story. I don't know if I can do this as well as JJ does, but I will give it a try.

I STOOD AT THE DOOR TO ALICE'S OFFICE, SO VERY nervous. To be honest I was there more for me than you. My hope was that I could learn about you from her. That I could gain some insight that would help me process all of this.

I had my hand raised to knock when she opened the door. She's beautiful, John, with that long red hair and those bright green eyes. I felt an odd stab of jealousy.

"Can I help you?" she asked, adjusting her glasses.

"Umm... I hope so. I... Can I come in?"

"My office hours are over. If you have a question, you can come back next Monday."

"I'm not a student. Actually, I just did a guest lecture over at the College of Engineering."

"Oh," she said, taking a closer look at me. I am not sure if she recognized me. She might have, we've been getting some press lately. She invited me in.

"My name is Tamara Watson," I said.

She sat slowly down in her chair and indicated for me to sit. "I was kind of expecting you a few years ago," she said.

I nodded. "John never really told me about you. I just found out about you and Jill recently."

She frowned deeply and slowly nodded. "I thought of seeking you out after... well, I never did. Such a terrible thing."

Our conversation was awkward at first. But we found our way through it. I think the whiskey she had stashed in her desk drawer helped.

And, you know what? I am not going to give you all the details of our conversation. Our conversations, actually. We've kind of bonded over this.

I didn't expect it. Actually, I don't know what I expected. I went to her to try to understand you. To try to come to terms with all of this. I wasn't trying to make a friend.

Jill is adorable. I met her at the park. The three of us had a bit of a picnic. She is smart, John. That's not a surprise with the two of you as her parents. She loves to play the clarinet; actually she played a little recorder for me at the park—she's quite good. She's obsessed with butterflies. It's more the fact that caterpillars turn into butterflies that captures her imagination. That metamorphosis is what she couldn't stop talking about.

She knows a lot about insects in general. It really creeped me out when she went to great lengths telling me about scorpions and how the venom works.

I gave Alice some of the pages that JJ has written that talk about your time together. She knew what I did, but hadn't asked if I had heard from you. I told her how and why the SECI project got started and handed her the pages.

Jill and I went off on a bug safari while Alice read.

When I came back, she said, "He's OK now, right?"

"Yeah. He's OK. He's trying to get past regretting this," I said, looking at Jill. "But he's OK."

She cried. Well, for her crying is more of a misting up, not the full water works that I do. "You know," she said, "I didn't plan it. I wasn't using him. It's just that... He was so young. Not in terms of intelligence, but in other ways, in the ways of relationship, he was so young. He wasn't ready to be a father, and I couldn't see us being a long-term thing."

I nodded and handed her a tissue from my purse.

"Can you tell him that? That I didn't try to do this, that I didn't want to hurt him. But look." She gazed at her daughter, who held an ant in her hand. "Look at her. She is the best thing I ever did and John made that happen."

"You know, if you want," I said, "you can record a video for him and he'll see it."

She shook her head. "Oh, God. No, no way. I can't do that. Just tell him for me. Tell him I am so grateful."

I nodded and said, "I will."

Later as we watched Jill play on the jungle gym, I said, "John asked me to check in on Jill from time to time. And having met her, I think I would like to do that. If it's OK with you."

She looked at me, her green eyes intense, her lips in a frown for a few moments. She then smiled and nodded. "I think I would like that. I think we both would like that."

So there you have it, John. I don't know if this helps you. I hope it does. I hope it brings you peace.

Jill is a beautiful girl, and she seems to be doing well. Alice and I talking has helped us both to sort out our feelings about you.

And now, I need to say good-bye. Please don't write back, at least not for a while. I still have a ways to go sorting this all out. I need to get through it and focus on the relationship that I have. I need to get past this.

I know that might sound harsh. I created SECI to communicate with you and now I am asking you to not communicate back, to give me some time to deal with this. I promise if it seems appropriate, I will leave another message for you. But I don't expect to do that anytime soon.

I love you, John. We had some good years together, and

I am so happy you are in a good place now. I hope that is enough.

Transmission #51
Received 2012/03/03 16:16:49

AFTER THE VIDEO ENDED, I LOOKED AT JOHN, HIS FACE blank, unreadable. I studied his form, it had gone a bit wispy, but he didn't appear to be in any real danger.

"We should go," I said.

He nodded, but didn't move. "Play it again," he said.

I triggered playback, and we watched the whole thing again. I studied Tam's face this time. She was clearly on the edge of tears. What she was asking for was very hard for her.

"Again," he said.

I played it a third time, and then he wanted a fourth time and a fifth time.

"Again," he said.

"No," I answered.

He looked at me, his jaw set and his eyes a bit too wide. "Again!"

I just stood there letting silence be my answer.

"Again, please," John asked.

"Let's go, John."

"Please, I need to see it again."

I wasn't sure what to do. John's way of grappling with this was to watch Tam's message over and over again. I didn't think it was for me to judge. I almost triggered playback again but stopped myself. I realized that it *was* for me to judge. I was in a role here with him, and I had a responsibility to do what was best for him, not what he wanted.

"Let's go," I said, and not looking back I exited the SECI chamber.

Different ghosts have different talents, and John wasn't good at manipulating his form in the way the SECI chamber required. I didn't think he would be able to trigger the playback himself.

I waited right outside the chamber for ten minutes. I knew he was in there trying. I worried that he would go bardo, but having been through what the two of us went through, my hope was that he was motivated, more than most, to stay out of that place.

I was relieved when he finally came out. "Please," he said. "Please play it again for me."

We all grieve in different ways. Much is the same, but much is different too. I opened up myself to Awareness, I felt all that I could. John was in pain, deep and terrible pain. I understood it, I empathized with it, but I didn't see any value in playing Tam's video over and over again.

"Why?" I asked, my arms crossed. I had this strange sense of Banquo as I stood there, as John's mouth moved silently, as he struggled for the words to say. I realized that I was acting like Banquo, that this is what he would have done with me if I was acting like John.

I again felt a sense of gratitude for my mentor but something else, too. I felt compassion. This role is not an easy one, and it really doesn't come naturally to me.

"I... It... She..." John stammered. "Damn it! Just play the video for me again." I felt for the guy, I did, but this obsession was poison, it was destructive.

In the distance I heard a siren approaching and an idea sparked in my mind. "No time," I said. "We're needed, now!"

I turned and flew out of the building towards the sound of the siren. I didn't look back but sensed that John was following.

I didn't fly at my top speed but at one John could keep up with. I flew up to get a better view of the streets and spotted the ambulance and then spotted where it was headed—a nasty wreck at a busy intersection.

Now, Banquo had not officially taken me on as his apprentice, and "chasing ambulances" was not something I normally did. But when I saw John struggling so, I imagined what it would do to me to go through that, and when I heard the siren I knew he needed something to get him out of himself.

I wanted him to do something instead of stewing in his grief, and wherever that ambulance was going, there just might be someone that needed our help.

And honestly, I needed it too. What was keeping me sane right then were the things that got me out of my own head. Writing, somehow, did that. Helping John did it. And helping a stranger, I knew, could potentially do that for both of us.

Transmission #52
Received 2012/03/03 18:23:04

"OH MY GOD! OH MY GOD!" THE WOMAN CRIED. SHE had blood running down her face as she stumbled out of her car. She slipped on the broken glass and fell to the pavement. She was in her thirties and had dark hair.

Her car, a bland, grey minivan, had been T-boned by a red two-seater. Airbags went off in both cars. Two figures were unconscious in the red car and one in the minivan on the side where the red car had smashed into it.

"Help him," the woman cried as she tried to stand up. "Someone help my husband."

I glanced at the minivan again and could see the soul of the woman's husband separating from his body. I saw the same happening to the male driver of the red car.

I looked at John and said, "You want the car or the van?"

"What?" he asked, his eyes darting back and forth from the wreck to me. His confusion was understandable, I had just thrown him a hell of a curve ball, but it was time for him to see the wider world, and these people needed help.

"Which of these souls do you want to help?" I asked. "The man in the van, or the man in the car?"

"I... I... I don't think I..." he stammered.

"Somebody, please!" the woman cried as she looked around the intersection. Cars had stopped and a few people were milling about, but they were giving the wreck a large berth. I could hear a siren as the ambulance approached.

I turned away from the wreck and looked at him. "Listen to me, John. You are here for a reason. We are here for a reason. And right now that reason is to help these two men. To do something that matters. To make a difference. Now which one do you want?"

"What? What do I do?" John asked, his eyes wide.

"Just talk to him, calm him. If he starts hearing the Call, encourage him to move on."

"I..." John stammered.

"It's OK," I said, smiling at him. "You can do this. You take the car, I'll take the van. With that woman, his wife, carrying on, that one's going to be tougher."

John nodded, his face pinched. "Good!" I said, leaving him and going to the now separated soul of the man. He was bald with a big belly and was following his wife around talking to her.

"Honey, it's OK," he said. "I'm OK. I don't know how, but somehow I'm OK. Look, I'm not even hurt. Grace, can you hear me, Grace?"

"I'm sorry, but she can't hear you," I said gently as I landed next to him.

He turned, his eyes wide. I positioned myself so I could see him and keep an eye on John as he approached the second ghost who was hovering right above the red car.

"Who are you?" he asked.

"I'm one of the paramedics," I said, and felt my form shift to fit what I was saying. Kind of like my police uniform. It wasn't perfect, but it was good enough for this.

"Please," he said, "help my wife."

"She is being attended to, sir," I said, seeing one of the real paramedics approach her. "Let me examine you."

He nodded. "It happened so fast. The light was green. Why did they, why did they..." he turned towards the red car and saw John hovering above it talking to the other ghost. "What? What the hell."

"Sir, can you please look at me, sir?" I said, drawing his attention back. "I need to check your pupils."

"What?" he said as his head swiveled back around to me.

"Now, look me in the eye," I said as I started to remember the Call. Even the memory of it was sweet, and as I remembered it, I began to hear it. Vague and distant, but I could hear it.

The man's face relaxed, and I held his eye contact. "Do you hear that?" I asked. "It's the most beautiful thing I've ever heard. My God, it is so amazing."

"I do," he said. "I hear it. What is that?"

"I don't know," I lied. "But I can't stop listening to it. I can almost taste it... and smell it... and..."

The man smiled, his face showing the bliss of the Call heard. "Grace, come here, hon," he said, "you've got to hear this. It's..." he swiveled his head to try to see his wife, but I kept myself right in front of him, so he couldn't.

"Listen to it closely," I said. "It's calling to you. It wants to take you home."

"Take me home?" he asked. "Yes, it does. It wants to take me home. It's so beautiful It's so—" and he was gone.

I glanced at John who was still taking to the other ghost

and went and checked on the woman. The paramedics had her on a stretcher with a neck brace on. "My... my husband, Hal... Can you help him?" she said. "Can someone please help him?"

"I'm sorry, ma'am," the paramedic said. "There is nothing we can do."

I had a moment of doubt then, sharp and visceral. Had I done the right thing by helping Hal move on? Maybe he would have been better off as a ghost, maybe he had things to finish in this life. I worried that I shouldn't have brought John to this accident. Who the hell was I to judge whose time it was to move on?

I took a deep breath and let it out.

I let go of the thoughts and tried to be Aware, tried to feel. I felt Grace's shock and grief—she would have a lot to go through, but that was the way of it. I felt for Hal, for what might have been if we hadn't come along, and I felt confusion, great, great confusion.

I didn't know if what I had done was "right." I didn't even know if that was the best way to think about it. I longed for Banquo and realized that while I was capable of helping others move on, I needed help. I needed Banquo if I was really going to start "chasing ambulances."

I flew over towards John and the ghost he was talking to. I stopped short when I could hear them. "It's OK, really it is," John said to the ghost. "What's done is done. You've got to focus on what is happening now, what your future holds for you, not get caught up in the past."

"But... I..." the ghost said, as he looked back over his shoulder at the van he had run into.

"Look at me," John said. "We all make mistakes—God

knows that I did—and we all need to find ways to move on after those mistakes."

I smiled and felt John. He was in the moment, he was helping this ghost, he wasn't back in the SECI chamber watching Tamara say good-bye to him over and over again. I wasn't fool enough to think he was suddenly over it, suddenly OK. Grief is not like that. But, at least for this moment, he was experiencing a future that was not about that grief. He was doing something that mattered.

Smiling, I flew over and introduced myself to the new ghost.

Part 3

Rhiannon

"Oh, I am fortune's fool!"
Romeo and Juliet: Act III, Scene I, by William Shakespeare

Transmission #53
Received 2012/02/22 02:03:41

WHEN I SAW RHIANNON LYING IN HER HOSPITAL BED IN her bedroom, the bardo came knocking and I sent it away with a polite, "No thank you." Don't get me wrong, this was one of those moments when the bardo was tempting. An escape, any escape, at this point, was tempting.

But, saying "no" was easy, even though I knew what was to come would be anything but.

I wasn't a brand new ghost anymore. I had been around the block, as it were. I knew what to do.

I positioned myself at the end of Rhiannon's bed, I put my hands under her head, and I summoned the warmth. This was what I had done for Anna-Beth after I had injured her. This is what I had done to get through to Ma. This is what Banquo would have told me to do if he had been there.

Tap into the warmth. Let go. Be with her.

And that is what I did. I focused on her face, her beautiful face, and let it become my world. I reached for and felt the warmth flowing through me, into my hands, and into her.

I wasn't trying to "heal" her. The warmth doesn't work that way. I was just trying to be in the flow with her, in the flow of love.

For I do love her. I love her with all my heart. Her love permeates the twisted passages of my psyche. She was my first real love, my only real love, and someone I will always love. Whether she's young or old, alive or dead.

I slipped right into that place with her and time slid past. Her best friends, Jeri and Gail, would sit and read to her for hours at a time. Her husband, Thomas, and her father, Kyle, spent a lot of time with her. Her sister and some other friends came for brief visits. And Thomas would bring in the baby.

The baby. They named him Joey. I almost lost it then, I almost said yes to the bardo. He was a chubby thirteen-month-old bundle of energy, with wisps of brown hair and piercing blue eyes.

They named him Joey.

My first name is Joseph, and while no one ever called me Joey, it was always JJ, could it be a coincidence that we had the same first name? Rhiannon had been pregnant when I died, could it be that she named her son after me?

At first, Rhiannon would wake from time to time. A few hours here and a few hours there. She would sip water, eat a little Jell-O, but I could tell she was doing it for them, not for herself. She could see the looks on their faces. She could feel the fear they felt. It was obvious what it meant if she didn't eat, if she didn't drink: she was really going to die.

The trouble was, she was going to die. All she wanted was enough water to soothe her dry mouth and the drops of morphine they put under her tongue that pushed her pain away.

Dying the way she was dying is hard work. The hardest work. And by the time I got there she had gotten very internal. She was most at peace when Jeri or Gail just sat or read to her.

Because of the location of the brain tumor, she couldn't talk, not really. Sometimes she could manage yes and no, but most of the time she said "no" when she meant "yes." They had all come to rely on her head, either nodding or shaking, to communicate yes and no.

You might be wondering how I "know" all this. How I know what she wanted and didn't want. There is a lot to it, and we'll get to all the details, but at first it was Awareness that served me.

I knew Rhiannon, but being in the flow of the warmth with her, being focused and Aware of her, I knew more. It got so that I was aware of her feelings. Not her thoughts, but her feelings.

I could feel the nauseousness that never really went away. I could feel the pain that insidiously crept in, that the morphine never totally banished. I could feel the shame she felt when those that loved her and feared her death looked at her. I could sense the fear she didn't want to acknowledge, of what was going to happen to her, what it would be like to die. And I could sense how hard this was for her, this dying.

And I have to tell you something. If I thought my own death was tough, the toughest thing I would ever do, I was wrong. Dead wrong.

Being witness to her death was much harder.

I don't want to even get started on the fairness of one so young, one with a baby, one so brilliant and promising, dying. There is no use going there, there is nothing to say that can be helpful to anyone. She was young, had a thirteen-month-old baby, had a promising career, was happily married, and she was dying. Nothing could be done about it.

And that part really wasn't the hard part. It wasn't the details of her life or the story of her life as she met her death. In some ways all those details didn't mean much. The crux of it is this: it felt wrong. It wasn't the story around her circumstances, it was this feeling deep within me that her dying was wrong, a violation of the most primal variety. She shouldn't be dying. She should live. If anyone in this world should live, she should.

And here's the hard part: letting that go. That righteous feeling of right and wrong. The knowing that the situation was unjust. I had to let that feeling go.

You see, those feelings were the problem. I don't know if I am going to explain this right, and I will get into particulars, but they were my biggest problem.

Every time I felt or thought what was happening to her was "wrong," I was thrown out of the flow and the warmth abandoned me. And when I could just be with her, where she was, the warmth returned and I could sense her, I could feel her, and I could tell that she liked it. She fed back in subtle ways, her face relaxing, her pain diminishing a bit, a sigh.

And the opposite would occur when I sat there thinking how unjust and horrible it was. Because, you know, it was unjust and horrible, wasn't it?

I wasn't the only one doing this to her. Almost everyone that came into the room did this. They brought their fear and their judgments. They brought her death and missed being with her in the moments she was alive. They were too involved in her future, her impending death, to be present with her.

And all this activity swirled around us for four days until she didn't wake up anymore. And then things changed.

Transmission #54
Received 2012/02/22 03:49:21

SUDDENLY I SAW RHIANNON LYING IN A HOSPITAL BED WITH a curtain drawn around. Jeri sat on a stool next to her.

Rhiannon looked healthy, her brown hair long and tied back in a ponytail.

"Taking a damn long time," Jeri said, her hand pushing her blond hair behind her right ear.

"You know how this works. It's the ER, Jer," Rhiannon said, "they are always slow."

Jeri nodded and bit her lower lip. "I know, but I don't like it."

Rhiannon shrugged and checked her phone. "Thomas will be here soon."

This thing I was experiencing was memory. I wasn't in the hospital room. I mean, I had no body or presence, I was just aware of it. Kind of like a dream. As I sat with Rhi on her deathbed, her mind was remembering, and I was witnessing those memories.

I was still vaguely aware of the room in Rhiannon's

house and what was going on, but most of my mind was experiencing her past with her.

Rhiannon's eyes widened when the doctor walked back in. He had kind eyes, with pronounced dark smudges below them. He pulled up a stool and looked directly at Rhiannon.

"We saw something on the CT," he began. "It's a mass sitting right between the two hemispheres of your brain." His words were simple and straightforward, but his furrowed brow and deep frown told the whole story. This was clearly the worst kind of news.

"A mass?" Rhiannon asked, her face pale. "Are you saying I have a tumor in my brain?"

The doctor nodded slowly, "I am sorry, but yes, I am telling you that."

"Is it... is it cancer?" Jeri asked the doctor as she bit down on her lip.

The doctor looked briefly at Jeri and then returned his focus to Rhiannon. "It is hard to say at this point."

I WATCHED AS THE SMALL MOMENTS UNFOLDED. IT KIND of felt like Rhiannon knew I was there, that she was trying to tell me the story, that she wanted me to know.

When Thomas brought her home from the ER and the babysitter had left, she said, "Can you get me Joey, hon?"

"Are you still feeling dizzy?" Thomas asked.

"No, I'm fine," she said. "It was that hot bath, it made things worse."

"But... if you are holding him, if you do get dizzy... if you fall..." he didn't finish the thought.

Rhiannon sighed and sat on the couch. "Look, I'm sitting down. I won't get up. Please bring me my son. I need my son."

"What did they call it again?" Thomas asked. They were in bed having gotten home from more tests and more doctors.

"A Glioblastoma Multiforme," Rhiannon said, pronouncing the words carefully.

Thomas looked drawn and tired, more tired than Rhiannon looked.

"But," she continued, "they won't be sure until they take the sucker out."

Thomas nodded. "I haven't studied brain canc..." He stopped speaking, his words turning into a sigh.

"It's all right," Rhiannon said. "You can say it. You should say it. We're both doctors, for God's sake. Brain cancer."

Thomas took a deep breath and let it out slowly. "I didn't study brain cancer in my coursework. Do you know about this?"

Rhiannon nodded. "It is an aggressive variety involving the glial cells. It has one of the worst prognosis of any central nervous system malignancy. Mean survival rate, for my age, is a year, maybe eighteen months with aggressive treatments." Her tone was flat as she said it, as if answering a professor's question in a classroom.

Thomas nodded, his eyes wide. They were silent for some minutes, both of them lost in their own thoughts.

"I'm afraid," Rhiannon said, tears falling silently down her cheeks.

Thomas nodded and gathered her up in a fierce embrace. Silent tears flowing down his cheeks as they both wept.

HERE'S THE THING ABOUT A SERIOUS ILLNESS. YOU KNOW, they say "it takes a village" in reference to raising a child. Well, it takes a village too when someone is seriously ill. And the stress and strain of an illness like this affects the whole village.

Thomas's Mom, Carol, moved in with them and took over much of Joey's care.

Rhiannon's friend, Jeri, who was a new doctor too, took Rhi to all her appointments taking notes and helping to ask questions of the doctors. Thomas, in the middle of a surgical residency, took off all the time he could.

The disease completely took over their lives.

Transmission #55
Received 2012/02/23 01:22:01

"OK," Rhiannon said. She sat stiffly on a chair in her living room surrounded by other women. The chair sat on an old sheet and a towel was wrapped around her neck. "I'm ready."

Jeri walked up behind her and turned the clippers on, the sharp buzz cutting through the heavy silence. "Are you sure?" she asked.

"As if there is a choice," Rhiannon said. "If you, my friends, don't do this, someone I don't know at the hospital will."

Jeri nodded, but turned off the clippers and handed them to a tall dark-haired woman that was right behind her. She slowly pulled the hair tie out of Rhiannon's hair and ran her fingers through it.

"You'll still be beautiful," Jeri said. The sentiment was echoed by many of the women in the room: "Like Sinead O'Connor"; "Smoking hot!"; "Natalie Portman"; "Sigourney Weaver"; "If Thomas won't have you bald, honey, I will."

Laughter ensued as Jeri caressed Rhi's head. After the

laughter ended, Jeri took the clippers back and turned them on. "Here we go, honey," she said as she put the clippers to Rhiannon's head, and her long beautiful hair fell to the sheet on the floor.

Jeri didn't take much hair. She stopped, kissed the bald patch she had created and handed the clippers off to Gail.

Gail was a round woman with a loud laugh. Her, Jeri, and Rhiannon made up with they called the "Witches of East Houston." They had bonded in medical school and had all stayed in Houston.

Gail shaved a small spot, kissed it, and handed the clippers to the next woman. Each one did the same, shaving a portion of her head and kissing the new bald area before passing the clippers on.

It was like a ritual, a blessing, a grand spell they were casting by honoring Rhiannon and preparing her for the journey that was to come.

In the end Jeri finished, cleaning up the parts others had missed. She turned off the clippers, walked in front of Rhiannon, and squatted down. She smiled gently. "You look beautiful, my dear, just beautiful."

Rhiannon nodded. "Let me see."

Gail handed her a mirror and Rhiannon looked for a long time. She rubbed her bald scalp, and tears started to run down her cheeks, silent and swift.

"You do look beautiful," Gail said.

"My God, yes," a brunette echoed.

"I know, I know," Rhiannon said nodding her head. "It's..."

"What is it, honey?" Jeri asked. "You can tell us anything—it's just us girls."

"It's... I..." Rhiannon sniffed loudly and wiped at the

tears on her cheeks. Someone handed over a tissue box, and she took several out and dabbed at her face. "Everything changes tomorrow. They are going to take that thing out. They are going to find out exactly what it is." The words came tumbling out of her as if eager to escape. "I... I'm just so scared. I don't want Joey to grow up without a mother. I don't want to leave Thomas. I... I..." Her tears no longer silent, the sobs overwhelmed her and she couldn't speak. Jeri took her up in a tight embrace as Gail and many of the other women gathered around her in a group hug.

She cried for a long time, her body convulsing as the emotions ran their course. The women attended to her. Handing her tissues, bringing her water, touching her, holding her.

As I witnessed this, I felt something strange and unexpected. I felt deficient. What I saw was so difficult for everyone involved, but nobody hid anything. During the course of it every woman there cried, they all participated, they all experienced it, they all let it out.

It wasn't perfect, I am sure, but it was honest and real. And I felt deficient because, as a man, I had never experienced that. Not really. I guess the closest I came was during the intervention that my family held for me shortly after Rhiannon kicked me out, when I was deep in my alcoholic phase. But here, in this room of women, it was natural, and beautiful, and healthy. They knew how to do this.

I felt guilty, as if I shouldn't be seeing it, as if I should leave. But I was also touched and fascinated and riveted.

After the tears stopped, Rhiannon said, "Let me see that mirror again."

Jeri held it up for her.

"I just want to say one thing to all of you," she said, a

smile growing on her face. "Don't quit your day jobs, ladies. You'll never make it as hair stylists."

Just as the tears were plentiful and unrestrained, so was the laughter that ensued.

When Rhiannon stopped laughing enough to talk, she shouted, "Wine!" The cry echoed throughout the room. "And bring the good stuff, no more cheap wine for me."

"ARE YOU AWAKE?" THOMAS ASKED, HIS VOICE SOFT AND gentle. "Are you listening?"

"Yeah," Rhiannon said, her voice weak and her eyes closed. Her hand went to the bandages on her head and then pulled up the sheets of her hospital bed. "Tell me again how the surgery went."

Thomas took a deep breath and sighed. "The surgeon said they got all they could, the margins looked good."

"And?" she asked

"...and they will have it typed in a few days and the oncologist will direct the next course of treatment."

"OK," she said, her eyes fluttering open and meeting Thomas's, but he couldn't hold her gaze for long. He looked down to the manuscript in his lap. I knew it was an early version of *Shuffled Off*—laser printed pages in a three-ring binder.

"Should I keep reading?" he asked.

"Please," she said, "it is very comforting."

Thomas shook his head, but continued reading. "*He opened the shed, rummaged around until he found the ammo can it was kept in, and pulled out the gun. The gun was sleek and long, dark grey metal, with a weathered wooden handle. Nate picked it up and hefted it in his hand and then passed it from his right hand to his left and back to his right again. He pulled out a cloth and rubbed it down. He put it down, and paced in front of the shed—back and forth, back and forth."*

Thomas paused, taking off his glasses and rubbing the bridge of his nose. "You know Nate, right?"

Rhiannon nodded, "Yes, Thomas, I know Nate. I know him well."

"Would he do this? I just don't know if I'm buying it."

Under the sheet Rhiannon shrugged, "Nate sent a note with this. He said it is accurate, this all happened. This is real."

Thomas nodded slowly, his brow furrowed. "I know you know these people, but... Ghosts? Bardo? How that woman, Anna-Beth, nearly died? It just seems unreal."

Rhiannon smiled a small and gentle smile. "Remember that part at JJ's funeral? Where I went to his casket, talked to him, and kissed his cheek?" she asked. "You read that part to me, didn't you?"

He swallowed and nodded.

"I was the only one there at the casket," she said. "No one could have heard what I said. And, that is exactly what I said and did."

"I don't know... Maybe someone overheard you. Maybe this Jin and Tamara are out to make a buck. Maybe—"

"And Nate?" Rhiannon asked, her voice rising. "That man is honest to a fault. He would never lie about something like this."

"It just seems kinda far-fetched," Thomas said, taking his glasses off.

"Occam's razor, my love. Isn't it a simpler explanation that this is real?"

Thomas's mouth formed a half-smile, and he shook his

head. "But it's not the only explanation. There could have been a hidden camera at the funeral. Maybe Nate really needs the money. Maybe none of this is real."

Rhiannon laughed. "Well, if you must resort to a grand conspiracy to explain this, to explain away the witnesses and my own experience, I think your assumptions are in need of reevaluation."

Thomas smiled and nodded. "I'm just not comfortable with the idea of ghosts."

"There we go," she said with a weak smile. "I knew you could do it."

"I am trainable, my love, as I have proved time and time again."

Her smile widened, but she did not comment.

"Should I continue?" Thomas asked.

"In a minute. Where's Joey, where's my boy?"

"With my mom, at home."

"When can I see him?"

"You need to get stronger. They are worried about infection. You'll be home in another couple of days. You'll get to see him then."

Rhiannon nodded, closed her eyes, and Thomas kept reading.

Transmission #56
Received 2012/02/23 03:02:30

THE MEMORIES KEPT COMING. I STAYED THERE, AT RHIAN-non's head, pumping the warmth into her, keeping every-thing exactly the same. I didn't want to interrupt the flow. I knew this was clearly Awareness of Others, but I was surprised by just how vivid these memories were.

It was a bit like the bardo, vivid and real. But, even though the events were intense and full of suffering, they lacked the hopelessness of the bardo.

It became clear that these were slightly more than memories. For example, sometimes what I experienced was through her eyes and sometimes I was like another pres-ence in the room witnessing. And sometimes I experienced things she had no memory of, but was there for—we'll get to that soon.

The memories flitted by as I watched Rhiannon recover from surgery and saw a real reduction in her symptoms. When her strength returned, her vertigo was gone.

She threw herself into caring for Joey and fighting her illness.

"I've got him, Carol. Thanks," Rhiannon said to Thomas's mother. Rhiannon was dressed in jeans and a white blouse with a purple scarf tied around her head.

"Really, it's not a problem," Carol said, the smile on her face stiff. "You need your rest. It's what I'm here for."

Rhiannon held her child, now five months old, close, rocking him gently as she walked the floor. She stopped, her voice low but fierce. "I'm fine, Carol."

"I... It's... I just..." the older woman stammered.

"Spit it out."

"Well," Carol began, her arms crossing her chest. "What if you get dizzy again? What if you... if you drop him?"

Rhiannon gave Carol a look that used to make my blood run cold. It wasn't that overt, a tilt of the head, a narrowing of the eyes, a setting of the jaw. But, it was clear as a bell. She would go as many rounds as it took. "I'm sorry, Carol," she said cheerfully. "Are you implying that I would knowingly put my son, my own flesh and blood, at risk?"

"No... No! Of course not. I'm just worried about... about both of you."

Rhiannon walked Joey into his room closing the door behind her, ending the discussion.

RHIANNON AND THOMAS WERE LYING IN BED. HE WAS reading, she was biting her thumbnail and staring at the ceiling. She had taken the purple scarf off showing the hair that was starting to grow and the obvious scar on the top of her head. "Your mom is driving me crazy," she whispered.

"She means well," Thomas said, rubbing his face and looking away.

"Oh, I see. She's already given you an ear full."

Thomas nodded and pursed his lips. "She kinda has a point."

"What?" Rhiannon said, her voice no longer a whisper.

"At some point, if that thing grows back, your symptoms could return. Is it worth the risk?"

"Jesus, Tom. They just took the thing out a few weeks ago. They don't grow that fast. Radiation starts next week."

"It's just... if..." he stammered, ending in a long sigh.

"So, you want me to act like I'm dead already? Is that it? I should spend my days sitting in a chair holding Joey from time to time when Carol thinks it's 'safe.' Is that what you want? You want me to turn over the care of *my* son."

"No... Not exactly. I—"

"Then what, Thomas? What?"

I felt for Thomas. He was in a no-win situation. No matter what he did someone would be angry at him. And it wasn't as if this was a simple situation. Clearly there was risk, but the question seemed to be, could Rhiannon manage that risk herself?

He was silent for a long time before he said, "I just think that Joey's well-being has to come first."

Rhiannon's jaw clenched. She crossed her arms over her chest and glared at him.

"You have to agree," he continued, "that he comes first."

Rhiannon nodded, her mouth set in a thin line.

"Even a small risk of you falling while you are holding him is not worth taking. Right?"

"A small risk?" Rhiannon asked, her voice soft and sharp.

"Yes," Thomas said.

"Like tonight, when after two glasses of wine your mother picked him up and carried him to bed."

Thomas's mouth opened and he blinked several times.

"Because," Rhiannon continued, "I think two glasses of wine constitutes a 'small risk,' don't you?" Thomas didn't speak as Rhiannon continued. "And really, isn't it possible for any of us to trip and fall? Toys in the living room. Improper hydration. Moderate alcohol consumption. Being distracted by people hovering over your every move because you have cancer. All of those things constitute a 'small risk,' don't you think?"

Thomas pursed his lips and nodded. "But we don't have what you have," he said.

"You mean cancer, don't you?"

He nodded.

"And you don't trust me to know my limits with my own son, even though I have cancer?"

"I'm just afraid, Rhi. I'm just afraid." Thomas's face crunched up as tears began to flow down his cheeks. "If anything happens to him, I just don't know what I'll do."

Rhiannon pulled him close and held him. "I will be careful, OK? I will be super, extra careful. But I have to care for my son while... while I can. You can see that, can't you?"

He nodded and they held each other as they both cried.

Transmission #57
Received 2012/02/23 04:45:36

Rhiannon paced with Joey, holding him as he cried. "It's OK, little man. It's OK." A few months had passed and her hair had grown out enough that she didn't always leave it covered.

She was having a "good" day. With the tumor removed and her radiation treatments finally ended, she felt almost normal, almost her old self.

As I watched her life spin past, though, I realized that the old "normal" was long gone and would never return. The "C" word was always there, always present, always lurking in every choice, every interaction, every breath.

"What is it, honey?" she asked the baby. "You're not wet, you just ate. Are you just tired, Joseph? Is that it?"

She was alone in the house. She had fought for and gained a level of independence. Thomas was working and Carol was out shopping.

She went into the baby's room and sat in the rocking chair holding him to her chest. She began to rock slowly as she sang to her son.

Her voice was soft and sweet. Not exactly in tune, but beautiful nonetheless. I wanted to slow that moment down. She was relatively healthy and doing exactly what she wanted. As she sang and rocked, Joey's eyes fluttered and then closed as he slept.

She sat there rocking Joey for a long time as tears slowly flowed down her cheeks.

Maybe she felt it, maybe she knew that this moment of balance, of health, wasn't going to last long.

It seemed innocent enough at first. She felt weak on her left side and a bit dizzy. It wasn't serious, she told herself. It wasn't anything. She was just tired, she didn't feel well.

That night as they were getting into bed, she told Thomas. His face went slack and his eyes went wide. "I'm calling your oncologist," he said, reaching for the phone.

She laughed. "Really, Thomas? You're a doctor and you're going to be one of *those* spouses? The one that calls every time their person sneezes."

"That's right, I am a doctor," he said, standing up. "Swing your legs over and sit on the edge of the bed."

Rhiannon nodded, she knew what was coming.

Thomas extended his two index fingers and said, "Squeeze." She grabbed them, one with each hand, and squeezed as hard as she could.

He nodded and said, "Palms up, resist." She complied and he pressed against her palms. He had her smile and stick her tongue out and move it to side to side and a few other things.

"OK," he said, sitting on the bed next to her.

"Well?" she asked.

He nodded slowly. "The left side is a little weaker, but not much."

She nodded, looking close to tears.

"When is your next MRI scheduled for?" he asked.

"About three weeks?"

"Let's call the doctor in the morning and see if we can move it up."

Rhiannon nodded. "Do you think..." she began. The unfinished phrase hung in the room. Neither of them acknowledged it, neither of them finished it.

Without another word they crawled into bed and turned out the lights, but neither one of them slept for a long time.

DOCTOR CALLAGHAN'S OFFICE WAS CHEERFUL ENOUGH with light green walls, potted plants, and sunlight flowing in from the window. But it wasn't enough, not to disguise the heaviness that permeated the space.

Every day people sat there with the stout man discussing their cancer. Everyday people got bad news, news they didn't want to hear, news they would give anything to change.

Today was Rhiannon's turn.

She sat in one of the padded grey chairs. Jeri sat in the chair next to her. Doctor Callaghan studied her file and the image on his screen. He took a deep breath and said, "I'm sorry, but the news isn't good."

The air came rushing out of Rhiannon, she had been holding her breath. "Can I see?"

Callaghan's brow furrowed before he nodded. "Right. Doctor, I forgot." He swung the monitor around and showed them a close-up. "Here is the original site of the surgery, that's scar tissue, here and here. In the center, you can see the mass is growing again, it's the lighter colored part."

Jeri looked closely, took a picture of the monitor and tapped notes on her phone.

Doctor Callaghan left the monitor facing them and went back to his seat.

"So this is it?" Rhiannon asked. Her face was calm and her voice strong, but her eyes were wide.

"No," Callaghan said. "We try chemo now."

Rhiannon swallowed, her eyes going wider. "And what will that do to my quality of life?"

"The tumor is growing quickly now. If we don't slow it down the quality of life you have now won't last long."

"You said slow it," Jeri said, "not stop it."

The doctor nodded. "That is correct."

"How long?" Rhiannon asked.

"The chemo will buy you a few months."

The color drained from Rhiannon's face as she blinked rapidly. This wasn't really news to her, she had researched the disease relentlessly. But reading it and hearing it said about you are two vastly different things.

IT HAD GOTTEN TO THE POINT WHERE I DIDN'T WANT THESE memories anymore. I didn't want to witness the days that brought her to where she was now—in a coma, near death. I didn't want to see and feel her pain. I didn't want to witness her family's pain. I didn't want any of it.

And I could have stopped it. I could have stepped away from her bed, stopped feeding her the warmth, flown back to Arizona. I "could have," but I couldn't. I couldn't deny

Rhiannon sharing her memories, this one last intimacy between us.

Her decline was so difficult to witness. I saw her, during these memories, go from robustly healthy, to deathly ill. And let me tell you, this wasn't some well-lit montage in a tear-jerker movie. This was a real and visceral display of the human biological form and what happens when it fails.

It was traumatic to experience, and it was traumatic to witness. I could feel the trauma of my own witnessing and see it in the eyes of those around her.

Transmission #58
Received 2012/02/24 03:16:58

THAT NIGHT AFTER RHIANNON TOLD THOMAS ABOUT THE appointment and after the tears had run their course, they talked.

"You've got to promise me, Thomas," she said, "that as this thing progresses you let me have time with Joey. As much time as possible."

Thomas nodded. "Of course."

"I won't be carrying him around anymore. But I can still feed him. I can still hold him and play with him."

He nodded again.

"Promise me."

"I promise," he said.

"And a will, I need a will."

Thomas nodded again, his eyes far away.

"And we need to tell people. Jeri said she would email for us when we are ready."

Again Thomas nodded, but didn't speak. I think it was all too much. The reality they had all been denying was now undeniable.

THE CHEMO TOOK AWAY HER ENERGY AND MADE HER SICK. The steroids she took to reduce the swelling in her brain made her face puffy and her appetite voracious. She struggled with the nausea and hunger, each telling her to do different things. She...

I don't think I can write about this anymore. Banquo sent me here, told me to write, said it would help, and dangled the huge carrot of being his apprentice in front of me. But I don't know. What good can it possibly do for me to tell you how the love of my life suffered and died?

What good can come of it?

Whoever you are reading this right now, you know you are going to die. You know your time in this world is limited. You know you only get so many chances to do the things you want to do, to experience the things you want to experience, to make a difference.

You know that, don't you?

Maybe you do, maybe you know it intellectually, but I am here to tell you that when it happens to you, it's different. It's not simple or clean or easily captured in words. Right now if you are healthy, these are stories, these are concepts, they are not "real." Not until you are in it and can't escape. Then it's real. Then you get to see what you are made of.

If an accident doesn't take you quickly, like one did me, how will you die? Will you be courageous? Will you do it with your eyes open? Will you be strong?

You can try to answer those questions, but you don't really know, and you won't know until it is your turn. But I can tell you there are clues to how you will die in the way that you live.

Rhiannon was a bright, intelligent, and curious woman. She was strong, and loving, and imperfect. She was often self-conscious and worried too much about what others thought. She was loyal and surrounded herself with loyal friends.

And that all came into play in how she died. She was intelligent enough to know what was going on and strong enough to accept it, and she constantly worried about those around her, about being a burden to them.

I could go into much more detail about her physical decline, how she slowly lost control of her body, but that's just about enough. I think you get the idea of what she went through as her body slowly failed.

Actually it wasn't her body exactly, it was her brain. As the tumor grew, the weakness on her left side first became pronounced and then debilitating. As the tumor grew it affected her speech center, and she had more and more trouble communicating. The words just weren't available to her any more. And eventually the tumor grew enough so that curative medical interventions were no longer useful and she went into hospice.

And for a time, a brief time, hospice was almost perfect, almost a blessing. Almost.

Transmission #59
Received 2012/02/29 01:43:22

OK, I'M BACK. I COULDN'T TAKE IT ANYMORE AND STEPPED away from this for a few days until Banquo talked me down, literally.

After my last writing session I went back to the grave-yard. Actually I spent most of my time at elevation only coming down for the Midnight Circle. I started to go higher and higher above Tucson until I must have been twenty or thirty thousand feet up.

I needed to be that high. I needed to be high enough so that the city became one cohesive mosaic surrounded by the desert. Up there I couldn't see anything as separate. No people, no cars, nothing individual. It was only one thing. Then I couldn't be aware of the many, many stories the million people and ghosts were experiencing.

Up there I could pretend that everything was OK.

On my third day of doing this I heard a pop behind me. It was about noon on a crystal clear winter day with the city below me, small enough to seem inert, and the sun above me, eternal.

"Hello, Banquo," I said without turning. Who else would it be?

Banquo moved beside me and surveyed the view. "Nice. Good choice, I can see why you are spending so much time up here."

"Thank you," I said.

"You know," he began, "this is the equivalent of what the Earth Sleepers do. You favor air, instead of earth."

"Earth Sleepers?"

"Yeah, you know. What Old Man Perkins and your friend John do. Spending the day with their bones."

"This is the same?" I asked.

He chuckled. "It's similar. You come here to remove yourself from the world. To rest. To rejuvenate. That's what they do when they go down with their bones."

I nodded. It made sense, but hanging with my bones still did not appeal.

"I must say," he continued, "the view is better from up here."

I didn't answer. I could feel the lecture coming and I didn't want it. Not then. "What do you want, Banquo?" I asked, forcing the issue.

Banquo smiled at me and nodded. "You're not writing anymore."

"Yeah. Done with that," I said.

"Yet the story is unfinished, and if the story is unfinished, our deal is..." he trailed off, not completing the sentence.

I looked at him. I was going to ask how he knew, but realized it was perfectly obvious. A three-day-long brood would make it clear to anyone who cared to look. "So?" I ended up asking.

He shrugged. "Write or don't write, study with me or don't. Just do both for the right reason."

I sighed. I wasn't in the mood for a lecture, especially one peppered with such fortune cookie wisdom.

"So why aren't you writing?" he asked.

So I told him. I let it come gushing out in a torrent of words. I told him how much it hurt reliving what had happened to Rhiannon. I told him how I would much rather die myself again and again than to watch someone I love die.

I wanted to stop speaking. I wanted some control over what I was saying, but once the words started, I couldn't stop them. I hadn't realized just how much I had needed to talk about it.

When I was done, tears flowed down my cheeks, and I looked at Banquo. His eyes were moist with tears too. "I am sorry, my friend," he said gently. "That is so hard."

Well, an open display of kindness and compassion from Banquo just made me cry more. Not that he wasn't compassionate, I knew he was. Everything about what Banquo did with his days screamed of it. But the direct, unambiguous expression of it caught me by surprise.

The tears finally stopped and I thanked him. He said, "You need to keep going, you know."

I laughed. I couldn't help it. It was, in some ways, a relief. My mentor was back to telling me what I needed to do. Not what I wanted to do, not that I agreed with him. But just that we were back to our typical way of relating was a relief. "Why should I?" I asked.

"When you were alive did you ever have a splinter that got in deep?" he asked. I nodded. "One that you had to dig out, that hurt like hell in the process? And once you finally got it all out your finger began to quickly heal?"

"Yes, of course," I said.

"Well, this is like that."

"Are you saying my grief over what happened to Rhiannon is a splinter in my finger?"

"No," he said shaking his head. "Of course not. The splinter in the finger is an analogy. I am only saying it is the kind of wound that will hurt a lot more while you do what you need to do to take care of it."

I nodded, he was right. Damn it.

"And once you do have it out, you will know. Because just like a finger with a splinter removed, healing will happen quickly. You're almost there, JJ. Don't give up now."

I looked at him and held his gaze for a long time. "This isn't something I expect to ever go away," I said.

"No, of course not. But you've been through this kind of thing before. You can get to a place where it doesn't rule your life anymore."

I nodded. He was right. Floating thirty thousand feet above Tucson didn't hurt as much as writing about Rhiannon, but I wasn't getting better either.

Transmission #60
Received 2012/02/29 04:02:39

OK, SO BACK TO RHIANNON. BACK TO WHAT HAPPENED to her. I've decided that I am going to tell the story, but I am going to leave out some of details of what happened to her physically.

Just trust me that there are points along the journey with a disease like this that are messy and humiliating and very difficult for the one experiencing it and the ones witnessing it. A slow death is a biological process, a decidedly messy one.

So where were we? Between that first trip to the ER, and the last trip to the ER, right before hospice, was about nine months.

First surgery, then radiation, and then chemo.

Each intervention helped, by either removing the tumor or slowing its growth. But each intervention came with its own cost.

So, after chemo and before hospice she did pretty well. Her balance was poor, and she started having a lot of trouble finding the right words, but her quality of life was pretty good.

It wasn't the life she once had, but it wasn't bad. She could get around OK, she could feed herself, and she could spend time with Joey.

Joey was growing so fast, and changing every day. And that is what she wanted most, to be with him, to watch him grow while she could. But her family didn't allow enough of it, not enough for her.

And watching it, I got so angry. I could feel her emotions, not theirs. The concerns they expressed were for Joey's safety, which was understandable, but it doesn't really explain their behavior.

She looked different with her short hair, her steroid puffed face, her keeping her hand on walls as she walked, her trouble with finding words, but it was still her in there. She could think and reason clearly, but she didn't look normal and she couldn't communicate clearly.

And this scared those around her. She would beg for her son, and Thomas would bring him for ten minutes while she sat on the living room floor and played with him, with Thomas sitting and watching the whole time.

"No!" she said when Thomas took the baby. "Need Joey."

Thomas shook his head and said, "It's time for his nap, honey."

Rhiannon's brow furrowed as she tried to speak. "No! Play time."

Thomas just shook his head and took the baby away.

I could feel her anger. She was aware that she sounded like a child, but she wasn't one. The one word she always had access to was "no" and she used it a lot, and as the disease progressed she used it when she didn't mean to.

For example, one time Carol asked Rhiannon if she wanted to see Joey and she said, "No!" after which she scrunched her face and shook her fist expressing her frustration at the wrong word coming out. This was becoming her "yes," but Carol took the "no" at face value and left her there with only the TV to keep her company.

Jeri seemed to understand. Maybe it was because she was a doctor, too (but then again so was Thomas), maybe it was because she had been with her own mother in hospice as she died from cancer, a story I heard her tell Rhiannon. I'm not sure, but Jeri didn't treat her like a child. Jeri didn't focus on her dying, she did her best to help Rhiannon live those last days to their fullest extent.

Jeri created a set of 3x5 cards with words printed on them that Rhiannon could use to communicate clearly: "Joey," "Hungry," "Leave me alone," "Hug please," "Bathroom."

And because of this, as the days slipped past, she began to cling to Jeri.

She did pretty well, finding enough words, right until close to the end. Right up until the seizures started.

Have you ever seen someone, in person, have a seizure? Have you ever seen someone you love have one? If you've answered "no," count yourself as blessed. It is a horror.

Well, at first they weren't. At first Rhiannon would sit very still, her eyes blank for a bit, sometimes a minute or two. These were her first seizures, but they went unnoticed and were only recognized in retrospect.

When the real seizures started, everyone knew about it. Jeri was with her and called 911 when it happened.

She was rushed to the hospital where they did a CT

scan on her. While they were waiting for the results she had another one.

Nope, I'm not going to describe the seizure. Sorry, I just can't. It was horrible to watch. But I did learn that Rhiannon never remembered them. She lost time and had no memory of the trauma her body went through. The seizures were hard on those around her, but not her. And that was some comfort to me as I watched.

This was one of those moments when I got to see something she couldn't remember—the power of Awareness of Others. Whatever I was tapping into was pulling in everything I needed to understand her experience.

When her oncologist, Doctor Callaghan, came in, his round face was sad. He gave the bad news gently, but it was "the" bad news. "There is nothing more we can do medically. It's time to think about hospice."

Thomas was there, and Rhiannon's father, Kyle, as well as Jeri. Kyle is a good man, but this whole thing had been too much for him. He would come in and visit for a day or two, but for the most part he wasn't very present.

"Well, there must be something we can do," he said to the doctor a little too loudly. "Can't you operate again? Take that thing out?"

Callaghan shook his head. "I'm sorry. The cancer has spread. It's moved into the left ventricle, this is what is causing the seizures."

"I can't accept that," he said, his arms crossed. "I want a second opinion."

Doctor Callaghan shook his head. "I understand." He turned to Rhiannon and asked, "Do you want a second opinion?"

Rhiannon's eyes got wide, and I could see Jeri squeeze

her hand and slowly nod, encouraging her. She looked at her father, and then her husband and then back to Jeri. She swallowed and then slowly shook her head "no."

The doctor waited a beat, the room was dead silent. "Just to be clear. You are saying you don't want a second opinion, correct?"

Rhiannon, her eyes wide, tears starting to form, shook her head, "yes."

"Well, I don't accept that," Kyle said. "That's not good enough. I've already lost my wife, I can't lose my daughter. I can't."

I felt for the guy, he was about to lose his daughter, what could be worse than that?

He turned to Thomas, "Are you going to let this stand?"

Thomas blinked, his jaw moving as he ground his teeth under clenched lips. "Yes sir, I am. This is her choice to make."

Well, that made up for a lot of the Joey crap in my book.

The argument escalated until Rhiannon, weak from the seizures and grieving the news herself, shouted "No!" She held up her "Leave me alone" card and pointed at her father and her husband as tears flowed down her cheeks. "No!"

"Rhi," Kyle began. "You're so young. There must be—"

"No!" Rhiannon shouted again, cutting him off. She swallowed hard as she struggled for the words. "Please. Leave."

Kyle nodded, blinked back his own tears and slowly walked out of the room.

After he left a thick silence descended. The doctor interrupted it when he said, "Should I send in a social worker to talk to you about hospice?"

Rhiannon stared at him for several breaths. Then she

quietly said, "no." Then her faced scrunched and she made a fist.

"That means 'yes,'" Jeri offered.

Rhiannon shook her head and pointed at the cards. Jeri pulled out the "yes" card, and Rhiannon held it up.

"So," the doctor said, "you do want to talk to the social worker about hospice."

She shook the card and said, "no," her hand coming to her mouth as she laughed and shook the "yes" card some more.

KYLE WAS GONE FOR A FEW HOURS, BUT WHEN HE CAME back he had changed. The look on his face was grim and stony, but he didn't argue with his daughter anymore. He stood guard over her like some great she-bear protecting her cub, and he made sure she got what she wanted.

It was stunning, really, and touching. I don't know what he did on that walk, but he left not accepting what was happening and came back her fierce protector.

From then on he was the one that handled the tough decisions. He made the funeral arrangements, he made sure legal matters were taken care of, he coordinated with the hospice so Rhiannon could die in her own home like she wanted.

I was impressed, and I can tell you I don't know how he did it. I don't know how he could have turned that corner so quickly, from resisting her death, to embracing it. And frankly, I worry about what it cost him.

But he did it and that evening Rhiannon was in her home in the hospital bed I was now standing beside as I let the warmth flow into her and witnessed her memories.

It took a village to help her die. Her father, Kyle, handling the gritty details, Jeri and Gail communicating with her friends and coordinating some good-byes with the closest of them, and Thomas and Carol taking care of Joey and the household.

But the hardest work was Rhiannon's.

Transmission #61
Received 2012/03/01 01:28:56

"Hey sweetie," Nate said when he entered the room. Rhiannon smiled as he leaned over and kissed her cheek. "I like the new look," the big man said, his hand going to his own head and his very short black hair.

She nodded.

Jeri offered him the chair she had been sitting in and Nate lowered his bulk down into it and took Rhiannon's hand.

As the days slipped by in hospice, Rhiannon had lost all her words but "no," but was having pretty good days. She was on anti-seizure medicine and morphine for the pain. Jeri arranged for her to eat her favorite foods when she wanted and coordinated these visits.

Communication was tricky. It was twenty questions, with Rhiannon answering "no" most of the time.

"Umm..." Nate began, looking at Jeri. "I..."

"Just sit," Jeri said. "Talk to her, tell her stories. Remember the good times." With that she left.

Nate nodded, but then sat there silently and awkwardly for a time. "Ma sends her best," he said finally.

Rhiannon smiled and nodded.

"She wanted to come but... Oh hell, Rhi, the truth is she couldn't come. Not after JJ."

Rhiannon's face lit up and she put her hands together and then opened them up, her eyes tracing a horizontal path back and forth.

"You want me to read to you?"

She shook her head and held one hand up and shakily wrote "J" on it twice.

"JJ. You want me to talk about JJ's book? Or you want me to read JJ's book?"

Rhiannon looked straight at him and frowned.

"Sorry, two questions." He paused, and then laughed. "This is just like when JJ came as a light. I had to ask simple yes/no questions one at a time."

Rhiannon smiled and nodded.

"So," Nate continued. "Do you want me to talk about the book?"

Rhiannon shook her head up and down enthusiastically.

"Well, it's all there. How Jin and Tam created the SECI chamber. How JJ died. All the crazy stuff he did." His face fell as he added, "All the stupid stuff I did."

She squeezed his hand and slowly shook her head "no."

"Not stupid?" Nate asked.

She kept shaking her head no and touched her own heart.

"I do miss him," he said. "God how I miss him." He paused, his eyes looking far away. "I know he's out there. Hell, he could be here right now. But it's just not the same."

She smiled and signaled for Nate to come close with her

hand. Nate did and she, with great effort, leaned up and kissed his cheek.

When Nate sat back down, he said, "You miss him too?"

She nodded her head and pointedly looked around the room.

"Do you think he's here?" he asked.

She shrugged.

"He might be. I left a message for him a few months ago. If he finds it in time he'll be here. If he can, you know he will."

Her eyes widened and she flapped her hand back and forth.

"More?"

She smiled and shook her head.

So, Nate sat there and told her about the foundation and SECI 2.0 and Anna-Beth, and then eventually he started talking about the past. About when Rhiannon, Nate, and I had spent so much time together, when we had been young and foolish and in love.

That may be a strange way to say it, "in love," but we were. Rhiannon and I were in a romantic relationship. But Nate and I loved each other, and Rhiannon and Nate loved each other. It was a love triangle, the good kind.

We had lots of good times. And Nate, being no dummy, once he got Rhiannon laughing, he just kept telling stories and they both laughed until she became too tired to hear them anymore.

Beyond the laughter I could see how Nate looked at her. He was in pain, for what she had been experiencing and for what was yet to come.

Transmission #62
Received 2012/03/01 03:56:32

HOSPICE WAS FASCINATING. PART OF ME, AS I WATCHED her memories flow, was intrigued by the processes. It was this abrupt turn from "anything to keep you alive" to "anything to keep you comfortable."

The medical journey Rhiannon had been on had been about survival, and everything was sacrificed in the name of that survival. Dignity, comfort, quality of life. It was all about extending life. There was some attention to quality, but it was kind of perfunctory. The real focus was on quantity.

When hospice came in, it shifted to the other extreme. Since death was assumed to be close, everything was about quality of life. From morphine to battle pain, to the anti-seizure medications, it was about making her final days the best they could be.

And that's the thing. Before, when they were fighting the cancer, the interventions were about the cancer. In hospice it was all about Rhiannon.

Don't get me wrong, I am not saying that quality of life should not be compromised in fighting cancer. What I am saying is that it was a relief when quality of life became the focus.

It was clearly a relief to Rhiannon. The morphine alone did a lot to help her feel better.

Led by Kyle and Jeri, her remaining days became about quality too. Visiting with friends and family, rewatching her favorite movies, eating whatever she wanted, when she could eat, that is.

It was beautiful and it was heartbreaking.

The one battle that Kyle lost was the battle for Joey. When it became clear that that was what his daughter wanted most, but wasn't getting enough of, he went to war.

You have to understand what it took for Rhiannon to express this. It took an hour with Jeri, who understood her best, and Kyle for her to get it out. She couldn't speak, just a long arduous game of yes/no, with her often saying "no" and shaking her fist instead of saying "yes."

"You want Joey, as much as you can?" Kyle asked, his eyes hard and his jaw set. "Right, honey, that is what you want?"

She shook her head vigorously.

"What about seizures?" Kyle asked.

Rhiannon looked at Jeri and widened her eyes.

"She hasn't had any, not the violent kind, not since she has been on the meds. She occasionally has the spaced-out kind, but those aren't a danger."

"OK," he said as he stood. He leaned and kissed his daughter on the forehead. "Consider it done."

The fight that ensued was loud and protracted. I couldn't hear the exact words but the tone was obvious.

Rhiannon's emotions during this were complex, but shame topped the list. Jeri did her best to distract her, turning the TV up, offering to play *Titanic* again, but it didn't help.

Rhiannon felt guilty that she had gotten sick, that she had cancer. As if she had done something wrong, as if it was her fault. That shame was deep and dark, and one of the hardest feelings she battled with during that time.

After the loud voices ended I heard the front door slam hard, and we didn't see Kyle or Joey for the rest of the day.

I wish I could say that I understood, but I can't. There were obviously concerns for the baby, now over a year old, and his safety around his mother. But she wasn't having violent seizures, and she didn't have much time. What the hell was the problem?

And I have thought long and hard about this and there is only one explanation. They feared something beyond the seizures. Thomas and his mother Carol feared death itself and they could not look at Rhiannon and not see death, not see their own, and Joey's, eventual death.

The other thought I have had, when I am being my most charitable to them, is that the contrast was too much. They were caring for a baby, which was all about life, and Rhiannon, which was all about death. That contrast was just too much, so they pulled away, and pulled Joey away, long before it was necessary or appropriate.

It brought Rhiannon great pain, this withholding of her son, being limited to pitifully short visits, most of those with Thomas holding the baby.

And since it brought Rhiannon pain, it made me angry. Mad. Furious.

Kyle kept trying, kept fighting for what his daughter wanted, but before long it didn't matter anymore. Rhiannon started pushing everyone and everything away. She began to use the "leave me alone" card more and more. She was unconscious a lot more, and when she was conscious she only wanted Jeri or Gail with her.

At first I was confused by this, but I think now I understand why. Rhiannon was letting go. As her body failed her, she was emotionally letting go of the world and the people around her.

Jeri, somehow, was the only one that could gracefully allow her that. She could sit in silence with her or spend hours reading Harry Potter to her. Jeri was clearly going through her own experience around Rhiannon's dying process, but somehow she managed to leave that at the door and focus on living with Rhiannon to whatever degree she was able to live.

Rhiannon even got to the point where she refused to see Joey.

"Joey's awake and fed, Thomas can bring him in. Do you want to see him?" Kyle asked.

Rhiannon shook her head once.

"Why not, honey. He wants to see his mama."

She shook her head again and looked to Jeri.

"She's tired, Mr. Pope. She needs more space right now."

Kyle left, but I could tell that he was hurt and confused. It was understandable considering all the battles he had fought to get Rhi more time with Joey.

Towards the end, food became a big issue. Meals were something that Thomas did a lot of when he was home. He was a good cook, the main cook for the family, and found some joy in making her whatever she wanted.

But towards the end it became a bone of contention. He wanted to feed her, she didn't want to eat.

Both impulses seem natural. Thomas wanted to feed her

because it was normal, it sustained life. Rhiannon didn't want to eat because she was dying and letting go of life.

There was a brief period when she ate to please Thomas, but it made her feel worse. The anti-nausea medication was increased but eating was no longer the right thing for her to do. Her body, with what strength it had, needed to do other things besides digesting food.

"You've got to eat," Thomas said. They were alone; Jeri was gone and Gail hadn't arrived.

She shook her head and pressed her lips together tight like a petulant child.

"Just some soup, dear. Please."

She shook her head again.

"Please," he repeated, bringing a spoonful of broth close to her mouth.

She looked hard at Thomas and slowly shook her head. It wasn't a childish "no," but a grown-up one.

It wasn't enough, he harangued her until she opened her mouth and took the broth.

I wanted to kill him, right then and there. It was a memory, of course, and I wasn't really there so I couldn't do anything. But the emotion that hit me was intense and overwhelming. Some of it might have been Rhiannon's, I'm not sure. Maybe I'm naïve, but it's hard for me to believe she could have felt that same emotion so strongly.

She took two spoonful's and refused again on the third. After more emotional pleas she accepted it, but didn't swallow. Rhiannon spit it back out at Thomas and fumbled through her stack of cards.

"What is wrong with you?" he shouted as he stood, wiping soup off of his face.

She said, "No!" as loudly as she could, which at that

point wasn't very loud. She continued to fumble with her cards.

"You have to eat," he said.

"No!"

"Please. Please don't do this." Thomas shook his head, tears running down his face. I don't think he consciously understood what he was doing and why he was doing it. I don't think he wanted to cause his wife suffering on her deathbed. I don't think he's a bad person.

What I do think is that even though he is a doctor, he had no grasp of death or the dying process. I think he wasn't ready to let his wife go, even though it was almost time. I think that, even though when I witnessed that memory I wanted to kill him, he was doing the best he could. Letting go the best way he could.

But here's the thing. I know what he was being asked to do was beyond difficult, letting go of his love, his wife, the mother of his young child, but what Rhiannon was doing was much harder.

She was letting go of everything.

Transmission #63
Received 2012/03/02 01:59:48

IN THOSE MEMORIES SHE BEGAN TO SLEEP MUCH, MUCH more. It was clear because when consciousness came things kept changing. Jeri or Gail would still be sitting there reading Harry Potter, but their clothing would be different and they would be in a different place in the story.

What I saw through Rhiannon's eyes also changed. Light became hurtful, and through a long, desperate session of yes/no she managed to convey to Thomas that the drapes should be kept closed.

I was aware that she felt this growing distaste for her body. As it became heavier and heavier she felt she had little or no use for it. It felt like a boat anchor, a throwback, or a vestige, kind of like an appendix. It didn't seem "right" anymore.

There were flashes of faces as the final visitors came. Tim, her high school sweetheart, the one she had been with right before me, her Aunt Judy, her cousin Bobby. But they were all too late. She didn't care, she couldn't care. A dim part of her awareness recognized them, and memories of them flitted by, but it was a distraction from what she was trying to do. And what she was trying to do was—

I think this is going to sound strange, but bear with me. This experience I was having with Rhiannon, that I was witnessing so intensely, was a very different death from the one I had. Very different. Honestly, I am still coming to terms with it. It is not one of those things you can just shrug your shoulders with and move on. It requires introspection and thought. A lot of both.

So, I am sure it looked like she was dying, but to her it felt different. It felt like she was trying to escape the body. The body had failed, the body was dying, and Rhiannon, the essential Rhiannon, was trying to climb into the life raft and escape the sinking ship.

But, the meat, her body, had a hold on her, a tight grip. She was so used to it, she was so attached to it—literally and psychologically—that it was difficult.

So while it looked like Rhiannon was dying, it felt like she was being born. This pressure bore down on her, and it was clear in that memory state with Rhiannon that at some point that pressure would drive her forth and she would be... she would be born.

I don't use that word "born" lightly, but it is the best word I can come up with. Maybe this state is like a caterpillar transforming into a butterfly. Its old form no longer useful, the caterpillar creates a cocoon and emerges as a butterfly. A completely new entity.

With that in mind, the way she withdrew from the world, from the people focused on her "dying," even from her son, makes sense. She was working very hard on making that transition from caterpillar to butterfly, from living to...

I still struggle with the whole "dead" thing. Sure, I'm a ghost, sure I'm "dead," but I am still alive. Language fails.

So, her transformation was from life to death, but maybe the clarification I can make that will help is this. It was from biological life to biological death. The soul lives on, clearly.

Soon the memories ended and I found myself back in the room with Rhiannon, left with this sense of pressure and anticipation.

And then I heard a voice say, "JJ?"

THE FOOL

Transmission #64
Received 2012/03/02 03:54:34

In the dark room, I heard Jeri quietly reading and saw Thomas sleeping in a chair next to Rhiannon's bed.

I had been vaguely aware of their comings and goings during my memory time with Rhiannon, but now I was fully present and quite disoriented. I stood at the head of her bed, my hands under her head, pumping the warmth into her.

I heard a wet rattling breath, slow and uneven coming from the bed.

"JJ?" I heard a voice say again. It was a female voice, sweet and light, tinged with fear, and as familiar to me as my own.

I shook my head and saw Rhiannon. She was sitting up in the bed, her head craned so she could see me. She looked like her old self with long hair and a slimmer face.

What the hell? I kept the warmth flowing, it would have felt unnatural to stop at that point, and moved around the bed, staring at Rhiannon.

She was sitting up in bed, but she was lying down too.

"Rhi?" I asked. As I moved, things became clearer. Her

body was still in bed, a shuttering, rattling breath coming from it. Her breathing was inconsistent, with some long pauses in between. But, her spirit, her ghostly form, was sitting up—it had somehow partially separated from her body.

"I thought it was you," she said, smiling thinly. "Have you been here long?"

I shrugged. "Not sure. A while. I'm so sorry, honey."

"It's OK," she said, but then her face fell. "No, I take that back. This dying stuff sucks!"

"I'm here, Rhi. I can help you."

"Am I... am I dead?"

I shook my head noticing how her bodies, biological and spirit, separated at the waist, but were still joined in the legs. "Not yet. Soon, though."

"What will happen?" she asked quietly.

I blinked several times and felt woefully unprepared. I wasn't sure what would happen, Banquo hadn't covered this phenomenon in any of his lessons. "I'm not quite sure. I think you will continue to separate from your body."

Rhiannon's eyes grew wide as she twisted around to look at her physical form. The body was quiet now, in the long pause in between breaths.

"But I'm not breathing, JJ," she said her eyes wide. "I'm not breathing."

"It's OK, just wait a—" I said, stopping in mid-sentence when a moist shuddering inhale occurred.

"Sorry," she said turning to me, "I guess I shouldn't be afraid, huh?"

"It's OK to be afraid. You have every right to be."

"Thank you for coming, JJ. Did you get Nate's message?"

I nodded. "I'm glad I'm here for you, Rhi."

Rhiannon nodded and sat silent for a long time, her

gaze traveling the room to her sleeping husband and her reading friend. Her gaze went back to Thomas. "He did his best. This is not the kind of thing you expect to have to deal with at our age."

Her statement stunned me. The anger that I had acquired during the memories was still with me, and here she was forgiving him already. Empathizing with him. Having compassion for him.

"He did," I agreed. It was more than anyone should be asked to bear.

"Oh," Rhiannon said, a look of surprise on her face.

"What is it?" I stood next to her bodies, my hands still pumping warmth into her, right under her lower back.

"I think it's... I think it's time. Oh!" I couldn't tell if what she was experiencing was fear or surprise or ecstasy. Maybe it was a little of each.

Her body took one last shuddering breath and let it out in a long slow exhale. Rhiannon's ghostly form separated from her body and floated up about a foot. I could see the silver cord I had not seen before going from her physical body's belly button to her ghost form's belly button.

Jeri stopped reading, closed her book and came over to the body. She pulled out a stethoscope and placed it to the chest of the body. She held it there for several moments before looking at her watch and saying, "Time of death 5:16 a.m." She let the stethoscope dangle from her neck and put her hand on the chest of what was once Rhiannon. She stood there, silent tears flowing down her cheeks. "Goodbye, sweet Rhiannon, I love you. I will miss you. Find peace."

The silent tears became a strangled sob. Thomas woke up and stared at her, his eyes blinking as he looked from her to Rhiannon's body and back again. Jeri gave a small nod to his questioning look and Thomas began to cry. It wasn't a quiet sob but a loud wracking cry. It enveloped his body as he got up and stood by the corpse. He gestured for the stethoscope and Jeri gave it to him. He stopped sobbing, by holding his breath, long enough to confirm what Jeri already knew.

As the tears came back, Jeri leaned over Rhiannon's body and grabbed him. They both stood there weeping, holding each other for a very long time.

THE FOOL

Transmission #65
Received 2012/03/04 01:26:31

I USED TO THINK THAT A LONG DEATH, A PROTRACTED death, like Rhiannon experienced would be easier. Easier on the dying and easier on the survivors. Now, I'm not so sure.

Going quick has its advantages. No tearful good-byes, no misbehaving relatives, no having to endure the difficult and messy process of your body shutting down.

Going slowly has its advantages too. You get to say good-bye, and at least have a chance to come to terms with your passing—you have time to adjust and let go.

And here's the truth. They both suck. Whichever one you experience with a loved one, you will probably wonder if the other one would have been better. And whichever death you experience, if you end up a ghost like me, you might find yourself wishing you had experienced the alternative.

But either way, it's hard. How isn't really that relevant. It's hard any way it goes.

Rhiannon floated above her body watching her husband and her best friend fresh in their grief. She seemed calm, but I was worried and had no idea what to do. Should I get her out of here or encourage her to stick with it? Should I try to comfort her or let her find her own way? I did my best to turn away from my own thoughts and emotions and to become aware of her emotions and needs.

After a few minutes, Thomas and Jeri separated and blew their noses.

"Thank you so much," Thomas said, "for all you brought to her in this... her..." he trailed off in a long sigh.

"Of course, of course." She blew her nose again and looked around the room. "I guess I better go tell her dad."

Thomas nodded, looking down.

"Where is he?" Jeri asked.

"He's asleep in our bedroom," Thomas said.

Jeri nodded and slowly walked out leaving Thomas alone with the body. He stood there blinking hard, took a step to leave the room but then reversed and stepped right back. He slowly sat down next to Rhiannon's corpse.

"I don't... I don't understand why," he said. "Why this had to happen to you. Why you had to leave us so soon. What... what am I going to do?" The questioned trailed off into more tears.

Rhiannon turned from the scene below and said, "I don't think I can handle this."

I nodded, because I didn't think I could handle it either. "Let's get you out of here," I said. I looked over her form, it was wispy, but relatively well formed for a new ghost. I modulated my hand to match hers and took it. That feeling of touch, that ghostly numb sensation was a thrill for me. It was the closest we ghosts get to the sensation and really the thing I missed most, touching and being touched. Rhiannon's eyes widened; she felt something too.

I knew there could be a problem, her cord not stretching

far enough for us to leave the house, but I didn't say anything. I smiled and slowly pulled her to the back wall of the room where the window was.

She looked back, watching her grieving husband as we flew, and soon we were out of the house.

Rhiannon looked around and so did I. I hadn't been out of that room since I had gotten there. We were in a little backyard with some raised garden beds, a patio, and a small section of grass.

"What happens now?" she asked.

I shrugged. "Well, at some point the mortuary will come for your body. There will be a funeral, you know." I felt inarticulate, my mind struggling to know what to do or say.

Her brows furrowed and she got a serious look on her face. "When they take the... my body away, will I go with it?" She looked down at the silver cord that went through the brick wall of the house back into the room that contained her body.

"Yes, unless we can cut the cord."

"How?" she asked.

"You have to want it enough. You have to let go of your body, accept that you are dead. It's not easy, it's—" I stopped speaking when I heard a "crack" and her cord disappeared.

She looked down and smiled, "Well, that wasn't so hard."

It had taken me days, had been a major ordeal, and here she did it with just a thought. "Wow," was all I could say.

"What now?" she asked.

"Let's get some elevation," I said.

"What?" she asked as I took her hand again and guided her straight up.

It was pre-dawn in Houston and as we slowly flew, the scene below us resolved into the lights from streets and the highways and the houses of the city with a few car head-lights cutting through.

"It's lovely," Rhiannon said, "but what am I doing here? Why am I a ghost?"

"I don't know, honey. Generally it's because we have something left to do. You read what I wrote. I had a lot to go through after I died coming to terms with it."

Rhiannon looked puzzled, and it scared me. What she said next scared me even more. "JJ, I know I'm dead. I get it. I will grieve my life, I understand that. But, I don't think I want to be a ghost."

Ever since I found out from Nate's video that Rhiannon was dying I had been harboring a thought deep in my sub-conscious, one that I was only dimly aware of. Like a weed, it wormed its way through my consciousness, permeating deeply into my psyche. An unexpressed desire, a dream really, one that would make everything OK, one that would make me happy.

That hope, that dream, was of Rhiannon and I being together as ghosts. Back at the graveyard, Jim and Jane are one of the happiest couples I have ever known, living or dead. That dream, that insidious dream, was that Rhian-non and I would have our second chance in the afterlife. That the love of my life would finally come back to me, that I would finally be complete again.

That realization came sweeping over me when she said, "I don't think I want to be a ghost." I floated there in front of her, gape-jawed, as I realized how badly I wanted it and how wrong it was.

Wanting to love her, to be with her, wasn't wrong. What was wrong is that I needed it, that I wasn't OK without her, that this one thing would magically make my life—excuse me, afterlife—suddenly OK.

The world doesn't work that way.

"Are you OK, JJ?" Rhiannon asked.

I saw her looking at my form and I looked down, I had gone all wispy. I tightened it up and answered, "I'm fine. It's... I..."

"I'll always love you, JJ," she said as if she had been reading my thoughts, as if she had mastered Awareness of Others as quickly as she had mastered Cutting the Cord. "I don't want to stay and watch my family grieve. I don't want to live in a graveyard."

"What about..." I stammered, feeling guilty for even thinking of it, much less saying it. "What about Joey?"

Rhiannon's face darkened and she turned and stared back down at her house hundreds of feet below us. She turned back to me, crossed her arms and said, "I'll be able to see Joey from heaven. I can't imagine a heaven where I wouldn't be able to check in on my loved ones. Can you help me, JJ? Please."

Rhiannon and I both had a background in the Christian faith, but when we were together it wasn't an active thing. This surely wasn't what I was expecting and certainly was not what I had experienced.

I took a deep breath and nodded my head. "Of course, Rhi. Please excuse my momentary lapse." I smiled at her and made her believe it. She smiled back and gave me a small nod as if to say she was ready.

Turning my back on my own desires, I focused on Rhiannon. I opened myself up to her, to Awareness and felt. I felt her fear of staying, of being a ghost like me, and I felt that she was ready to go.

I looked back down at my form and saw that it was crisp but too transparent. I focused until it was as good as I could make it and turned my attention back to her.

"Do you hear it, Rhi?" I began, my voice calm and deep, my fears pushed aside, my focus on her. "Do your hear the Call? It's like music, the most beautiful music you ever heard. But it's not just music, you can feel it and see it and taste it. It's all around you, it's here to take you home."

As I spoke, Rhiannon first looked confused, then looked around, and then her face relaxed and a smile grew. As she smiled I could sense the Call too. It sang to me of unrelenting beauty, of peace, of redemption, of an end of suffering.

"You hear it," I said.

She nodded. "Oh my God, JJ. It is extraordinary. How did you say no to this?"

I shrugged and smiled at her. Her form changed, becoming brighter as if someone turned the color saturation of a picture way up. She was dazzling to look at.

"It's... Oh my God, it's so beautiful. Thank you, JJ. Thank you!"

I smiled, really smiled. Seeing her suffuse with color and joy and life was a wonderful thing. "Just say 'yes,' hon, and you'll be there."

She took a deep breath, her attention turning back to me. "Come with me, JJ," she said, her face radiant, her hand reaching towards me. "We can explore this... this wonderful place together."

Now, I had managed to sublimate my own desires, turn my back on my terrible need to be with her, and now this. My mind reeled. And as she issued the invitation, the Call became louder, more intense. Not like it was just here for her, but maybe it was here for me too. That I could go too.

At war in me was... well, it is hard to explain, hard to draw clean lines around, hard to express, but I will try. On one hand, I didn't think I was ready, I didn't think I deserved redemption yet, and didn't think I had lived enough or learned enough. I wanted to learn more from Banquo, I wanted to know how my friend Jesus was doing, I wanted to be here for Nate and Ma, and my sister Jean when it was their time.

On the other hand, there was Rhiannon glowing with the beauty of the Call, beckoning me to go with her, to be with her. But I knew there was something not right in my "need" for her. Something not healthy, something codependent.

And finally, there was the Call itself, whispering to me of an end of suffering, an end of guilt, of redemption.

I gave her my best smile and shook my head. It was the best I could do, I couldn't speak it, I couldn't say "no" to her. When I did, the Call faded, it was still there, but clearly not there for me anymore.

She smiled and nodded, "I understand." And I am sure she did. I suspect she understood better than I did.

"I have always loved you, JJ," she said, and with that, she was gone.

"I have always loved you, Rhiannon," I said to the empty space that once was her.

Transmission #66
Received 2012/03/04 03:45:47

I JUST FLOATED THERE, FOR HOW LONG I DON'T KNOW, stunned, staring at the empty space that once contained Rhiannon. It happened fast and for a time I was numb.

That didn't last, though.

The desire, the need, that had wormed its way through my psyche—to be with Rhiannon again—turned on me soon enough. It wasn't gone, I had just ignored it while I did what I thought was the right thing. Once the numbness faded, I was left with that need, a need that could never be satisfied.

And you might think that desire would just give up and die now that what it wanted couldn't be. You might think that, but you would be wrong. It turned on me. Or, rather, I turned on me.

I berated myself for making the wrong choice. I regretted not going with her. I hated myself for letting her go and not convincing her to stay. I could have convinced her if I tried, couldn't I?

This was grief, pure and simple, but I can't really tell you what stage it was. Anger, there was certainly a thread of anger in it. Denial, I wanted to pretend that I hadn't just completely screwed up. Depression, I wasn't quite there yet, but the shame and fear was a precursor. Deals, right then and there I would have done almost anything to turn things back.

But this wasn't just one of those stages, this was a chaotic blend of all of them descending on me together. And I was grieving not only her death, but her sudden, irrevocable disappearance. Once you answer that Call, that's it. You don't come back. End of story.

I silently floated there watching the spot that Rhiannon had been in. Afraid to leave it, afraid to move, as if that somehow would make it more real. But my inner turmoil became too great and I let out a howl and flew straight towards the moon.

It was the smallest of crescents, low on the eastern horizon, forming what looked like a white smile in the night sky. I focused on it and flew as fast as I could. I wanted to fly to the moon. Maybe that would give me enough elevation, enough perspective, to deal with what I was experiencing.

My flight felt strange, my gaze so focused on the moon as it rose that I had no point of reference. I could feel the effort I exerted, but I couldn't tell how far or how fast I was going. The moon didn't change; it just sat there in the sky mocking me with its sly grin.

A few hours later, the sun came up and started chasing the moon, but I only had eyes for the moon. She became Rhiannon to me, beautiful, distant, and untouchable.

Eventually I did look down, and saw Houston far, far below, nestled above the Gulf of Mexico. I had flown a long ways, but I really can't tell you how far. I had nothing to gauge it on. I could see the whole of Houston as well as Galveston and a long stretch of the Gulf Coast.

I turned from the moon and stared. I had never been up this far, except in an airplane, of course. The sliver of wonder I felt was a very small thing, but it distracted me from my pain, so I dwelled on it.

Maybe I was twenty or thirty thousand feet up. Maybe I could fly all the way to the moon. I turned back to the glowing crescent and immediately realized the foolishness of it. The moon orbits the earth. At the rate I flew I would, at best, just chase it around and around the planet. I could never catch it. Never.

And for some reason this struck me as funny. Some archetypal quest of foolishness, like Don Quixote tilting at windmills. I would be a fool to try.

And that made me laugh even more. High above Texas I lost it. Only a fool would try. Well, if I was anything, I was a fool. I remembered the gypsy Helen back at the graveyard and what she had told me of the Fool in the Tarot.

Laughing, I turned away from the city below and back towards the crescent moon and resumed flying.

Why not? What did I have to lose? I mean, really, what the hell did I have to lose? I was a ghost. I had just let the love of my life slip through my fingers. I would never get a chance to be with her again. What the hell did I have to lose by chasing the moon?

And in retrospect, I can only think of one thing. Sanity. Tilting at this windmill could cost me my sanity. The Fool seems to walk that line—he'll try things others won't because he's not burdened with the same load of notions and beliefs as those around him. He doesn't know what won't work so he'll try anything. And sometimes he does amazing and surprising things. And sometimes he's just a fool.

And to tell the truth, my sanity was pretty much gone there. On a long vacation, at the very least. What I was going through needed expression and chasing the moon was my way of expressing it.

So, I alternated between laughter and tears and just kept flying towards that crescent moon as it made its transit in the sky.

Now, I'm no astronomer, and I can't use Google to look this stuff up, so bear with my vagueness here, I am going from a rather poor memory of high school science classes. My improved ghostly memory doesn't help—I wasn't paying much attention.

So the moon takes about thirty days to orbit the earth, and the earth rotates once a day producing the moon-rise and moon-set. And moon-rise and moon-set are roughly twelve hours apart.

I started with the moon close to the eastern horizon, so that gave me around eleven hours before the moon set, a bit more since I was moving towards it.

I flew at maybe a hundred miles per hour, maybe more. I didn't have a useful point of reference, so I don't know. It felt like I was going faster than usual.

So I did my Fool's quest, laughing and crying most of the way, chasing the moon as it fled behind the curve of the earth. The path I took was roughly 1,000 miles, in a curve. At first straight east, and then straight up, and then arcing to follow the moon as it fled to the west.

Yeah, I know I'm geeking out a bit here, but I have to.

Where my grief and my Foolishness ended up taking me is kinda cool, and that ended up being kind of important.

So I ended up, roughly, three hundred miles above the earth's surface.

It was stunning. Jaw droppingly stunning. I knew, of course, it was happening, I could see it, but once the moon got close to the horizon, I stopped and really looked at where I was.

I could see the curve of the earth and space beyond the horizon. I could see the lights from Dallas and Phoenix. I could see Mexico and a storm brewing off of the Pacific.

It was extraordinary. It was a gift. I just floated there for the longest time and cried. Not just for the loss of Rhiannon but for the beauty of this world and the opportunity I had been given to see it like few have ever had.

I was the Fool then and I knew it. I embraced it, and I moved into gratitude and acceptance. But only for a moment, my grief still had a long ways to go.

Transmission #67
Received 2012/03/05 02:12:43

THAT MOMENT OF ACCEPTANCE DIDN'T LAST VERY LONG. It was a wonderful and hopeful moment, but brief. Soon the bardo came calling.

And it's really a good thing I took myself so far away. Who knows what I might have done if I had been around the living or the dead—I was not fit company for either.

Banquo's Rules of the Dead #5: *First do no harm.*

Yeah, I know, that is part of some oath doctors take. But it seems like an idea worth living by.

So in orbit, I couldn't harm others, which was great, but I could harm myself. When the bardo did come calling, I laughed at it and I cursed at it and I sent it away. I laughed because it seemed funny, how the hell could the bardo make me suffer more than I was right then? It could, of course, but in that moment I couldn't imagine it. I cursed at it because... well... hmmm, why did I curse at it? Because I was a little off my nut, because the bardo was an interference, a distraction, and at the same time, my worst enemy. Spending all that time in the bardo with John had changed me. I knew the bardo well. I knew how horrible it could be, but I also knew that I could defeat it.

So, I floated above Texas, the sun moving west.

I became fascinated with the idea of the terminus, that point where night becomes day. I wanted to see it. And somehow in my foolish madness I managed that. When I started my orbit, the terminus was far to the west, so I kept myself fixed over Texas until the sun came up in the east and the terminus was right below me. I then kept the sun fixed and watched the terminus as it made its slow way across the planet.

It was most interesting when the big cities went by: Phoenix and Tucson, Los Angeles, Tokyo, Moscow, London and much of Europe, New York City and the eastern seaboard, Chicago, and finally Dallas and Houston.

I loved watching how the cities transformed from night to day, from being lit by lights to being illumined by the sun.

As the earth turned I cycled through, in random order, these things: remembering Rhiannon and how I had lost her twice; weeping at my loss; laughing at what a fool (or Fool) I was; cursing at the bardo until it went away; remembering the trauma of my own death; and wondering about my friends and family below.

I was mad, as in crazy, but it felt safe to be mad up there. I couldn't hurt anyone or anything. The emotions I needed to feel could come out and express themselves. The earth and the perspective from this distance provided comfort and solace.

Just like the Grand Canyon, for me, always provides perspective, orbiting the earth at several hundred miles up did the same thing, only more. A lot more. Humanity and all its cares and concerns were still down there, but from up there it wasn't discernible, everyone and everything, all life, ran together to create the mosaic that I saw. It was the complete opposite of my experience when I was helping Jesus search for Javier. That was like looking at humanity under a microscope. This was like looking at all of life in one glance. All that was left was the awe and beauty of our planet.

It helped. Not that I wasn't still mad as a hatter for a few days, but without it I don't know what it would have taken for me to settle down.

After the earth had rotated below me for about six days, I started to get bored and sane. I wasn't over what had happened, I wasn't done grieving Rhiannon—not by a long shot—but I was stabilizing.

On that sixth rotation, I was aware enough to notice something. When North America was farthest away from me, when I was above Australia, it felt like my energy was a little thin.

I discounted it at first. I was way past the need to fade, to have some serious rest, but as I became aware of the feeling, I felt more energy as North America rotated closer. And actually this mystery, this mini-obsession, helped. It gave me something else to ponder besides my life and all its tragedies.

And here's what I came up with. The farther you are away from your "bones," as a ghost, the weaker you become.

It's only a theory at this point, and I have no idea what it means, but it's interesting, isn't it? What if I had been cremated and my "bones" had been distributed to the Pacific Ocean, slowly circulating over the years. How would that affect my energy levels? What if my remains had been put in a rocket and left on the moon or on a rocket that was slowly making its way out of the solar system? What would that do to my ability to be a ghost on Earth?

I'm not saying it's one of the great mysteries of the universe, just that it was enough to help pull me a bit further out of my funk.

I HAVE TO TELL YOU THAT THIS WORLD OF THE AFTERLIFE is strange, very strange. I mean, that's obvious at this point, right? It was obvious to me as I floated above the earth, off my nut grieving the loss of Rhiannon.

But what happened after several days in orbit, I would never have guessed.

This warm feeling came over me, concentrated around my head, and then my vision transitioned until I wasn't seeing just the earth below me, but a woman and two men staring up at me.

Yeah, weird. Three hundred miles up and I see the earth below, but I also see these people staring at me. And their faces are big, all three of them taking up the same space as the earth.

"What! Who... Who are you?" I asked. "I think I've finally lost it."

One of them, a sickly looking man with grey hair and a well-manicured goatee, looked at me, his eyes wide.

The pretty woman had sad eyes and brown hair pulled back into a ponytail. She didn't look like Rhiannon, but there were enough similarities to send me for a loop. She said, "I apologize, JJ. My name is Viki Dobos, and I have a gift."

A gift? What the hell kind of a gift could she have? I was several hundred miles above the earth seeing huge floating faces overlaid on my home planet. "You're real?" I asked. "I... I am not imagining this?"

"No," Viki said. "No, you are not. I can assure you this is quite real."

So, if they were real, I was kind of annoyed. I wasn't at my best and this was a hell of an interruption. "OK," I said. "And you do what?"

"I am a medium. I draw the dead and the drawing comes to life and the dead talk to the living."

"You know," I told her, "this is not a great time. I'm ... I'm kinda going through something right now. I came up here for privacy, not to get on some mystical skype call."

"Please, Mr. Lynch," the sickly looking man said. "Can you confirm you wrote this book?"

He held up a book, but it was kinda hard to see, overlaid on Eastern Asia as it was. I first recognized my name on it, and then I saw the title and knew what it was. "*Shuffled Off*... Nice title, Banquo's gonna love that," I said. "If you are asking, did I use the facilities at U of A to write a memoir of my life and death, then yes. Can I go now?"

The woman looked at the sickly man, who was apparently in charge. He gave her a small nod.

"Sorry to bother you, JJ," she said. I saw her lean in close and exhale toward me and then the three faces faded from my view.

As annoyed as I was by the interruption, I think it helped me. I spent the next few hours marveling that such a thing was possible (the living communicating directly with the dead), that this was somehow done by people (or at least one person) with a "gift" and by "drawing." I knew that Tam and Jin had turned my words into a book, but actually seeing it. Well, that was thrilling. I never in my whole life, not to mention my afterlife, expected to be an author.

The incident wasn't the end of my grief, only an intermission.

Transmission #68
Received 2012/03/05 03:59:17

WHEN NORTH AMERICA ROTATED BELOW ME FOR THE eighth time, I was almost ready to go. I was still struggling, but acceptance was coming for longer periods of time and my thoughts had turned to the future. I had an idea. Something that made me want to move forward in my life instead of looking backwards. Something that would require me to be the Fool again.

As I contemplated whether to fly back down to the ground or just let myself fade, I heard a "pop" and Banquo appeared.

His mouth fell open when he saw the earth far below us. "What? Oh... Oh my... JJ, you... Wonderful, just wonderful."

I laughed. Banquo was not one to be at a loss for words, and his reaction delighted me. "Nice view, huh?"

Banquo took a deep breath, recovering his composure and said, "Indeed, very nice view. What are you doing up here?"

I turned away from the earth and looked at Banquo and said, "Grieving."

He nodded. "Rhiannon?"

"Yes. She moved on. I helped her."

Banquo's appraising, awareness-filled gaze was longer than usual. "Well done, JJ. That must have been very difficult."

"I'll say. I've been a bit bonkers for a while."

Banquo nodded, as if me being bonkers was the most normal of things. "And now?"

I was surprised at how quickly this conversation was going. I had something to ask of Banquo and when I imagined asking him, it didn't look anything like this. I figured I'd have to tell him everything before he would hear what I wanted. But now, after one long look, he had invited me to ask.

"And now," I said, "I have an idea. Something I want to ask of you. Something big."

Banquo nodded and smiled, indicating that I should continue.

"I'm not ready to move on, Banquo. I summoned the Call for Rhiannon, she wanted to go, and she asked me to go with her. I said no."

"Why?" he asked.

I laughed, a brief snort, really. "I've been pondering that for the past week. And I can't tell you I completely understand besides saying that I'm not ready. But, I can tell you this. I was always obsessed with her in a way that wasn't all that healthy. Going with her would have been giving into that. I don't want to be that person anymore."

"OK," Banquo said.

"And I don't want to be one of those 'rest in peace' guys. I don't want to sleep with my bones every night like Old Man

Perkins, John, Walter, and all those folks. I'm not ready to be at peace."

Banquo smiled at me and laughed with his eyes. Me not wanting to rest in peace... I know, totally obvious, right?

"So I want to do something," I continued, "I want to do something of value while I am here like this." I pointed at myself indicating my ghostly state.

"And what is it that you want to do, JJ?"

"I want to be an 'ambulance chaser,' like you. I want you to teach me, really teach me." I felt fear in my belly as I said it. The kind of fear you might feel when you said you wanted to go to college for the first time, or when you said you were going to travel the world, or decided to have children, or do anything big and new and scary.

"Ambulance chaser?" he asked. "I don't think I follow."

"You showed up at the wreck Nate and I were at on I-10. When I was communicating with Nate and he was all messed up about it. You showed up. You helped the new ghosts move on."

"Ahh," he said nodding his head.

"You didn't exactly 'chase' the ambulances, you beat them there, but you get what I'm saying."

"I do," he said, turning from me to gaze at the earth below.

I followed suit and resisted my urge to say anything. God how I wanted to, but I didn't. There was a large storm over the Midwest and I stared at it, trying to catch flashes of lightning.

After many minutes, Banquo cleared his throat (a very conscious gesture for a ghost, since we don't have throats) and said, "It is an honorable request, JJ, and I am touched that you would ask it."

"But?" I said. I hadn't meant to speak, it just slipped out.

"No buts," he replied. "You are asking a lot."

"I know," I said. "I just want to do something worth doing."

Banquo's smile was soft and full of compassion. "And you have. You are."

I nodded, thinking of this last year. Helping Jesus find Javier, helping John out of the bardo, and helping Rhiannon move on. "Thank you. I get that, but I want to do more."

Banquo rotated away from the view of the earth and faced me, his arms crossed. "Very well. What you are asking is to be my apprentice. Is that correct?"

My mouth opened in a silent gesture of surprise. I hadn't associated my request with the word "apprentice," but as I thought about it, my belly tightened, the fear grew, and I realized that that was exactly what I was asking for. "Yes, that is correct," I said slowly and deliberately. "I want to be your apprentice."

"With all that implies?" Banquo asked.

"Umm... I guess. What all does it imply?"

Banquo laughed heartily. "To tell you the truth, JJ, I'm not exactly sure myself. But I can tell you this, I will ask much more of you than I have in the past. I will expect you to abide by rules that I set down and to do what I ask of you."

I nodded and swallowed, the lump in my belly growing heavy. I was scared but also excited. In many ways I have wanted Banquo to let me further in, teach me more, since we first started this. "OK, I am willing."

"Very well," he said with a sharp nod. "I have three conditions before we get started."

"What are they?" I asked.

"First, you are still deep in this experience with

Rhiannon." I opened my mouth to speak, but he kept talking. "You have done well to come up here and vent your emotions, but I need you focused and present. So, if you truly want to do this, you need to go to the SECI chamber and write the story, all of it."

I nodded. I had my doubts about the consequences of these stories—I still do—but I was willing to do it.

"Second, you must tell me the story, all of it, leaving nothing out."

"Of course," I answered.

"And third, you must complete your obligation to John. Take him to the SECI chamber and let him say what he needs to say to Tamara. You must also continue to keep an eye on him as time progresses."

"I agree," I said. And after thinking it over, I added, "I have two requests of my own."

Banquo looked amused, but said, "Let's hear them."

"First, I want to learn how to travel. I need to be able to 'pop' especially if I am doing things like keeping an eye on John."

Banquo nodded and said, "I agree." I was surprised, it took a lot for Banquo to agree to progress to the next lesson. "And second?"

"Second, I want to hear the rest of the Iliad. You kind of left us hanging."

Banquo smiled and laughed. "Of course, of course. I would be delighted to recite the entire story to you. We will have to move into the Odyssey, which is the true completion of the story."

Silence descended as we watched the continents slip past below us, brown and green floating in the blue ocean, haloed in white clouds.

That had been too easy, Banquo agreeing to teach me. I kept waiting for the other shoe to drop. As if on cue, Banquo turned to me and said, "This deal we just made. It's going to be hard, much harder than you are thinking right now. You've got a lot to do before we can even begin the apprenticeship."

I bit my lip and nodded and then looked back down at the earth below as I gathered the threads of the story I needed to tell him.

Transmission #69
Received 2012/03/06 02:45:58

BANQUO AND I STAYED THERE, FOR ANOTHER TURNING OF our world as I told him everything that had happened, basically as I have told it to you here. He asked lots of questions, as you would expect, which helped clarify my thinking.

When it was over he said, "Thank you," and with a pop was gone.

I stayed up there for a while. The fatigue I felt was getting heavier, and I knew I would have to fade soon, but I fought it like a little kid.

I didn't know when I would have the time to get up there again. I was in orbit, for God's sake, how cool is that? A ghost in orbit.

I really missed Jesus then. I would have loved to share this with him. When Mexico swung into view again I thought of him and imagined, that from my great height, I could see him down in Mexico City. Fredrick had said that Sister Dominga had died, what was he still doing down there? It had been a year since we parted ways—I had been in the bardo for a very long time. Was he attending to other issues around his own death? Looking up long lost relatives? Or had he gotten himself in some huge mess by being the Fool like me and having trouble extracting himself?

As I stared down at Mexico, I had a flash. I didn't know if it was my imagination or maybe Awareness. I saw Jesus smiling and laughing with a brown-skinned woman with long, jet-black hair that was braided in the back. They were walking hand in hand across the desert.

Who was this woman and what had happened to Jesus while he was away?

With unanswered questions on my mind, I gave in to the need to rest as the earth below me slowly faded, and I knew nothing for a time.

Transmission #70
Received 2012/03/06 04:21:32

I CAME TO HOVERING OVER MY GRAVESTONE. I DIDN'T RUSH away, like I usually did, I lingered. "Joseph Jeffery Lynch. November 5, 1980 – August 22, 2010." It seemed so final, as if those letters and numbers engraved in granite spoke the truth, the final truth about my life.

But I floated there conscious, alive—albeit without a body—staring at that granite-engraved finality.

I needed to go to the SECI chamber. I needed to tell my story, but I just stared. What would happen, I wondered, if the world truly knew that even though your end date gets engraved in granite, it is not the end of you? I still wonder.

It seems to be an odd dichotomy that the world's religions all speak of an afterlife, but the world's population is scared to hell of death.

Now, this is the kind of question that I need Jesus for. He would have a sharp, illuminating perspective on this. Me, I have no perspective, only the question. Why do we fear death when every faith talks of an afterlife? Why?

Why do we struggle so mightily against death if we truly believe heaven is what awaits us?

Why do we expend so much of our resources on last-ditch, ineffective medical interventions that only delay the inevitable a little bit and compromise the quality of life left to us?

Why?

It seems to me that all this indicates that we are still scared shitless of death despite our "faith."

And no, I don't have answers here, but I do have another question. Would you live differently if you knew—not just believed, but knew—that there was an afterlife, that consciousness goes on after the death of the body? Would your life be different? Would you be different?

The possible answers to that question, frankly, scare the hell out of me. I saw firsthand what Nate tried to do when he knew there was an afterlife. What happens when thousands or millions start reacting to "knowing" that death is not the end? Not believing but knowing. Humans are unpredictable and there would be an entire spectrum of reactions, all the way from "living in peace," to "yeah, I knew that," to "death is not the end, so I'm out of here," to... Well, I won't take it further than that. I leave it as an exercise for you.

I FOUND JOHN WELL AND HAPPY. HE HAD TRULY SETTLED into life at the graveyard and seemed content. He rested with his bones during the day, went to the Midnight Circle, and hung out a lot with Anton as well as some others he had made friends with.

What a relief. I wasn't up for another epic adventure

into the bardo to save him. I just wanted to complete what I had started.

"Are you ready to go?" I asked.

He nodded, a shy look on his face. "I am."

"Do you know what you want to say to Tamara?" I asked.

"I guess. I've had a lot of time to think about it and it has afforded me some perspective, but it's hard."

I smiled and nodded and we flew off to the SECI 2.0 chamber, and I transcribed John's message to Tamara.

"How's Jesus?" I asked Banquo the next time I got a chance. I had started writing this manuscript and had settled back into life at the graveyard. It was good. I appreciated a simple life, and knowing it wasn't going to last long, appreciated it all the more.

"He's... actually he's been through a lot," Banquo said with a frown, "but he's doing well now."

"Is he coming back?" I felt funny asking. I really wanted to talk to my friend and feared that I might be developing an unhealthy fixation on him like I had with Rhiannon. But I shook that off. I had always had close male friends and never went off the rails like I did with Rhiannon.

"Yeah, he's headed in this direction. But because of certain circumstances he's been taking his time." Banquo had a bemused smile on his face.

"It's a woman, isn't it?" Banquo's eyes widened, so I continued. "She's got long black hair, down to her waist. She wears it in a braid. Her eyes are blue and her skin is brown but not quite as brown as Jesus's." Banquo's look of surprise delighted me, so I just kept going, not really knowing where this was all coming from. "Her name is Lela.

She's Native American and they're... they're..." this last bit shocked me and it was my eyes that widened.

"Go on," Banquo said with a small smile.

"They're in love," I said. I didn't want to say it. I really didn't. It didn't feel like something I was making up, it felt right, it felt real.

"Well done, my boy. Well done," Banquo said, his voice booming as he slapped me on the back. He had done it properly so his hand didn't go through me, and I felt that numb, vague sense of touch. Banquo had never "touched" me before. I think it was a big deal.

"Was all of that right?" I asked.

Banquo nodded and beamed. "Every bit of it, JJ. Well done. You are starting to get the lesson of Awareness."

A thought occurred to me, one that delighted me and eased my confusion about Jesus and this woman. "So, since I've got Awareness down, I am truly ready for Traveling now. Right?"

He chuckled and shook his head. "Awareness, JJ, is the one lesson none of us are ever done with. Ever. There is always more we can be aware of, always further we can go."

Banquo's Rules of the Dead #6: *In the meat life or the afterlife, Awareness is the name of the game.*

I nodded. It made sense, and frankly I didn't care as long as we could move on to Traveling.

THE FOOL

Transmission #71
Received 2012/03/07 02:16:46

A FEW DAYS AFTER MY TALK WITH BANQUO, JESUS
returned. I was talking to John when I felt this tingling
along my back and heard, "Hey, JJ."

I knew it was him before he spoke—I could feel him.
I had been practicing my Awareness and thought he was
close. I turned slowly, a huge grin on my face, which I saw
mirrored on Jesus's. "Hey, Jesus," I said.

It was strange and a bit awkward. I mean, I really missed
him, and I was so glad he was back, but all I came up with
was, "Hey, Jesus." I thought back to the assemblage of
women that shaved Rhiannon's head. If it had been any
one of them meeting each other after a long absence there
would have been immediate hugs and tears and carrying on.

But not us. Me and my best dead-friend, just said "Hey"
to each other.

Standing next to Jesus was a petite woman with brown
skin, long black hair in a braid, and piercing blue eyes. I
hesitate to describe those eyes, my words will fall far short,
but I will try. They were a light blue, like the blue you see

reflected in pictures of icebergs. Luminous, pale, piercing. She appeared to be looking not at me, but into me, at my soul. It was distracting.

I took a step forward and Jesus did too and I got a closer look at his eyes. I could see that he had been through a lot since he left. There was joy there, that was plain, but there was pain too.

We each took another step and then suddenly the distance was gone and we were slapping each other on the back in a ghostly hug.

"I missed you, man," Jesus said in a whisper.

"Me too. Me too," I said. "So much has happened."

"Yeah," he replied.

We parted suddenly as if we had realized what we had been doing. "So, yeah," Jesus said. "I want to introduce you to Lela, Lela May Sykes. Lela, this is JJ Lynch."

She smiled and extended her hand. I noticed a few things. She appeared to be young, maybe twenty-five, her form was impeccable—only a tiny bit transparent—and she had a tattoo of a lynx on her right shoulder.

Her grip was perfect, and as we touched I felt something deep within me stir. I'm not sure exactly what it was, but it seemed like I recognized her or that I knew her. It was some strange déjà vu kind of thing.

She was attractive enough, but she wasn't "pretty," not in the conventional sense. Her face was lean and wiry, much like her body. She had a prominent jaw and a small nose. But really it's hard to get past those eyes. Iceberg-blue eyes.

"Jesus has told me all about you," she said.

I nodded and smiled and then blushed. I got the impression that she knew all my secrets, the good, the bad, and the ugly.

We spent the rest of the day together walking and talking. Jesus gave me bits of his story, but I didn't really learn much about Lela. It was awkward having her there. It disturbed our dynamic, and I found myself unsure of how to act.

It reminded me of how Nate had acted when Rhiannon and I had first gotten together. We had all had an adjustment phase when Rhiannon came into the picture. And while that had been difficult for me and Rhiannon, it took the biggest toll on Nate.

And in this case, I was Nate. I was the one coming into the middle of a romance trying to learn how to be with my friend with a woman in the picture.

That evening, before the Midnight Circle, Banquo took the three of us aside.

"JJ, how's the writing going?" he asked.

"Maybe a quarter done," I said.

He nodded, "Good. I want you to show Jesus so he can start writing too."

"Jesus?" I asked.

"Writing?" Jesus asked.

"Yes," he said, turning and looking at Jesus. "I need you both clear and ready to learn. Writing his story has helped JJ a lot, Jesus. I think it will help you too."

I looked at Jesus and back to Banquo. "You're going to apprentice us both?" I asked.

Banquo nodded and smiled, "And Lela too."

I looked at Lela, her expression was inscrutable. "Does she need the SECI chamber too?" I asked.

Banquo paused, looking at me closely before answering. "Look in her eyes, JJ. Does it look like she is grieving right now? Does it look like she needs to get something off her chest?"

I looked into those cool blue eyes and opened myself to feel what was there. I felt confidence and wisdom with a hint of trepidation. And there was something else, a shadow of something I couldn't quite identify. She had a secret, but I couldn't discern anything about it.

I looked away and shook my head.

"OK then," Banquo said. "You two tell your stories. Get yourselves in balance and then we will start."

As I WRITE THIS MEMOIR, I FIND MYSELF SPENDING MORE time alone. Not just in the SECI chamber but in general. Part of my process, I guess. Every few days after a writing session, I fly alone to the Grand Canyon. I find a majestic perch and as the sun rises, I play my silly plastic guitar.

No one can see me, no one can hear me, but yet I keep doing it.

At first I tried to imitate songs I love, mostly classic rock, but I don't anymore. I try to come up with new music, new sounds, new expressions.

Often times it's a horribly discordant mess that emanates. But sometimes the music is sweet and interesting, and all mine.

And a thought keeps running around my head about this: *I am the instrument.*

I'm a ghost, the cheap plastic guitar is just a prop, it's no more "real" than I am. But it is a focal point for the noise I am creating. I could do it without the guitar, or without looking like "JJ" for that matter. But I don't. We ghosts try to present as normal a life as possible, but it's anything but.

I have no idea what this means, but I kinda think it's important. I am going to have to talk to Jesus about this, I think he'll have some perspective.

I am the instrument.

THINGS WITH LELA ARE, WELL... THEY ARE COMPLICATED. She is smart and intense and very much a distraction. Jesus is distracted by her presence in the most pleasant kind of way, and I am distracted by the sudden changing in our dynamic. Jesus and JJ has become Jesus and Lela and JJ.

Go ahead, call me a third wheel. I can take it, though the truth does hurt. I had just said a permanent good-bye to the love of my life, and my best dead-friend was deep in the throes of new love.

But still we hung out. I wanted to get to know her. I wanted to spend time with Jesus. I wanted normal. But normal is not what I got.

One day all four of us were walking the graveyard. That would be Jesus, Lela, Banquo, and me. Banquo was grilling us on our writing progress when I felt a warmth overtake me and my vision began to bifurcate.

"Hey!" I shouted as the other three kept walking. They looked back puzzled. "I think I'm getting another call."

Banquo nodded, I had told them all about the first one. He held his arms in front of the other two, indicating that they should stay put.

When the dual vision was fully upon me, I could see three people directly in front of me. They were large, taking up the entire space I could see, and would shift and stay in front of me no matter where I looked.

I saw Viki Dobos, her face drawn and concerned, a man

of about forty years with short blond hair and angular features, and a girl with brown skin and long black hair.

"Hey, it's the lady, the lady that skypes the dead," I said waving to my friends. "Come on, guys, check it out."

"Hello, Mr. Lynch," Viki said, "please excuse the intrusion. I hope this is a better time."

"'Mr. Lynch,' seriously? Please call me JJ," I said to her. "And yeah, now is fine, we're just hanging out." I turned to Banquo who was approaching cautiously from my left side, his eyes wide. "Do you see anything?" I asked him. "You guys look kind of dim to me."

"Yes," Banquo said slowly. "There is this column of light coming down around you. It is beautiful with scintillating colors. What do you see?"

"It's this kind of double vision," I said. "I mostly see them and the room they are in."

Banquo had signaled Jesus and Lela over and they all stood to the sides of me. "I'm going to touch your shoulder now, and so is Jesus," Banquo said. "Lela, touch Jesus's shoulder. We might be able to see what JJ sees. Are you OK with that?"

"Sure, why not, give it a shot." I felt two light, ghostly touches on my shoulders and felt that warmth traveling towards them too. "Can you see them?" I asked Viki, although judging from the looks of wonder on their faces I thought I knew the answer.

"Nice. OK," I said, looking to my left. "This is Jesus, my best dead-friend."

"Thank you, JJ," Jesus said with a big grin.

"Sure, bro. To his left is Lela, Jesus's... What should I call you two?"

A smile played upon Lela's lips as her eyes drilled into me. "You haven't figured that out yet, huh?"

I knew what they were, I just wasn't quite ready to name it yet. But the occasion called for it, so I said, "This is Jesus's significant other." I turned my head to the right and said, "And this is my friend and mentor Banquo."

Banquo nodded and smiled, I could tell he was delighted. Something new, something different. "You must be Ms. Dobos," he said. "JJ told us all about your first encounter."

Viki nodded and said quickly, "It's nice to meet you all. I don't mean to be rude, but I have an important matter I need help with and these connections don't usually last very long."

Banquo looked carefully around and said, "I think we can do something about that." He turned towards Jesus and Lela and said, "Do you see that? That halo of energy around JJ?"

They nodded. "What?" I asked. "What halo, I don't see anything?"

"It's OK, JJ, take a moment and look carefully," Banquo said. "Jesus and Lela, focus on the halo, feel it, make it stronger."

I could feel the warmth growing stronger and Viki and the man and the child became sharper and clearer.

"That seems to be working," Viki said, a look of surprise on her face.

"I don't see any damn halo!" I said.

"That may be because you are the focus of the energy," Banquo said gently. "Just focus on Ms. Dobos, try to make her as clear as you can."

After I stopped looking around like an idiot and concentrated on the hazel eyes of Viki Dobos, the energy became stronger and clearer.

Viki gasped, her eyes blinking rapidly. The other two with her looked surprised too.

After a moment of silence, Banquo asked, "Better?"

Viki nodded. "Yes. That is amazing. How do you—"

"One thing at a time, my dear," Banquo said with a smile. "You needed JJ for something. How can we help?"

Viki took a deep breath, looking at the man and the child. The man was serious, he gave her a small nod, but the girl was obviously lost in the wonder of it.

"With me is Tim and his daughter Anela," she said. "I just drew Tim's wife, Anela's mother, and..." her voice trailed off and her face fell. The images I saw of them wavered for a moment and then Viki's face hardened as if she were exerting herself. "She is in what you would call a bardo state, reliving her death over and over. She drowned."

Bardo. The thought of it filled me with dread. After all that time in John's bardo, I was not eager to return.

"How long has she been dead?" Jesus asked.

Viki looked to Tim who replied, "Almost two years."

"Please help my mama," Anela said. Her plea cut through me. She was just a child, obviously missing her mother.

"I'm sorry," I said, hanging my head. "I can't, not again..."

"I don't understand," Viki said.

"My dear," Banquo began, "as you know, the bardo is one's own personal hell, a place ghosts sometimes get trapped in. JJ has recently had a very long and very difficult encounter with it. None of us go there willingly."

"Then you won't help?" Viki asked, her disappointment obvious. I felt the warmth beginning to fade, and it became harder to see the three of them.

"Focus now," Banquo said to us, his voice stern. "We are not done here yet."

I focused on their faces and felt things return to normal. "Reaching someone in the bardo is very difficult. You," I said, looking at Tim and Anela, "have the best chance. You knew her, you loved her, you are the ones that can reach her."

"How?" Viki asked.

"Simple, my dear," Banquo said. "You have to find something more important to her than her suffering."

"While it may be simple," Jesus added with a kind smile, "it's not easy. Not easy at all."

Viki's face loomed large as she seemed to exhale on me, and then they were gone.

I stood there feeling guilty. I knew how to go into the bardo. I knew how to get through to someone. Yet I couldn't consider doing it again. I couldn't risk losing another year, or more, of my afterlife. But the pleas of a young girl asking me to save her mother haunted me.

It was something worth doing. The kind of thing I kept saying I wanted to do. But I just couldn't.

I mumbled something to Banquo, Jesus, and Lela—who were talking about the encounter with great enthusiasm— and wandered off. I needed to be alone. I needed to think.

Transmission #72
Received 2012/03/07 04:12:28

THE FUNK THAT DESCENDED ON ME AFTER OUR ENCOUNTER with Viki, Tim, and Anela was like a black cloud. I continued writing but missed a few Midnight Circles, choosing instead to wander the graveyard grounds alone. After two nights of this Banquo found me and insisted I come.

"Ladies and gentlemen, ghost and spirits," Banquo said as he strode into the middle of the circle. "We have something very special for you tonight. One of our own, Jesus Manuel Rivera Dominga, has returned, and he has brought another to join our ranks. If you haven't met her yet, please give a warm welcome to Lela May Sykes."

There was smattering of hoots and hellos.

"We have a tradition here at our humble home. That is of celebrating our first death-day. It is a coming of age of a sort. If you make it a year as a ghost, then you are truly one of us, you are truly part of this family."

I was standing next to Jesus and Lela. I looked around wondering whose death-day it was. I had been witness to one of these before and it was pretty fun. The person who had just reached their first year dead would be given the circle and asked to tell a story for the group.

"We usually observe this tradition on the actual death-day, but in some cases that is not possible." As Banquo's voice boomed out, he slowly turned and looked at the ghosts around him until he got to Jesus and me.

I felt a cold stone in my belly as I realized who he was talking about.

"Jesus," Banquo began, beckoning him forward. "You were gone on your death-day and what better way to celebrate your return than giving you the circle." Banquo gave a gesture that called Jesus forward and then transformed into a bow.

Applause and shouts greeted Jesus as he walked to the center of the circle and Banquo took his place in the circle next to me.

Panic claimed me then. I knew I was next, and I had no idea what to do.

"Thank you, thank you," Jesus said. "You are most kind, and I am glad to be back. Tucson is not where I was born, but it has become my home. Not because it is a beautiful place, or because it reminds me of my own home, Mexico, but because of all of you. You have become my family, and where else could I possibly call home?"

There was an uproar of hoots and shouts and cheers.

"But I owe you a story, don't I? I have been gone a long time and there are many tales, but one that stands out." Jesus proceeded to tell the story of how he and Lela met. I won't record it here. I know Jesus is going to be spending time in the SECI chamber and I want to let him tell it himself. I will tell you this, the story had me laughing and crying and cheering along with the rest of the ghosts. It is interesting to note that Lela didn't seem exactly pleased with how much he told. Some of the details were a bit intimate. But our ghostly society is all about story and he told a good one.

When he finished, Banquo strode back to the center of the circle. "Our dear friend, JJ Lynch, was in the bardo on his death-day. Doing what few have the courage or the strength to do. He was helping someone he had never met, someone who is now a part of our family, find his way out. JJ, the circle is yours," Banquo beckoned to me with a flourish and a bow.

I moved forward, feeling butterflies exploding in my stomach. "Thanks for the warning," I hissed at Banquo as he walked by. He just smiled.

I looked around the circle at the people there. Jesus, Banquo and Lela. Jim and Jane. John and Anton. Fredrick. Helen. Old Man Perkins. Marilyn holding Motor. Little Emily holding Walter's hand. And all the rest.

I didn't speak, at first I couldn't, I was overwhelmed. This was my family now. This was my home.

I struggled to come up with something worthy to say, something entertaining, something amazing. But my mind seemed to be mush. I thought of whipping out my guitar and playing some really bad music, and that would be fun, but not the right thing.

I thought of regaling them with tales of all the messes I made right after my death. But that's old news, and they all knew the story.

I needed something special. Something unexpected. Something that had meaning to me.

"Rhiannon Elizabeth Pope," I began before I had really thought it through, "died on January 22, 2012, at 5:16 a.m."

I stopped and looked at the audience. Banquo smiled, Fredrick gave me a small nod, Jesus's hand went to his heart.

I began again, letting my voice get loud and full like Banquo's. "Rhiannon Elizabeth Pope died on January 22, 2012, at 5:16 a.m. She answered the Call and moved on about an hour later. She was thirty-two years old and is survived by her husband Thomas, her one-year-old son, Joey, and her father Kyle."

I paused, licking my lips. They were listening, this sounded like a story of death which is always welcome at the Midnight Circle.

But I couldn't speak of her death, of how she died. Not in detail. It was too much for me yet. But what I could speak of was her.

"She died like she lived, with courage and grace. I know, I know, that's what we always say about the dead when they are gone. All the good and beautiful things in this world were contained in the one that has passed. They said those kinds of things about us when we died."

As I spoke my voice grew stronger and deeper. I felt this wave of emotion building inside that I couldn't deny. I let it go and gave it voice.

"But you know what? She was courageous and graceful in death and life. And she was also fearful, shy, and full of doubt. She was human, just like all of us. She wasn't just one thing. She was a bit of everything. And I loved her. No, I *love* her.

"Her favorite color was purple. From the first day I saw her to the last, her fingernails were painted purple. And for her, purple is not just a color, but a constellation of colors. There is plum, and mauve, and eggplant. There is royal purple, light purple, and purple with sparkles in it. She knew them all and loved them all. And the way she loved that color, is the way she loved everything she cherished. Always varied and subtle and unending in variety.

"She loved to dance. She loved to play racquetball. She loved her husband and her son. She was loyal to a fault—I should know—and she was... she was the love of my life.

"And she is gone now. She left this plane of existence with hope for the next step. She left sure she was going to heaven, sure that she would be able to watch her son grow up from there. She did what I could not do, let go of this world once her body had failed.

"She left with courage and grace and hope.

"Rhiannon was small, petite, but could level you with her eyes. She was smart and driven, and could focus like a laser when she wanted to, or be diffuse as a cloud when the work was done.

"She had a laugh that sounded like music to me and her touch was magic.

"She was—is—way out of my league, but still she tarried with me for a time. Brightening my life with her grace, and like all things in this life, that came to an end.

"But don't feel sorry for me. We had love, and how can you feel sorry for those that loved? How can you regret the end when the journey was beyond compare?

"Not that it wasn't difficult. It was. I don't know about all of you, but I really started living after I died. I found my life in the afterlife. And I can only be grateful that I got to be there for my beloved Rhiannon as she left this world and moved on to the next."

I paused and laughed. "OK, I am more than just grateful. I am also angry and sad and grieving. For it is the way of us humans, isn't it? Change hurts, and this change hurts like hell. But tonight I celebrate the love that we have, for I still love her, and wherever she is right now, I know that she loves me.

"And like our loved ones that still have their meat bodies and miss us even though we are still so close, I miss her because I cannot see her or touch her or talk to her. But that does not make her less real. That does not make my love for her, and her love for me, less real."

I paused, I needed a big finish, but I wasn't sure what to do. I turned slowly looking at the faces of my tribe, my ghostly family. I saw tears and nodding heads. I saw those who looked down and couldn't meet my gaze. I saw Banquo, his arms folded, but beaming at me.

"So, if you will indulge me. Let's assume that Rhiannon is in heaven and watching those that love her. Let's assume that, and why not? Let's assume she is watching right now, with her purple nail polish and her beautiful brown hair pulled back into a ponytail.

"And if she is watching, then it would make sense for me to address her directly. To tell her what I feel in my heart. To say the things that I might not have said to her, or didn't say well."

I trembled at what I was doing. I really had no idea where this was coming from, but I felt it so strongly that there was nothing to do but follow it.

I spread my hands and looked up at the sky. "Rhiannon, words cannot express how grateful I am for you in my life. For the love you gave me and the love you allowed me to give you. From the moment I saw you, I wanted us to be together, forever. But that is not the way it was supposed to be. I was not ready, I was such a screw up. I struggled with so many things when we were together. But, my love, you made me a better man. And because of your love, because of your faith in me, I will continue to try to be better than I was, better than I am.

"I hope you can see Joey from where you are. I hope you found what you wanted. I hope you have peace if you want that, but mostly I hope you have passion and purpose and joy. And plenty of purple fingernail polish.

"I love you, Rhiannon."

As the tears flowed, I felt something release. I knew I could go on without her.

I had an apprenticeship to look forward to and being with my friends. I wasn't unrealistic about it—I knew I had a long way to go. But at least I had a plan, and a future, and a purpose.

Transmission #73
Received 2012/03/07 06:45:32

LIFE IS GRIEF. REALLY IT IS. AS WE TRANSITION FROM ONE phase to the next, from one place to the next, from one relationship to the next, we have to let go. And letting go is grief.

Where there is life, there is grief. Whether it is the meat life or the after-life.

This is not a bad thing, because the corollary is also true. Grief is life. That you are changing and experiencing the emotions of that change, of that letting go of the familiar and finding something new, means you are living. That is life. That is wonderful.

And maybe we can all be like the Fool of the Tarot that Helen told me about. We can dive innocently and enthusiastically into our lives and the change it brings.

I know I am often a fool (lowercase "f"), the kind of fool that society has no room or respect for. The kind of fool that is just plain dumb. But, I am finding, that I am often a Fool (capital "F"). The kind that does things for the right reason without fully considering the consequences, or even being capable of considering those consequences.

I was a Fool when I set off with Jesus to find his killer. I was a Fool when I entered the bardo to help John. And I was such a Fool when I went to Rhiannon's deathbed to help her.

And if I hadn't been a Fool, if I hadn't gone forth with innocence, doing those things just because I knew they were the right things to do, they wouldn't have happened. If I had really known, if I had really thought them through, I would have run away screaming and not done a one of them. If that had happened, what kind of an afterlife would I have?

And now it is time for me to be the Fool again.

Jesus has love in his life, so I must be the Fool and find a way to be with my best dead-friend while he explores this love.

I must be the Fool with Banquo as he has agreed to allow Jesus, Lela, and I to be his apprentices.

I don't know what the future will bring, but I do know it will be interesting, and difficult, and wonderful. I do know that I will continue to be the Fool.

This is Joseph Jeffery Lynch signing off to go continue on his Fool's journey. Be well.

Epilogue

Video Transcript #7
Nate Luca speaking to JJ Lynch
Recorded on 2012/03/10 4:18 p.m.
Playback triggered on: 2012/04/12 2:34 a.m.

OK, BRO. TAM AND JIN HAVE ASKED ME TO KIND OF WRAP this thing up. We've been reading your transmissions eagerly as they come in and... Wow, what do you say?

I mean, on one hand I am not at all surprised. JJ Lynch, in the afterlife, fighting the good fight, damn the consequences. I mean, that's totally you, bro. But... Damn!

It doesn't sound like you are having the typical ghostly experience. No "resting with your bones" crap, no taking it easy, no going slowly to resolve your life. Not you.

OK, so enough of me being all amazed at your adventures.

I have a few updates. Agent Franks is behind bars, and it doesn't look like he is getting out anytime soon. Let John know the prosecutor thinks the murder charge is going to stick, so Franks won't be able to bother anyone ever again. What happened to Professor Aldridge is still a mystery, but maybe that is one you guys can handle from that side.

On a more mundane note, there's Anna-Beth... Ah hell, let's talk about ghosts and the afterlife all day, but trying to talk about women, now that's hard. I appreciate the advice you gave and how it made me laugh. So I just settled in and got patient. And that patience has been rewarded. William is out of the picture. Let me see, how do I put this delicately? She's grown, he hasn't, so they are quite incompatible now.

And you know with the JJ Lynch Foundation stuff, we've been spending some time together, and with where things are going, quite a lot of time.

So I guess I should explain that. The first year was for fundraising and planning. We are moving into the implementation phase now. "The Garage" is about to open. It's a vocational training program for at-risk juveniles. Look at me, bro, using big words.

This whole thing has forced me to grow too. Step up, take some responsibility. I've been learning a lot about business and non-profits and grants and stuff. It's all very complicated—Anna-Beth has a much better head for it than I do.

Anyway, "The Garage" is opening up next month. It's a pilot program, to see how it works. We're taking a dozen kids in trouble and working with them after school. We're gonna get them dirty fixing cars.

I don't know if it'll fly, there are so many unanswered questions. We're going to have to prove that this works to get more funding.

So there's that. And there's Anna-Beth, suddenly single. She is amazing, JJ, and as you said, so far out of my league. But hey, if you could land Rhiannon...

Oh, shit! Sorry. I am sure that's got to be a sensitive subject.

I went to Rhiannon's funeral. It was so hard. I just

thought someone should represent us and say good-bye to her. I am really glad you were there for her. It makes a lot of this worth it. I know it sucked, and I know you are still sorting it out. But, man, am I blown away by you. What you did for her. How you put her first when it meant...

OK. Let me try to get my act together here and be coherent. Let's just say where Anna-Beth is concerned you have been my inspiration.

We went on our first official "date" last week. It wasn't anything spectacular, just a nice dinner, but it was a date. I... She...

I remember how you were about Rhiannon back in college, back at the beginning with her. I didn't quite get it. She was just a girl, right? Well now I get it. Anna-Beth is not "just a girl." She makes me feel weak, she makes me want to be strong, she inspires me to grow.

It was just a date, nothing fancy. I have no idea where it is going, but I can say she has agreed to a second date. So there is that!

I just wanted to tell you about her because I know you'll get this. I know you'll be there cheering me on.

We talk about you, quite a bit actually. I told her she could make a video herself for you, but she is being shy. She did, though, want me to convey a short message.

Let me see... Where the hell did I put it? OK. Here goes:

"JJ, I somehow feel I should call you Mr. Lynch, but Nate assures me that would be insulting. So, JJ.

"There are many things I could say, but only one thing that is really relevant. Thank you. I know that might sound strange, after all we went through after your death. But you did me a great service. You woke me up.

"I am grateful for that. I know the circumstances were

not anything any of us could have anticipated. And I am so glad no one was hurt worse, or killed.

"We are doing our best to honor your memory, and I hope that counts for something.

"Well, thank you, JJ."

OK, that's her message. And I guess it's time for me to wrap it up too.

SECI 2.0 is here at your disposal. We've also started to receive transmissions from Jesus, which is very cool. He's telling a hell of a story so far.

So be well, JJ. Tamara, Jin, and Ma send their best. We all love you. We all are rooting for you. We all welcome hearing from you whenever you can.

I... we... Oh, hell, JJ. Since our big night—and I mean, what the hell can I call that time when I almost died and you almost... Anyway, since our big night and I recovered from my injuries, I find my emotions a lot more on the surface, a lot harder to hide.

And maybe that's a good thing. Anna-Beth assures me that it is. I don't know, though. It doesn't feel like a good thing, all this "feeling." But, you know, it sounds like from what you're writing something similar has happened to you too. Look at us, bro, all growing up and stuff.

OK, JJ, time for me to sign off. I miss you, man. I love you.

Author's Note

THANK YOU SO MUCH FOR READING. WHAT FOLLOWS IS A really fun deleted scene, an excerpt from *Of Things Not Seen*, which follows Jesus down to Mexico city, and then acknowledgements and a bit about me.

But, before you proceed, I have a favor to ask you. If you've enjoyed this book, then do me the honor of spreading the word. Write an honest review on Amazon (just a few sentences is fine), loan the book, or tell your friends. Word of mouth is the best endorsement a book can get, and only you can do that. Thank you!

If you want to know as soon as new books come out please sign up for my email newsletter. Go to RobertJMcCarter.com, you'll see the signup offer on the home page. As of this writing I am giving away ebooks of the first episode of my Superhero/Love Story series.

Deleted Scene

What follows is the equivalent of a deleted scene you might find after a DVD. And just like those scenes, it belongs in this story but doesn't quite fit into the main flow.

It also contains some spoilers for Drawing the Dead. If you've already read it, then proceed, I hope you find it interesting. It documents JJ's side of the climax of that book.

This little scene also gives us a tantalizing glimpse of JJ's future as Banquo's apprentice.

Transmission #74
Received 2012/04/12 03:02:16

Sometimes you get what you ask for. Sometimes it's not quite what you thought it would be. Hell, it almost never is.

Our apprenticeship with Banquo has officially started, and I keep thinking about this incident that happened a few months ago. I guess the memory keeps floating up because it is a part of this story that I haven't told yet. It's also my first taste at being Banquo's apprentice. So here I am, back banging on this keyboard for ghosts. Consider this an encore, if you will.

My memoir writing days were predictable. I would spend my days resting at elevation and come down to the grave-yard after sunset. I would then walk the graveyard, ponder-ing the portion of the story I would tell, or hang with Jesus and Lela until the Midnight Circle. After the Circle I would fly to the SECI chamber, type away, and then go back to the graveyard and go to elevation and rest.

One evening, about a week into the writing process, I wandered through the graveyard, my mind deep in the story I wanted to tell. My story. Me. And, yes, I was totally focused on myself again.

After our second encounter with Viki Dobos, the skype with the dead lady, I had often thought of her. She had been so desperate for help with Tim's wife, Anela's mother. I hoped they had gotten through to her. I hoped they had gotten her out of the bardo. I felt guilty for not being able to help.

I comforted myself with one of my Banquo's Rules for the Dead. *If you can help, then you must try to help.* Well, in this situation the corollary is what made me feel better: *If you can't help, then you must not try.*

But that didn't stop me from thinking about Viki. We seem to have this strange link. She helps the living communicate with the dead, and I am one of dead communicating with the living. Different sides of the same coin.

As I strolled the manicured lawns of the graveyard alone, my mind wandered back to her and I felt this nebulous sense of desperation. It wasn't focused, I didn't know what it was about, but it was intense. I stopped and instead of pushing the feeling away, which I would have done before the whole Awareness of Others thing, I embraced it. I went with it. I focused on Viki and opened myself up to her.

Heart beating fast, palms sweating. Not much time. Must save him.

I looked around, I was in the graveyard still, but for a moment I thought I was somewhere else, sitting at a table, drawing someone. That sick grey-haired man with the goatee that I had seen when Viki first drew me. She was desperate. She was in danger.

I flew up a few hundred feet and searched for Banquo. I didn't see him and cursed my inability to pop. I needed

Banquo, and fast. I forced myself to calm down and look carefully, taking slow ghostly breaths as I scanned the graveyard.

Time ticked past and my sense of urgency increased.

A spike of pain in my kidneys. Nausea. Must keep pushing.

I spotted him over by the mortuary talking to Fredrick. I flew down fast and interrupted them. "Banquo, I need you. Viki needs help. Now."

He glared at me and then pursed his lips. "Excuse us, Fredrick," he said before walking away a few paces with me.

Room spinning. Must hold on, must give him time. The sound of sirens in the distance.

"It's Viki Dobos," I began, "she is in danger, something is wrong. Can you take me to her? Please."

I have to give Banquo credit. He didn't doubt me, he didn't ask questions, he just looked carefully at me and then took action. "Give me your hand," he said. I extended my hand and he modulated his form to match mine so our hands were overlapped, together, one. "Now think of her, see her, feel her."

A drawing of the grey-haired man. A table with two other men at it. Pain, unbearable pain in my head. Falling. I hear shouting. Darkness comes.

I saw Viki Dobos first, still, unmoving, lying flat on the ground. I saw her spirit next, hovering over her body with a gaped mouth, bardoed-out expression on its face with a silver cord connecting it to her body.

"Come on, V!" a large grey-haired man with a ponytail said as he did CPR on Viki's body. Sweat ran down his face.

He turned to Tim, who I recognized from the second time Viki communicated with me, and said, "Where the hell is that ambulance?"

I wanted to take action, but I couldn't. I just stood there shocked by what I saw. I heard the siren of an ambulance in the distance as I looked around. We were in a large room with high vaulted ceilings and an outward facing wall of glass. Outside I saw palm trees, sand, and blue ocean.

I looked at Banquo, his eyes narrow as he appraised the scene. I tried to calm myself and do the same. I looked at Viki's bardoed spirit and opened myself to Awareness.

I felt her fear, her shame, her terror. I saw her spirit grasp her belly and I dimly heard her say, "No, Mother. No!"

"What do we do?" I asked Banquo.

He looked at me and nodded at my form. I looked down and I had gone wispy and had a sickly chartreuse hue flicking along the edges of it. "Awareness of Self, JJ. First and foremost."

I bit back a retort and firmed up my form. The chartreuse flicker faded but stayed, my feelings too strong to just dismiss. I wanted to help, but I didn't want to end up in the bardo. I felt for what she was going through, having spent all that time in the bardo with John and his mother.

"Good," Banquo said. "This is your show, JJ. What do you want to do?"

I took a deep breath and pushed down the anger I felt. The stakes were high, why the hell was Banquo turning this into a lesson? Why wasn't he just telling me what to do?

I looked back at Viki, her body and her spirit. Was she alive or was she dead? Did I want to help her survive or help her spirit move on?

"Can she survive?" I asked.

Banquo shrugged his shoulders and continued to stare at me.

"She can survive," I said. "If she can wake up from the bardo, she can survive. Right?" Banquo just kept looking at me, his eyebrows raised as if he had asked the question. "She *can* survive this," I affirmed.

Two paramedics came in carrying handfuls of gear and took a look at the situation.

"How long has she been down?" the blond-haired one asked.

Tim looked at his watch and said, "About three minutes." The paramedic nodded, but his downcast eyes worried me.

The brown-haired paramedic took over for the big man who fell back panting and exhausted. "Please, V," the big man whispered. "Don't leave. Please."

I watched as the first paramedic pulled out an automatic defibrillator and started to get it set up, opening Viki's blouse and attaching the defibrillator pads.

"You must focus, JJ," Banquo said. "What does she need?"

"Right," I said, pulling my gaze away from the paramedics and focusing on Viki's spirit. "We don't have much time, not enough time to enter the bardo. We need to reach her though, give her a fighting chance."

I looked at Banquo, he nodded encouragingly.

A plan popped into my head, one that scared the hell out of me, but seemed like it might work, so I took action.

I walked behind Viki's tortured spirit and intentionally matched the quality of my form to hers. I let it go wispy, transparent, and diffuse. This was the first step I had taken when I entered the bardo with John. I then intertwined my arms with Viki's until they were one. I gasped as the strength of her emotion crashed onto me like a tsunami. Shame, deep and pervasive, nearly overwhelmed me. That shame kept her locked in the bardo, kept her spirit from returning to her body.

I let my Awareness of her shame grow. I heard someone saying to her, "First you embrace that gift and then you deny your heritage as a woman." The voice was condescending and full of vitriol.

I felt the bardo, I felt it inviting me in, calling me down. I had my own shame, it whispered to me. I have done so much harm to those I love. I have so much to hide from the world. I am not worthy. I am not loved.

I hardened my will and said no to the bardo. I was dimly aware of the paramedics shocking Viki's heart, but I was more aware of her screaming in her bardo experience.

I needed to get a message to her. Something that would help her wake up. Something that would give her the smallest of edges against the bardo. But I didn't know this woman at all. We had two brief paranormal skype calls and that was it.

I felt her bardo experience shift as a cold chill flowed from her and permeated my form. She was going deeper, it was getting worse. The defibrillator shocked her heart again. There wasn't much time.

On the edge of the bardo, my ghostly form intertwined with Viki Dobos's, I summoned the warmth. Just like I had done for all those days with Rhiannon, I summoned it for Viki to fight the cold of her bardo experience. It wasn't much, but I could feel it traveling through my form into hers. I could sense the smallest of disturbances in her bardo experience.

"You are worthy of love," I whispered. I didn't shout it,

somehow I knew that would have been inappropriate. I just whispered it once and let it flow down the warmth to her.

VIKI DOBOS CAME BACK TO LIFE WITH A SHARP, DESPERATE intake of breath. Her spirit started moving towards her body, and since our hands and arms were still entwined, my spirit moved towards her body too.

"Separate!" Banquo yelled, the urgency in his voice shocking me back to what was happening.

By instinct I firmed my ghostly form up which made it incompatible with hers, and we separated as her soul sunk back into her body. We were face to face, inches apart, when her hazel eyes flew open and she coughed.

I flew back to Banquo and watched the aftermath. The paramedics attending to Viki, the two men nervously looking on.

As they loaded her onto a gurney, she took the large man's hand and said, "Reg, I saw my mother. I was in the bardo."

"It's OK, honey," the big man replied. "Just rest. Everything is OK."

"I'll be there when you wake up," Tim said, a strained smile on his face.

After they took her away, we flew out of the house and started walking down to the beach.

"Where are we?" I asked.

"Hawaii, I think," Banquo answered.

I nodded, distracted by what had happened, and what had almost happened. "That was close. Thanks for the warning. What would have happened if I hadn't separated our forms?"

Banquo shrugged. "Oh, her body probably would have rejected your spirit but..." he trailed off.

"But what?"

"But," he said with a wicked grin, "it might not have."

I stopped walking and stood there blinking. Two spirits, one body. That didn't sound like fun to me.

"Seriously?" I asked.

"Seriously," he said.

A chill passed through my form, and I shook my body in an attempt to throw it off. "So, is that what an apprentice-ship with you is going to be like?" I asked.

Banquo laughed, his booming voice drowning out the surf. "Well, JJ, I could ask you the same thing. Is that what having you as my apprentice is going to be like?"

My laughter joined his as we walked down the beach.

*Want to know what happed to Jesús when he went to
Mexico City and met Lela?
The following is a sample of* Of Things Not Seen

"The wry humor and raw emotional truth of JJ's journey will have readers
rooting for him from death to eternity."   *Kirkus Reviews* on *Shuffled Off*

OF THINGS NOT SEEN

A GHOST'S MEMOIR, BOOK 3

ROBERT J. MCCARTER

AUTHOR OF *SHUFFLED OFF*

Chapter 1

"Bless me, Father, for I have sinned," I whispered to Father Finnegan who sat placidly in the other side of the confessional booth. "It has been seven months since my last confession. In that time I have felt anger towards my killer, and since I found him and brought him to justice, I have found myself in a place of deep despair, a place of confusion. I have begun to doubt my faith."

Father Finnegan took a deep breath and sighed, his thumb moving his rosary beads smoothly along his index finger as his mouth moved silently in prayer. His hair was grey, with only a hint of the red that was there when I first met him, and his face was deeply wrinkled. He didn't say anything.

"I'm a ghost, Father," I continued, moving my face right up to the brass confessional screen so I could see him clearly. "I sit here, I see you, I speak to you, but you can't hear me. You can't tell me how to confront this crisis like you helped me so many times before. You can't tell me to do Hail Marys or Our Fathers. You can't assign me an appropriate act of contrition. You can't..." I trailed off, fighting back the tears. I longed for the life that was past, for the body that let me communicate with the living, for the faith that used to seem so unshakable.

"Sister Dominga is up there in her room dying. I am down here, dead, wishing you could hear me. There is another ghost, a strange woman, who keeps appearing in Sister Dominga's room. She is probably there now. I don't know who she is. I don't know what she wants.

"I have left my ghost friends up in Tucson and walked here to Mexico City, walked home. But I have no one to talk to. I have no one to help me. I can't leave Sister Dominga, but I don't think I can stand this. The Bible doesn't talk about souls in my state... It doesn't mention ghosts. What does this mean, Father? What can I do? I am so confused, I..."

A woman, large and middle-aged, walked into the confessional. I didn't want her to sit on me, nor did I want to hear her confession, so I flew up and out of the confessional. As I did, I heard her say in Spanish, "Forgive me, Father, for I have sinned," and I heard Father Finnegan reply in his Irish accented Spanish, "I will hear your confession, my child."

I felt a sharp pang of jealousy that such a simple act of comfort was now beyond my reach. I slowly flew out of the church and into the nunnery, back towards Sister Dominga's room.

I didn't know what I was doing or what I needed, but I did know that I would be there when Sister Dominga died. If she, by some chance, became a ghost upon her death, I wouldn't let her go through it alone. Not after all she had done for me.

I flew slowly to the old wooden door of her room. It was

thick and scarred with age and use. I stood there listening—was the other ghost in there?

I heard her voice, soft yet strong as she whispered to Sister Dominga. "I am here, Grandmother. I am here. I heard your call and I came. I will show you the way if you need. I will be here for you." Her words were in Spanish with an accent that I couldn't quite place.

Grandmother? Did she say Grandmother? Sister Dominga was a nun, she had been a nun almost her entire life, how could she be a grandmother? She had been like a mother to me, rescuing me from the streets and saving my life, teaching me, raising me, how could I not know she had a child, much less a grandchild?

I wanted to rush in, to demand an explanation, but I pushed that impulse down. I had surprised this ghost before, and she would disappear if I rushed in. So I moved slowly through the door until I could see her. She was petite and slim with long black hair that was braided in the back and skin a shade lighter than mine. As soon as I was far enough through the door for me to see her, her head turned towards me and our eyes met.

Those eyes made me feel just a little bit alive, and they scared me too. They were blue, shockingly blue, ice blue, the kind you see reflected in the depths of icebergs. Her gaze penetrated me. I just knew that she saw deep into my soul and could see my doubt and my weakness.

This was the third time I had seen her and the longest she had stayed.

"My name is Jesús," I said. "I just want to talk."

She continued to stare at me, her lips turning down into a frown, her head moving slowly back and forth. With a gentle "pop" she was gone.

I STOOD AND STARED AT SISTER DOMINGA FOR THE longest time. Her face drawn and pale, her breathing slow and unsteady, her eyes closed, looking like they would never open again. A soft moan escaped her lips and I feared the worst. I was here because I needed her, and in case she needed me. And what if she did need me, could I even help her when I didn't know how to help myself?

I longed for the round-faced Sister Dominga with the hard, uncompromising eyes that hid an endless capacity for compassion. I wished she would open her eyes and give me one of her looks, the kind that used to make me scared and excited. The kind of look she gave me as a boy that said she knew exactly what I was up to and that I would not get away with it.

I stood there and felt the doubt that had brought me to walk from Tucson, Arizona, to Mexico City. It was like a disease, a cancer, a darkness inside me, eating me from the inside out.

The mystery of the other ghost, calling Sister Dominga Grandmother, was maddening, but it was drowned out by the noise of my own doubt and fear. I had been back for three days and done nothing but watch Sister Dominga, wander the church and the orphanage, and hope...

But I didn't know what I was hoping for. A dying woman to wake up? My doubts to magically disappear? To suddenly know what I was doing with my afterlife?

I had been here before, bereft of faith. I had been down low, much lower than this, and had survived. And it was Sister Dominga that had saved me body and soul.

"How can I do this without you?" I asked her. She had been like a mother to me, and it was always the mothers that had brought me to faith.

When I spoke, I saw the smallest change in her face. A slight relaxing of her now gaunt features, as if the pain that plagued her had eased for a moment.

"My first memory is of Mass," I continued, studying her face. "It was around 1972, I was maybe three, my mother had dressed me in my best shirt—which was admittedly not much back then—and walked me to the church. I remember all the people, beautiful in their suits and dresses and shiny shoes. I remember the hard wooden pews, and how my mother had me kneel on the padded bench when she did."

Sister Dominga let out the smallest of sighs and I felt a tear run down my ghostly cheek. Maybe there was something I could do for her, some small way I could help her while she still lived. It was like the tiniest sliver of sunlight after a terrible thunderstorm.

"You want to hear my voice?" I asked her. "Does that help somehow?"

She didn't answer, but I could feel it. I could feel just a glimpse of the woman who had saved me and raised me. I could feel her longing for company, to not feel alone as she passed from this world. I could see her, in her coma, physically relax.

I laughed, a brief awkward bark. A tiny bit of the pent-up pressure I had been feeling for the last several months escaping. This I could do. This would help Sister Dominga. This would help me.

WHEN THE DEACON CAME AROUND SWINGING THE THURIBLE full of incense, I remember that scent was so sharp and strong that I wrinkled my nose and sneezed, the smell of frankincense overpowering me. I moved closer to my mother;

the man in his white vestments scared me. He looked so old and so serious. Like if I didn't do what he told me I would receive much worse punishment than the scoldings my mother gave or the spankings my father gave.

I slid still closer to her on the pew, enjoying how I could slide on the polished wood. I might have turned it into a game, but my mother took my hand and held it tightly.

Her hand was warm and so much bigger and stronger than mine. She looked down at me, a thin smile on her face. I needed to be quiet—she had told me before we had left. I needed to behave. I bit my lip and nodded so she would know I knew what she wanted. Her smile became full and wide and she gave me a small nod before turning her attention back to the deacon with the old brass thurible.

My mother was so beautiful. I remember staring up at her and thinking there was nothing more beautiful in the world than my mother. She had light-brown skin and big brown eyes. Her black hair was swept up in the back and piled on top of her head. She wore a blue dress, worn, but the best she had. She sat with her spine straight, her eyes on the priests.

She felt so strong, so true, like nothing bad could ever happen to us just so long as my mother could go to Mass. She prayed all the time, for our health and well-being, for God to give her and my father another child.

I didn't know it then, but in that church as a three-year-old boy, I was experiencing faith. Faith in my mother.

She was smart and beautiful and could do anything.

Faith came easy. Faith came naturally. It has not been easy or natural since then.

"START AT THE BEGINNING, AND DON'T LEAVE ANYTHING out, Jesús."

Sister Dominga would say that to me when I came back to her orphanage with a black eye, a split lip, or a guilty look on my face. She had a knack for listening and would always seem to know when I was leaving something important out. She would stand there, her arms crossed, her lips pursed, her eyes relentless until I spilled the essential facts.

Start at the beginning, and don't leave anything out.

That was a long time ago, when I was a boy, when I was such a terrible mess. My family had been killed, I had been living on the streets, and was nearly beaten to death when Sister Dominga found me. She saved my life, she got me off the street, and eventually, she saved my soul.

Sister Dominga ran a small orphanage called *Orfanato de San Miguel Arcángel* (the Orphanage of Saint Michael the Archangel). It sat in Miguel Hidalgo, one of the sixteen boroughs of Mexico City. Just an old brick building behind a humble city church, the *Iglesia de San Miguel Arcángel* (the Church of Saint Michael the Archangel).

When she found me, nursed me back to health, heard my story, I was eleven years old. I was older than the kids they usually took in, and way too old to be adopted. So my role there was a bit different. Sister Dominga wanted me to act as a big brother to the other kids, watching over them, making sure they followed the rules. I saw my role a bit differently. I saw myself as their protector. I wanted to make sure no one ever did to them what had happened to me.

The one thing we didn't have any trouble with was my role as storyteller. There were anywhere from six to eight boys there at a time, and we all slept in the biggest room of the old building, beds lining all the walls. When it was time for lights out, I would read stories to the younger boys. I would first read them in Spanish, and then in English. Sister Dominga loved it that I knew English so well and thought I should pass it on to the other boys.

When I first got there I had this habit of reading the ending first. Sister Dominga would give me the books, something like Hansel and Gretel, or a Hardy Boys mystery. I would always skip ahead and read the ending before I sat down to read it to the boys. I wanted to know how it would end so I could do a better job of reading it. That's what I told Sister Dominga. But she knew better—I skipped to the end so I could brace myself for what was coming. It's just the kind of life I had lived.

And here, now, as I stand here trying to figure out how to tell my story, I would love to jump to the end. But I can still hear Sister Dominga telling me to start at the beginning and don't leave anything out.

I talked this over with JJ, my ghost friend, who's done this whole memoir thing before. I told him what Sister Dominga used to say and asked him what he thought. He looked me over with those intense blue-grey eyes of his and said, "Yeah, that works, as long as you leave the boring stuff out. Stick to the story you need to tell."

I have to tell this story. Not that I think my life is all that interesting. Maybe it is, I don't know, though. It's my life, so it's completely normal to me.

So, no skipping to the end. No leaving out anything important. JJ tells me it takes some guts to do this. I believe him. I hope that I am up to the challenge.

My name is Jesús Manuel Rivera Dominga. I was born without the Dominga on the end. I added it once I was an adult to honor Sister Dominga and what she meant to me.

This is for you, Sister Dominga.

Chapter 2

MY FATHER'S HANDS WERE BIG AND ROUGH AND HE ALWAYS
had this musky, sweaty smell to him.

About the same time I was going to Mass with my
mother, I would sometimes go to work with my father. It
was a rarer thing, but sometimes when my mother couldn't
watch me, he would take me.

My father was a short man with broad shoulders and a
barrel chest. In the early days, he had a big mustache and
often had several days' growth of beard.

He was a stone mason, working with heavy rock all day
long. He was strong and quiet, and seemed to love his work.

The day I remember when I was very young was a Saturday. We were in *Naucalpan* (one of the boroughs of Mexico
City) working on an outdoor patio in one of the big houses
up on the hill. The house seemed like a castle to me, with
big wooden doors, tall ceilings, and large paintings on the
wall. We didn't go in, I only glimpsed these wonders from the
outside, but it seemed like a magical place. I wondered who
could possibly live there and have so many beautiful things.

My father was smoothing out sand in a wooden frame, getting ready to lay in the large pieces of flagstone.

"Papá?" I asked quietly. I knew he didn't like to be disturbed when he worked. My "job" there was to bring him things when he asked.

"Yes, Jesús. What is it?" he said in his thick English. My father almost always spoke to me in English. He wanted me to learn it well. To him it was a symbol of a better life.

"How did they get all that?" I asked, my gaze going to the window and the riches within.

He shrugged his broad shoulders and looked back to his work. He pulled the piece of wood across the uneven sand creating an area of flat, even sand that just begged to be played in, but I knew better.

I moved towards the window, it was the largest window I had ever seen, very wide and much taller than me. The sill of it was low enough that if I just moved one of the potted plants that rested there and jumped up, I would be able to see right into the house and get a better view.

My father grunted as he picked up a large piece of tan flagstone and moved it towards the flat sand. I looked at him and marveled at how strong he was, how big his arms were, at how the muscles in his neck bunched. The sight distracted me from my quest to see better into the house for a moment. It was clear to me then, there could be no one stronger in this world than my father.

After he got the piece of flagstone into the sand, I turned back to the window. It had a collection of cacti on it, some of them I had never seen. They were full of sharp needles, colorful flowers, and bright greens all in a row. I found one plant, a small barrel cactus, that I thought would be light enough for me to move. I reached up and started to move it towards the edge of the sill. It made a scraping noise and I turned and looked, but my father was intent, studying the assembled flagstones, looking for the next piece to lay.

I slid it farther, my arms stretched up above me. I just had to see fully into that house. As I got it to the edge of the sill, I realized it was heavier than I had thought. I tried to get a grip on the clay pot, but it was glazed in a bright blue and slick. Fear spiked through me as I realized the pot and large cactus was going to fall on my head.

"¡*Dios mío*!" my father cried, as one strong arm grabbed me and pulled me away, with his other hand he managed to get a grip on the lip of the pot. His hand arced down with the pot as he arrested its momentum, the sharp needles of the barrel cactus penetrating the skin of his arm. He set both the pot and me onto the ground and I saw the look of pain on his face.

"¡*Lo siento*!" I cried, telling him I was sorry.

"English," he said as he gritted his teeth and slowly pulled his arm away from the cactus, the barbs of the needles doing more damage as they pulled away from his skin.

"Sorry, Papá. I am most sorry," I said. "I wanted to see."

He nodded slowly as he plucked some of the larger needles out of his skin. The smaller hairlike ones, I knew from experience, were too small to come out and would bother him for a long time. Small droplets of blood formed where the large ones were pulled out. My stomach lurched and my heart pounded.

"Papá, I... Please..." I stammered.

He looked up at me and smiled. "No problem. Next time, you ask." He then grabbed me with his uninjured arm and lifted me so I could see into the house. The floor was made of glittering stone tiles, the inside door to the room was carved with a rearing horse. There was a colorful woven rug on the floor, and furniture made out of leather.

I gasped at the sight of it. Such wonders, such magic, I was sure wizards or princes lived there.

My father chuckled at my reaction, but put me down, put the cactus back, and said, "Enough."

He went back to his work, the pain of the injury I caused him seeming to be nothing at all.

Then I had faith in my father. Faith that he was strong enough to meet any challenge and that he could protect me from any danger.

THE STORIES I WAS TELLING SISTER DOMINGA HURT. NOT because they were bad stories or about bad things, but because they brought into sharp contrast the difficult things that were going to happen. These old, old memories of my childhood were not anything I had thought about in a long time. And, I think my ghostly form aided in this. JJ and I have discussed how the ghost's memory is better than the living. JJ said it has to do with the "meat" being gone and "not getting in the way anymore."

Whatever the case, the vividness of these memories as I told them was shocking.

"It's funny," I said aloud, "but as a ghost I can't smell at all. But as I sit here and talk about that pungent incense as I went to mass with my mother or the powerfully musky scent of my father as he labored, it is almost as if it's real. As if they aren't long, long gone." Again Sister Dominga visibly relaxed when I spoke to her, so I kept articulating my thoughts.

"I am so confused. But this seems to be helping, this

talking to you. So I will keep doing it, it is the least I can do after all you did for me." I felt some relief that I was able to help, even in a small way. Without thinking much about it, I moved my ghostly hands underneath Sister Dominga's head and summoned the "warmth."

It's hard for me to tell you what the warmth is. It is something Banquo, my ghostly mentor, taught JJ and me about. Actually, JJ used it to great effect in several situations, but I had never tried until now. It required that I be calm and clear and let go. Just be present. Just allow love to flow through my hands into Sister Dominga. At first it felt horribly awkward. How was holding my hands near her going to help? I was a ghost. I couldn't really help her. I couldn't even touch her. But then I felt the smallest sensation of warmth in my hands. It felt... Well, it was shocking at first. Temperature is another thing that ghosts don't experience, so feeling something akin to the heat of sunshine on my skin was surprising and delightful. I laughed and smiled, something that had been rare for me lately.

I moved closer, stepping into the bed, my ghostly form overlapping with it, so I stood right next to her. I put my right hand under her head and my left hand under her back where her heart was. I felt the warmth again flowing through me and into her. Sister Dominga took a deep breath and sighed. It was a small thing, but it made my heart sing. This was somehow easing her suffering, and for that I was grateful.

As I stood there, I thought about the warmth. It felt like it was coming from outside of me, like it wasn't a part of me, like it was from...

I cut the thought off. I wasn't ready to contemplate where the warmth came from. I was confused about the fact that I was still a ghost, that I was still stuck on Earth, that I hadn't heard the Call (it happens when a ghost moves on—more on this later). So I just relaxed and let the warmth flow and kept telling my story.

"So where were we?" I said. "We were talking about faith. About how as a child I had faith in my mother and faith in my father. But that simplicity of my early childhood didn't last all that long."

Chapter 3

NOW THAT I THINK OF IT, WAS IT REALLY "FAITH" THAT I had in my mother and father?

What is faith?

Doesn't it have to be devoid of proof to be truly faith? I had faith in my mother's faith, and had ample proof of how it made her stronger, how it kept her steady. I had faith in my father's strength, which was evident in nearly everything he did.

Was that faith? I think it was, but what happens to my faith when I see evidence that contradicts those views of my parents?

And maybe this is my essential issue: confronting the remains of a faith that has been proven to be unsound. I had great faith in what would happen when I died and... well... nothing of the sort happened. I am here. I am a ghost. I have not been taken home.

But back to my mother and father. As a child, I sort of had blinders on. My mother, while very religious, was also very superstitious—those things used to seem very different to me, but I am not so sure anymore. My father, while a hard worker, didn't make much money, desperately wanted a better life, and drank too much tequila. I, of course, was not aware of all this when I was three or four, but time and maturity has made it obvious.

"Come, Jesús, we must go now," my mother said. Her eyes were wide and she spoke rapidly.

"Where are we going?" I asked. I had been playing with some blocks, constructing what I thought would be a grand tower on the floor of our one-room house, while my mother cooked at the stove. Her brother, my uncle, had just been over, and they had talked in hushed tones.

"To church," she said, grabbing my hand and pulling me up. Her leg brushed against the colorful blocks and toppled my tower.

"No!" I cried, upset about my tower and not even thinking about church.

"I need my Jesús to go to church with me," she said, yanking my arm uncomfortably and crossing herself with her other hand.

I began to feel her desperation and started to cry. Something was wrong with my mother, something only church could fix. This trend became more pronounced as the years passed. My mother would have to go to church more and more, and if I wasn't in school, I would have to go with her.

My blocks forgotten, I kept glancing at my mother as she pulled me out the front door of our casita onto the narrow dirt road that led to it. She walked quickly, her eyes staring forward, her grip tight. She still wore her white kitchen apron over an old pale-yellow dress. There was a smudge of flower on her cheek—a white stain on her brown skin.

"Uncle Francisco?" I asked quietly as I tried to keep up with her.

"Yes," she said, sharply. "He... Uncle Fran has... well..." she stuttered and stammered for a few more strides before stopping and squatting in front of me. "He did something, Jesús. We must go light a candle and pray. Can you be my big man and help me?"

I nodded solemnly. I knew how to pray. My mother had often told me that Jesús Christ and I had the same name, so he had to listen when I prayed to him. "What should I pray for?" I asked.

Her brow briefly furrowed and moisture sprang to her eyes. "Pray for his soul," she said in a whisper. "Pray he finds his way."

My mother then stood up and started her fast walk towards our church. As we walked, I started mumbling a prayer, "Jesús, please watch over my Uncle Francisco. Please help him. Please help my mamá." I said it over and over while we walked to the church, while my mother lit a candle, while we kneeled before the altar, while we walked out of the church.

After it was over, my mother seemed calm and back to her normal happy self. I smiled because I knew my prayer had already worked.

SISTER DOMINGA LET OUT A DEEP, SHUDDERING SIGH. The warmth that I felt flowing through me, into her, was surprisingly strong. It felt sacred, it felt holy, it felt like communion.

For a moment after I had stopped talking, it was perfect—this bright sharp moment of beauty and peace. I had been lost in my story, deep in my past, and had forgotten about everything. That Sister Dominga was dying and that I was broken, my faith gone.

As the present tumbled onto me, the warmth fled, and I felt alone again.

When my faith was strong, I never felt like I was alone. There was always God there with me, watching over me, helping me. And the times when I didn't have faith, the feeling of aloneness has often been overwhelming. After my parents were killed... after the gang of boys I spent some time with, the Muchachos, left me for dead... and then there with Sister Dominga.

Pain crept back onto her face and I stepped back out of her bed. Right then the door opened and a nun entered. "How are we today, Sister?" she said.

She was short and round, wearing a simple white habit, consisting of a loose white dress, a white coif on her head, a wool belt, and her rosary beads hanging from the belt. Sister Helen. "Time to tend to you, dear. We must keep you comfortable." I moved farther back as she brought a basin with warm water and a sponge over to the table next to her bed. "You do look better," she commented as she looked at her face. Sister Dominga didn't look as good as when the warmth had been flowing into her, but she didn't look as bad as when I arrived.

I floated out of the room. I never stayed for her care. I couldn't bear to see how the most base of her physical needs were dealt with. Keeping her clean, changing her clothing and bed pads, feeding her... I couldn't watch.

So I left and contemplated my past and what I would tell Sister Dominga next.

UNCLE FRANCISCO ALWAYS HAD A READY SMILE AND A booming laugh. When he came to visit he always brought me a piece of *leche quemada*. It literally means "burnt milk," but it is a caramel candy with pecan halves on top. I loved them. Francisco was tall and lean and had lighter skin like my mother.

My mom and Uncle Francisco were *criollo*, of pure Spanish decent. My grandparents had immigrated to Mexico from Spain. My father was *mestizo* with a strong dose of Mayan. I, of course, had no idea what any of this meant as a child, but in Mexico lines were drawn between the criollo and the mestizo. The criollo tended to be more affluent, had a greater representation in government, and tended to have better jobs. As it seems to happen all over the world, many lines were drawn around race in my home country.

My mother's family were proud of their heritage and did not think my father was an appropriate mate for her. Not only because of his mixed blood, but because of his lack of an education and his simple trade. They thought him below her. They had basically disowned her when she married my father, and my mother had to give up a lot to be with him. She was used to nice things and enough money. Their early life together had little of each.

Uncle Francisco was my mother's only contact with her family. He would come around every month or so, give me my piece of *leche quemada*, talk to my mom, drink with my father. I loved his visits. He was full of amazing stories, wore fancy clothes, and had this thin, well-trimmed mustache that I found fascinating. And he would never speak in English. His Spanish was fluid and flowing, and oh so dramatic.

One day he came and shared tequila with my father. I didn't really know what it was then, but I knew the strong smell and I knew how it could change my father. "Juan, I have a job for you," Francisco said to my father, his long frame draped over one of our kitchen chairs. My father's face brightened. He had been home more lately, work being slow, and everyone seemed very serious about it. "I am redoing the courtyard in my restaurant, and I need a job done, such that will be talked about far and wide. I will spare no expense on materials, it will be the jewel of my establishment!"

My father nodded his head slowly, "Thank you, my brother, you can count on me."

Francisco's eyes narrowed and he leaned close to my father. I was on the floor not far away playing with a wooden truck and they were not paying attention to me. Francisco whispered to my father, but it was the kind of loud whisper that men that drank tequila often used. "I need someone I can trust, someone that can keep quiet."

My father nodded solemnly and filled their glasses with more tequila. "I am your man, Francisco." I saw a hunger in both men's eyes as they clinked their glasses and drank. My uncle's hunger I did not understand, but my father's I had an inkling of. It was the look he had when he so carefully practiced his English, and insisted I do the same. It was the hunger he had for a better life, the desperation he felt to prove himself worthy of my mother to her family.

At the moment, of course, the four-year-old me didn't understand this intellectually, but I could feel it.

I could feel change coming, and it scared me.

Chapter 4

THE DAY OUR LIVES TRULY CHANGED IS SO CLEAR TO ME. I remember dirt under my bare feet. Dry and fine, cool to the touch, the kind of dirt that fills your nose so that is all you can smell. I was four years old. This is where it all started.

I was standing there being inspected by adults. My father was there with his stubbly face and mustache and my mother with her bright brown eyes, wearing her best dress. There was another adult; a man in a clean, unwrinkled white suit with a red tie. He had a wide smile and very white teeth.

They were talking about me, but I didn't really understand what they wanted. It was adult talk. I just knew that I was the center of attention. I stood tall and smiled back at the man in the suit.

My father asked me to say hello. He said this to me in English. I looked at the man and said, "Hola, Señor. Buenos días."

My father frowned and shook his head. "English," he said. "Talk to Mr. Langold in English."

"Hello, Mr. Lan-gee," I couldn't manage the pronunciation of his last name. "How are you today?"

English and Spanish weren't that different to me then. Words were words. It wasn't until I grew older that I understood that the differences in languages go far beyond the words and reflect much of the cultures that created them.

The man squatted and said, "I am just fine, Jesús. How are you?" He spoke his words in English, slowly and carefully.

"¡Bien!" I said, clapping my hands together. My father gave me a look, so I added, "Fantastic," and everyone laughed.

My father and Señor Langold walked into our house and started talking. My mother came over and put her hand on my shoulder. She was shaking a little bit. I knew what was happening was important, I just didn't know why. I peered into the open door of our little house. It was made out of cinder blocks with a tin roof—a simple rectangle with one room.

I saw my father grab a bottle of Tequila. He took out two glasses and filled them, giving one to Señor Langold. They clinked their glasses and drank the amber liquid.

I stepped towards the door, but my mother caught my hand, pulling me away. "Want to go to the park?" she asked in Spanish. While my mother could speak English, she preferred her native tongue, and that is what we spoke when my father wasn't around.

The playground was a long walk away, but I loved the swing and eagerly agreed.

I looked back at the two men in the house. The bright sunshine made it hard for me to see them clearly, but I could see how my father looked at Señor Langold, and it made me uncomfortable. The look he gave Señor Langold was the kind of look I gave him—hanging on every word, eager to please, somehow innocent.

That look scared me.

I started to ask my mother, but she pulled me towards the park and my worries were soon forgotten.

I RARELY LEFT SISTER DOMINGA'S ROOM WHILE I SAT VIGIL. The only time I felt comfortable leaving was when Sister Helen was there tending to her.

When I left, I would mostly wander into the church. With its high vaulted ceilings, tall stained glass windows, altar, and statue of the crucifixion up front. It was in many ways your typical Catholic church. It was old, but so was Mexico City.

I could have wandered the halls of the little orphanage, or I could have gone outside and wandered the neighborhood, or I could have spent time in the rectory, or the quarters for the nuns and priests, but I didn't. I always ended up in the church, staring at the life-sized statue of Jesús Christ on the cross.

It was hallowed space, and even though I couldn't feel my faith, the space kept calling me. My questions kept taking me there.

"Why?" I asked the statue of Jesús. "Why haven't you come for me? Why am I still here?"

It was a Thursday evening and the church was deserted. I could feel the quiet that only an empty place of worship can hold, but it wasn't soothing. It bothered me profoundly.

"Why?" I asked again, my voice louder. I could feel my

confusion slipping to anger. "I have believed. I have done my best to be a good person. *¿Por qué? ¿Por qué?*"

The statue with its crown of thorns, with its pierced hands and side, did not answer, did not move, did not provide me with the answers I sought. It was inert, a piece of painted wood, what was I expecting?

My gaze went up as I looked at the ceiling of the church and I caught a flash of movement and thought I heard a soft, mournful moan—or maybe laughter, I couldn't really tell. It was just a flash and then it was gone.

"Oh, my. Now you've done it," I heard a voice say behind me.

I whirled around and saw a man standing there. He looked like a Mayan native. He stood there wearing a plain white shift, with a deeply lined brown face, and the telltale transparency of a ghost. He gently moved his head back and forth.

"What have I done?" I asked, taking a step back.

"Disturbed the lurkers," he said, pointing his finger straight up towards the high arched ceiling.

"Lurkers?" I asked. I was more than a bit off balance. When I first arrived I was surprised not to see any other ghosts besides the woman in Sister Dominga's room. I thought a place like this would be filled with them, having offered comfort and solace to many. I figured ghosts would come here when they died. But I hadn't found any until now.

"They are spirits that are stuck," the man said and then pointed at me. "Kind of like you?"

I stood there and stared. First at the Mayan man and then up at the ceiling where I caught another glimpse of what now seemed to be ghosts.

"Who are you?" I asked.

"My name is Yochi."

"What are you doing here?"

"What do you mean?" he asked, looking around the church.

"This is a Catholic church, you're dressed in traditional garb. You don't seem to belong."

He smiled. "This was not always the conqueror's church. Once my people worshiped on this ground."

When he smiled I saw missing teeth, and I felt my heart lighten in a strange way. For a moment, everything seemed OK.

"See, Jesús, all is not so bleak as you imagined." With a gentle pop he was gone.

I stood there for a moment looking around, confused, and then said, "Wait! How did you know my name?" I thought I heard laughter echoing among the rafters of the church and I felt my heart lighten. But then I heard a noise from above and caught movement up there again. A chill went down my spine and I headed back to Sister Dominga's room. I wasn't ready to meet the "lurkers," whatever they were.

That's the end of the sample. To find out what happens next, pick up a copy of Of Things Not Seen. *For more information go to:*

RobertJMcCarter.com/Books/OfThingsNotSeen

Acknowledgements

FIRST AND FOREMOST I WANT TO THANK THE READERS OF *Shuffled Off*. It is your enthusiasm for JJ, Jesus, Banquo, and their adventures that inspired me to keep going. And those of you that gave me feedback, thank you! Your thoughts have influenced this book.

And now, if you will indulge me, I would like to talk about my dog Jake. He was a talking, howling, wild coyote mix. He was part of my life for twelve years and walked thousands of miles with me in the forest. He died in January of 2012. I had been mulling over this book, and the day he died I sat down and started writing it. It may sound weird, but thematically these books are about grief, and the grief I was feeling about his passage got me right to where I needed to be. JJ's rant about "life is grief" (Transmission #2) is what I wrote that day, and it led to much of what happened in the book (Part 3, specifically).

For me (and JJ, it seems) grief requires action. When Jake died, writing the first draft of this book was the action I had to take.

I need to also thank my amazing wife, Aleia, and the

non-profit she runs, Further Shore (www.FurtherShore.org). It is her work with the dying that has had such a profound effect on what and how I write (and on me in general). I may take on these issues in fiction, but she does it every day in the real world. I am humbled by the person she is. And my thanks to the volunteers, caregivers, and practitioners of Further Shore. You guys do something worth doing each and every day. My hat's off to you. Further Shore's work also had a great deal of influence on Part 3.

Thanks to the winners of my "Name the Ghost" contest: Jennifer Star and Lenny Gingello. They named the ghosts Lela and Blinky respectively. I really appreciate your support!

As always, a hearty thanks goes to my amazing band of beta readers: John Bifano, Roni Hornstein, Chris Kalinich, Michele Lytle, Gary D. McClellan, Susanne One Love, Aleia N. O'Reilly, Eliot Schipper, and Janine Schipper. I seriously couldn't do this without you.

Thanks to my amazing proofreader, Diana Cox (www. novelproofreading.com).

And as always, my greatest thanks go to you, the reader. I appreciate you taking the time you took to read this book and to spend some time with JJ and the gang. And if you got all the way to the end of the acknowledgements, you must truly be extraordinary!

About the Author

ROBERT J. MCCARTER IS THE AUTHOR OF FIVE NOVELS, three novellas, and dozens of short stories. He is a finalist for the *Writers of the Future* context and his stories have appeared in *Adomeda Spaceways Inflight Magazine*, *Everyday Fiction*, and numerous anthologies. His short stories have been published alongside such luminaries as Brandon Sanderson, Peter S. Beagle, Jody Lynn Nye, and David Farland.

He has written a series of first person ghost novels (starting with *Shuffled Off: A Ghost's Memoir*) and a superhero / love story series (*Neutrinoman and Lightningirl: A Love Story*). Ten of his short stories were published in *Life After: Stories of Life, Death, and the Places In Between*.

He lives in the mountains of Arizona with his amazing wife and his ridiculously adorable dog. Find out more at RobertJMcCarter.com.

Books by Robert J. McCarter

Novels in the "Ghost's Memoir" world:
Shuffled Off: A Ghost's Memoir, Book 1
Drawing the Dead
To Be a Fool: A Ghost's Memoir, Book 2
Of Things Not Seen: A Ghost's Memoir, Book 3

Books in the Neutrinoman and Lightningirl Series:
Meteor Attack!
    Lightningirl and Neutrinoman, A Love Story. Episode 1
Toxic Asset
    Lightningirl and Neutrinoman, A Love Story. Episode 2
Protocol X
    Lightningirl and Neutrinoman, A Love Story. Episode 3
Season 1 (Omnibus edition of Episodes 1 - 3)
Off Book
    Lightningirl and Neutrinoman, A Love Story. Episode 4
    (Coming soon)

Short Stores and Collections
Life After: Stories of Life, Death, and the Places in Between
Probability: Resolve
The Turing Test Will Be Televised
Ghost Hacker, Zombie Maker

For a complete list, go to RobertJMcCarter.com

www.ingramcontent.com/pod-product-compliance
Lightning Source LLC
Chambersburg PA
CBHW051539250626
47157CB00001B/115